(A Novel)

Elisa Lorello and
Sarah Girrell

PUBLISHED BY

Published by AmazonEncore
P.O. Box 400818
Las Vegas, NV 89140

ISBN-13: 9781935597575
ISBN-10: 1935597574

ACKNOWLEDGMENTS

The following deserve our eternal gratitude:

Terry Goodman, Sarah Tomashek, and the team at AmazonEncore for believing in our novel before they even saw a word of it.

Kate Hagopian (aka "Cool Kate"), who read the manuscript and gave us fabulous feedback.

Glenn Volkema, who gave us the guy's perspective.

Eda Lorello, who was generous enough to share her home and heart with us.

Jim Paquette, whose profound patience, support, and ability to share allowed us to write.

Our parents: Michael and Eda Lorello, and Kris and Celeste Girrell, fans from the start.

The Lorello siblings: Michael, Bobby, Ritchie, Steve, Mary, and Paul.

Mary Mottola, who taught her granddaughter Elisa that the key ingredient in any recipe is love.

Rebecca Clark, equal parts friend and sister to Sarah.

The Undeletables, who made sure the coffee cups were full and were more often than not the intended readers.

Elspeth Antonelli, whose blog *It's a Mystery* offered smiles and sage writing advice at just the right moments.

Numerous coffee shops in the Raleigh, North Carolina, area, especially It's A Grind! in Cary for their input and service, and Crema Coffee for making a vanilla chai latte as good as Mirasol's Café and Uncle Jon's in southeastern Massachusetts.

Libraries and independent bookstores everywhere, for all they do.

Kindle owners who put *Faking It* and *Ordinary World* on the map.

Our friends, families, support networks, creative minds that have inspired us throughout our lives, and all the other people who are forever in our hearts.

~ *Sarah and Elisa, October 2010*

With respect and gratitude for all of the teachers
and mentors I've had over the years, especially:
Sue, who let me read in class,
David, who made classic lit cool,
Magali, who taught me to think,
question, and think again, and of course,
Elisa, who helped me find my voice.

~ Sarah

For my sister Mary, with love

~ Elisa

1

Valentine's Day

I LOVE THE smell of freshly baked anything.

Bread, muffins, cookies, cake—*especially* cake—the smells of vanilla and yeast and butter and chocolate can be an aphrodisiac one day, a childhood memory the next, a promise of prosperity the day after that. Freshly baked anything is the smell of love.

The scents of vanilla and hazelnut lassoed me in the parking lot and pulled me toward the open doors of my café, The Grounds. Rather than use the back alley entrance, I passed through the main door and was greeted by Spencer, Tracy, Jan, and Dean—the Originals—from their corner window table. As Spencer and Tracy resumed recapping last night's episode of *The Office*, I passed Minerva buried under her anatomy books at the table directly across from them. She'd moved a vase of faux roses to the empty chair opposite her.

On my way to the counter, I stopped to re-stick the handmade paper and lace doily hearts to the walls before moving on to the self-service bar and disposing of stray napkins, empty sugar packets, and used coffee stirrers. In the back corner near the entrance to the seldom-used reading room, Car Talk Kenny sat in his usual upright chair sipping a mocha hazelnut latte and scribbling something in the margin of the book he was reading. He looked up long enough for me to make eye contact and wave to him, which he returned with a grin.

"Happy Valentine's Day, Norman," I called as I circled around and behind the counter, grabbing an apron from a hook on the wall.

"You're early," he called back from the kitchen.

"I missed you," I teased.

"Good. You can start on the muffins."

My afternoon shift underway, I immediately went to work on a batch of jumbo chocolate chip muffins while Norman took his break and the lunch rush slowed to a lull. Just as the muffins finished baking and I removed them from the oven—swollen, luscious, seductive—a college student and his girlfriend walked past The Grounds's open door, arm in arm. I could see the moment they smelled it: his spine straightened, and she slowed to crane her neck in the direction of the doors. The girl stopped and pulled her young lover inside by his arm, her ponytail swishing back and forth. They held hands while I retrieved their order—hers, a sweet iced tea; his, a large black coffee that he nearly flooded with sugar—and a freshly baked muffin for them to share. He let go of her hand only to pay for the order while she held the muffin close to her nose, breathing in its scent, the pleasure registering on her face.

The Originals seemed captivated by the young lovers, conversation stopping momentarily in order to observe them. And yet, the couple remained unaware of their observers and exited The Grounds the same way they'd entered—blissful and obliviously in love.

"The Topic of the Day is first loves," Spencer announced seconds later, his arm resting naturally around Tracy's shoulders.

On cue, Dean spoke first. "Nineteen-ninety. I was eleven. Janet Jackson in that video that's all sepia-toned, after she lost all that weight and got really buff. I think I became a man that night." He turned to Jan and tugged at the sleeve of her pastel pink scrubs. "Babe?"

"Spin the Bottle party at someone's house—I can't remember the date," said Jan. "Jason Belk. He was my first kiss, too. I guess I lumped the two together."

Spencer followed. "Angela...holy crap, I can't remember her last name! And she was the love of my life at fifteen. I think I even proposed to her."

"And you can't even remember her last name?" teased Tracy. "Geez, it's gonna be like that with every wedding anniversary, isn't it. I'm going to have to tattoo the date on your forehead!"

Jan asked Tracy, "What about you? Who was your first love?"

"Robbie Smitts, my next-door neighbor," Tracy answered. "He used to walk me home from the bus and carry my books."

"I didn't know people still did that," said Dean.

"I carried Tracy's books all throughout college," said Spencer.

"That's 'cause you're a gentleman," said Jan to Spencer, eyeing Dean as if to imply that he could take lessons in such thoughtfulness.

"Minerva, you're next," called Dean.

"Jay," a voice chirped from behind an anatomy book that had been propped up against two other textbooks. She held up her hand and flashed her wedding ring as she spoke her husband's name, at which Jan cooed.

Minerva, my best friend, was as much a fixture at The Grounds as the Originals, Norman, the lumpy reading chairs in the corners of the café, and the Cookie of the Week. I've never known how she managed to switch her concentration from coffee shop banter to the functions of the circulatory system, but she aced every exam and lab, even after swearing the next one was going to be the end of her. After soaring through nearly three-quarters of an intense program to become a midwife, I was amazed that she still worried.

"That is so sweet," said Jan. "What, were you high school sweethearts or something?"

"What about Sebastard?" I called from behind the counter. It didn't occur to me until after I blurted his name that she might not want that that bit of information getting out. She turned around in her chair to face me, tilting her head so that her eyes looked over her horn-rimmed glasses, and shot me a death stare. I sheepishly shrugged my shoulders and ducked behind the cappuccino machine, my face flushed with foolishness.

"Who?" the others asked. "Spill it!"

"Sebastian," she corrected. "Just a guy I dated in high school, before I met Jay."

"Dumped him for Jay, eh?" asked Dean.

"Actually, he broke up with me," said Minerva. "Don't get me wrong—I thought I loved him. But Jay's the real deal. That's why I call him my first love. Nothing before him can possibly count."

The women ooo-ed and awww-ed while the guys rolled their eyes and informed Norman that he was next.

Norman yelled over the cappuccino machine, "I don't kiss and tell, but I will say that I promised to name my firstborn after her, even if it's a boy." He then turned to me. "Eva?"

Finally, I chimed in. "You mean aside from Nicky Bates, my boyfriend from nursery school who always shared his cookies with me at snack time?"

"So that's how the whole baking thing started…" Dean interrupted.

"Eight years old. My sister Olivia's friend Kevin. He had a mullet. He also, I later found out, became a pothead," I said as I placed a freshly baked jumbo chocolate chip muffin, still warm, on a white plate and sprinkled red sugar crystals around it in the shape of a heart. Smiling in satisfaction at my design, I emerged from behind the counter and presented it to Spencer and Tracy.

"A two-year dating anniversary deserves a complimentary muffin," I said to them.

"Aw, thanks Eva," said Tracy. She separated the muffin's top from its bottom, then further split the top in two before passing it to Spencer and taking a bite, making a thumb's up sign as she chewed slowly. I beamed. First bites, first sips, first batches are a lot like first loves—so savory, so pleasurable a moment that you want it to last an eternity. Compliments and accomplishments were nice, but nothing quite matched seeing people enjoy something I made, especially when I made it just for them.

"So Eva, isn't it about time you split one of these muffins with someone?" Tracy asked.

I floundered for a moment, unsure how to answer. "Nah," I parried, "I can eat the whole thing by myself."

"Come on," Spencer wheedled. "Quit teasing. For real, when are you gonna get yourself a guy to boss around?"

"I have Norman."

"I heard that!" Norman called from behind the counter.

"Seriously," said Spencer.

"Who says I don't already have one?" I replied.

"Because we'd have heard about it by now," Tracy said. "Or seen him here."

"What can I say? I like being single."

Spencer and Tracy exchanged skeptical glances before looking back at me.

"*Really*?" they said together, followed by, "Why?" while another asked, "Who *likes* being single?"

"It's not some horrid disease," said Sister Beulah, the nun from Saint Someone-or-Other who had slipped in as the lovebirds were leaving. She retrieved her usual order from Norman and sat at Minerva's table, relocating the roses yet again. "Granted, my valentine doesn't send me cards, but I sure don't miss dating."

"Come to think of it, when was the last time you even went on a date?" Norman asked me as I joined him behind the counter. The Originals followed with choruses of "Saayyy, yeah."

"It has been awhile," said Jan.

"Yes, you should put yourself back out there," Sister Beulah added.

I looked at her, incredulous; I detested the phrase "put yourself out there" almost as much as the phrases "any guy is lucky to have you" and "I just want to be friends." The first two were supposed to be phrases of encouragement, but I had always seen them as patronizing. The third, however, was the cold kiss of death in the dating world.

"I really don't mind it. Besides, who has time? Ever since I left teaching, I've put all my energy into getting The Grounds up and running. It's only in the last few months that I've even had a second to breathe."

"Bull," said Norman, careful not to curse in front of the clientele. "I have plenty of time for dates. In fact, I just took a girl out for dinner last week."

"All due respect, Norm-o, managing a business is not the same as owning it."

"Suit yourself," he said. "But I think it's a crock."

⤳⟲

At the end of the shift, as Norman headed out the door, he ran through a list of reminders for me.

"Oh, and don't forget to update The Grounds Web site and Facebook page. It's your turn."

"No problem, Norman. Second date with that girl tonight?"

"Nah. The dinner last week was nice, but the date wasn't. You're my valentine this year."

Leave it to Norman to turn my face a shade of pink that matched the paper hearts.

After a shower and pizza delivery that night, I opened my laptop and surfed to The Grounds's profile page on Facebook. After adding an event sponsored by North Carolina College of Liberal Arts and uploading a new photo of Vanilla-Macadamia Supremes, I opened a new window to *Groundskeepers*, our networked blog.

The idea of splitting a muffin with someone had lingered in my mind all day. I stared at the screen for a moment before my fingers danced across the keyboard.

Why I Love Singlehood

Is it me, or is society split into two ways of living: couplehood and singlehood? And the former is vastly preferred over the latter. This afternoon my customers looked at me as if I needed prescription medication because I opted for singlehood. As if I needed to be exiled to a special singles community, quarantined until my desire to procreate was restored. As if I needed to buy a condo and adopt a cat, two prerequisites for the modern bachelorette.

I am thirty-three years old and extolling the virtues of singlehood while dispelling the stereotypes of lonely, desperate people hungering for their weddings and becoming wine connoisseurs in their spare time rather than going to a restaurant or a movie by themselves. And I—gasp!—have both dined and done the movies solo, and survived.

Here are just a few of the many reasons why I love singlehood:

Bathrooms

It's been two years since I've shared a bathroom with a guy. Since I've shared a bathroom with *anyone*. This is enough time to condition anyone to hold on to the luxury of not having to step over a pile of wet towels to mop up the puddles of water post-shower, wash my hands in a sink of stray shaved facial hair, or clean up gobs of toothpaste. To say nothing of his impatience over my taking up time for primping, and coveting counter space for jars and tubes and bottles of lotions and oils and sprays and gels.

Should I meet someone new and fall in love and move in with him, we're gonna have to get a place with *at least* two fully equipped bathrooms. Faulty wiring, cockroaches, peeling paint, freezing pipes, and two bathrooms? We'll take it! (OK, maybe not the cockroaches…) Affordable central air, dishwasher, washer-dryer, hardwood floors, fireplace, balcony, cleaning service, big kitchen, picture windows, swimming pool, tennis court, and only one bathroom? Thanks, we'll keep looking.

Schedule Confirmation

Case in point: my sister wound up having to call off her plans to visit me two weeks ago. The kids had soccer practice and music lessons, her husband had business trips and golf tournaments, etc. No one could get their schedules to mesh. When I try to get together with my married friends, they've got to consult with their spouses and BlackBerrys days in advance, coordinate who's got what car, check in on walkie-talkies and send smoke signals, and that's not even including the ones with kids. When someone sends me an invitation, the only thing I need to consider is my calendar and whether I'm in the mood for a drive. (I admit that being my own boss helps.) And, of course, I'm usually the one that has to drive to their house because it's more convenient for them and their others.

I can get on a plane, a train, or a ferry with as little hassle and as much ease as possible. And I can go anywhere I choose: Raleigh.

Gainesville. Canada. Dollywood. I am home every Christmas without having to also do the in-law thing. I am sitting on my couch choosing from my pick of TV show marathons on New Year's Eve without having to worry about an office party full of people I've barely met. And don't even get me started on the joys of no babysitters. Not that I don't love my married or parental friends, or kids, even. I love them dearly, and their kids, too. I especially love my niece and nephew. But I love my freedom more.

The Avoidance of Creeps

They're out there, trust me. Granted, there are more good guys than creeps. Exponentially more. But creepy guys are like vampires; all it takes is one to spook you forever.

Granted, a wedding ring may be the ultimate creep repellant, but I'll sacrifice meeting a few good guys if it means avoiding a few creeps along the way.

Fiscal Responsibility

Spend thousands of dollars on a gown I'm only going to wear for six hours at best? Spend thousands more on flowers that will wilt before day's end? Spend still more on a DJ who plays music that could be easily downloaded from iTunes? Granted, you get thousands of dollars in gifts if you've got generous and rich friends and family. But in that case, why not just have a yard sale?

The one concession I'll make is the bridal registry. I couldn't care less about china patterns; but new cookware, a popcorn popper, ice cream maker, and every kitchen utensil there is, not to mention fluffy new towels and bath soaps—well, that's just cool.

Ah, but what about eloping? you ask. Isn't that fiscally responsible? Beats paying for that enormous tent, yes, or making sure all the chairs' slipcovers have the right bows on them. But why not just splurge on an annual cruise and skip the wedding part?

What It's Really All About

One of my most vivid memories from childhood is staying home from school sick and watching soap operas with my sister. My mother didn't approve of me watching soaps because she thought I was too young, but fortunately she was at work. The kissing part is what I remember. At twelve years old, I was all in favor of kissing. Dating, being in love, romance, the bride and groom, etc.—I wanted in on all of it. Couplehood, essentially. That intention was as authentic and natural and lovely as could be.

But these days, it's not so much about soul mates as it is about best friends. When the romance dies, when the breasts go south, when you wake up and the person next to you has the same dog-breath as you do, what really matters is that your best buddy remembered that it's the anniversaries of your parents' deaths and gave you a hug. And you don't necessarily need to be married to him or her. S/he could be your brother or sister, your dog or cat, your partner in crime or brother in arms.

Do I miss companionship? Not really. In my line of work, it's impossible to be alone or lonely. Even at night.

Do I still want couplehood? I honestly don't know. Depends on what day you ask. But what I do know is love doesn't understand numbers or logic. Doesn't know race or culture, gender or age. Love just is. And it's as simple as that.

Relationships, however, are an entirely different matter.

All you need is love, sang the Beatles, but they never said what kind. Give me companionship and camaraderie, but keep your bathroom to yourself.

∽

"You have *got* to make it its own blog," Minerva said the following afternoon at The Grounds, where the Topic of the Day, to my surprise, was "Why I Love Singlehood."

"I concur," said Norman. "We want more. You can be Wilmington's own Carrie Bradshaw."

"Hardly," I retorted, then looked at Minerva. "Really?"

"See for yourself," said Minerva, who proceeded to read out loud while I looked over her shoulder: *This post is the anti–Sex and the City. You are dispelling—*and 'dispelling' is misspelled with two *s*'s and one *l—the belief that being single is being less than, and that the sole—*spelled s-o-u-l—*the sole goal in the life of a single woman is to not be single, especially when you consider that half of all marriages end in divorce. Hello? Doesn't that signify that jumping into a relationship just for the sake of not being alone is not a good idea?*"

"Who says that's why they're 'jumping' into marriage?" said Spencer.

"Good point," I said.

"Here's another one," said Minerva, and read out loud again. "*It's a testament against the Prince Charming myth that says he's going to come and rescue you. Please. He can't even pick up his socks off the floor.* Hmmm...disappointed, are we?"

Sister Beulah laughed and read another. "This is in response to the other comment," she said. "*Who said that's the only reason people get married? And who said that's the reason people are getting divorced?* Your point exactly, Spencer."

"I know. I wrote that comment," said Spencer.

The comment that caught my attention, however, said: *Wake up and smell the bullshit. You are rationalizing your loneliness and disguising it in clever writing.*

"You can ignore that one, Eva," said Minerva. "Probably just projecting his own loneliness."

"How do you know it was written by a he?" asked Dean. "The screen handle was Anonymous."

Frowning, I retreated behind the counter.

"I think you should do it," said Norman. "You know it'll catch on like wildfire, and it'll be good for business. We already have a large clientele of singles."

"Norman's right," said Minerva, avoiding Norman's raised eyebrows. "I know—shocking, isn't it, Norman being right. You're a great writer, Eva. When was the last time you wrote anything other than a recipe?"

"I write all the time. Menus, Grounds's updates, invoices…"

"You know what I mean. You haven't written anything since your novel. This could be a good creative outlet for you. We can call it WILS," she said, pronouncing it "Wills" like the Brits called Prince William.

"C'mon, Eva," goaded the Originals from their table. "Say you'll do it."

The comments swirled in my head: Wilmington's own Carrie Bradshaw. Dispelling the myth. Wake up and smell the bullshit.

"Why not," I said. "It was kinda fun to write it."

⌒◗

In the shadow of Valentine's Day, writing something so anti-marriage seemed sacrilegious. And yet, I felt idealistic rather than cynical, like a millennial woman casting off her dating shackles.

For the record, I meant everything I said when I wrote that post. I was so in the moment as I was writing it. Hell, I might as well have been Mary Tyler Moore flinging her hat into the air in the middle of the city street.

Then Shaun called.

2

The Jeanette

"HEY, EVA. IT'S Shaun," I heard him say upon my answering the phone.

"Hi!" I said, happy to hear from him. "What's up?"

"I read your new singles blog."

The revelation that Shaun regularly followed The Grounds's Facebook page and read my blog created a tingling sensation in my chest.

"Really?" My voice sounded like I'd just sucked on a helium balloon. "Well, what'd you think?"

"It's definitely a conversation piece. And it's nice to see that you've got such a great attitude."

"Well, I didn't expect it to be such a sensation, but what the hell."

"I'm just glad you're doing OK," he said.

"Why wouldn't I be?"

"Well, I wasn't sure if you'd heard, which is why I decided to call before the grapevine got to you first."

"Heard what?"

He paused before speaking again.

"I'm engaged."

The tingling of hope in my chest—that's what it was, I'd realized: *hope*—turned into the familiar feeling of post-breakup knife gouging.

"You're what?" My helium voice was back.

"I'm engaged. To the new professor in philosophy. Her name's Jeanette."

Jeanette. He's engaged to a Jeanette.

"You've met her, actually," he said. "Or at least you've seen her. She's been to The Grounds. She has long red hair."

As if that description alone would clarify everything for me.

"She wrote a book on Kierkegaard, in fact," he added after several seconds of silence passed between us.

Yeah, like that helps.

I wrapped the coiled cord of the antiquated phone around my finger so tightly that my fingertip turned purple. "Why didn't you tell me you were seeing someone?" I asked.

"Um…" he started. Meanwhile, my brain frantically searched its databases in an attempt to recall a redhead spewing on about a Kierkegaard book. No hits. "I don't know," he said. "I guess I was afraid of hurting your feelings."

I summoned all the strength in my body, as if I were about to lift a hundred-pound barbell, to sputter, "Well, congratulations! Mazel tov. Really."

"You're not mad?"

"Why would I be mad? Really, Shaun, I'm happy for you."

Kill me now. No, kill Shaun. I'm already dead inside. Then kill the Jeanette. Thank God he couldn't see me. I thought I would actually break a tooth, they were clenched so tightly. I thought my jaw would lock into a creepy grin like the Joker. I thought the phone cord would actually sever my finger.

"Thanks. It means so much to me to have your blessing. You're still one of my best friends, you know," he said.

"Well, you deserve to be happy," I said, wondering what "best friends" really meant to him. To me it meant not keeping your fiancée a secret. Better still, it meant not getting engaged before I did.

"Well, um, I just wanted you to know, and I'm glad to see that you're doing so well. Hey, I'll bet you're glad to be out of academia, huh," he said without missing a beat. "You know it's midterm this week. Bet you don't miss that."

"When's the wedding?" I asked.

"Huh? Oh, we haven't set a date. I'll let you know, though."

Yes, because I'm dying for that piece of information. Then again, I was stupid enough to ask.

"Great," I said. "Well hey, I gotta get going. It's my turn to open the shop tomorrow, and you know how I am about getting my eight hours of beauty sleep."

"It's eight thirty, Eva."

"Well, we open at seven, so that means I've gotta get up at five thirty, and you know what a morning person I am—not. Besides," I rambled, "I like to read a bedtime story first."

We bid each other cordial good-byes, with me congratulating him and his bride-to-be one last time. I hung up the receiver, my hand shaking as I did. In fact, my whole body trembled.

He's getting married.

What the hell just happened?

I hadn't dated anyone since Shaun Harrison. We had met in the lobby of the campus library five years ago, expecting to attend a reading by author and NCLA alumnus Jack Sandoval. In fact, we were the only two people in the lobby because apparently we were also the only two people who didn't see the sign or receive the campus notification that the gig was canceled because Jack had the flu (six months later, I found out that he had actually been too drunk to read—his wife had just served him with divorce papers). So we went out for coffee instead, and afterwards spent the better part of three years living together.

Shaun was one of those guys with chiseled features—green, catlike eyes; long lashes; brown sugar–colored hair that fell in waves over his ears; glistening, white, straight teeth; and quarter-bouncing abs. He was five foot eleven to my five foot five. I was much more turned on by the fact that Shaun could recite all the amendments of the Constitution, in order, than the fact that he could do twenty one-handed pushups. I delighted in seeing his face light up every time he talked about the Continental Congress or Thomas Jefferson. Whereas I had taught creative writing at NCLA, he taught American history—still does.

We were the epitome of every romantic cliché: we enjoyed traveling, dining out, and long walks on the beach. We rooted for the NC State Wolfpack over the Carolina Tar Heels. We both grew up on Long Island and went back twice a year to visit our families. We were both Cancers and in our early thirties. We had great sex. We laughed at each other's jokes, liked each other's cooking, and even shared the same taste in television and movies.

You could've choked on the perfection. Or so I thought.

He didn't cheat on me, if that's what you're thinking. One thing about Shaun—he was loyal to a fault. No, one evening as we sat on the couch reading our respective books, he just closed his, looked up at me, and said it.

"I don't think I'm in love with you anymore, Eva. In fact, I'm not sure I ever was."

I swear I heard the *wham* of my familiar world crashing down on me. I looked over at him, my neck actually snapping from the severity, and opened my mouth.

Nothing. Dumbfounded.

I checked the book he was reading to see if that had anything to do with it: *The Lincoln-Douglas Debates.* Unromantic, yes. But I wouldn't think relationship-threatening.

My mouth still refused to work.

"I mean, I love you," Shaun went on without me. "I really, really love you and all that. You're my best friend in the world. But that's it. I just don't feel anything past that. I don't feel that *feeling* you're supposed to feel when you're in love."

A sound finally came out of my mouth. Lots of sounds, actually.

"Which feeling is that? The one that feels like everything is right in your world? The one that makes you feel like you want to spend the rest of your life with this person? The one that lets you know you're standing next to your soul mate?"

"Well, yeah."

"You mean the one I've been feeling for the last three years? The one I thought you've been feeling all this time? The one you *told* me you've been feeling?"

"I thought I was," he said.

"What changed your mind?"

"I don't know. I just somehow know it's not there."

"You know, the romance fades at some point, Shaun," I said. "It happens to everyone. If Romeo and Juliet hadn't offed themselves, it would've happened to them, too. One day Juliet would've gone apeshit on Romeo for leaving his boxers on the bathroom floor and wondered what she ever saw in such a heathen, and in turn, Romeo would've gone out for a couple of beers with his fellow Montagues and complained about Juliet's incessant nagging and how she let herself go."

He was unfazed by my literary tirade. "It's not that. I know the romance fades. It's just…I mean…I just feel like we've been stuck in the middle part of the movie, ya know?"

I stared at him, wondering to which movie he was referring.

"And I've been waiting to get to the end, but I just don't see it happening. I'm sorry, I really am. It's not you. I know that's a typical thing to say, but it's really not. You're a wonderful woman. Any guy is lucky to have you. I just don't think I'm that guy."

Have I mentioned how much I hate that "any guy is lucky to have you" line?

"So," I said, "if any guy is lucky to have me, then you're opting to throw away that luck? You're telling me you're less deserving? Are you just some humanitarian sacrificing your good fortune?"

"Stop trying to logically analyze this, Eva. Love is not logical."

He had moved out by the end of the month.

The worst part was when he said he still wanted us to be friends. He meant it, too. Real friends. I didn't believe him at the time. But since then, he'd lived up to his word and we actually did remain friends, once I was able to be in the same room with him and not feel the urge to either get on my knees and beg him to take me back or bludgeon him with a skillet. I'm not even sure of the exact day it happened. After months of going out of my way not to run into him—parking in a different faculty lot on campus, avoiding the pizza place where he grabbed a slice in between his classes—one day I walked into the auditorium to see a guest lecture by *Washington Post* reporter Bob Woodward, when I heard a voice behind me.

"Hey, Eva."

My head turned slowly, almost in slow motion, and instead of my body going stiff as a board, my face relaxed into a smile as I saw his own face light up.

"Hey, Shaun."

And that was that. I didn't go out of my way to see him, but in the two years since, we occasionally exchanged phone calls or e-mails when there was a new book or movie or *Family Guy* episode out that we thought the other would like. Granted, we weren't spending all of our spare time together in museums or downtown, but since he started showing up at The Grounds (almost to the point of being a Regular), I'd brought him his mochaccinos and cookies and joined him at his table and we shot the breeze for anywhere between five minutes to an hour, or until I was needed by Norman or a customer. In fact, his occasional presence at The Grounds was something I looked forward to. And yet, all that time he'd not said one word about dating anyone. About *the Jeanette*.

I'd denied that all along I'd been wishing for his pleasantries to turn into pleas for me to take him back, or that I'd been looking for some hint of desire in those cat eyes. But *this*. This was something different. *He's getting married.*

I reeled my mind back to the present moment and unraveled slowly. At first I just stood there, leaning against the wall and still clutching the phone's receiver. Then I robotically dialed my sister Olivia's number before sliding to the kitchen floor, unable to close my mouth or stop the trembling.

She answered without saying hello. "What's up, Eva?"

"Shaun's getting married," I sobbed.

She paused for a beat. "Wow."

"Yeah."

"When did this happen?"

"Tonight. He just called me."

"He got engaged and called you first?" she asked, a touch annoyed.

"No—I mean, I just found out tonight. Just now, actually."

"Why'd he call you at all?"

"We're still friends."

Silence.

"Don't start, Liv," I said.

"I said nothing," she replied.

"You didn't have to."

Olivia changed the subject. "Hey, Eva, what's with the pot shot at my calling to cancel plans with you in the blog post?"

"Aw, Liv, don't take it personally."

"You need to think of other people's feelings when you write."

"And you need to examine your own guilt."

I could hear my nine-year-old nephew Tyler screaming, "MOM!" in the background.

"Do you need to go?" I asked, my heart sinking.

"In a minute," she said. "Tyler needs help with his math homework. Are you OK?"

"Yeah," I lied. "I just thought I'd tell you the news."

"OK. Well, I've gotta go before Ty has a conniption."

"Give him a hug for me," I said.

"Will do. I'm sorry I can't be of more comfort to you right now. And Eva, just think of it as having dodged a bullet. You're doing fine without him. Love you."

"Love you too."

I hung up the phone, feeling dissatisfied. Should I call Minerva? Should I whip up a batch of brownies? Should I immerse myself in Meg Ryan movies? What would make me feel better?

Who was I kidding? Shaun was getting married. Nothing could make that better.

How could I have known that disaster would strike so swiftly, so completely, so unnervingly? How could I have known that Shaun was such a jerk?

OK. It wasn't Shaun's fault. I knew that. But any rate, disaster struck, and I was totally screwed. I had to act fast otherwise my cover would be blown. I'd be Valerie Plame-ed, outed, discredited. I'd have to delete the entire WILS blog, and I'd barely started it. Hell, I'd have to change my identity and move. Because all of a sudden, in the blink of an eye, I didn't want to be single anymore. Rather, I wanted to prove to Shaun that I was just as desirable as the Jeanette was. More to the point, I wanted to make him *jealous*, make him crave to get me back. So what if he'd never once hinted at any interest in getting back together during the course of our post-breakup friendship? Perhaps he didn't know he wanted it. Not until he saw me blissfully happy with someone else.

Worst of all, I knew that Shaun's engagement was the end of his and my friendship—or, at the very least, our friendliness. My comfortable, familiar life had been overturned and its contents spilled out. And once again, it happened at the hands of Shaun Harrison.

3

You Can't Handle the Truth
●●●

BFFs

I was only 15 when the movie *When Harry Met Sally* came out in the theater, but by the time I was 20, it topped my list of favorite films of all time. Feed me a line—any line—from the movie, and I'll feed you the next three lines.

Some say that Nora Ephron ruined relationships because the likelihood of marrying someone you were friends with was even more remote than meeting Prince Charming. And I confess that I bought it—hook, line, and sinker. When it came to my ex-boyfriend, I had thought we were headed in that direction. I had thought we were best friends as well as lovers. But instead we were lovers who managed to become friends.

But can you really be friends with your ex? I say why not, as long as you both agree that it's over. Isn't it better than having all that animosity? Isn't it better than carrying that baggage around with you?

And that's another good thing about being single: you can be friends with your exes without your significant others going green and

needing restraining orders after hacking into
your e-mail account and stalking your ex's old
hangouts in a bout of temporary insecurity-
induced insanity. I'd rather have the former
than the latter. At least with the former, you
get to relive the good moments, and you never
have to change your phone number.

But these days, I'm more taken with the idea
of being my own best friend. Because if you
can't live with yourself, you'll never be able
to live with anybody else.

I did everything in rhythmic lethargy the next morning:
opened The Grounds, made the cookies, cleaned the espresso
machine, wiped down the tables, reorganized the books in the
reading room, prepared the pita wraps, and so on.

By midafternoon, the Originals arrived along with the
post-lunch Friday crowd. Just as I removed a newspaper that a
customer had left on the table, I turned to find Minerva glaring
at me, arms crossed, the sleeves of her lab coat scrunched up
to her elbows.

"What?" I said.

"What's wrong?" Her words sounded more like a demand
than a question.

"Nothing," I lied. "I'm fine. I just didn't get enough sleep
last night."

"You're not fine."

"Min, really, I—"

"You made almond biscotti."

I went behind the counter, straightening the stack of paper
menus by the register as I did so. "So? It sells a hundred percent,"

I argued, discarding one scribble-laden menu that someone had used to test a pen.

Minerva followed me. She was perhaps the only customer I let behind the counter, not to mention the only one ballsy enough to go without permission in the first place.

"It also goes well with a cup of steamy something and childhood memories of your Nonna," she said. "Which means you want a cup of steamy something to cradle while you escape to said memories. Which means something's up. So what is it?"

"I told you, it's just sleep deprivation."

"I read your post," she said without hesitation.

"The BFF one?"

"Yeah. Did you see the comments?"

"Already? Geez, doesn't anyone sleep?"

"An anonymous commenter pretty much said that anyone foolish enough to live life by a movie line deserves what they get. So you know what Norman wrote in caps? YOU CAN'T HANDLE THE TRUTH!"

I laughed.

"The rest of the comments get into the men-and-women-can't-be-friends argument."

"Ah," I said, wiping down the counter.

"Did I ever tell you about the last time I saw Sebastard?" she asked, still not missing a beat. "Last time I saw him, he was carrying his toddler and buying a bagel sandwich for his wife. I mean, I'm sure she's great for him—she's a Katie," she said, as if that explained everything. "It's just that he was always so clear about not wanting any of that domestic crap—his words. So obviously, she had something that made her marry-able and me dump-able. I mean, I'm happy with Jay. Blissfully happy. You know how happy. But just seeing them? I think my heart broke right there. Like some big, silent announcement that she had something I lacked."

"She did. A baby."

She wanted to laugh, I could tell, but didn't. Instead, she shot me a look. "Point is, even though I know we were never right for each other, I cried for forty-five minutes at least. Hard. It sucked."

What, had she wiretapped my phone last night?

"Seriously, Min? The Katie's got nothing on you."

Minerva grinned in appreciation for the validation, and we both let the silence hang in the air until the moment presented itself. *Be brave,* I told myself. *She's your best friend, after all.*

"She's a Jeanette," I said under my breath. Minerva made a face that registered equal parts shock and disgust, as if I'd just said, "*I have scurvy.*"

"Shaun's got a girlfriend?"

"Worse."

"Ohmigod, *mistress?*" she said loud enough for the nearby customers at the counter to turn their heads in our direction. Then she covered her mouth, as if doing so would erase the word from their memories.

"No!" I said, my voice still hushed. "And shut up, will you? Fiancée."

"Oh. Oh, Eva, I'm sorry."

"It just took me by surprise, that's all. I didn't even know he was dating anyone. And how'd you know I was talking about Shaun in the blog post?"

I selected a sunny yellow plate for Minerva and placed two biscotti on it.

"Who else would you be talking about? And he never told you? That shmuck...he didn't do all this via e-mail, did he?"

She fumbled in her purse for the correct change, hardly taking her eyes off me.

"No, he called me last night. And he's not a shmuck."

"Yes he is. He's a shmuck because when he was with you, he had everything he needed right in front of his face and was too blind to see it. He's chasing something that doesn't exist."

"She does. She's a philosophy professor."

"I rest my case."

"Well, it's what he wants, I guess. I'm fine. It was just the shock, like you and Sebastard. I'm still happy, still loving singlehood. All's well."

Minerva gave me one of those motherly looks that says, *You're full of shit*, that makes you feel like someone opened the door on you while you were sitting on the john.

"You know what I wish?" I said. "I wish that just for one day my customers stayed on the other side of the counter and left me and my cookies free of psychoanalysis."

Minerva opened her mouth, about to utter a comeback, reconsidered, and closed it. Then she grinned.

"We wouldn't even make it till noon." With that, she bit into her biscotti.

I didn't deign to respond.

4

Lemon Torte Day

I MAKE A lemon torte on March twenty-sixth every year. It's my mother's recipe; she made it every Easter for as long as I can remember, saying that the lemons tasted like spring. I didn't even used to like it until I (almost sacrilegiously) added a raspberry drizzle to sweeten it up, but I've made one every year without fail since the last Easter Mom celebrated, the year I'd sneaked it into her hospital room so that she, Olivia, and I could eat it together—right out of the pan—while sitting on her bed (it was a girl's thing).

My mother died on March twenty-sixth, from breast cancer. I was fourteen years old. Olivia was eighteen.

Mom was my Girl Scout troop leader, and we always outsold all the other scouts in the troop when it came to the cookies. She was also a great cook, and Olivia and I often helped her prepare meals, hopping up to stir some pot or check the oven in between algebra problems and vocabulary quizzes. She baked almost every night, stopping only to shoo our fingers out of the bowls while we helped. Even as a child, I excelled at baking, and Mom encouraged me by giving me my own set of mixing bowls and a handheld electric mixer and measuring cups and spoons. Every Friday after dinner, the four of us would play *Scrabble* or *Monopoly*, and on nights when Mom was too tired to play, Dad taught Olivia and me to play poker and—better yet—how to count, stack, and bluff. Our father was a crack mathematician and a movie buff; he especially loved vaudeville and slapstick comedy. Whereas Mom and I bonded over bundt cakes and buttercream icing, Dad and I routinely watched and reenacted scenes by the Three Stooges and the Marx Brothers and Abbott and Costello.

When we were children, Olivia and I were best friends. She taught me to read and write and helped me with my homework, and I taught her how to do French braids and play Chinese Jacks. I told Olivia all about my first kiss with Nicky Bates, and she told me all about the first time she went all the way with Bobby Ackerman. Together Olivia and I tried (and hated) smoking, and she always let me tag along with her friends. She taught me to drive, and I taught her how to get out of jury duty.

After Mom died, Olivia dropped out of college to help my father take care of me and see me through high school, despite his begging her not to. I have always felt guilty but to this day can't decide if the guilt comes from her decision or the fact that in secret I was grateful that she did it because I needed her; she was someone to talk to and hug and interact with, and I was afraid to be with just my father. Not that he was some monster—far from it—but our mother's death had shaken him to the core. He'd retreated inside himself to the point that he was no more than a shadow that lurked about the house when he wasn't working twelve-hour days to avoid a place that was short on laughter and long on sadness. Besides, I'd lost count of the number of times he told me how much I looked like my mother.

My father died sixteen months after my mother, also of cancer, although I still believe it was brought on by a broken heart and not genetic predisposition, as the doctors told us. He had emotionally left us long before, so grieving for him was more an act of longing for the days when we were all young and carefree and close than an exercise in shock and loss. I'd thought such grief would be easier to manage. Turns out I was wrong.

After barely graduating high school, I went to work full-time at a bookstore for almost four years. It was a perfect fit for me—I couldn't remember a time when I wasn't escaping to some story. Time outside the kitchen was spent reading and spinning stories. Meanwhile, Olivia worked as a receptionist in a doctor's office, where she met the man she'd eventually marry.

When I was twenty-two, the age at which the few friends I had left had graduated college, Olivia finally snapped.

March twenty-sixth, to be exact.

We had just finished the last slice of torte when she put her fork down and asked, "Eva, when are you going to get out from under your rock?"

I looked at her, bewildered. "What?"

"This has got to stop."

"Mom's torte?"

"You need to get a life! You're twenty-two, and where are you?"

"What are you talking about?" I asked, feeling panic and anger rise. "This is our *home!*"

"This place hasn't been anyone's home since the day Mom got diagnosed."

I sat back hard, as if she'd struck me, while she charged full steam ahead. "You should be *writing* books, not selling them! You should be out living *your* life, not what's left of theirs." She glanced up at me, and I was surprised to see tears lining her eyes. "And don't even give me that look—Mom and Dad would've told you the same thing."

"Oh yeah?" I shot back, my vision blurred with tears I refused to blink away. "And you think they'd be so proud of you answering phones? That takes a lot of skill!"

She made a strange, strangled sound, and several moments passed before she spoke again.

"I can't believe how selfish you are," she said. I'd never heard her voice so cold. "Didn't it ever occur to you that I might want to get married and have a family of my own? You're my sister, not my daughter! You think I wanna spend the rest of my life taking care of you? It's time to grow up! For both of us!"

She pushed away from the table and left me crying in silence that pounded at my ears. I didn't see her again until later that night when she slipped into my room and onto the corner of my bed. I pretended to be asleep, but she saw right through it. She sat with me and rubbed my back for nearly an hour. It was probably the worst fight we'd ever had.

⤙⤚

The food processor interrupted my memories as it pulverized organic graham crackers while the butter melted in a saucepan on the stovetop. I combined the two and pressed the mixture into Mom's torte pan—I refused to use any other—before putting it in the oven and moving on to the custard.

The best part of lemon torte is making the custard. Today I had chosen two perfect lemons—bright yellow and blushing green in just the right spots—and I could almost hear my father behind me trying to coerce me into doubling the sugar, just like he used to do with my mother. Like me, he had no taste for sour things and would squinch his face after every jaw-pinching bite of the torte before licking his fork clean and spearing more. I think I could make lemon custard with my eyes closed, letting the pull of the spoon tell me when it's heated enough to set just right. After removing the custard from the stove to cool in the fridge, Mom would give Olivia the spoon. We had a system: Olivia got the custard leftovers (her favorite part), and I got the crust crumbs (my favorite part).

I slid the bowl into the fridge, and my memories continued.

I had been vehemently opposed to selling the house at first, but Olivia said that it would be nothing more than an empty tomb if we held on to it. She didn't want to live there, and I didn't want to live there without her. The truth was that I was afraid to leave home, to lose the last remnant of the family I once had, to never know the feeling of home again. And I didn't want to go out into the world where nothing was safe or sure, but I'd never considered that Olivia was itching to get out into the very world I was avoiding.

So that was that. We sold the house and split the money, of which my half went towards my tuition and living expenses at SUNY Stony Brook as an English major. From there I went on to a master of fine arts degree in creative writing at NCLA, thanks to a scholarship. And when I'd written a novel as my thesis project and it was published, receiving favorable critical reviews, my value increased tenfold.

Sitting at an oval-shaped table in yet another English department conference room, facing yet another hiring committee for yet another tenure-track position, my novel and copies of my curriculum vita were spread out like evidence in a police interrogation. Words like "impressive" and "promising" danced about the air.

And then I smelled it: *bread.*

A nearby sandwich shop in the campus student center had just finished baking several loaves, and the wind directed the heavenly aroma right into the open conference room window, like a telegram delivered just for me. My academic life then flashed before my eyes—but instead of seeing myself delivering papers at conferences and attending guest lectures or book signings, grading papers and advising students, the images were of me bringing chocolate chip cookies to study groups and baking birthday cakes for my fellow grad students. When I was a TA, I'd been invited to serve on faculty committees with hopes that I'd attend meetings armed with pitchers of smoothies or platters of lemon bars. The other stuff—grading and lecturing and publishing and all that—suddenly seemed like an indefinite sentence of manual labor.

"Eva?" the creative writing program director had piped. "Is something wrong?"

I hadn't heard a word she'd said.

I left the interview that day vowing to never go on another, and the following day, I applied for a business loan to open a coffee shop. For the next year, I turned down job offers and stayed on faculty as an adjunct at North Carolina Liberal Arts College until The Grounds was up and running. Of course, being a tenured professor would have given me prestige, my own office with a window and my name on the door, and some job security. But being in a place where I could both bake and gather with the college crowd less than a mile away from campus seemed like the natural thing to do.

Leaving Olivia in New York was probably the hardest thing I've ever done—worse even than selling the house and packing up all of our parents' belongings. For the first two weeks, I had called every night (and sometimes the following morning) and cried, pleading for her to either come get me and take me home or to pack up and move down South with me.

"It'll get easier," she promised. "You'll see."

"Don't you miss me at all?" I once cried.

A quiet sob followed a long pause before she answered, "You'll thank me later."

She was right. On all counts.

⌒⊙

After pouring this year's custard into the shell, I drizzled the raspberry glaze on with darting strokes, the spoon leading my hand and wrist.

When I dialed Olivia's number and got her voice mail, I hung up without leaving a message, satisfied at having heard her voice, at least. I sliced the torte into slivers and arranged them on a plate for my customers to help themselves.

"What's the occasion?" Scott asked as he sampled a sliver. I shrugged without saying a word. "Whatever it is, we should celebrate it more often. This rocks."

I had not been conversational all day, not even when Shaun walked in and ordered a mochaccino, looking at the plate that still contained a few slivers.

"I thought so," said Shaun.

"Excuse me?" I asked while handing him his drink and collecting his money.

"It's Lemon Torte Day."

He remembered.

I looked into Shaun's eyes, and time stopped. They reflected compassion, the warm gaze of a lover who held me on the anniversaries of my parents' deaths, when Olivia wasn't there to rub my back while I cried. The man who kissed me after one bite of lemon torte; I could taste the custard on his tongue. My Shaun. Soon to belong to the Jeanette. Where had he been all this time? Why had he left?

"Thank you," I said, my voice breaking just above a whisper.

I excused myself and went into the back room, where I sat on the edge of the desk in the cramped office and took several deep breaths. A photo of Mom, Dad, Olivia, and me at Disneyworld—all wearing Mickey Mouse ears—watched me from the upper right-hand corner of the desk. I was ten, Olivia was fourteen, and Mom and Dad were in their midforties. They looked so young and vibrant and healthy. We were all so happy. I buried my face in my hands and cried.

The door to the office opened, and I uncovered my face to see Norman holding it for Shaun. I'd never seen that look on Norman's face, one of paralyzed uncertainty, as Shaun entered and hugged me close. How I wanted to hate Shaun in that moment, to tell him to go away and never come back, to curse him for leaving me just as my parents had done. At least they had a good excuse. But instead I held on to him, inhaling his scent and wishing for the moment to last, if only to have him back again.

When I regained my composure and emerged from the back room with Shaun, my eyes still glassy, Norman didn't ask why I was upset, didn't say a word. Just whispered in my ear that I could go home if I wanted to. I shook my head; I was already home, I said. He kissed me on my cheek.

The torte was long gone by the time Olivia returned my call.

"Hey," she said.

"Hey," I answered. "Happy Torte Day," I said sadly.

"Yeah," her voice was soft, faded like the edges of my memories. "You too."

5

Friends First

SITTING ON MY bed after work, perusing Facebook and other blogs, I stared at my laptop screen before opening up Google's homepage. I then stared at the empty Search box, waiting for me to make a move. As if my hands were on automatic pilot, the letters appeared in lowercase form, one by one: l-o-v-e-m-a-t-c-h-.-c-o-m.

Enter.

The homepage appeared and two more blank boxes stared at me, asking for my username and password. *Not a member? Sign up now!*

My focus remained fixed on the screen. An abnormally gorgeous couple practically batted their eyelashes at me. The next thing I knew, I was filling in more blank boxes with my name, address, date of birth, ethnicity, height, body type, eye and hair color, astrological sign, religion, political affiliation, likes and dislikes, and checking boxes of my ideal match. Blue eyes. Non-smoker. Six feet tall. Average build. No terrorists, stalkers, or Toby Keith fans. Libertarians and/or Independents optional. Divorced fathers optional. Married fathers definitely out.

I paused again, the cursor hovering on the tagline. *Friends first*, I finally typed. Then I found a photo—one of me leaning my elbow on the counter, wearing a slate gray shirt that almost perfectly matched my eyes. Minerva had taken it with her cell phone, I think, as I rested my chin on my hand, my unruly chestnut hair spilling down to frame a half smile. I uploaded it and clicked *Submit*.

A half hour later, as I lay in the dark on my back, staring at the ceiling and waiting to fall asleep, I spoke out loud: "Aw, crap. What the hell did I do that for?"

6

Busted

WITHIN THE FIRST week of posting my profile on Lovematch.com, I'd received three "winks," two invitations for coffee (I'd made the mistake of admitting that I spend the majority of my time in a coffee shop without mentioning the crucial detail of owning it), and one guy told me I was "incredibly sexy"—how does one discern that from a snapshot of someone who's leaning on a countertop?

I read each prospective profile. Many of them lived in Wilmington or the surrounding towns, although one was as far as Chapel Hill, and I concluded that he either owned a beach house here or a really cool car. Many of them promised to treat me like a queen, were "fed up with game-playing" (I assumed they didn't mean *Scrabble* or *Guitar Hero*), were loyal, loving fathers and good, God-fearing Christians.

The key to a successful ad, I decided, was audience awareness and brevity. Unfortunately, many failed. For one thing, too many false assumptions were made—that I had or wanted kids, that I was seeking financial security, or that I'd been dumped or neglected, and that I was not to be trusted. For another thing, some were trying so hard to establish that they were reliable, rich, or sensitive that they seemed to ignore me altogether. And I couldn't help but reject the profiles with excessive run-ons and fragments, spelling errors, or those typed in all capital letters.

What can I say? It was an occupational hazard, even if I was no longer in the occupation. All indicated a lack of attention to detail and proofreading, not to mention poor Internet etiquette. I mean, really, DIDN'T ANYONE TEACH YOU GUYS THAT ALL CAPITAL LETTERS MEANS YOU ARE SHOUTING AT SOMEONE? And besides, why ask out the former-English-teacher-geek-bookworm when you the only book you've ever read was the ghostwritten autobiography of Tony Hawk?

As I read profile after profile, one notion nagged me: these were all personal *advertisements*. Buy me! An investment of a lifetime! It was catalog shopping, at best. Worst of all, it was so unromantic. But some pushy curiosity kept me reading, clicking, scrolling, and searching, perhaps hoping I'd eventually find a gold nugget in all that sand. Another Shaun, or someone even better.

❧

Minerva, Sister Beulah, Car Talk Kenny, and I huddled around a table cluttered with ceramic mugs, crumpled napkins, and Minerva's laptop and study notes. So far, they were the only people I had told about joining the site. I hadn't even told Olivia or Norman.

As Minerva scrolled through the list of available men, one of us occasionally interrupted in a hushed voice, "Oooo, what about this one?" and Minerva discreetly read the profile out loud. We then discussed and debated.

Car Talk Kenny winced at one. "He'll cheat on you first chance he gets."

"How do you know that?" Sister Beulah asked.

"The picture was taken at a bar."

"So? How does that lead you to the conclusion that he'll cheat on her?" said Minerva, while I asked, "How do you know it's at *a bar*?"

"Look at the lighting," he said.

By the second week, I'd still managed to keep the endeavor a secret when one night Lovematch.com alerted my iPhone to a new message. I opened it and my jaw dropped when I saw the photo of Scott, Norman's best friend. One of the Originals.

> *Cool profile, Eva! So much for singlehood—you are so busted! Well, how 'bout it? Wanna grab a coffee? Haha.*

I stared at my phone, mortified. Was he seriously asking me out? I had a strict rule about not dating any of The Grounds's customers. Norman, however, exercised no such rule and was always on the lookout for potential dates or, as he dubbed them, "future Mrs. Norman Baileys," as if he was going to keep backups.

Later, I scanned Scott's profile, beginning with the photo. Strange, he resembled the Scott I knew, somewhat: cowlicked, milk chocolate–colored hair with eyes to match; long face; thin, pale lips. Leaning against a railing offset by a red, rocky backdrop. The Grand Canyon, I guessed. Adventurous looking. This Scott, however, looked older. Less attractive. Perhaps he wasn't photogenic. Or perhaps I had just gotten so used to seeing him day after day that I never really studied his features before. His profile name was "babelfish360." (Mine was "groundskeeper-silly." Long and corny as hell, I know, but I couldn't resist.)

Computer geek seeks sci-fi chick, he wrote. Didn't do much to warm the cockles of my heart. Then again, at least he made no promises of queen treatment or to be the final destination on my quest to find Mr. Right. The rest of his profile contained quotes and lists of books and movies that the sci-fi chick would know and appreciate. And, to my surprise, I knew most of them.

Rather than reply to his message, I shut down my laptop and went to bed, dreading the awkward moment when I'd see him again. And sure enough, my stomach did somersaults the next day when he entered The Grounds, laptop case strung over his shoulder and thick computer manuals in hand (he was some kind of software programmer, that little I knew). He greeted Norman at the counter, high-fiving him in midair and morphing it into a handshake. While Norman prepared his latte, I occupied myself by loading a stack of dishes into the dishwasher.

"Hey, Eva," Scott called, extending himself just short of climbing across the counter to get a glimpse of me. I pretended not to see or hear him. He said it again.

I turned and feigned surprise. "Oh, hey, Scott." He possessed a devilish grin that worried me.

"Eva, those are *clean*," said Norman, pointing to the dishes. I stopped and sighed and stared at them, silently cursing myself.

"You OK?" Scott asked.

"Fine," I said.

"You look a little nervous. Got a hot date or somethin'?"

I turned and shot him an angry glance. Scott was never one to be an asshole, but something apparently had gotten into his water supply, and I had to nip this in the bud.

"Actually, I should be asking *you* that question," I said. "Any good hits on Lovematch-dot-com lately?"

"You're doing Lovematch-dot-com?" asked Norman.

"Well how else are you supposed to do it, dude?" replied Scott.

"Duh! Look around you!" Norman said, gesturing his arms in a round-up motion of the café.

My eyes panned across the café. A group of Originals was clustered in their usual corner by the counter. Neil, the Regular who came in like clockwork every day at one thirty for a coffee and Cookie of the Week and stayed precisely for twenty minutes, sat on a bar stool facing the picture window. In the opposite corner, two students were hunched over their laptops. And Car Talk Kenny occupied his perch just outside the reading room.

"It's all couples and impoverished grad students! Isn't that right, Eva?"

"Hardly," I said, ready to list any number of academics, telecommuters, and independent contractors. "And who are you—Steve Jobs? That's a helluva low opinion of my clientele you got there."

"I'm just sayin'," said Scott, "I'm not waiting for the woman of my dreams to walk through those doors. Instead, I'm being proactive. Obviously you got the same idea, although I thought you were all gung-ho for the single life. Or are you doing some kind of sociological experiment for your blog—you know, like *30 Days with Morgan Spurlock*?"

I handed Scott his BLT pita wrap, shooting him another murderous look, but it was too late; Norman caught on and opened his mouth, pointing at me.

"You didn't!"

He said this within earshot of the Originals.

"Didn't what?" asked one of them.

"Eva joined Lovematch-dot-com," Norman announced. Like a first-grader, I folded my arms on the counter, buried my head into them, and groaned.

"You're kidding! Let's look her up!" I heard Dean say.

"Oh my God," I moaned, the words muffled in my folded arms.

"Hey, Eva, can we not violate the sanitary codes, please?" said Norman.

"Here she is!" said Dean. "Hey, that's a great picture—that's here, isn't it? When'd you take it?"

I lifted my head and eyed Dean suspiciously.

"How'd you get into the site?" I asked.

"My username and password."

"You subscribe to Lovematch-dot-com?"

"How'd you think I met Jan?"

This revelation rendered me speechless. I'd just assumed some serendipitous event brought them together, like a fender bender or a mistaken dental appointment or side-by-side seats at a football game.

"Are you actually looking for a mate?" Neil asked me. "What happened to you loving singlehood?"

"Nothing happened. It's just that so many people on the blog are telling me what I'm missing out on, so I decided to see what all the fuss is about," I replied, hoping I sounded convincing.

The Originals, including Scott, crowded around Dean's laptop. Dean read aloud: "*Friends First*—that's her tagline."

"Nice alliteration," interjected Car Talk Kenny, who had crossed the café to join in on my humiliation. He seemed to be directing the remark to me, however, since he glanced at me when he said it.

Dean continued, "*Take 1 cup of 30-something ex-Yankee, 1 cup of entrepreneur, 1 cup of a master's degree, and add generous helpings of books, TV shows, and movies.*" He looked up. "This is cute. It's a little recipe." He returned to the screen and read out loud again. "*Mix with a tablespoon of humor, a teaspoon of pluck, and a sprinkle of TLC.*"

"Aw, Eva, I love it!" said Jan. "I didn't write anything nearly as creative when I subscribed."

"I don't even think I read what you wrote. Your smokin' picture did all the talkin'," said Dean to Jan. "Little did I know you spend your life in scrubs."

"At least they're pretty scrubs," said Tracy in an effort to comfort her visibly wounded friend. She gently touched the sleeve of Jan's pastel blue scrubs with daisies.

"Keep reading," prodded Scott.

"*Bake in up to 95-degree temperatures on the beach, but be sure to use sunscreen. Let cool in temps no lower than 40 degrees, or suffer the consequences of crankiness. Enjoy with a sweet chardonnay or a slick Sam Adams.*" Dean looked up again. "Sam Adams? Really?"

"Better than your frat-boy Bud Light," Norman zinged. "And you're what, thirty years old now?"

When the Originals started sparring over the movie quotes (I knew they'd be stumped on the one from *Animal Crackers*), I slunk away into the reading room to retrieve stray coffee mugs.

About an hour later, as I wiped down tables, I went over to Scott's, sat opposite him, and leaned in. "So, were you seriously asking me out for a cup of coffee?" I asked in a hushed voice.

"Hey, I'm sorry about outing you. I just couldn't resist."

"Yeah, right. Because you're Mr. Funny."

"What's the big deal? Everyone does it these days. Fifty bucks says half the faculty and administrators of NCLA are on Lovematch-dot-com, including the chancellor."

"You didn't answer my question."

He looked down for a moment and looked back up, his cheeks red. "Let me put it to you this way," he started. "If you weren't you and I only had your profile to go on, I would've asked you out."

I leaned back in my chair, mouth opened, wounded. "Thanks a lot."

"No no no no no," he said quickly, and he lightly took hold of my wrist to keep me from standing up and walking away in a huff. "I didn't mean it like that. I mean I've got too much to lose this way, that's all."

"What way?"

"This way," he said, smacking the table. "I don't want to lose all of this."

"How do you know you would lose it?"

"I'm too much of a coward to find out either way."

With that, he went back to his open computer manual and highlighter, and pretended to get lost in the text. Or at least I thought he was pretending. Saying nothing in response, I got up and finished wiping down the rest of the tables.

7

Dating Rules

I HAD BEEN in a funk since Lemon Torte Day, missing my parents and Olivia all over again, not to mention Shaun. He hadn't called or come into The Grounds since. But at some point, I decided that enough was enough—it was time to be proactive, get back into the swing of things, try a new hand of cards.

Time to go on a date.

When I swung open the door to Mike's Seafood restaurant, Nick from New Bern—my first Lovematch.com date—was already waiting for me, standing stiffly in the lobby. I instantly recognized him, although he was both taller and heavier than I'd imagined (I hadn't seen any photos of him from the neck down). He straightened his posture when he saw me.

"Eva?" he asked tentatively. He pronounced it EE-va, despite my telling him otherwise during the ten-minute phone call to finalize plans for the date.

"It's pronounced AY-vah," I corrected.

"Sorry," he said, looking relieved. "I'm Nick." He shook my hand. "So why'd your mother insist on giving you a name that's spelled one way and pronounced another?"

He's just met me face-to-face and already he's criticizing my parents?

"Actually, it was my father's influence," I explained. "I'm named after my paternal grandmother. She's European and that's the way they pronounced and spelled it. My sister was named after our maternal grandmother. Her name is Olivia, and it's spelled the same way it's pronounced."

The hostess sat us at a table in the middle of the restaurant.

"Well," Nick said once we were seated, "you're even lovelier in person."

"Thank you," I said, taking a sip of water and feeling uncharacteristically shy. I'd dressed in black pants and a sleeveless blue top along with Nine West pumps.

"What do you think of *me*?" he asked. His bluntness surprised me.

"You mean, appearance-wise?" I asked.

"Of course. Be honest, now."

Thinning hair. Close-set eyes. Tweed and khaki, buttons straining.

"As advertised," I said, willing myself not to blink. "No complaints."

He seemed satisfied with this answer. Just then, my eyes brightened as our server and I recognized each other.

"Professor Perino!"

"Caleb Collins, as I live and breathe," I said. He was obviously pleased that I remembered his name. "What's a nice guy like you doing in a place like this?"

"I'm on the five-year plan at school," he replied with a chuckle. "I work here on the weekends and during the summer."

"I see. And what comes after graduation, or are you sick of everyone asking you that?"

"Not at all, ma'am," he said with a twinkle in his eye. "I'm moving back to Virginia to work for my dad's company. It was too late to change my major and transfer to NC State, but I've decided to get into engineering."

I looked at him, my face frozen with shock. This was the same kid who was hell-bent on moving to New Hampshire to live a bohemian lifestyle and drive a hybrid, who was a Civil War buff and whose first short story in my class was about a Confederate soldier who breaks ranks of his father's command and defects to the North.

"What changed your mind?" I asked.

"My girlfriend has a Hummer," he said.

Nick interjected, "Sweet ride!"

Caleb turned to him and nodded. "Dude, you know what I'm talkin' about. They never shoulda discontinued them." I thought he was going to high-five him.

I seized the moment to introduce the two, telling Nick, "Caleb was one of the shining stars from my teaching days at NCLA. He took my Introduction to the Short Story class."

"Professor Perino is a great teacher," said Caleb.

"You can call me Eva now, you know."

Caleb laughed politely. "Yes ma'am."

"So, what's an outsider got to do to order a drink?" said Nick. Apparently the Hummer-bonding thing had a short lifespan.

Caleb turned his attention to Nick. "I'm sorry, sir. What can I get for you?"

"I'll have a Coors Light."

Caleb wrote the order on his pad before looking at me.

"Glass of wine?" I said. "But I think I'll have it with dinner, and when I figure out what that will be, I'll let you know what kind of wine."

"Sure thing, ma'am." He flipped his pad over and tucked it in the front pocket of his apron. "I'll get that Coors for you and take your dinner orders in a jiff."

"Thanks. It's great to see you, Caleb."

He smiled widely. "You too, ma'am."

"*Eva*," I reminded him.

"Yes ma'am."

As he walked away, I looked at Nick. "I've been living in the South since oh-one and I still can't get used to guys calling me 'ma'am.'" I paused for a beat before adding, "He's a great kid," thumbing in the direction that Caleb walked away.

"Were you that intimate with *all* your students?"

I sat back, wondering if he was deliberately trying to creep me out. Shaun used to tease me about baking cookies for my classes, but he knew there was a line I wouldn't cross. Most people thought I was friendly with my students because I wasn't much older than they were, but they (including Shaun) never understood how personal writing could be regardless of the genre and discipline in which one wrote, or the bond that formed between teacher and student because of it.

"I was fond of my students, but I would never use the word *intimate*," I said.

"Well, he's gonna comp those drinks, right?" said Nick.

"Excuse me?"

"The drinks. He's not gonna charge us for 'em, is he?"

I frowned. "Why would he do that?"

"Seeing as how he knows you…"

I glared at him, trying to stave off the disgust that was seeping in.

"I would never expect such a thing. He's probably making less an hour than those drinks cost."

He shrugged as if this fact was inconsequential. I took another sip of water.

"So, Nick from New Bern. Why don't you tell me the story of your life," I said in deadpan, Billy Crystal–Harry Burns voice.

Nick proceeded to do just that. He began with the hospital in which he was born, moved on to his four-year-old birthday party, then elementary, junior, and senior high school, college, graduate school, first job, second job, marriage, divorce, and finally, Lovematch.com—all in a Southern drawl and pausing only when Caleb returned with the beer and took our dinner orders, not even allowing Caleb and I to resume our small talk. He talked until our dinner orders arrived while I nodded robotically the entire time.

"Why did you divorce?" I asked like a sucker when I finally got a word in.

"Truth?"

"You think lying on the first date is a turn-on?"

He laughed. "Well, if you must know, my ex-wife was a real bitch."

I put my utensils down (which was probably wise), dabbed my mouth with the corner of my napkin before returning it to my lap, and took a rather forceful drink of wine. He noticed my offense.

"You said to be honest."

"Yes, I did. Thank you for that. While your wife was busy being a bitch, what were you doing?"

"I was working my ass off trying to keep her happy."

"So what about her bitchiness was so endearing it made you want to marry her?"

This is probably not the best line of questioning, said a voice in my head.

"She wasn't a bitch when we were dating," Nick replied.

"Someone give it to her as a wedding present?"

"Excuse me?"

"I'm just saying that people don't change that drastically. Either she was always the alleged bitch that you say she was and you were subconsciously blind to it, or you saw and chose to ignore it."

He took a swig of his beer. "I think it's time for a subject change, don't you?"

"Right-o," I said.

"So why are you still single?" he asked. "What's wrong with *you*?"

I took another sip of wine. Strike two. Three, if you count him calling me EE-va.

"What's wrong with me?" I said, looking at my plate of half-eaten grilled salmon. "What's wrong with me..." I said again, my voice trailing off.

"How'd your last relationship end?" he asked.

"My lover decided that he wasn't in love with me after all," I answered, wanting to ask Caleb to bring me another glass of wine and a Taser.

"How come? What, did you pressure him to get married or somethin'?"

Strike four.

"Hardly. Actually, I have no idea why."

"I guess he just wasn't that into you."

"Guess not."

If I could, I would've fired lasers out of my eye sockets and exploded his head. Thankfully, Caleb returned with the check.

"So, where've you been, Professor? I never see you around campus anymore."

"Oh, don't you know? I left teaching. I own a coffee shop now."

"Really? How come? Is it near school?"

"Here," I said as I reached into my purse and pulled out a business card. "That's good for a free coffee on your first visit."

"Oh, I know this place. I've never been there, though. Cool," he said, avoiding Nick's invasive eyes. "I'll definitely stop by sometime."

Caleb left the table again, and I wished I could follow him.

"So why'd you leave teaching?" Nick asked me.

"I wasn't really interested in the academic conversations and all the responsibility that came with tenure—you know, that whole publish-or-perish thing."

"What's 'publish-or-perish'?"

"It's an expression. If you don't publish scholarly articles—or for me, another novel—you could lose your chances of getting tenure or grant funding or whatever else they can lord over you. I liked being in the classroom with the students, but I was more interested in telling my stories and reading theirs than I was in grading them."

"So how long have you been at The Grounds?" asked Nick.

I froze. Never in our communications did I mention my business by name.

"I already Googled you and scoped out your shop," he said. Then he added, slightly agitated, "Relax—I'm not gonna camp out in front of it or anything like that."

Google: the stalker's best friend. Strike five.

Nick picked up the tab while I left a cash tip for Caleb amounting to fifty percent of the bill. Once outside the restaurant, Nick and I looked at each other, paused in the awkward moment.

"So, Eva." He mispronounced it again.

Please don't kiss me, please don't kiss me, please don't kiss me...

"Yes?" I said.

"Thank you for an enjoyable evening."

"Same here." I extended my hand, and he took it and folded it into his own for a brief, damp-palmed minute before returning it to me.

"I won't be seeing you again, will I."

"No, you won't."

"How come?" he asked.

The words of Louis Armstrong in response to a reporter's question "What is jazz?" came to me: *Man, if ya hassta ask...*

"I don't like when women are referred to as 'bitches,'" I said. "Regardless of how your wife treated you, she doesn't deserve that, even if her behavior was reprehensible."

"Fair enough," he said. "May I walk you to your car?"

"I'm all set, thanks."

When I got home, I flung off my heels, slipped out of my outfit, threw on a T-shirt, and flopped into my reading chair in my bedroom, taking in a deep breath and exhaling deliberately.

I *love* my reading chair. I had purchased it from a furniture showroom in Port Jefferson on Long Island years ago. I maxed out a credit card for it. Its cream-colored suede is soft as butter. Its firm wood legs don't make a sound when you sit in it. Its cushion is like sitting on a cloud. It's roomy enough to either sit upright or curled up. I can fall asleep in that chair for a full eight hours and wake up without a crick in my neck or stiffness in my lower back. Reading has always been my reward after a long day, even after grading drafts of short stories or freshman compositions. I've escaped to many worlds of books in that chair. I've written my dreams in that chair. I sat on Shaun's lap, and later missed it, all in that perfect chair.

Sitting in the stillness, a thought came to me: *Tonight was my first date in almost two years.* I'd never gone so long without even one date. And certainly I'd never experienced anything as contrived as this. Even blind dates had the element of surprise going for them.

I stood up and padded over to my writing desk, turned on my laptop, and stared at the screen for a moment. First I checked e-mails. Lovematch.com alerted me to two new messages. A wave of disgust came over me after perusing them. More promises of happily ever after. More photos of strangers trying to impress me.

"Damn catalog shopping," I muttered aloud.

I hopped on and off Facebook, then skimmed The Grounds's bloglist hastily, in a daze, before looking at the clock; it was getting late. I didn't want to call Minerva or Olivia or anyone else and start going through the play-by-play of the date. But I felt the need to say *something*.

The WILS Dating Rules

I love singlehood like I love vanilla chai lattes and cookies. But that doesn't mean I don't date from time to time. For fun, you know? Anyway, it has come to my attention that there are some things that cannot be excused, some things that should never have happened in the first place. And should you decide to leave your single lair to enter dating territory, you should be aware of them. So here, dear reader, are a few simple rules for the dater.

Rule #1: Get her name right.

Know it, use it, and for God's sake, say it correctly. Especially if she makes a point to say it for you, and particularly if she insists that no one ever gets it right. It's her name, for crying out loud. It's part of *her*. Show some respect. However, should you find yourself tripping over your own tongue, cursing the day you decided to try to become un-single and wishing that all girls were Jills and all guys were Larrys, do not blame her parents. Do not ask what they were thinking. Ask what her name means, ask where it's from, ask her to repeat it or spell it, but please, please, please, I am begging you, don't ask what *possessed* her parents.

Rule #2: Don't monopolize the conversation.
If you're in the middle of your life story and you feel the need to come up for air, stop. If her eyes are glazed over and she's past the point of fidgeting, *stop*. If the waiter comes to take your order and you're still going strong by the time he returns with your meals, stop, Stop, STOP.

Please.

Rule #3: Never admit to having Googled your date.
That one is self-explanatory, yes?

Rule #4: Don't call women "bitches."
Even if you're sure she is one, it's just not right. In fact, let's try to steer clear of foul language in general when one is in a classy

location and out to impress. Think about what you're saying. Think etymology. Think sexism. *Think*, for crying out loud! I understand that vernacular language is strewn with things you'd never say in front of your grandmother, but the slurs relegated to degrading humans by calling them womanly? Frankly, I think they could be erased from the English language altogether.

And I can't stand when women call men dogs either, by the way.

Rule #5: Never utter the words "So, why are you still single?", "What's wrong with you?", "What's your problem?" or any combination thereof. Ever.

8

The Deal Breakers

HAVING SPENT THE last two months going on Lovematch. com dates, I was ready to call the whole thing quits. Despite subscribing to an introductory three months with a few more weeks to go, I stopped checking the site and started deleting the e-mail alerts to new messages or winks, not to mention the barrage of invitations to extend my membership for another six months at a reduced rate, assuring me that finding love takes time. But I was sick of the fabricated constructions of myself and my dates, sick of the endless parade of first dates that felt like interviews, sick of conveyor belt dating. Even though the majority of men were cordial, gallant, and complimentary (some of them warranted second dates, and one even made it to three), none of them offered anything by way of chemistry. I don't even know if "chemistry" is the right word. Even in terms of my "friends first" criteria, they all fell short.

Although I shared common interests and a couple of laughs with these guys, we failed to connect in terms of eliciting long conversations into the night, or the passage of hours in what seemed like minutes. None of them inspired lengthy e-mails or endless phone calls. None of them made me feel giddy, or smile when no one was in the room. None of them prompted me to share my life stories, my hopes and dreams, strengths and vulnerabilities. Few, if any, even made me horny.

The last one was a combination of Denny Crane and Voldemort. Disenchanted yet again, I decided it was time for a report card.

The Deal Breakers

I was going to begin this post apologetic for being superficial and demanding perfection where none is to be found, but after two months of steady dates, and a few choice decades on this planet, I've decided against it. Because we all have 'em, and we all know it. You know, pet peeves, worst-habit-evers, nerve-graters. Flaws that are just not acceptable, would never be considered "cute" during that dreamy in-love phase, and will never turn into something you just have to live with. The relationship-enders. Deal breakers. Won't-get-to-first-base deficiencies. And what can you do but laugh? As the musician Emily Saliers once said, "You have to laugh at yourself sometimes, because you'd cry your eyes out if you didn't." So here, in good fun, are a few that have crossed my path, unfortunately. (I've changed names to protect the guilty.)

Deal Breaker #1: "William from Wrightsville Beach" brings home recyclable trash. Here we are, at one of those cute grill shacks that sells hot dogs loaded with krout, hamburgers and greasy fries, and frozen custard. The kind of place that only has picnic tables outside.

We are having a good time, me with my burger so pink it could moo, him with his chilidog, and the two of us sipping our cans of Coke, swapping our favorite scenes from *The Office*. We finish, and as I get up to throw out our trash, he swivels his head like a cornered dog searching for an exit.

"What's wrong?" I ask.

"I don't see a recycling bin anywhere for the cans. And these cardboard boats, they can be recycled, too."

"Not with all this ketchup dripping all over them, they can't."

William then proceeds to go into the shack and asks for a bag, to which the poor teenager behind the counter informs him that she can only give him a full-size garbage bag. William comes back outside, grabs a few more napkins, wipes down the cardboard boats with them, flattens them, and then wraps them in two more napkins. So here I am, trying to rationalize how sweet, how caring, how *conscientious* he is when he goes over to the trash can. Oh yeah, the trash can. The trash can to end all trash cans. The thing looks like it hasn't been emptied in *weeks* and is dripping with crusted ketchup. I can smell it all the way from where I am standing, watching in horror as he gently opens the lid and begins extracting cardboard boxes as if they're jewels on some exotic archaeological dig. I wish I were joking.

Oh, but that's not all. Nope, he's *muttering* as he's doing it. He's actually *picking through the nasty, food-crusted, grease-drenched trash can* and *talking to himself.* At this point I can hear a voice telling me that the highest rate of murder victims in the country are white females— a good portion of which are murdered by people they've only had one social encounter with... like a date. I seriously consider hitchhiking, he looks that unstable. I am scoping out a car full of college students when he comes back, his garbage bag at least half full. He then places it in the backseat of his car, along with the empty cans, and drives me back to The Grounds.

"You do realize that you wasted like twice as many napkins just so you can take those cardboard thingies home and recycle them in your own bin, don't you," I say. "And besides, they're like totally germafied."

"Most of them can be recycled, too," he rationalizes. "Don't tell me you are one of those people who thinks the planet is going to sustain itself."

"I—"

"You think global warming isn't real?"

"Wha—"

"How much waste comes from your store?"

"Hmm, I can't keep track, what with all those Styrofoam cups we use and plastic water bottles we give out."

I could tell him that half our power comes from solar energy and that we use fair trade ingredients, and the shop has three—count 'em, three!—recycling bins, but dammit, he's pissing me off. To make matters worse, flies follow his car and hover over the cardboard thingies. That's just skeevy.

Deal Breaker #2: "Joe from Wilmington" chews too loud. Was-probably-a-horse-in-a-former-life kind of loud. Might-actually-be-a-horse-in-a-man-suit kind of loud. We go to dinner at Mario's on Front Street and both order lasagna as well as the softest, fluffiest dinner rolls ever (God help 'em if I find out they came from a can). The conversation is fine, enjoyable, even. And at least he doesn't eat and talk at the same time. But I can't get past the chewing. Like a slow-motion jackhammer. How does one chew lasagna loudly? Salad, I understand, but *lasagna*? Not to mention that he loads so much Parmesan cheese on top you'd think it snowed. And even though I am itching for some tiramisu for dessert, I skip it because I don't want his chewing to turn me off to tiramisu forever.

Deal Breaker #3: "Randy, originally from Rhode Island," has an unhealthy attachment to Trent Reznor from Nine Inch Nails. I understand the concept of "fan" (short for "fanatic," in case you've forgotten); I still listen to all my U2 albums on a regular basis and will travel across state lines to catch one of their concerts, but Randy has tattoos. He has pinups on the walls in his bedroom (not that I've been to his place, mind you—he proudly bragged about it). I haven't had a pinup since I was sixteen. And his license plate is 9 IN NAILS. His e-mail handle is tr_NIN_genius. His Lovematch.com profile name is Trent. In fact, he's seriously considering officially changing his name to Trent. Eek.

In hindsight, I'm not sure what made me agree to go out with him in the first place, or what drew him to me considering I had, among other things, a *You've Got Mail* movie quote on my profile. I should've denied my identity when he approached my table in dark skinny jeans all frayed at the knees, dyed jet-black hair, and a sterling silver skull earring. More astounding is that he has a master's degree in early childhood education.

I make the mistake of innocently suggesting that Nine Inch Nails was one of the pioneers of techno music, when he nearly rips my head off. "It's *industrial rock*, not techno!"

"What's the difference?" I ask.

"It has *a soul*, for chrissakes! How can you not know that? What's in your car stereo right now?"

I cringe at the thought. A Genesis CD.

"I mostly listen to the radio," I say.

"Trent's a genius who crafted a well-produced sound, and it's like, raw and powerful, with like, anger that spits in the faces of the corporate material machine, you know?"

I have nothing against Trent Reznor, but I can't resist needling Randy. "My friend Norman claims that there's more anger to be found on John Lennon's first solo album."

He shakes his head vehemently. "Tell your friend that he doesn't know shit."

I smile an evil smile; he's asking for it now. And he should thank his lucky stars he didn't actually say this to Norman's face.

"Wasn't Trent Reznor a middle-class kid from Ohio?" I go in for the kill. "If you ask me, I'd say he was a whiny little narcissist. What did he know about anger and despair other than the Cleveland Browns?"

He looks at me in disgust. "He grew up in Mercer, Pennsylvania, not Ohio."

"You say to-MAY-to, I say to-MAH-to. Tell me he's from the South Bronx and I'll take it all back."

I might as well have called Trent Reznor the Donny Osmond of techno—no, excuse me—*industrial* rock. "Listen, we gotta end this date right now. I just can't be with someone who doesn't, like, get it."

To his credit, Randy—er, Trent—pays the bill, but leaves the diner without, like, even saying good-bye to me.

And so, readers, I've decided to compile a list of other deal breakers for future potential dates, and I invite you to please share your own…or ones you possess.

- Uses one of those shampoo-conditioner-body-wash all-in-one products.
- Doesn't get the appeal of *Weekend at Bernie's*.
- Secretly watches *The Bachelorette* and wonders if he has a chance.
- Double-parks his car so no one messes with it.
- Prefers microwavable brownie mix to scratch.
- Calls tortellini "noodles."

The next day, the Originals and Regulars ranked their top ten favorite comments.

min-imalist: Yells at the TV during sports games.

Normal: doesn't properly wrap leftovers

hot_heather: won't kill spiders or any other bug.

PC: Expects me to kill the damn bugs for her…and then complains about gender equality and women's lib shit.

jonesin: Flosses his teeth and leaves spots all over the mirror.

Anonymous: leaves her hair in the sink, the tub, the shower…my god, it's *everywhere*!!!

Mysterio: Hell yea, guy. and she uses my razor on her legs.

Anonymus 2: color-blind

That last one elicited a bunch of follow-up comments.

tracingpaper: he can't help that!

SVU: That's cruel, dude.

min-imalist: How can you tell he's color blind?

PC: How do you know it's a he?

And finally, my favorite deal breaker:

jayblue: can't stand to lose at Scrabble

To which someone replied:

Anonymous: i effing hate this game. this one and monopoly. there's nothing fun about spending a whole freaking day *thinking* about a *game*. where's the fun in that??

Which then provoked:

Normal: You hate Scrabble *and* Monopoly???? What kind of communist are you? Please don't tell me your idea of a good game is Hungry Hungry Hippos. And btw, what's your beef against capital letters? That's *my* deal breaker.

SVU: Dude, I love Hungry Hungry Hippos. No joke!

Some people's ideas of deal breakers rather frightened me. I had been expecting the typical toilet seat up, toothpaste cap off, toilet paper roll facing up or down, and other such bathroom hygiene issues. I also felt relieved that I was not as shallow as I thought. And yet, I couldn't help but wonder if my expectations were too high. Shaun had his own idiosyncrasies, of course (such as having to organize the pantry according to the size and height of cans and boxes), as did I, no doubt. What made anyone bearable to live with?

I called Olivia.

"Hey, Liv, what's your deal breaker?"

"My what?" she replied, sounding frazzled. I could hear pots and pans banging in the background.

"Your deal breaker? You know, what could David do that would send you packing?"

"Aside from cheating on me?"

"Well, I wasn't going for anything so dramatic. You know, like leave the seat up or track mud on the carpets or something."

I heard Tyler and Tara bickering while Olivia tried to referee. "I don't really know, Eva. Things that seem horrifying in the beginning are rather inconsequential when you're cleaning up your kid's puke and taking him to the emergency room at three a.m.—WOULD YOU GIVE HER BACK HER ELEPHANT AND BE DONE WITH IT ALREADY??"

"Ugh, thanks for filling my head with that image."

"That's family life, kiddo."

Olivia hadn't called me kiddo since I was, well, a kid.

"Look, I'd love to talk more, but I'm trying to clean up from dinner and get the kids settled with their homework. Everything OK?" she asked.

"Yeah," I said. Just before she could say good-bye, I asked if Tyler was OK, being that she mentioned emergency rooms and "him." Everyone was healthy, she assured me.

"Talk to you later," I said.

"Sorry," she said before we exchanged I-love-yous and good-nights. Just as I hung up the phone, I heard a last cry for help from Tara and a final reprimand from my sister.

I sat on my deck, looking out at the horizon, watching the sunset. I couldn't for the life of me picture being with someone long enough to warrant the kind of complacency with which marriage seemed so filled. Moreover, I wasn't sure I wanted it. What was the middle ground? I wondered. *Was* there a middle ground? Was there a place between unrealistic expectation and complacency in a relationship? And if there was, did it have a shelf life?

Maybe Shaun and I had gotten complacent before we got to marriage. Maybe that was what falling out of love was all about. Or, at least, the end of romance.

⸎

Summertime didn't signal a lull in business at The Grounds—in fact, the Originals and some of the Regulars would hang out almost all day, communing in the café when they couldn't stand the excessive heat or the crowds at the beach, the overflow of tourists, or visitors from the Triangle and Triad looking for a getaway without leaving the state. On mild, sunny days, half the clientele would sit outside the café. Additionally, I started making ice cream with Cookie of the Week pieces in it—we always ran out before three o'clock.

Since the spring semester ended, Shaun stopped by almost daily for an iced coffee. As always, I'd sit at his table and chat with him, talking to him about almost anything but philosophy, the Jeanette, or weddings. Our conversations felt comfortable, just how they had always been when we were together. Many times we wound up laughing, playfully touching each other's arms as we recalled an anecdote from our respective or collaborative pasts. Or we'd challenge each other to television and film and music trivia (I beat him at *The Munsters*; he beat me at *The Godfather*). I looked forward to seeing him each time, my heart doing a little jig whenever he came in. Minerva, however, would glare at us from behind her medical books; I knew this because I could feel the lasers from her pupils boring a hole into my spine.

One day after Shaun left, I fetched a giant macaroon for Minerva and accidentally smacked the plate on her table with enough force to make Car Talk Kenny glance up from his reading. (Unbeknownst to Norman and the others, or so I thought, I often gave Minerva at least one free cookie per week.)

"So, you gonna do that every time he comes here?" I asked.

"Do what?" she replied, not looking up from her notes or acknowledging the cookie. Minerva hides her true feelings about as easily as one hides a carton of sour milk in a refrigerator.

"You know what. You're like a cat ready to pounce. If your eyes threw daggers, there'd be several protruding from Shaun's chest right now."

She still didn't look up.

"It's not his fault he's getting married," I said. "So it didn't work out for us. It happens. Life goes on. Why hold a grudge?"

Finally, she picked her head up, her horn-rimmed glasses perched on the bridge of her nose, as if she realized for the first time that I was sitting there.

"That's not the problem," she said.

"Then what is?"

"He doesn't deserve your friendship."

"Why not?"

She tried to speak softly. "Because you don't just wanna be his friend. I can see it on your face when you talk to him, Eva. You're practically begging him to *see* you, and it's just not happening. You don't need that. You don't need him to sit there blindly, throwing it in your face."

"Throwing what in my face?"

"The fact that he's got you wrapped around your finger, and you both know it."

Anger swelled inside me like a slow whirlpool.

"You are way off base," I said, trying not to raise my voice.

"He's taking advantage of your feelings for him just so he can feel good about himself, and you're letting him."

"Min, you know I love you, but sometimes you're just too damn judgmental for your own good. I mean, I appreciate that you care and don't want to see me hurt, but this isn't a black-and-white world."

She looked hurt. "I am not judgmental."

"You're telling me he's blind. Well maybe, you know, he's just not that into me, like the book says."

Minerva dropped her pen and looked at me, incredulous. "Oh God, you didn't, did you?"

"Didn't what?"

"Read *He's Just Not That Into You*. Please tell me you suffered a minor brain injury. Please tell me you bumped your head on a shelf one night or you couldn't sleep and needed something to dull your senses."

"It actually makes some good points once you get past the condescension and banality."

"When? When did you do this to yourself?" she demanded.

"Um, I don't remember."

I'd taken a copy home from the reading room the day after my date with Nick from New Bern but hadn't actually read it until a couple of weeks ago, after I'd overheard Shaun mention the Jeanette to a colleague who'd joined him for an iced coffee, referring to her as his fiancée. I finished it in two nights. I even made notes in the margins.

"So then why aren't you cutting ties with him?" Minerva asked.

"Because we're friends. And as long as he wants to be friends, then that's fine with me. And may I point out that *he*'s always been the one who wanted to remain friends. He never once said that we should part company."

As I said the words, I could actually hear them saturated with rationalization. What's more, I could picture the *He's Just Not That Into You* authors saying something in response like, "If you want a friend, get a dog."

"And that's exactly what worries me," Minerva said, her voice hushed. "He knows how you still feel, and he's taking advantage of that."

"I don't 'feel' anything," I said in defiance. "Can't you be friends with your ex? Is there a constitutional amendment banning it? I mean, really, who says you can't?"

"And how does the Jeanette feel about it? Does she even know about you?"

"Who cares?"

Minerva opened her mouth in disgust. "Oh, that's a great attitude. Eva, put yourself in her shoes: imagine that you're Shaun's fiancée and he's still friends with his ex-girlfriend of three years—his former, *live-in lover*. Would *you* be OK with it? Wouldn't you be wondering *why* Shaun insisted on remaining friends with this woman? Furthermore, would you trust a woman who said, 'Who cares what she thinks?'—*she* meaning *you*?"

Shitters.

I had never seen it from that point of view before. Maybe Shaun wasn't the one who was blind. Minerva was right. Blatantly right. But my ego was too proud, too wounded, and feeling too foolish to tell her so.

I looked past her table.

"I've got a customer," I said, and stood up to attend to him without saying anything more to Minerva for the time being. She went back to her books, calling out as I walked away, "By the way, the macaroons are perfect today."

Later in the afternoon, after Minerva and most of the Originals had left, Car Talk Kenny remained perched in the corner with a J. D. Rhodes novel. As I straightened up the end tables, I heard him utter, "She's right, you know."

I stopped in mid-straighten, and looked at him. He revealed only his eyes for just a moment.

༄ঔ

The first time I met Car Talk Kenny, rather, the first time I'd *noticed* him, it had been one of those days where the espresso machine went on the fritz, the gourmet beans were sold out, orders got mixed up, and the line never shortened.

"What can I get you?" I'd asked as soon as he'd stepped to the counter.

"Hi," he said. "How are you?"

"Good. You?"

"Liar," he grinned.

"Excuse me?"

"How *are* you?" he repeated.

I blinked. "Tired," I said with a weak laugh.

He gave me a look that said *that's more like it* before saying, "I can imagine." He then ordered a plain café au lait and a maple nut muffin at my recommendation. As I handed him his muffin—warmed just because I thought he'd like it that way—and finally asked him how he was, he smiled and said simply, "Better."

I'm pretty sure he was the one who slipped a five into the tip jar on the counter that day, although he never copped to it. He'd been a Regular ever since. Kenny was one of those people to whom you can only ever tell the truth, and I found myself always glad to see him; somehow, just knowing that I *could* tell him I felt like crap made me feel inherently less crappy. There were still days when he'd quirk an eyebrow if I said I was "great, thanks" with a little too much fervor, or chuckle to himself if I emerged from the kitchen covered in flour and all the markings of a battle lost against the mixer and still managed to say I was "fine."

༄ ༽

"I'm sorry," he said in the present moment. "I didn't mean to listen in, but she is."

I wasn't offended. In fact, in that moment I felt the impulse to hug Kenny and not let go. Something about this scared me, though, and I tried to mentally shake it off. Still, I could not escape from the truth in his eyes.

"I know," I said. "And she knows I know."

With that, I went back behind the counter and into the kitchen.

9

Possibilities

"THE TOPIC OF the Day is speed dating," I announced to the café, filled mostly with Originals and Regulars, on an uncharacteristically mild Monday afternoon.

The idea had consumed me ever since I gave up on Lovematch.com. I'd always wanted to try speed dating; I likened it to a game of *Twister* or Musical Chairs, only the winner winds up picking out china patterns and reserving an expensive catering hall two years down the road.

"What about it?" asked Jan.

"Anyone ever done it?" I asked.

"I did!" said Tracy.

"Me too," added Jan.

"Really?" Dean asked. "When?"

"Years ago, during my *Sex and the City*–wannabe days," she replied to both Dean and us.

"What'd you think?" I asked.

"It's more fun if you have a couple of cosmopolitans in you," said Jan.

"I did it once."

Heads turned to meet the tall, tan, sun-bleached blond, twentysomething stranger at the counter dressed in Dockers shorts and a polo shirt from which this admission came. I guessed him to be a windsurfer in town for the summer.

"And?" I asked, handing him a strawberry smoothie in exchange for a twenty-dollar bill.

"It was fun, but I didn't like the women I met," he said, accepting his change and stuffing it into his front pocket.

"What kind of women?" Norman asked, sounding especially curious.

"Superficial," the guy said. "Shallow. Kept asking me how much money I made or what I did for a living, but not in a small-talk kind of way. Just to mess with 'em I started telling 'em I was a garbage man."

A couple of the Originals laughed.

"Then I followed it up with 'I'm CEO of my own garbage company. Gives new meaning to being a garbage man.'"

More laughs.

"They didn't know what to do with that," he said.

"Where did you do it?" asked Norman.

"A few years ago, when I lived in Boston. Your friend was right when she said it's more fun if you put a few drinks away beforehand."

Funny, I didn't detect the New England accent until he mentioned Boston. He held up his smoothie as if to toast all of us, and then he walked out as we thanked him for his input and bid him a good day.

"You thinkin' of speed datin', Eva?" asked Spencer, whose Southern accent became even more apparent following the smoothie-drinking-speed-dating Bostonian.

"Thinking about it, yeah."

"How come? I mean, what ever happened to you loving singlehood?" asked Spencer.

"Trust me, if she does speed dating, she'll love it even more," said Jan.

"So, did you hook up with anyone that night?" Dean asked Jan.

"Dean!" she said, exasperated. "Enough already." He frowned and sipped his iced latte.

"It just seems that you're saying one thing and doing another," Spencer remarked to me, ignoring Jan and Dean's little spat.

"Who says dating can't be a part of singlehood?" I said. "Besides, I'm just curious. It's a process of elimination. For all those people who keep telling me what I'm missing and that I should be 'out there.'" I made quote marks with my fingers. "So, I'm going 'out there,'" (gestured the quote marks yet again) "to prove to them that it doesn't work and is not detrimental to my lifetime happiness."

I turned to a table of Regulars. "So, any of you singles wanna come with me sometime?"

Dara, one of the new Regulars since the summer began, shook her head. "Not me. You might as well auction me off on eBay."

"That might be next," said Spencer.

Sister Beulah also shook her head. "I'm spoken for," she said as she winked. I smiled back.

"I'll go," said Norman.

I whisked around. *"You?"*

"Why so surprised?"

"I don't know, I just thought—" I stammered. "I didn't know you were interested."

"Why not? It's been awhile since I've been on a date."

"OK then," I said, my voice shaky. For some reason, going speed dating with Norman seemed like the equivalent of going to the senior prom with my brother, if I'd had one.

"I'll go," Minerva chirped with a sly grin.

I gaped at her. Was she serious?

"Yeah," she said as if she'd read my mind. "It'll be fun."

"But, you're—"

"Look, I'm going to want all the details, and not just the WILS version, either. Just think of this as a favor to you—I'm saving you the trouble of recounting it all."

I could actually feel my jaw flapping as I searched for something to say. "But, Jay—"

"Maybe he'll come, too." Her perpetual grin was so mischievous I thought she could've been playing a trick on me. And yet, I feared otherwise.

"Come on, Eva, let her go," Jan coaxed.

"Yeah, and then you can have dueling blog posts afterward," Tracy added.

"Nice! Like a news report–style thing," Dean added.

"But," I tried again, "she's *married.*"

"So?" said Tracy. "You're only doing it to prove how stupid it is anyway. What does it matter, so long as her husband doesn't mind." She then turned to Minerva, "Would he?"

"Nah. Knowing him, he'll wanna come along. You have no idea how bored he gets with me studying all the time."

Dean laughed. "Minerva, don't take this the wrong way, but I'm not sure I've ever actually seen you study."

"Dean," Jan chided, "what do you think she's doing here all the time?"

"Uh," he gestured at the group of Originals and Regulars all engrossed in the conversation, "*this*?"

"The cookies are good, but they're not *that* good," Tracy said, backing up Jan. "She's obviously one of those people who studies best with a little background noise. Right, Minerva?"

Minerva considered the stack of notes next to her, under a crumb-dusted plate. "No, the cookies really are *that* good."

The group laughed as Minerva licked her fingers, dabbed at the remaining crumbs, and finished them off before taking her plate to the dish bin at the far end of the counter.

"Would your husband really want to go?" Tracy asked, obviously finding the thought as absurd as I did.

Minerva returned to her seat and brushed stray crumbs off her notes. "Sure. We haven't been out in ages. At this point, the poor boy will probably take whatever he can get. And it's like you said, she's not looking for a soul mate or anything—and neither are we, mind you—just a bit of fun. Right, Eva?"

I tried to read Minerva's expression, searching for ulterior reasons behind her newly found interest in a social life…or was it *my* social life she was trying to keep an eye on?

"Well, I guess when you put it that way," I said. What did it matter anyway? She was right. It wouldn't matter if Jay and Norman went any more than if Spencer or Scott did. It was all in the name of good fun, nothing more. Right?

"So," said Jan, "whaddya going to wear?"

I rolled my eyes. My co-manager, my best friend *and her husband*, and I were all going speed dating. How was I supposed to think about what I was going to wear?

❧

The next morning Dara came in an uncharacteristic fifteen minutes early—most days you could set your watch by her punctuality.

"Hey, Dara, what gives?"

"I've got an early meeting."

"The usual?" I asked, already pulling a blueberry muffin from the display case. "To go?"

"Today, yes."

I slipped her muffin into a bag. "Anything else?" I asked.

"Actually," she sounded pleased with herself, "there is." She then slid a folded, neon pink flyer across the counter to me. I opened it to find a full-page ad: *Romance in 8 Minute's!* and mentally chided the printers for not catching the unwarranted apostrophe.

"What's this?" I asked.

"Speed dating," she said, "for you and Norman." She grabbed the bag and her latte, and left me agog. This from the woman who said she'd rather auction herself on eBay. Where'd she get it? The flyer included date (this Friday), time (9:00 p.m.), place (Pub on the Pier), and a suggestion (Dress to Impress!). When Norman came in, I showed it to him, and I left Minerva a text message on her cell phone since she was in labs all day. She texted me later that evening: *j and i will meet you at the grounds fri 8:30.*

My stomach dropped. This was really gonna happen, wasn't it.

⤫

By six thirty Friday night, I had scrubbed off the lingering scent of The Grounds, scarfed down a slice of cold pizza, emptied the entire contents of my closet, and scattered them around my room in a frenzied attempt to outfit myself; by seven thirty, I was fast approaching an all-out panic attack.

No, it wasn't panic. One does not panic about something that one is doing simply as an experiment. And I'd decided that that's what this was: a social science experiment, to be followed up with a written report. That's why it mattered; it'd throw off the study if I didn't dress appropriately.

So what was "appropriate"? The flyer said Dress to Impress. What if I didn't want to impress? What if I was merely window shopping, just looking? What if I wanted to intrigue rather than impress?

I checked my closet again—the remainders were either not fit for public viewing, hadn't been worn since I'd last power-washed The Grounds, or were the wrong size in one direction or the other. Faced with a closet devoid of any further possibilities, I confronted my disheveled bedroom again, taking stock of my options.

My bureau was buried under dresses. Sundresses. Cocktail dresses. Funeral frock. No go. None of them. Too frilly, fun, cute, bright, busy, sexy, formal, or—in the case of the funeral frock—churchy (and although Nora Ephron recommends that every woman should have a little black dress, I doubted my funeral frock was what she had in mind).

I turned to my reading chair, covered with my collection of business suits—relics from academic conferences and teaching days. Big thumbs down. Too formal, drab, dry. Said all the wrong things about me. Said, power-hungry. Said, I-could-eat-your-liver-for-lunch-if-I-wanted-it. I mentally crossed suits, pantsuits, and skirts falling below the knee off my list.

Jeans? They beckoned from my dresser, inching their way out of half-closed drawers. Ugh. Not the image I wanted. Too twentysomething, too comfortable, and too casual.

I was left, then, with combinations of skirts, pants, and tops, a myriad of choices blurring before me in piles on my bed. I eyed the few skirts not belonging to suit sets that lounged across my pillows.

What would Elizabeth Bennet wear? What would Bridget Jones wear? What would Carson Kressley wear?

I considered an option: a black pencil skirt, slit up the back. Hemmed just above the knee, it accentuated my legs and hips. With the right top, it could be sophisticated and sexy without crossing any lines. Definite possibility.

On the other hand, the cream, cotton-linen blend pants were versatile, comfortable, flattering to my figure, and adaptable to almost any social situation depending on the pairing of shoes and blouse. Also possible.

Ten minutes to eight.

Shitters.

Pants. No, skirt. Skirt?

"Argh," I grumbled, moving blouses from one pile to another, then back again. I called Minerva's cell phone, but it went straight to voice mail—geez, don't tell me they left for the shop already!

Time to think logically. I turned to my bed, lecturing to an imaginary class of denim rejects and using my most scholarly voice.

"Objective: To assess the validity of speed dating, and make conclusions about..." I stopped sorting shirts, searching for the right word, "its ridiculousness?"

If they could've, my suits would've rolled their button-eyes at me. I plowed ahead, sorting through my shirts by hanger again.

"Hypothesis: Speed dating doesn't net long-term relationships. It's too full of superficial hopefuls trying too hard to get—" I grimaced "—*out there*." My jeans seemed to agree. "No. Trying to get *laid*."

"Methods and Materials," I recited, eyeing my bed again. "First, Materials. Me, my clothes, my conversation...or are clothes and conversation part of Methods?"

Aw, hell.

"Screw it." I grabbed a floral print skirt with a ruffle hem at the knee, stepping into it before I could change my mind again, and matched it with a solid violet cap-sleeve, wide V-neck top that I'd purchased ages ago because it reminded me of my favorite shade of tulips and looked good on me, the way it practically fell off my shoulders. Come to think of it, Shaun always loved it.

Methods: Researchers will meet at The Grounds prior to the Event to be Observed, and will enter the bar together, and we will feign...no, forego...bias? Let's see...a married couple, a thirty-two-year-old guy who's not been on a date since February, and me, who willingly walked into this mess.

Nope, no bias there.

As I moved from the bedroom to the bathroom to apply my makeup, my memory took me back to fourteen-year-old Olivia's bedroom, helping her get ready for a school dance. As I handed her various pots and compacts and tubes of cosmetics, hues of eighties ostentation, I'd dabbed my cheeks with hot pink blush and imitated her sharp, angular eyeshadow using my fingers as brushes. I studied her honey-colored hair, teased and standing straight on top with puffy bangs, the rest falling to her shoulders. Her face was round; her skin, fair; her eyes, the shape of almonds, with blue diamonds for irises.

"Do boys like all this stuff?" I remembered asking her, lining her lip glosses in a row.

"They like the way it looks on girls, if that's what you mean."

I glanced at Olivia's Culture Club poster. "It looks like they like to *wear* it, too."

"Boy George does."

"Does the lipstick get all shmudged when you kiss?" I asked.

Olivia giggled. She had sporadically dated all through high school until our mom got sick and she broke up with Bobby Ackerman. And me? I had kissed boys at parties and went to the occasional movie, but by my mid to late teens, most kids didn't know how to talk to me. I was the girl whose parents died of cancer, who was living with her sister on welfare, so the rumor went despite it not being true. Dating just wasn't on my mind, not even after I graduated high school and went to work in the bookstore. College coaxed me out of my shell, and I'd finally started doing all the things most girls would've done in high school.

Not that I minded being a late bloomer. It made me appreciate my dating experiences more. But perhaps it explained why I fell so hard for Shaun—he was the first guy I *lived* with, the one with whom I shared all my secrets and fears and hopes and dreams.

As I brought myself back to the present moment, staring at my reflection, blush brush poised in midair, studying my slate eyes, my pointy chin, and searching for wrinkles, I asked my reflection out loud, *"What are you doing?"*

I mean, really—why was I going through all this? Was it to please a bunch of people who read *Why I Love Singlehood*, people who responded to my posts as if they actually had a say or a stake in my life? My blog readers were mostly singles like myself, sometimes cheering me on and sometimes complaining about their own lonely existence. Some seemed to be waiting for me to make a bold move, almost so that they'd have something to emulate. But no sooner had I written that inaugural post did I realize that I didn't want to be the Singles Spokesperson. It was too late to surrender the title, however.

This dating thing seemed much easier in Olivia's day. There was nothing to analyze. You dressed up. You moussed and crimped your hair and wore bracelets all the way up to your elbows. You put on makeup. You went out and came home when your parents told you to. You wrote about it in your diary and then hid said diary somewhere your little sister couldn't find it.

The whole damn dating thing was easier in Shaun's day, too. No tearing about the closet or striking poses in front of the mirror. I wore jeans and a blazer and heels the night we met, with subtle makeup and my hair long and straight. Of course, I wasn't intending to meet anyone that night, but my wardrobe didn't change much throughout our courtship. Why bother? I'd already impressed him that first night.

If only it could be that simple again. The last great Relation-Ship hadn't sailed away without me, had it?

⌐◦

I arrived at The Grounds by 8:35, having only changed my top two more times (out of the purple V-neck, and then back into it), flaunting three-and-a-half-inch strappy sandals (the hottest part of the outfit, as far as I was concerned—I considered maybe putting my feet on the table during the dates to have the guys get a look at them), and keeping my hair down and makeup simple. After a failed attempt at an updo, I brushed it out and let it flow past my shoulders, soft and unruly.

The Grounds closed at seven o'clock; Norman and I both took the night off and had our favorite part-timer, Susanna, close for us. By the time I arrived, Norman, Jay, and Minerva were already there. Norman was dressed in dark khaki chinos, a light cream button-down shirt, and black Oxfords. He was clean-shaven and had also gotten a haircut. A John Cusack lookalike, Norman Bailey had jet-black hair, puppy-dog brown eyes, and a nose so well shaped it could be featured in a rhinoplasty catalogue. He wore paisley shirts and blue jeans with black Chuck Taylors or brown moccasins, and gave up wearing cologne after working at The Grounds for one week and being nauseated by the combination of aromas (although he smelled faintly of Kuros tonight). Totally adorable and datable.

Jay wore black Dockers (Minerva gave him a hard time about wearing black during summertime) and a golf shirt. Minerva had on her "date dress"—a hot little red number with a slit on the side and a low-cut back, all for Jay's benefit, I knew. The moment I walked in and saw them, I turned around and Minerva had to grab me by the arm to keep me from walking back out, as if the door was a revolving one.

"Wow, you look lovely, Eva!" exclaimed Norman. "That color is perfect for you."

"Lovely?" I said. I wasn't sure I was going for "lovely."

"Seriously, you look really good," said Minerva, who at that instant pointed her cell phone at me and clicked a picture.

"You look hot," I said to Minerva. "I don't look hot."

"You look sexy," said Norman.

Sexy. Norman thought I looked lovely and sexy. Was there an eclipse of some kind taking place?

"Thanks, Norman. You clean up pretty good yourself."

"Thanks. So…are we ready to go?" Norman asked. We all looked at each other and nodded in agreement.

"Shotgun!" called Jay, and Minerva rolled her eyes. Norman had offered to be the designated driver, so we all thanked him for that.

With Jay and Norman in the front listening to a local band that Norman had downloaded from iTunes, Minerva and I sat in the back and chirped away like two teenage girls.

"So," she said as she leaned in to me, her voice lowered. "I have to tell you something."

"What?" I said.

She was giddy and her eyes sparkled. "I might be pregnant."

My mouth fell open, and she put up her hand to keep me from speaking.

"Don't say anything. No one knows but you, Jay, and my lab partner, and I don't want anyone else to know."

Thankfully the music, along with Jay's and Norman's conversation, was loud enough that they wouldn't have heard anything even if I could've found words.

"Min!" I finally managed to spit out. "Are you serious?"

She giggled. "Totally."

"Did you do one of those home pregnancy doohickey thingies?"

"My lab partner at school gave me a test."

"Ohmigod. Wow. Min."

"I know!" she said, scrunching her shoulders as if we were talking about a prom date. "Isn't it great?"

"I didn't know you and Jay were planning anything."

"Oh, it's totally unplanned. I mean, it couldn't come at a worse time, with me still in school and him paying off his student loan. But who cares? It's a *baby*, Eva. A little Minerva and Jay. A Baby Brunswick. Can you imagine my bringing a little one to The Grounds? She'll have her own Cookie of the Week."

"Strained biscotti?"

Minerva laughed.

"So, Jay's excited?" I asked.

"Well, he doesn't want to get his hopes up, but yeah, he wouldn't be upset if it's positive."

"Wow. A mini-Min."

"Oh, please tell me you'll never say that again."

We both giggled, and I gave her arm a squeeze. "I'm not sure what to say. It's too soon for congratulations, isn't it?"

Minerva scrunched her shoulders again. "I've got a good feeling about it. I'm not even gonna drink tonight, just in case. But don't tell Norman, OK?"

"I promise, I'm not gonna tell anyone."

She hugged me.

"Hey, no lesbian hanky-panky back there—not if I can't watch," said Norman, looking through the rearview mirror.

When we arrived at the bar and the four of us entered together, scoping the place out, I couldn't help but feel hopeful to meet someone by the end of the night.

"This is gonna be fun," said Jay.

"Is it?" I said. At that moment, as Minerva inconspicuously slid off her wedding ring and sneaked it into her clutch purse, I had the urge to snatch it from her, put it on my own finger, and never take it off.

10

The Social Experiment

The Just Barely Morning After Speed Dating

OK, here's how it went.

Jay, Minerva, Norman, and I arrived at the club just moments before it was to begin. Ten guys total, one guy to a table.

The Rules: Everyone gets a number. Women start at one table, and you have eight minutes to make conversation or whatever. When the eight minutes are up, a bell rings and you move on. No chance to wrap up the conversation, get a business card, nothing. You stop in mid-sentence and move on.

Guy #1 goes something like this:

<u>Him</u>: Hey, good-lookin'. (I shit you not.)

<u>Me</u>: Hi, I'm Eva.

(I extend my hand for shaking. He kisses it. Eiw.)

<u>Him</u>: Ay-va, you said?

<u>Me</u>: Yes.

<u>Him</u>: I'm Peter.

<u>Me</u>: Hi, Peter.

(At this point, I'm thinking that introductions can actually kill a lot of time when you only have eight minutes. He's wearing a button-down rayon shirt with a Harley Davidson on it, by the way.)

<u>Him</u>: So, why speed dating?

<u>Me</u>: I'm conducting an experiment. And you?

<u>Him</u>: (laughs) An experiment? What are you, some kind of witch doctor?

<u>Me</u>: Just curious about the social behaviors of dating, I guess.

<u>Him</u>: Well, I'm on the hunt for Mrs. Right. You wouldn't be her, would you?

<u>Me</u>: Ummmmmm…

(How many seconds does it take to say 'Ummmm,' I wonder.)

<u>Still me</u>: Probably not. But thanks for asking.

<u>Him</u>: You sure are pretty, though.

<u>Me</u>: Thanks. Nice shirt.

<u>Him</u>: (looks down at his chest and pulls it down to show it off) You like Harleys?

<u>Me</u>: I used to pretend I was riding one when I was ten and had a chopper bicycle with the banana seats.

<u>Him</u>: (laughs again) Pretty *and* funny. You sure you're not my dream girl?

DING DING DING
(Actually, there was more conversation than that, but why put you through it?)

Guy#2: Good-looking, actually. I think he Botoxes, though.

<u>Him</u>: Hi.

(extends his hand.)

<u>Still him</u>: I'm John.

(Am I going through the Apostles?)

<u>Me</u>: John? I'm Eva.

<u>Him</u>: That's a pretty name.

<u>Me</u>: Thanks.

<u>Him</u>: So, tell me about yourself in eight minutes or less.

<u>Me</u>: I own my own business.

(Gosh, those two bookend *own*s look terrible on the screen. Didn't sound so repetitive at the time…)

<u>Him</u>: (eyes widen) Wow! What kind of business are you in?

<u>Me</u>: I own a coffee shop near the college.

<u>Him</u>: Wait a minute…are you talking about The Grounds?

<u>Me</u>: Yep.

<u>Him</u>: Oh my fucking god! I been there!

(Whoa. Too much excitement there…)

<u>Me</u>: Cool. Did you like it?

<u>Him</u>: Well, it seemed to be a bunch of bookworms in there, but the coffee was pretty good.

DING DING DING

Guy #3: Pudgy. Bald spot. Looks like he lives with his mother. Poor guy. Isn't stereotyping awful? Let's just ring the bell and move on.

Guy #4: I forget his name. Something with a Q, I think.

<u>Him</u>: What kind of business do you own?

<u>Me</u>: Coffee shop.

<u>Him</u>: Well that's not much of a lofty enterprise, is it.

<u>Me</u>: What do you mean?

<u>Him</u>: What're you pullin' out on a yearly basis?

<u>Me</u>: Ask my accountant, you moron. (OK, so I said the second part in my head.)

<u>Him</u>: You don't even know how much your business makes?

<u>Me</u>: I know exactly how much my business brings in. I just don't think it's any of *your* business. (Moron)

<u>Him</u>: I'm just sayin' that if you wanna make any real money, you don't go into food or retail to do it.

<u>Me</u>: Tell that to Howard Schultz.

<u>Him</u>: Who?

<u>Me</u>: The Starbucks guy.

(He's unimpressed. I would've been impressed. After all, how many people know that the guy who started Starbucks is Howard Schultz? How impressed am I that I can even remember that now, while I'm a little soused?)

<u>Him</u>: So how long you been in business?

<u>Me</u>: A couple of years. Before that I was a professor.

<u>Him</u>: Of what?

<u>Me</u>: Creative writing.

<u>Him</u>: You're a liberal, aren't you.

DING DING DING

Guy #5 was Norman.

<u>Me</u>: So, do you believe this?

<u>N</u>: I got a marriage proposal.

<u>Me</u>: (mouth opens) You're shitting me.

<u>N</u>: Absolutely not.

<u>Me</u>: And?

<u>N</u>: And she has fifty thousand dollars worth of credit card debt.

<u>Me</u>: She told you that?

<u>N</u>: Every last dollar.

<u>Me</u>: What was the context of this? I mean, how did this come into the conversation?

<u>N</u>: I think I mentioned something about my comic book collection.

<u>Me</u>: I'm not seeing the connection.

<u>N</u>: So how 'bout you? Any takers so far?

<u>Me</u>: I've got Harley Davidson, Botox Bob—or John, actually—and Donald Trump.

Norman winced. Minerva was at the table ahead of us, and truth be told, I had been trying to listen in on her dates. I mean, what was she saying to them? It occurred to me at that moment that sitting there talking to Norman was the most comfortable I'd been all night.

This was getting depressing fast.

Guy #6

<u>Me</u>: (very unenthusiastically) I'm Eva.

<u>Him</u>: I'm Todd.

(I eye him suspiciously.)

<u>Me</u>: How old are you?

<u>Him</u>: I'm twenty-four.

<u>Me</u>: I thought this was for ages thirty to forty-five.

<u>Him</u>: Aw hell, I knew I signed up for the wrong night…

DING DING DING

Guy #7

I don't even remember that one. Besides, by then I was on my third Rosebud and they put in more bud than rose.

Guy #8 was Jay, smiling ear to ear, like a big kid. Just like Minerva, in fact, earlier in the car.

<u>Me</u>: How goes it?

<u>Jay</u>: This is so much fun. We should do this every week.

<u>Me</u>: You're serious?

<u>Jay</u>: Our girl is really chattin' 'em up. Told every single one of them that she's married and is conducting a social experiment.

<u>Me</u>: Aw crap, that was *my* line. The social experiment, I mean.

<u>Jay</u>: You two have got to stop spending so much time together.

He looked past me at the next table and watched his wife. God, he was so smitten with her. Lucky bird, that Minerva.

Guy #9: Tom Cruise lookalike, minus couch-jumping. And sorry, I know that horse has been beaten to death, but I can't think of any other good Tom Cruise jokes at the moment.

<u>Him</u>: Nice to meet you.

<u>Me</u>: You too.

<u>Him</u>: I'm Tom.

(I shit you not!)

<u>Me</u>: Eva.

<u>Him</u>: Having a good time so far?

<u>Me</u>: It's OK. And you?

<u>Him</u>: The girl that came before you told me she's married and is doing a social experiment.

(I was in mid-swallow when he said this and nearly choked.)

<u>Still him</u>: Hey, you OK there?

Me: I guess you get all kinds here.

Him: Well, you know, what's the point of the experiment if you're gonna tell everyone what you're doing?

Me: Well, you know, there's academic integrity, and ethics.

(shut up, shut up. *shut. up.*)

Him: Let me guess: you're a professor over at NCLA?

Me: Used to be. Now I own my own business. Ever been to The Grounds?

Him: I knew you looked familiar! That's a great place! You recommended a bookstore when I was looking for an out-of-print anthology in 19th century British lit.

Me: Really? When?

Him: You were only open for a few months. I haven't been there in a long time, but maybe I'll stop by.

(What's this? Am I *liking* this guy?)

Me: Thanks.

Tom worked in the health care field and owned a house. Intelligent. Digs British lit, even if it is 19th century. Definite possibilities.

Me: How old are you, Tom?

Him: Just turned thirty-five last week.

(*Definite possibilities.*)

We made small talk. We made jokes that we laughed at. It was the only time I didn't check my watch, that the bell rang when I was in mid-sentence and didn't want to walk away.

Guy #10… Wait, there was a rosebud #4, but was there a guy #10?

At the end of the round, Jay, Minerva, Norman, and I all filled out our cards. Basically, you check a Yes or a No next to the number of the guy that you would be interested in going out on a real date with. You hang out, get a little more drunk, and then someone comes to you and tells you which guys matched with you. You only find out if both matched together.

Of course, Jay and Minerva got matched. Norman matched with me (we had agreed to check off each other's box just in case no one else did) and a girl named Samara. He was clearly excited about that and rushed to the other side of the bar to talk to her. She had long, dark hair and a sassy little pink dress with a skirt length that made mine look straight out of Amish country.

My turn: Norman, of course, and… *Please let it be the Tom Cruise-guy! Please let it be the Tom Cruise-guy! It has to be—we had all that chemistry…*

Just Norman.

Suddenly, Norman's and my idea to match each other up felt even more pathetic than if we hadn't.

Before we left the bar (we were waiting for Norman), I went over to the Tom Cruise-guy, who was chatting it up with a blond.

Me: Excuse me, may I just ask why you didn't check my box?

As the words lingered in my ear, I realized that something sounded very off-color about them.

He held up his hands as if I was about to make a scene.

Tom: Listen, no offense. You were just a little too know-it-all for me, that's all. Like you had it all figured out or were above it all or something. I mean, it's all good clean fun, ya know?

I shrank to the size of a stain on the floor.

Me: Thanks. Sorry to interrupt you.

Norman drove and talked incessantly about Samara. Minerva fell asleep on Jay's shoulder, while he kissed her head and closed his eyes. I sat up front and stared out the window, feeling like the world had gone and hooked up without me.

I thought I was so content not to be in
a relationship. And then it occurred to me: I
wasn't. What I mean is, I actually was *not* content to be with anyone who wasn't Shaun.

It's about him, isn't it. It's always been
about him.

I shut down my laptop and stood up, trying to catch my balance. Without even washing the makeup off my face, I slipped
out of my clothes, left them in a pile on the floor, threw on a
T-shirt, and fell into bed.

And the Tom Cruise-guy thought I had it all figured out.

11

Aftermath

FOLLOWING THE SPEED-DATING night, I had given myself my first weekend off in God knew how long, and spent most of it in bed. Not accustomed to drinking so much, I nursed a hangover using one of Minerva's home remedies consisting of alternating glasses of V-8 juice and Gatorade with a double dose of vitamins. I had also decided to give myself a much-needed sabbatical from my laptop. When I returned to The Grounds on Monday, however, I was barraged with questions about my WILS post and about the speed dating night. It turned out that I should've titled it "Never Post Anything When You're Drunk."

"I don't know," said Dara, sitting with Minerva and two other Regulars, "it sounded kinda fun."

"Wow, that's quite a turnaround for you," I said. "Whose post did you read—mine or Minerva's lab report?"

Not surprisingly, Minerva had taken the social experiment to heart and wrote a conventional lab report—she even used APA documentation when she quoted Jay's account of the evening as "snazzy."

Minerva rolled her eyes at me. "It wasn't *that* bad."

"Please. You could've submitted that thing to the *Journal of Behavioral Psychology* and they'd have wound up studying *you*."

Dara leaned in to Minerva, as if we were discussing a scandal. "So, did you take any cards at the end? Who was your favorite?"

"My favorite mini-date?" Minerva asked. "I'd have to say Norman."

Norman?

Jay shot Minerva a look. *Norman??*

She glanced around at our faces, all emanating confusion. "Yeah. I had a really nice time," she insisted.

I couldn't believe my ears. "Norman—as in, you-once-threatened-to-castrate-him-for-calling-you-Minnie, Norman?" I said.

Behind her, Norman blanched at the mere memory.

"I never threatened to castrate him," she corrected. "And yeah. He's a funny guy." She called over her shoulder, "You hear that, Norman? I think you're a peach!"

"You're married!" he shot back from behind the counter. "What good does that do me?"

"I dunno. References?"

"Do I look like the kind of guy that needs references?" he asked.

"Do I look like the kind of girl you want to answer that?" she retorted, turning back to the rest of us and continued nonchalantly to her husband. "Who was your favorite, Jay?"

He looked at her as if the answer was obvious. "You."

She scoffed, "Oh, please. You eat dinner with me every night! There must have been someone more interesting there. Come on, tell us! I promise, I'm not going to get upset."

"You're my favorite," he said, sounding like a boy defending his favorite teddy bear.

One side of Minerva's mouth tipped up in the rare, soft smile she reserved only for Jay. It was one of the things I admired about their relationship—they were never very affectionate in public—handholding was as obvious as it got, but the *love*…without kisses and cooing and gooey eyes, Minerva and Jay shared an almost tangible air of affection between them. I think that is what separates couples that look "natural" together from the rest of the love-struck, eHarmony world. Most couples demonstrate—hell, *prove* to each other how in love they are with favors and manners and declarations on Valentine's Day. Minerva and Jay never had to show each other; rather, it was an unspoken, unyielding fact. A covenant. Sometimes it was apparent in a look or a smile, or the way they finished each other's thoughts and sentences, but most of the time it was a presence that pulled everyone under its warm blanket.

Why didn't Shaun and I have that? I wondered. *And is it too late to get him back to find it?*

"Well, we all know Eva's and Norman's favorites," said Dara.

"How do you know?" I asked.

"You wrote it all down, silly! Yours was that Tom guy who turned out to be not that into you, and Norman's was the girl with the dress."

"Her name is *Samara*," said Norman.

Actually, I had forgotten a lot of what I had written that night. I momentarily covered my eyes with my hand, as if everyone would disappear when I took it away.

"Are you going out with her again?" Scott asked Norman.

"Tomorrow night, in fact," said Norman. "But if you want to know the truth, it wasn't my favorite date. And sorry, Minerva, but neither were you. It was Eva."

I felt my face get hot. *Me?*

"Well, that's not hard to believe, given the way she looked that night," said Scott.

I flipped around so fast I pulled a muscle in my back. "How do *you* know what I looked like?"

"Geez, where've you been this weekend, Eva?" asked Scott.

"Hiding under my covers. Now answer my question."

"Minerva posted it on her blog along with her report."

In mid-cookie chew, Minerva sheepishly smiled without opening her mouth and shrugged her shoulders. "It's a support document."

I then went over to Scott's laptop, surfed to Minerva's LiveJournal blog, and sure enough, there I was: the cell phone photo of me in the café before the event. It wasn't a half-bad picture, actually, but still. I looked at her again—she'd finished chewing by now, followed by the rest of her vanilla chai in one final gulp.

"It's a good picture, Eva. It needed to be seen," said Minerva.

"It's an *awesome* picture," corrected Scott. "Let's do a quick poll: who here agrees that Eva looked hot on Friday night?"

All the Regulars but Neil raised their hands. "Sorry," said Neil, "I didn't see it."

"Well come here, dude," said Scott.

Mortified, I looked at them all and announced, "I've got work to do in the kitchen," and headed in that direction as Neil peeked at Scott's laptop.

Later that day, Car Talk Kenny walked into the reading room where I was sitting cross-legged on the floor in front of the bookcase, sorting through a box of books that a customer had donated earlier that day.

"Hey, Eva."

I looked up at him.

"Hey, Kenny."

"What's up?" he asked.

"Come sit with me," I instructed, patting the floor. He obediently squatted to his knees.

"How was your weekend?" he asked.

"You see Minerva's LiveJournal?"

He paused for a beat while I handed him a pile of books that he gently placed next to him. "Yeah. Nice picture. I liked your WILS post better, though. Hers was a little too clinical."

"It was a rip-roarin' time. You should have been there with us."

"I had other plans, unfortunately," he said.

"Are you seeing anyone, Kenny?"

The question surprised both him and me.

He inspected the spine of one of the books. "Not right now," he answered. "Why?"

"Do you want to be? I mean, do you mind not being in a relationship?"

"Yes and no."

"How yes and how no?" I asked.

"No, I don't mind because life is good and I'm on track and ready for the right woman that comes along. Yes, I mind because she hasn't come along. Or she's not ready yet."

"You're just waiting for her to show up?"

"Something like that."

How does one get to that point, to be so satisfied or willing to wait? My very first WILS post was about that very satisfaction: but since then, I'd lost it. In fact, I suddenly couldn't remember ever feeling it.

"Why don't you go find her? How do you know she's not waiting for you?" I handed him another stack of books.

"You've got a point there," he said.

"I'm giving it all up—dating, I mean. It's an endless cycle. Friday night was just one more reminder of why I love singlehood."

"Well, OK then. If it makes you happy. But I think you're lying."

I stopped what I was doing and stared at him in shock. He smiled at me—a wide, bright smile. A Kenny smile.

Kenny didn't have Spencer's square chin and high cheekbones, or Dean's silky brown hair, or Norman's puppy-dog eyes. He didn't have Chris Noth's million-dollar Mr. Big finesse or Hugh Jackman's *everything*. He was six feet tall and gangly, with sandpaper hair that was cut unevenly and hazel eyes that were witness to the world around him. He was good-looking, but an awkward dresser. No, Kenny was someone you couldn't appreciate unless you sat close, stopped talking, and waited for him to smile. His smile was infectious, the kind that lit up his whole face. You couldn't forget Kenny's smile. It just wasn't possible.

Sitting on the floor with him at that moment, I really *looked* at him, and smiled back.

"You think I'm lying?" I asked.

He nodded. "Through your teeth."

"About what?"

"All of it," he said. "Here's the thing, Eva. Why don't you stop proving to yourself and the world that you're happier being single and just be happy for happy's sake? Date, don't date; get married, don't get married; have kids, don't have kids; do it because it's really right for you and not because a whole bunch of blog-people with too much time on their hands—present company excluded," he said, gesturing between the two of us, "are gonna lace into you for changing your mind or making a decision that doesn't warrant pithy prose."

It took a full five seconds for me to realize that my mouth was open and nothing was coming out.

"And I'll tell you something else. The Tom Cruise guy was likely a tool," he said.

I laughed out loud, the first time all day long. All weekend, come to think of it.

"And I would've checked your box had I been there, and not just because I know you. Pictures don't lie."

"Bullshit," I said in a hushed voice. "They lie all the time."

"That one didn't." He smiled again, and again I couldn't avert my eyes quickly enough.

I stood up, and he followed. "I'll buy you a cup of coffee, Sailor," I said, turning him around in the direction of the café tables, pushing him gently all the way.

⌒〇

That evening, when I got home from The Grounds, I reread the speed dating post in mortification. It was so blunt, so revealing. How could I have been such a yutz? Jay and Minerva and Norman didn't mind that I used their names, but I should have changed the others and kept Shaun out of it, for my sake and especially for his. Seventeen comments followed, all of which I perused until my eyes set on the last one, posted anonymously:

I didn't know you felt this way.

Could it have been Shaun? He had read the very first post of WILS, so who's to say he didn't read this one too? I furiously edited the post, changing names and other potentially comeback-to-bite-me-in-the-ass details, until I gave up, surrendering to the fact that the damage was already done. Sinking with defeat, I added one final line to the post:

The verdict: speed dating confirms my prereq— friends first.

Followed by a new dating rule:

Rule #6: Never, ever blog about your night out when you've had one too many Rosebuds to drink.

12

Stepping Up

THE NEXT DAY, when Car Talk Kenny stepped up to the counter, he neither greeted me nor ordered. Instead he leaned against the counter and watched me work.

"So, are we friends?" he asked.

"What?" I asked, taken aback by the question. "Yeah, sure. Of course we are."

"Good. Then you'll go out with me."

"*What*? No way."

"Why not?" he asked.

"You're a customer."

"Then I guess we're not really friends." He stuffed his hands in his pocket and gazed at the menu board. One thing about Kenny: he rarely ordered the same thing more than two days in a row.

I pulled away from the counter. "No, we are. I just...I don't know you well enough."

"No," he said, speaking more quietly. "You're friendly with me, but we're not friends."

"Why not?"

"I'll have the hazelnut decaf, by the way," he said, following me as I moved down the counter to select a cup and pour. "You're a watcher. And there's nothing wrong with being a watcher—I'm a watcher. I could watch people all day long. But I don't use it as a substitute for knowing people like you do."

Wow. Ouch.

Coffee sloshed onto the counter as I set his mug down and made direct eye contact. "For the first time ever, Kenny, you're dead wrong."

"Suit yourself," he said, handing me the exact change, "except I'm not. Read your blog."

He tucked a five-dollar bill in the tip jar and walked to his usual corner in the reading room.

By the time I had armed myself with enough comebacks to make my case, he was gone.

⤳◯

The next morning, Kenny entered The Grounds carrying a white paper bag. When he stepped up to the counter, he neither greeted me nor ordered. Again.

"We have twenty minutes," he said.

"For what?" I asked.

He held up the bag. "Lunch."

"It's eleven thirty, Kenny."

"Right. So we have twenty minutes until your lunch rush starts."

"I can't leave now."

He glanced quickly around the café to assess the action. "It's not like we're flying off to Fiji or anything."

"Where are we going?"

"Outside," he answered, arm outstretched and pointing to the door with the same hand that held the bag. "Come on."

I caved. "Fine," I said.

Checking on Susanna and the newest part-timer, I came out from behind the counter and followed him out.

"You brought food from another place into my shop?"

Shrugging, he led me around to the back of the building. "Sorry if I was a little too blunt for you yesterday. I have a tendency to say exactly what's on my mind and not think about whether it might hurt someone's feelings."

"It's OK."

"Good." He sat, patting the curb next to him. "So what are your thoughts on guacamole?"

"What?"

"Your choices are turkey with cheddar jack cheese and guacamole, or ham with apple slices and aioli on a Kaiser roll."

"Um, guacamole, I guess."

"Good choice." He handed me a large sandwich wrapped in deli paper.

"Thanks."

He plunged his hand into the bag again. "Barbeque or sea salt?" he asked, pulling out two bags of potato chips.

"Sea salt. Where did you get all this?"

"Sandwich shop on Market Street. I found it a while back."

"Are you planning to make that your new hangout? Swept off your feet by aioli and guacamole?"

"What can I say? I'm a sucker for avocadoes."

"Big deal. You can't put avocado into a cookie."

I took a bite of the sandwich. "Wow," I said after swallowing, "maybe I wouldn't blame you if you defected."

He smiled as I took another bite. "OK," he said. "My kindergarten teacher's name was Janeway McHolland, I wanted to be an entomologist when I grew up, and I hate peas."

"Are you speaking to me in code or something?" I asked.

"We're becoming friends," he answered, and continued. "Anyway, my favorite color is green, and I could eat blueberries like popcorn all day long."

I held up a hand to stop the onslaught of information. "Why aren't you eating?"

"It's eleven thirty, I'm not hungry yet," he answered, as if it were obvious.

"Well, you can't just sit here and watch me eat."

"Why not?"

"Because that's weird."

He nodded and took a sip of Coke. "Got it. Doesn't like to be watched while eating. Good to know."

The fresh air was a welcome change from the ubiquitous scent of coffee. Despite being hunched on the curb, my knees pushed up to my chest, I was enjoying my impromptu lunch. Kenny took a bite from his sandwich and set it back down, disinterested.

"When I was little I asked my mom to move my birthday," he said.

"OK, that one you have to explain."

"My birthday is January fourteenth. Everyone is all partied and gifted and wintered out. And really, how fun can you make a winter birthday party?"

I swallowed. "Snowball fights? Snow forts?"

"Not where I'm from. Just cold and gray."

"Where are you from?" I asked.

"Delaware."

"Delaware?"

"It's near New Jersey."

I huffed. "Well I knew *that*. You just don't look like you're from Delaware."

He snorted. "Delaware has a look?"

"Whatever," I said. "So no outdoor birthday fun. So what about indoor stuff? Laser tag? Chuck E. Cheese? There had to be something."

"Laser tag would've been fun, I'll give you that. But somehow my birthdays just always felt like a big flop. By my eleventh I'd had enough, so just on a whim, I asked my mom if I could move my birthday to *June* fourteenth, and she agreed."

"And?"

"And at eleven and a half I realized that my birthday wasn't the problem. I just didn't like parties. Period."

I laughed, which made him laugh, until he glanced at his watch and frowned.

"Oh, don't tell me. Already?" I said.

"You should probably get going. It's quarter of," he added apologetically. I wondered if it was in response to my disappointment or his own.

I wrapped up the remaining half of my sandwich. Kenny put his sandwich—he never took a second bite—back into the bag. We stood and I tried to read his expression—a sign of romantic interest, an ulterior motive—but all I saw was Kenny. Honest, friendly, having-a-good-time Kenny. I waited for the moment to become awkward, but it never did.

"Thanks for lunch," I said.

"It was my pleasure." He smiled, saying, "After all, what are friends for?"

13

Duck!

FOR THE NEXT two weeks, Kenny and I continued our get-to-know-you, tell-all routine. The first time following our impromptu lunch, he'd placed his order and added a little tidbit: "I'll have the Cookie of the Week and a Peruvian blend coffee, and I hate wet socks." And when I returned with his order he said, "Your turn." He had caught me so off guard that I stood there blankly before saying, "Uh, I hate millipedes?"

Good God, how lame. Of course I hate millipedes. Who doesn't?

"Well, there goes next year's birthday present."

He retrieved his order and sat down while I contemplated banging my head on the counter. Once I caught on, however, the game became a fun exchange of bits of trivia and did-you-knows. He left notes for me everywhere, too. He'd leave napkins on his table that read, *My favorite font is Garamond*. Or, *I like the smell of ink*. Or, *I hate polka dots, but love herringbone*. One night I found a coffee cup sleeve tucked under my windshield wiper that said, *I'd like to go green, but I'm kind of lazy*. Another time he scribbled on a credit card receipt, *I want to invent a word that rhymes with orange*.

And always, a demand: "Your turn."

By the end of the two weeks, I learned that Tuesdays are his favorite day, he hates wool sweaters because they itch, chocolate chip cookies and braided rugs make him nostalgic, he's a self-proclaimed "all or nothing kind of guy," and he's afraid of heights. In return, he learned that I'm overly competitive when watching *Jeopardy*, fireworks of any kind scare the crap out of me, and I once dressed up as one of the Robert Palmer girls for Halloween. It wasn't long before I found myself taking note of personal pet peeves or new quirks to share the next time I saw him. I'd even plan out what I'd say on my way to work. And then it occurred to me that I was *looking forward* to seeing him every day, if only to tell him that the sight of milk in cereal makes me gag.

ᑎᗧ

My alarm went off at five-thirty like a banshee with a vengeance. I hit the snooze button and my brain chugged to life, cogs grinding and wheels spinning. My eyes burned as I pried them open, trying to figure out what, exactly, was causing the feeling of dread pinning me to the bed. Were we expecting a large shipment? No. Was it hurricane season? (When was it not?) Was it possible that Norman threw a secret after-hours party and trashed the place? Nah. He would've invited me. Then cleaned up.

What day was it?

Oh. Crap.

As of 4:16 this morning, I was thirty-four.

The number slammed into my chest, pinning me to the bed. Thirty-four years might as well have been thirty-four tons.

Thirty-four years! And what did I have to show for it? I was neither who nor where I had thought I would be (back when I was, say, ten...or even twenty); not that that was necessarily a bad thing, but suddenly I wasn't sure if it was a good thing, either. And not that thirty-four was a super-horrible age—it wasn't a milestone, like forty, and I could still tell people I was in my *early* thirties. And yet, something about this particular birthday bothered me and filled me with a dread that made me want to duck and take cover.

I considered my options. The Grounds opened at seven o'clock. That gave me at least a couple of hours to pack the essentials and flee the country before anyone would notice the shop hadn't opened and track me down. Could I fit all my shoes into my car and still see over the steering wheel?

Scratch that plan.

Or I could hole up here, maybe in a closet—no, better yet, under the porch!—until after dark. Then, I could tunnel away, safely avoiding both humanity and sunlight. Although I wasn't sure how effective a garden trowel would be after a few miles of tunneling...to say nothing of the Chunnel I'd need to construct.

Invent a time machine? I could go back and stop myself from going to that cursed speed dating charade, for starters. But why waste a good time-travel on something so stupid when there were so many other moments worth doing over? A night of *Monopoly* with my parents and Olivia instead of four hours playing Nintendo, for starters.

My alarm shrieked again, and I hit the snooze a bit more forcefully, fumbling with the buttons until it clicked off for good.

Damn. Anyone who couldn't handle an alarm clock probably wouldn't fare so well at constructing a time machine from scratch.

Call in sick?

Instead, I forced myself out of bed and attacked my morning routine like a woman on a mission and was at The Grounds by

6:27 dressed in a *Life is Good* top, capri pants, and espadrilles. By 8:51, I'd spilled a smoothie down the front of my shirt, smeared coffee grounds on the capris, and changed into my usual mandarin orange Chuck Taylors.

The day brightened somewhat when Norman came in early bearing a bouquet of Gerbera daisies with a *Mutts* card for me.

After thanking him, I tucked the daisies into a vase and placed them on the counter.

"So how does it feel to be old?" asked Norman.

"How does it feel to have a bouquet of flowers shoved up your nose?"

"Point taken."

The place seemed to be busier than usual. Kenny, who had been showing up at 11:30 on the dot, was conspicuously absent today, and I found myself shifting my gaze between the door and my watch between every customer order.

I brainstormed a new cookie recipe, figuring that would take my mind off this day that had all the makings of a hurricane brewing. Testing new recipes was always akin to starting a new book chapter. The possibilities for combinations of the basics—flour, sugar, eggs, baking powder—were as appealing as the combinations of words and sentences. It was how you put them together and what you added to the mix that made the difference. The process could be equal parts exciting and terrifying, but when it worked, when customers took that first bite and let the flavors sit on their tongues for just a second, savoring the moment, I felt a gratification beyond anything that a well-written chapter or a good class lesson could ever give me. The writing process had never been as invigorating. Writing my novel was a chore, an assignment. And truth be told, the thrill of finishing it surpassed the thrill of publishing it. Of course I wanted readers to like it, and of course I wanted to sell books and make money. But given a choice between a favorable book review and a favorable cookie review, the latter mattered far more.

Minerva came in just as the lunch crowd was thinning out. As I started to fix her iced chai latte, she intervened, "Um, before you get too far into that, can you make it with soy milk?"

"Soy milk for the farm girl?" I teased. "And which cookie? I made ginger-molasses drops, just to test out a new recipe. Does it sound funny? I made them on a whim, but I'm worried they might be too weird."

She shook her head, and I stopped rambling soon enough to realize she was pale.

"You OK?"

"It's a vegan day," she said.

"Uh-oh. Another rough day in the lab?"

I knew enough to let Minerva's self-declared "vegan days" go unquestioned. I wasn't entirely sure what went on in her labs (although I've heard her say the word "cadaver" as casually as one says "hamburger"), but anything that was bad enough to make her swear off animal products even for a day was more than I wanted to know.

She studied her purse but didn't reach for her wallet.

"Tell you what, go sit and I'll bring your chai over in a second."

She smiled—barely—and headed towards the reading room. This was bad. No milk, no animals, and now the secluded reading room. Very bad.

Making sure that Susanna had the counter covered, I handed Minerva her chai and then plopped onto the overstuffed loveseat next to her. "What's up?"

She swirled the drink with her straw (although it was as mixed as it ever would be) before answering.

"You know how Jay likes to get our food from a co-op?" She took a sip and seemed to brighten for a second, remarking, "This is good."

I'd made it just the way she liked it—a little heavy on the chai, light on the ice, and enough milk to lighten it without it dulling the flavor.

I nodded and waited for her to continue.

"Well, this morning I was making an omelet, and when I broke one of the eggs open, it..." She shuddered. "It was dead."

"The yolk?" I asked. Being a suburbanite, the closest I ever got to rural living was visiting farm stands in the Hamptons when I was a kid and the State Fair in Raleigh.

"Which means there was enough of it there that it could have been alive. Eventually."

I tried not to make a face, but failed. "Eiw." Probably not the most supportive thing I could have said. "Well I can see why you're steering clear for the day," I offered, trying to be supportive.

"I almost threw up in the sink. And I made Jay eat his omelet by himself. In another room."

I lowered my voice to a whisper and leaned in. "Maybe it's just morning sickness?"

She shook her head, tracing patterns in the condensation on her cup. "False alarm."

It took me a moment to catch on. "Oh, Min." I wrapped an arm around her shoulder, pulling her into a sideways hug. "I'm sorry."

Minerva didn't seem to mind the awkwardness of the half hug; her eyes brimmed. "A fricken chicken can get pregnant, and I can't." She wiped her eyes quickly. "Fricken chicken. Ha. I like that."

I couldn't help but laugh a little. Even when she was at her lowest, Minerva still found ways to smile.

"It's not that you can't, Min," I said. "It just wasn't the right time—you said so yourself, between school and finances. Geez, can you imagine all that stress of having to learn how to deliver someone else's baby while carrying your own?"

"I know." She sounded younger than I'd ever considered her. "But Jay was so excited. And I was so happy."

I tried to think of the best thing to say. "When it's meant to be, it will."

She nodded, actually snuggling closer. "Is it wrong to miss something that never was?"

My thoughts immediately drifted to Shaun gazing at me from inside some fading memory, followed by my parents. I sometimes tried to picture what they'd look like today, silver-haired and wrinkled, voices changing in pitch and inflection. Thank goodness for videos at Christmas and Olivia's confirmation, otherwise I would've forgotten the sound of their voices altogether.

"I hope not," I said.

Minerva suddenly sat up straight. "Shit, Eva—today's your birthday! I completely forgot!"

I put my index finger to my lips. "Shhhhh. I'd rather not make a big deal about it."

"Why not?"

"I don't know. I'm just not into it this year."

She inspected the top of my head. "I don't see any grays."

"Don't think I didn't look."

"So what's the problem?"

I sighed quietly. "I guess I'm just wondering if this is really enough." I stood up. "Forget it. I'm being silly. Of course it is."

"Well, for what it's worth, happy birthday. I'm going to steal you after work tonight and take you out for drinks."

"Sounds good to me."

⌒〇

The rest of the day had gone quickly, and despite my disappointment that Kenny was a no-show, I was looking forward to going out with Minerva. With only an hour left of my shift, I kicked into overdrive filling customer orders, doling out samples of the new cookie, and trying to stay one step ahead of keeping the back counters clean and tidy.

"Be right with you..." I said to the next customer, then did a double-take when I saw who it was.

The Jeanette.

Even before I saw *him*, I knew it was *her*. I just *knew*. Her long, luxurious red locks, her fabulous proportions, her creamy skin tone. Her everything.

Damn.

Shaun stepped into my line of sight and smiled. "Take your time."

Double damn to holy hell.

Willing my stomach to stop doing somersaults, I moved in front of the register, hyper aware of my clothes covered in coffee grounds and smoothie stains.

"What can I get for you?" I said in an exaggerated, peppy tone.

"Eva, this is my fiancée, Jeanette. Jeanette, this is my good friend Eva," Shaun said.

I don't think she was ever real to me until that moment.

"Nice to meet you," I said, summoning sweetness and extending a floury hand. She took it by the fingertips and shook politely—whether she did this because she had dainty hands or because she didn't want to get them dirty, I don't know, but I instantly assumed it was the latter, and who could blame her?

"Same here. Shaun has told me so much about you."

A string of possibilities of what Shaun might have said, all in his voice, ran through my head in that split second: *Eva's my ex-girlfriend who wrote a novel. Good baker. A little on the batshit-crazy side, though.* Or, *Nice girl. Knows way more television and movie quotes than the average civilized person should know.* Or, *If she were in a Nora Ephron movie, she'd be the comedy-relief coworker who constantly has man troubles and watches Cary Grant movies.*

"I'm the one who wrote the Kierkegaard book," she added after a beat.

I nodded. "Ah, yes. Well, who doesn't love a good Kierkegaard book after a long day and a hot bath?"

She stared at me blankly for a moment, then picked up a napkin from the dispenser next to the register and wiped her hands. Definitely the latter.

"So, what would you like?" I asked.

"Tall iced coffee. Decaf, with skim?" She was the picture of polite.

"Sure. And for you, Shaun?"

"I'll have what she's having."

I'll have what she's having? I'LL HAVE WHAT SHE'S HAVING??

"Sure," I said.

Norman jumped in when he saw me jam the scooper into the bed of ice like I was spearing a fish.

"Why don't I take care of this for you," he offered.

As I walked out from behind the counter, I passed Scott (who was eyeing Shaun like a maniacal prison guard), as well as Sister Beulah, who was sitting with Minerva, who mouthed, "Are you OK?" to me. I nodded and headed into the reading room to straighten up, but dammit, it was immaculate. To my dismay, Shaun followed me.

"Can I talk to you for a second?" he asked.

I exhaled forcefully, flabbergasted, yet not wanting to show it. "Sure."

I leaned against one of the tall bookcases, obnoxiously tapping the book spines with my fingers.

"So?" I asked.

"I've been reading your singlehood blog lately."

Oh God. Here it comes.

"And?"

"And, well, I read the post about the speed dating," he said in his professor's voice.

I avoided eye contact and started straightening books that were already straightened, praying that he was referring to the edited post and not the original. "Yeah, well, I was a little tipsy when I wrote all that."

"I read what you wrote about me."

Shit, shit, shit!

"Oh."

"I'm not upset that you used my name or anything. It's just that I thought you were over it all already. Us, I mean."

"I was—I mean, I am."

"It didn't sound like you were," he said.

I shrugged my shoulders. "I told you, I was drunk."

He looked uncomfortable. "I just thought, you know, you were fine. You said you were."

"Yeah, well, I lied," I said.

He looked at me with an expression that was dangerously close to pity.

"I guess I don't understand," he said. "I thought I gave you plenty of time to let that all blow over."

"Blow over?"

He sighed. "And come on, Eva, what are you doing going out speed dating with a married couple?"

I looked up at him for the first time. He'd struck a nerve.

"What the hell is that supposed to mean?"

"I'm just saying, I'm concerned. You're above that."

"I'm above going out and having fun with my friends? Jay and Minerva Brunswick are my *friends*, Shaun. Not that anything I do is any of your business anymore."

"I'm your friend, too, you know."

I put up my hands, halting him right there. "You are not my *friend*. You are my *lover* who dumped me for a philosophy professor."

"You and I broke up long before I met Jeanette."

"Still, you think it doesn't hurt? You think I don't see in her what you never saw in me? She'd make Aphrodite want to call Jenny Craig." Shaun pretended to take interest in a water ring left over on one of the end tables while I steamrolled his attempt to put together a response. "You think I don't go to bed every single night wondering what I said or did after *three years* to turn you off? You think I don't want to go back in there right now and ask the Jeanette what her secret is?" I pointed in the direction of the counter, where she was waiting.

"Eva, what do you want from me? I'm sorry it didn't work out between us the way you wanted. It was nothing you said or did or didn't say or didn't do. I just...didn't...love you in that way. I'm sorry, I really am. Dammit, we've been through this already!"

My eyes burned as I swallowed hard, my mouth dry and throat constricted.

"I want nothing from you, Shaun," I forced out, and slunk away from him, farther from the café and closer to the restrooms. "Your fiancée is waiting for you."

"Wait," he called. "I want you to come to the wedding, Eva. You're still an important part of my life, and it would mean so much to me."

At that moment, I stopped, turned around, looked at the book I happened to be holding in my hand—a Stephen King novel—and then looked up at him, fuming.

"Duck," I said through clenched teeth.

"What?"

"DUCK!" I hollered as I hurled the book just far enough to miss him but close enough to scare the living daylights out of him. He crouched and banged his knee on an end table just as the book sailed past him and hit the wall. Minerva and Sister Beulah raced to the reading room when they heard the thud, while all activity in the café came to a deafening halt.

"Ow! Geezus, Eva, what the hell?" Shaun said, hunched over and holding his left knee.

I took a step toward him.

"You don't get it, Shaun. You just don't freakin' get it, do you. Are you insane? I don't wanna go to your stupid wedding. I don't wanna be friends with your perfect Jeanette, or you, for that matter. I wanna go back to the way things were! You loved me once, I know you did. What happened? Just tell me and I'll fix it."

"Eva, stop this, please. Nothing good comes of this."

I wanted to stop, to spare myself any further humiliation. But I couldn't. He was slipping away from me all over again, just as he had the night he broke up with me. Just as my mom and dad had slipped away into the oblivion of cancer. Just as Olivia had kicked me out of my own house so she could get on with her own life. There had to be something I could prevent from happening. There had to be something I could save, something I could keep for myself.

"Tell me, what does she have?" I asked in desperation. I would've sold The Grounds for the answer, the secret.

"I *never* loved you the way you thought, OK?"

Tears rolled down my face. "But *I loved you*, Shaun. For keeps."

At that moment, I couldn't for the life of me figure out *why* I loved him, why I still cared, why I was blubbering away when I really wanted to topple the bookcase over him. I hated him, and I hated myself for not having the moxie to just wish him well, turn my back, and never give him or our relationship a second thought ever again. I hated that it still hurt as bad as if we broke up yesterday. Most of all, I hated that if he asked me to, I'd take him back in a New York minute. But he was already long gone.

"I can't stand all this dating shit," I confessed. "I don't want any of it. There'll never be anyone else but you. You were it. And now you tell me that you shared my life and my bed for three years and you *never* loved me? Did I dream the whole thing?"

"I tried to want it."

Before I could ask what he meant, Minerva's voice sharply interjected, "Shaun, this is neither the time nor the place for this discussion. I suggest you and your fiancée leave Eva's place of business. *Now.*"

Thank God for Minerva.

Without looking at her, Shaun backed out of the reading room, met the Jeanette at the door—perfect, sane, engaged Jeanette—and left without their orders. God knew what she thought of me at that moment as she walked to the door without a backwards glance, clutching her handbag as if to protect it from muggers. God knew if she even cared.

After they left, Minerva shot Norman a stern look, and he informed the customers that the show was over. I sank to my knees and wept while Sister Beulah and Minerva attended to me. Minerva bent down and put her arms around me, our second awkward, sideways hug of the day.

"He forgot my birthday," I cried. "He remembered Lemon Torte Day, but he forgot my birthday."

"He never deserved you," said Sister Beulah as she rubbed my back, just like Olivia used to do. "It's a blessing in disguise, even if you can't see it right now."

"Got room in the convent for one more?" I tried to joke.

"And waste a pretty face like yours? I'd just as soon have you run off and join the Marines," she joked.

When I regained my composure, I stood up and entered the café as if I were about to be thrown to the lions—the pretend preoccupation amongst the clientele was worse than when they'd all been gawking at me. I caught a glance of Tracy holding her hand on her heart and mouthing something to me, although I couldn't make out the words.

"Norman, I'm going," I announced as I went behind the counter, looking for nothing in particular, my voice wavering.

"Do you need someone to take you home?" Norman asked, clearly concerned. Scott leaned against the counter so far I thought he was going to climb over it.

"I'm fine," I said. I could silently hear Kenny asking me, *No. How are you* really *feeling?*

"Dude, you shouldn't be alone," said Scott.

"Don't 'dude' me," I snapped at Scott, and everyone's heads turned and chatter stopped for the second time. "I am not one of your bar buddies. I am not a 'dude.'"

"You're right," said Scott. "I apologize, Eva. Let me make it up to you by taking you home."

"*I'll* take her home," said Minerva as she started to close her books and put away her laptop.

I looked at Minerva, Norman, and Scott; for a split second I hated all of them.

"For the love of...I am older than all of you," I said, ignoring the fact that Sister Beulah had a good fifteen to twenty years on all of us.

I removed my apron and went into the back, grabbed my purse, took two deep breaths, and stood there for a moment. *Stop it*, I thought. *Stop the madness. Stop the world from crashing down on you.*

I knew what I wanted. Not the comfort of a warm chocolate chip cookie, or the hug of a friend. Not a sister's hand gently rubbing my back, or a Marx Brothers marathon. No, I knew *exactly* what I wanted. What I needed.

When I came back out, Minerva was waiting for me. I turned to Scott.

"I accept your apology, Scott, and the ride."

Minerva's neck practically snapped as she turned and looked at me, wounded.

"I'll call you later, Minerva," I said as Scott lightly laid a hand on my back. The silence rang as we walked out. I said nothing in the car while Scott talked incessantly about what an asshole Shaun was and how Jeanette couldn't hold a candle to me and he should be the one begging me to take him back, blah blah blah blah blah…

When we got to my house, he accompanied me to my front door as I unlocked and opened it.

I should've said good-bye and left him there, on the porch. I should have never let him drive me home in the first place. I should have stuck to my original plan and tunneled the hell out of town that morning.

As if my brain was functioning separate from my body, I took Scott by the shoulder, pulled him to me, and kissed him.

Not bad.

I kissed him again.

Next thing I knew, we were in my house, making our way to the bedroom, kissing and pulling each other's clothes off along the way.

Bed or shower, bed or shower?

We showered first, then went to bed. Minerva had both called and left a text message, as did Norman and Shaun. I ignored them all.

14

Scott

I OPENED MY eyes in darkness, during what was presumably the middle of the night, to the sound of light breathing next to me. My head felt heavy as I turned it on the pillow to see the figure beside me, the source of the light breathing. I faintly smiled as I closed my eyes again, comforted by this presence, and fell asleep again.

Bright light streamed through a slice in my window shade and struck my headboard like a laser beam, leaving me with no choice but to wake up. The smell of sex and soap hit me first.

Uh-oh.

A tactile sensation struck next—soft, percale sheets that hugged my bare skin.

Bare. Skin.

Then I heard cabinet doors open and close in the kitchen.

Oh shit, what did I do this time?

It all came back at me like a crescent wave: the Jeanette, the confrontation with Shaun, the meltdown, the going home with Scott, the kissing Scott, the foyer, the shower, the bedroom, the sex, the sex, oh God, the sex!

I slid out of bed, stepped over the heap of clothes and damp towels, and found my robe. After sliding on the robe followed by slipping into flip-flops, I first went to the bathroom, splashed some cold water on my face and gargled mouthwash, and then flapped down the hallway, past the living room, and into the kitchen, where Scott was rummaging through my pantry and wearing nothing but plaid boxers. Odd, I hadn't even realized he'd been wearing boxers last night.

"Hey," I said, my throat froggy.

Wow, the eloquence.

He turned and saw me and smiled. "Hey, you," he said as he padded over to me and planted a kiss on my lips. "How are you? How'd you sleep?"

I cleared my throat. "Like a rock. How 'bout you?"

"Really good. Your mattress is really comfortable."

"Thanks," I said.

I'd had sex with Scott. I'd had a lot of sex with Scott.

"Um, where do you hide your coffee?" he asked.

"I don't have any coffee. I don't even have a coffeemaker."

He dropped his jaw and looked at me. "How is that possible?"

"I don't like coffee."

"You *what?*"

"I don't like—" I started before he interrupted me.

"You own a coffee shop!"

"You noticed."

He opened his mouth again, but nothing came out.

"It's the biggest joke at the shop," I said.

Not only had I just slept with one of my customers, one of the *Originals*, but he didn't even know that I don't like coffee?

He processed this. "You know, come to think of it, I've never actually seen you drink a cup of coffee. I've seen you drink tea, smoothies, water, pineapple juice, but no coffee."

"I used to hate the smell of it, too, but I got used to it."

"Wow," he said. "That's just too funny."

"I can't believe I'm about to say this, but there's a Dunkin' Donuts right around the corner. You want me to get dressed and go get you some?" I asked.

"Nah, I can wait. That's sweet of you to offer, though."

He kissed me again, this one lingering and tasting a little bit minty. He then looked at me, his brown eyes warm. Nice.

"Soooo…" he said.

"So."

"Last night…"

"Yep."

"You were amazing, Eva."

I blushed. "Thanks," I said shyly. "I had a good time, too." In fact, it was *really* good.

What now?

"Listen, Scott—" I started, but he interrupted me again.

"I know, Eva. This wasn't something you exactly planned. It was a rebound from the drama with your ex yesterday. I'm not clueless. If this is only a one-time thing, then I understand. And if you want to keep it quiet, then I understand that, too, and totally respect your privacy. I just want you to know that I meant what I said. It was really special for me."

Wow. Good in bed *and* thoughtful. What were the odds?

I took a deep breath and let out a dramatic sigh.

"To be honest, Scott, I'm not sure what I want at the moment. You were wonderful, too, and I really appreciate your offering to give me space. I want to be fair to you and not string you along. But..." I stopped, at a loss for what to say next.

"It's OK," he said.

At that moment, the urge to kiss him overcame me, and I did so, wrapping my arms around him. He nuzzled my hair as he slid a hand into my robe and onto my bare back.

"You smell good," he said in practically a whisper.

"You smell like morning," I replied, to which we both laughed. He let go of me and asked to use my shower. I was both grateful and disappointed for the killed moment—for sure we would've ended up back in bed again, and what surprised me most of all was that I wanted to be.

I retreated to my deck and curled myself in the cushioned patio chair, listening to the surf beyond the trees and cul-de-sac and forcing myself to think of things other than naked Scott in my shower.

Wilmington had always seemed like a logical move for me. Located on the southernmost coast of North Carolina, its beaches had beckoned to me immediately upon my arrival. I suppose growing up on Long Island, surrounded by water, had naturally predisposed me to wanting to be so close to it. Wilmington, how-ever, had the added bonus of little palm trees lining the properties of beach houses along private roads, something even the richest Hamptons residents couldn't buy. The sonorous rhythms of the ocean soothed me to sleep every night, and although the salty air wreaked havoc on my hair, especially in the summer, its lin-gering breezes were welcoming during the molten months. The NCLA campus was within walking distance of the ocean, and I had even occasionally conducted short story workshops there.

My house was a two-bedroom bungalow, complete with an open deck and skylights in the kitchen. I'd bought it just a few months after graduating, able to afford it thanks to the advance my publisher gave me as part of the contract for my novel. For years I had thought Shaun's presence had made it a home, but even after we broke up and Shaun moved out, my house was more a sanctuary from the pain of his absence than a reminder of it. I suppose it was one more reason why I'd been single for so long. Aside from being too tired to go out after work, I enjoyed the solace of my house. Although I spent more time at The Grounds, I loved coming back here at the end of a grueling day and flopping on my couch or reading chair, listening to the not-too-distant surf, even as the central air-conditioning whirred in the summer, followed by the central heat in the winter.

Cradling a cup of tea in my hands, my thoughts didn't stay distracted for long as the events of the last twenty-four hours crept in. The meltdown in front of Shaun; Minerva's disappointment; Scott in my shower; they all strutted past me like runway models, and I cringed with each sight. *You just slept with* Scott, *dammit. Scott, who propositioned you on Lovematch-dot-com. Scott from The Grounds. Scott the Original. One of your cus-*tomers. *Norman's best friend. Someone other than Shaun.* Sure, there had been guys before Shaun, but not since. *Why Scott?* I wondered. Despite my failed attempts to deny my motives, I had known exactly what I was doing when I accepted his offer to drive me home. But what if I had let Norman drive me home, or if Kenny had been there? Who would be in my shower right now?

I felt a twinge in the pit of my stomach, a cross between nerves and hunger, with perhaps a pang of longing.

Moreover, I had no idea what I was supposed to do now, or what Minerva or Norman would say if they found out. *If* they found out? Why wouldn't I tell them? And what about the other Originals and Regulars? Good grief, what had I done?

All these questions clamored for my attention.

Damn Shaun for coming into my shop with the Jeanette, for meeting her and getting engaged, for breaking up with me in the first place. And damn me for still caring.

When Scott reemerged, this time wearing nothing but a towel around his waist, he found me still sitting outside on my back deck, still in the robe, holding the cup of tea and staring out into the horizon.

"Hey," I said again when I heard the screen door open. He had a nice body, I noticed. His torso was muscular without being ripped; his biceps, well defined; legs, sturdy, well-suited for surfing, parasailing, and jet-skiing, sports I knew he regularly participated in. He was a beach bum and a water rat when he wasn't working or hanging out at The Grounds, and he sported a year-round tan that was much more attractive than a booth- or sprayed-on clay color.

I stood up, and he took a step toward me, blocking my path to the door. Good God, he's still horny, I thought. And good God, so was I.

"Eva," he whispered, and kissed me again, this time slipping his tongue over mine. He smelled clean and fresh and felt moist and supple, and I wanted to see what was underneath that towel. "I want you again," he said.

"I need a shower," I said to myself more than him.

"Can I join you?" he asked.

"You just had one."

"It was a cold one."

I blushed again. "You'll shrivel up like a prune."

"I like prunes."

"What happened to giving me space?"

"I'll give you space afterwards." He pulled me to him, and I knew exactly what was under that towel.

"Damn," I murmured, my face buried in his shoulder, "you're intoxicating."

He chuckled. "Good," he said.

"No, it's not good. This is crazy. You—we—*this*," I stammered, trying to find a way to say what looped obsessively in my head.

He backed away, and his smile disappeared.

"You're right," he said. "You're freaked out. I can see that. Do you want me to go?"

Yes. No. Please. Maybe.

"My car is at The Grounds," I answered.

"Do you want me to take you there so you can get it?"

"I can walk," I answered. "It's only about two and a half miles. The exercise will be good for me."

"OK," he said, without even a drop of disappointment in his voice.

"Listen," I said, "thank you for last night."

"You're welcome."

"And thanks for giving me space, too. I can't tell you how much it means to me."

"I understand."

I took his hand. "I think for now I just want to take it one day at a time. I'm definitely not ready to tell the world what happened."

"Sure thing. I think Norman's going to be a little disappointed that he didn't get to go home with you yesterday. For all we know, it would've been him you'd be having this conversation with."

I looked at him suspiciously. "What are you saying?"

"I'm saying Norman has a little crush on you."

My stomach dropped to my feet.

"Oh God. Oh, please don't tell me that. Not right now."

He grinned. "Sorry, but I think it's true."

"But he's seeing Speed-dating Samara. And he talks about her all the time. It's sickening how goo-goo-eyed he gets."

Scott shrugged. "I mean, he's never outright said anything, but being friends with him and all, I see the way he looks at you when you're not looking. I've not been your only admirer, Eva. I think we're ready to start a club."

Friggin' great.

With that, he kissed me one last time and bid me good-bye.

⟳

As I stood in the shower and let the cool water rain on me, I wondered what to do. It was bad enough that I'd posted my humiliation from the speed dating fiasco for the world to see, but this time I'd fucked up in 3D, with spectators and casualties. I was going to have to go back into my shop with my head held high and resume some semblance of routine, stop this runaway train from completely derailing, if it hadn't already.

One thing was for sure: singlehood was now a rug that had been pulled out from under me, and I was going to have to somehow regain my footing.

15

Come Back

AFTER SCOTT LEFT, I called in sick to work.

I viewed Facebook status updates but didn't change my own.

I made an egg-white veggie omelet for myself and ate half of it.

I straightened and dusted the rooms of my house and did laundry.

I called Olivia and left a message on her voice mail; I hadn't talked to her in two weeks.

I sat on the deck and tried to read a book, but gave up after reading the same paragraph three times and not remembering what it said.

I wandered from room to room again, as I'd done earlier that morning, like a lost puppy, not knowing what I was looking for or when I was going to get up the nerve to call Minerva.

I looked at my iPhone.

I watched TV, mostly consisting of a *Law & Order* marathon, *The People's Court*, and *30 Minute Meals*.

I sat outside on my deck.

I went back inside and cleaned off the smudges on the iPhone with the edge of my T-shirt.

I wandered around the house for a third time.

I picked up my phone and called Scott; he had given me his cell phone number before he left.

"Hello?" I heard him say, sounding tired.

"Hey, um, it's Eva."

"Hey!" The lilt in his voice reappeared.

"What are you up to right now?" I asked.

"I'm catching up on some programming. Working from home sometimes makes you procrastinate since no one's looking over your shoulder."

"Can you bring it over here?" I asked, almost feeling as if I'd stepped out of myself and was watching the whole thing—and thinking about how ridiculous it was.

"You want me to come over?" he asked.

I hesitated for a beat before answering. "Yeah, I do."

"When?"

"Is now too soon?"

"I'll be there in fifteen minutes," he said and hung up without even saying good-bye.

They were the longest fifteen minutes of my life; I thought I might die from the anxiety of waiting.

What am I doing?

When I heard the knock at the door, I opened it to find him standing there with his laptop briefcase in one hand and a can of Maxwell House in the other.

"Just in case you wanna pick up a new bad habit," he said with a boyish smile.

I smiled back and pulled him by the arm. "Get in here." He dropped his stuff as I pulled him close to me and kissed him hard. This time we went straight to bed.

I never did pick up my car at The Grounds.

16

The Club

SCOTT LEFT EARLY the next morning since it was my turn to open The Grounds, and I walked to work, which did me a lot of good as far as giving me time to clear my head. We'd had another night of great sex, and we even sat in bed and talked and joked around a bit. He was four years my junior, so it was strange to consider that when I was starting high school on Long Island, he was still playing Little League baseball in Silver Spring, Maryland. But Scott was low maintenance, and he was letting me be confused or distant if I needed to be, and that was comforting. Besides, he was nice. It wasn't that I didn't like Scott before—I had simply never considered us as a potential couple, even after the Lovematch.com incident. I still didn't, really. We were somewhere between being fuck buddies (although geez, how I hated that term, not to mention the concept) and dating (which, at this point, was just as undesirable as being the dreaded fuck buddies). And it disturbed me even more that I had slept with him twice before finding out that his last name was Vogel.

I don't know whom I was more nervous to face—Norman, after learning that he had a crush on me, or Minerva, whom I had blown off and had been avoiding ever since. I'd forgotten all about her news about the false alarm and felt guilty for not calling her back and being more available.

Shortly after I served the first two customers of the day, Norman called in sick—his first time in a year.

Mid-late afternoon that same day, Spencer and Tracy and Jan and Dean were sitting at their usual table, although Jan and Dean were sitting more apart than usual and seemed a little on the quiet side.

"So, Eva, what's up in the world of singlehood?" Tracy asked. "You haven't written much in your blog lately." Before I could answer, she said, "You know, you should pitch your blog to HBO as a TV series. Ever since *The Sopranos* and *Sex and the City* went off the air, there's nothing good on."

"Not true. What about *Entourage*?" said Dean.

"Isn't that on Showtime?" I asked.

"You're a writer," Tracy persisted. "How hard is it to write a script?"

"Do you even know how to write a screenplay?" asked Dean.

"Teleplay, actually," I said.

"You don't just sit down and write a script one day," said Jan. "It's a lot of work."

"Aaron Sorkin wrote most of *A Few Good Men* on cocktail napkins," I pointed out.

"Aaron Sorkin wrote *A Few Good Men*?" asked Dean.

"Isn't that the guy who wrote *Wag the Dog*?" asked Jan.

"David Mamet wrote *Wag the Dog*," said Dean. "Aaron Sorkin wrote *The West Wing*."

"And *Sports Night*," added Spencer. "Remember *Sports Night*?"

"You know that Aaron Sorkin wrote *The West Wing* but not *A Few Good Men*?" I asked.

"*Wag the Dog* was a good movie," said Dean.

"And *A Few Good Men* wasn't?" said Jan.

"Who writes *Entourage*?" asked Spencer.

Looking away from the table and at the door, I saw Minerva come in, laptop and messenger bag in tow, followed, coincidentally, by Scott, which made my stomach do several backflips in succession. I excused myself and went behind the counter to assist Susanna.

"Hey, Suze, would you mind checking on the cookies in the oven?"

"She's in the middle of my order," said Minerva tersely. "You can do it."

Ouch.

I entered the kitchen and pulled out a tray of pinwheels from the oven while watching Minerva from the window that separated the back counter from the kitchen. I could also see Scott at his usual table, already engrossed in his work, although he looked up once, made eye contact with me, and grinned before looking down again. My heart fluttered—it hadn't done that in a long time. At least not for someone who was neither Shaun nor Colin Firth.

When I exited the kitchen, Minerva was sitting at a table by the window, hunched over her books, studying.

"Mind if I sit here for a minute?" I asked. I never had to ask that before.

She shrugged. "Sure."

"I'm sorry I never called you, Min."

"S'OK," she said, not looking up.

"I was upset and needed time to cool off and sort things out. Surely you can understand that."

"I left a million messages for you," she said. For the second time in as many days, Minerva sounded young to me. Like a little kid.

"I know."

"Were you trapped under something heavy?"

I took note of the *When Harry Met Sally* reference, but didn't laugh.

"Something like that," I started.

She looked at me. She looked at Scott. Then she looked back at me.

"I knew it!" she said like a lawyer making a dramatic accusation, albeit softly enough so others couldn't hear.

There was no way I could lie to Minerva, so I leaned in and confessed. "It just sort of happened."

"My ass it sort of happened. You wanted it to happen. That's why you let him take you home."

"So maybe I did. But, Min, be happy for me. He's really nice—well, not *nice*," I said, searching for something more qualifying. "I don't know, he's fun and he's been really cool about the whole thing."

I could tell she was holding back, and suddenly I didn't want to know what she was thinking.

"I just—I want to be happy for you," she started, "but I'm not sure what to be happy about. That you finally rebounded over Shaun? That you spent a weekend with a guy whose favorite moniker is *dude*?"

She looked directly at me, apologizing with her eyes while she continued. "Eva, I promise you that the minute I know you're in a good place, I'll be happy for you. Until then, I'll be your biggest supporter—heck, I'm already your biggest fan. But one of us needs to keep our guard up. I mean, come on, the guy doesn't even like chai!"

I offered an obligatory smile to cover up the aching feeling that lately, no matter what I'd done, Minerva disapproved. Or maybe she was right—maybe there was nothing to be happy about yet. I recalled the past couple of days, both relaxing and wonderfully exhausting. Nah, there was plenty to be happy about. I just had to give Scott a chance. And once Minerva did, she'd be happy for me, too.

"Does Jay like chai?"

"Nobody's perfect," Minerva said primly.

I dropped the volume of my voice as well as my playful tone. "And how's everything else going for you guys, you know, since…" I trailed off.

She shrugged. "OK, I guess. I mean, you were right. It's so not a good time to get pregnant. But Jay's been his usual wonderful self. God, how I love that boy. He's my best friend, ya know?"

I pushed an image of Shaun out of my mind at the words *best friend*.

"In addition to you, of course," she obligingly added.

"I know. You're both lucky to have each other."

"Thanks to you," she reminded me, sarcastically.

"That's right," I said, sitting up straight. "You haven't thanked me lately."

When we were classmates, I had convinced Minerva to enter a poetry slam contest at NCLA, where she met Jay. He had recited a poem called "If a Tree Falls in the Woods, Who Cut It Down?"

Minerva touched a finger to her forehead in a lazy salute. "Hat's off to you, partner," she said.

I returned her salute. "I gotta get back to work. Norman called in sick today."

She looked astonished. "Norman? Sick? Is there a new strain of influenza going around?"

"Perish the thought."

"I hope he's OK," she said.

"Probably just needed an extra day off."

Before I got up, I hesitated. "You know, Scott said something a little unsettling to me the other day. He said that Norman has a crush on me, and isn't the only one. He cracked a joke about a club. What do you think of that?"

Minerva wore her studious face, as if I'd just asked her to explain the DNA chains of mitochondria.

"Hmmmm…I have noticed the way Norman sometimes looks at you when you're not looking. I'm not sure *crush* is the word I'd use—more like an attraction that he's not all too certain about. He cares about you, though. I mean, that much is obvious. You've got me on the club. Might be fun to guess, though." She nudged in the direction of a customer smearing a latte foam mustache off his lip. "He could be a member, for example."

I chuckled and looked for someone else. "Could be the guy who delivers my paper products."

"Could be Dara."

I laughed, incredulous. "Dara has a boyfriend!"

"Maybe it's a female crush; you know, like the one you have on Wonder Woman."

I swooned at the thought. "It's those red boots."

I left the table and went into the back room to speak to vendors and do payroll. Returning to the café, I spotted Kenny sitting at Minerva's table and stopped in my tracks. Determined to act casual, I strode past Scott and stood in front of them.

"Car Talk Kenny," I said in a forced friendliness that was as transparent as the plastic cup from which he sipped the last of his iced coffee.

He looked up at me, perplexed, chewing on his straw.

"Yesss…" he said tentatively and went back to making teeth marks on the straw.

"Where've you been?" I asked.

"Busy."

"No, really," I said, taking a page out of his book. "Where've you been?"

"I stopped by the other day, but you'd already left."

"What day?"

"Your birthday."

Oh shit. His words deflated me, the air *whooshing* out of my lungs.

"How've you been?" he asked.

"Fine."

"No, really. How've you been?"

"Fine," I insisted. Heading back to the register, I couldn't help but wonder whom I was lying to. Safely behind the counter, I spied him giving Minerva a *what the hell?* look. As the next customer stepped up, I caught Minerva in my peripheral vision leaning in close to him—he looked like he'd just been slapped in the face. *So help me, if she's telling him about me and Scott…* no. She wouldn't.

Scott stayed for two and a half hours, near closing time. I had gone out of my way all day to not avoid him completely, but also not be *too* friendly or flirtatious with him. Before leaving, he handed me a napkin with a note scribbled on it, which I shoved into my pocket. When I had a moment to slip away, I pulled it out and read it: *You're cute as hell when you're working.* Grinning, I re-folded it and went back to work. After closing, Scott came to my house and spent yet another night with me. As I lay next to him, waiting to fall asleep and replaying the scenes of the day, it struck me that I'd missed Norman all day long.

The next morning when I checked my e-mails, I found one from Minerva, subject heading "The Club." *Don't rule out Kenny*, was all it said. I quickly deleted the e-mail without a response.

17

Running

DON'T RULE OUT Kenny.

The words echoed in my head as I stood in front of the open fridge in my kitchen after work. My brain pieced the items inside together like a puzzle: bag of salad starters, veggies from the crisper, a piece of grilled chicken, a nub of Romano cheese. But I was too antsy to eat. My father's voice—or what I remembered it as; it'd been too long to be sure it was really his anymore—came to me as minutes passed without my making a move: "No sense in filling your belly when your head's already overflowing."

I closed the fridge.

Tugging my running shoes out from the back of the closet, I felt a small rush of anticipation as the road awaited me, but I knew better than to skip stretching. My thoughts swarmed as I dropped to the floor of my porch and slowly began to coax length from muscles that had gone too long without. It'd been months since I'd been running, a ritual I practiced regularly during my NCLA days. Whether it was circling the two-mile campus main road (twice) or stationary on the treadmill at the campus gym (to which I still had access as an alumna), my students would call out, "Hey, Professor Perino!" and I would wave a sweaty hand in acknowledgment, uttering more of a grunt than a hello. I wouldn't say that I love running (I'm definitely not one of those people), but I do relish the freedom and rhythm of it.

Some of my best thinking happens while I'm running. My best writing, too. In college I ran for term papers; later it was tough chapters, sometimes even recipes, but they always came to me after running, and usually after ten p.m.

I'd been thinking about the Club all day, keeping an eye out for Kenny (who never showed), watching Norman for signs of a secret membership, and feeling like a twelve-year-old fool in the process. The whole thing reeked of junior high, where I spent innumerable lunch periods engaged in this same behavior trying to determine whether I had a chance with Bobby Ackerman's younger brother Jason. The Club was all the more humiliating now that I not only had Norman to consider but an entire secret society, according to Scott. How had I gone from having no one in my life to a variety of potential suitors, not to mention one with whom I spent more time than I ever had with Shaun, and another who had already seen me naked on more than one occasion?

After ten minutes of stretching, I headed out, finding my pace easily and focusing on breathing, knowing that the tightness would leave my legs and lungs after a mile or so. I let each breath match the beats of soles on pavement—in (pound pound pound), out (pound pound pound), in (pound pound pound), out (pound pound pound)—as scenes from the day replayed before my eyes...

Although he never let a customer wait, never shirked a single duty, Norman had spent the day revolving around Speed-dating Samara. He was smitten and she loved it. She'd been in his sight from the moment she sauntered in with her Coach sunglasses tucked neatly into her trendy hairdo, the kind that comes after spending hours with your hair in big, fat rollers to give it big, loose curls. He brought her whatever she ordered, lingered just long enough to laugh over something trivial, and returned to the counter where he watched her, lest she need something else. I swear I even saw them texting each other.

And despite this alleged Club, I believed that the reasons for which guys liked me and the ways guys liked Samara were completely different. Every time I thought of her in that cute little dress she wore that dreaded speed dating night, I felt a twinge of jealousy—not because Norman liked her (after all, I was his favorite date, so he said) but because she was the kind of girl that lots of guys would like. It also reminded me of the Tom Cruise guy and everyone else who didn't like me that night. I bet he checked her box. I'll bet they all checked her box. I would have preferred that Samara and Tom had hooked up instead while Norman and I went out for a beer. She also happened to be dumb as a rock, with a laugh so piercing it could cut glass. Minerva and I secretly called her "Samurai" and thought Norman could do better if he randomly pointed to a name in the phonebook.

And yet, I couldn't criticize Norman too harshly. I wasn't much better. Although we didn't have "eye sex" all day (as Minerva called it), I'd kept Scott in my peripheral vision throughout the afternoon, and I'd tried like hell not to be disappointed when he'd mentioned he had to lay low for the night. He'd been talking to Norman (who was fixed on Samara, who was on her cell phone with someone named Gigi who was "*too* funny") but looked straight at me as he said that there was a big meeting in the morning with a client and he had to prepare for it tonight.

"Whatever, man," Norman had answered, eyes shooting back to Samurai as she pealed out in laughter again.

"Ohmigod, Gigi," she cried out, flicking something from underneath a fingernail, "you are just *too* funny, now. *Too* funny."

I found myself neither dreading nor loving the end of my shift. On one hand, it meant I had to go home to a quiet house (in other words, sans Scott); but on the other hand, there'd be no eye sex and shrieking blonds there. I figured it was a draw.

In (pound pound), out (pound pound). More images flashed before me: Norman swirling the steamed head of each latte he made into some design before handing it to the waiting customer. Scott's hands splayed on the counter as he leaned forward to tell Norman (and me) about his evening plans. Norman ogling Samurai as she uncrossed and crossed her legs. Scott's steady gaze from above his laptop. I replayed events from the past couple of days, too: Yesterday's awkward exchange with Kenny. Scott on my deck, all tan and buff and wearing nothing but a towel. Kenny yukking it up with Minerva. Shaun and his perfect Jeanette. Norman and Samara. Kenny, Minerva. Scott in bed. Shaun with me. Shaun and Jeanette.

In (pound pound), out (pound pound). *Breathe, Eva.* Is it possible to love one person your whole life? *Breathe...*

The Love of Your Life?

Is it possible to love one person your whole life? Does the myth of the high school sweetheart exist, or is it just a dream created at slumber parties and held on to for dear life by unhappy singles and desperate class reunion-goers?

Let's say for the time being that it does. That some people (albeit a depressingly decreasing number) fall in love, get married, and stay that way for the rest of their days not because they have to, are too chicken to change, or can't imagine life any other way, but because they *want* to. Let's say that for some, love endures, because for some it does.

Finding a love like that is like striking gold. There can be no luckier thing. Think of all the things that have to synchronize just so for so-called "true love" to happen—and stay happening. You have to meet, first of all. You have to recognize that something's there, and act on it. It has to work; you have to both be single and interested. You have to go through the steps of dating and falling in love, get married (or make some equivalent commitment), and then either your life is smooth sailing from them on or you have to love each other so fiercely, so completely, that no tragedy or amount of time can change the way you feel for each other.

The odds are against you every step of the way. If there are over six billion people in the world, isn't it a bit far-fetched to believe that there's one—and only one—out there just for you? Let's take the stars from our eyes and face the facts. Not only is that concept impractical, it's improbable. Think about it. See, all my life I've been clinging to the idea that "the right guy is out there somewhere," but I think as an adult I owe it to myself to admit that maybe he's not. Maybe there's not only one. Or maybe there's not even one. But with six billion to choose from, how does anyone know when they've found the love of their life?

As a kid I disliked people saying that relationships were hard work, that no relationship was 50-50, rather they should all be 100-100, and that you had to work to stay happy and in love. I thought that if a relationship was all work, then why bother? Is having to work at a relationship every day a sign that it isn't the love of your life because it's too hard (or even unnatural), or is it a sign that it *is* the love of your life, worth all the effort?

What if your relationship isn't any work at all? What if it just happens, just falls into place, feels good, goes with the flow? What then?

The problem with making up rules about how love and dating should be is that there will always be an exception—a time when they either don't fit or don't apply—and that leaves you in the dark. And no one wants to be on unsure ground when his or her heart and soul are on the line.

So I ask you: is there such a thing as the love of your life, and how do you know when you've found it?

Sprinting the last block to get to my laptop in time before I lost any of my mental composition, I typed it up before I even showered. After dinner (I tossed the grilled chicken into the salad), I revised the blog entry and posted it, then went to bed with Jane Austin's *Emma*. Better to get lost in someone else's world than in my own.

18

Two Loves

THE "LOVE OF Your Life" post elicited a slew of comments within the next forty-eight hours, some frighteningly harsh and painfully cynical ("Life sucks and then you die. Alone."), while others just dripped of sweetness ("I just *know* he's already here, so close you can touch him!"). Moreover, it seemed to bring out the storyteller in everyone, both in cyberspace and at The Grounds.

"My granddaddy told me that he knew the minute he saw my grandmama that she was the girl he'd marry," began Jan, with the Originals and most of the Regulars in earshot. "It was his favorite story to tell, and I remember it clearly because he used to tell it every chance he got, even after his mind started to go. It was the summer of forty-eight, a scorcher, and they were at his town's Fourth of July festival."

"Back then it wasn't about barbecues and shopping sales," remarked Sister Beulah.

"You got that right," said Jan. "He'd been in the parade with a couple of his war buddies, and was still wearing his uniform. She was a nurse, selling blueberry pies to raise money for the VA when he saw her. He tapped his friend and pointed to her. 'There,' he said. 'That's her. That's the girl I'm going to marry.' His friend said Granddaddy would be lucky if she even looked at him, so he marched right up to her and said hello."

"And did she?" asked Spencer while Dean looked on, uninterested, no doubt from hearing the story more than once. "Look at him, I mean."

Jan nodded, proud. "She smiled," she said, and paused for a beat. "Now my granddaddy, he was smart. He lived on a farm in New England, and she was from the South. And he knew that if he was going to get her, he'd have to have her married by the time winter came because no Southerner in their right mind would ever choose to live on a Yankee farm once they'd seen what winter really meant."

The Southern natives laughed.

"So that's what he did. They dated all that summer, and before she left, he asked her to marry him. She came back and they got married that fall, and every winter thereafter she'd curse him for fooling her. He'd say he was just a fool for love, and she'd always—every time—say he was *her* fool, and she'd have it no other way."

"That is just the sweetest story ever," said Tracy, giving Spencer's hand a squeeze.

"Isn't it, though?" said Jan. "It just goes to show you, Eva, that true love is out there; and when you find it, it lasts. Even through the winter."

My throat too tight to speak, I nodded and hastily left the group to assist Norman with the line of customers that seemed to appear out of thin air.

⌒♡

"Hey, Eva, a letter came for you. No return address," said Norman when I came in for my afternoon shift the following day. Retrieving it from under the cash drawer of the register, he pulled it across his face and took a whiff. "I don't smell any Old Spice. You got a secret admirer you're not telling us about?"

I snatched the creamy vellum envelope from him and studied it front and back. It was postmarked Wrightsville Beach, but I didn't recognize the cursive penmanship, almost calligraphy, that so elegantly and formally spelled out my name and The Grounds's address. Unable to resist, I too put it to my face and inhaled, looking for signs of scent that would offer some clue, but came up with nothing. *Another member of the Club?* I wondered as I grabbed my apron off its hook. Rather than open it here, my gut told me to save the envelope for when I got home at night, that it was deserving of my full attention.

And so I did. Showered and powdered and tucked into bed, Scott asleep beside me, I gingerly tore the envelope open and pulled out three sheets of the same creamy, vellum paper, carefully creased and filled with the same elegant script. With a fountain pen, I realized.

> *Dear Eva,*
>
> *When I read your post on WILS last night, I knew I had to respond, but not publicly. I know how close you are to Minerva and some of the others, but I would prefer that what I am about to tell you be kept between us.*
>
> *You asked about how one knows if the love of your life is indeed the love of your life. I want to tell you about my two loves.*
>
> *When most little girls were playing "house," mothering their baby dolls and cajoling their little brothers into being the daddy, I was playing "church," which consisted of my dolls taking turns reading from the Bible and my giving homilies and feeding Necco wafers to those*

same dolls at Communion time. Catechism classes far surpassed my interest in math or American history, and my parents practically had to drag me out of mass every Sunday. I studied every mannerism of the priests the way my friends studied every move of the Beatles. These were the days just after Vatican II, which probably means nothing to you, but it was an exciting time for the laity of the church. The masses ceased to be in Latin, and parishioners started to play a more important role. That, along with the women's liberation movement, gave me hope that one day I, too, could become a priest and pledge my devotion to God.

But sadly, women's lib stopped at the altar, and my dream was not going to be realized. I wasn't sure that a vocation as a nun was right for me, so first I went to college to find my way. There I met a girl named Lily, and to my surprise, I fell deeply in love with her, and she with me. In those days, the sexual revolution had come and gone, but homosexuality was still seen as a sin against God. But how could something like love ever be sinful?

I now had two loves of my life: God and Lily. We talked about moving somewhere like New Hampshire or Vermont, someplace tolerant where we could open a little store and sell homemade maple syrup or something wonderfully hippy-ish like that. I thought I could still serve God by getting involved in a small parish or volunteering at a hospital. Lily and I desperately wanted to be married, but same-sex marriage seemed to be farther from our grasp than female ordination. I confess that I was even mad at God for a while—how could She let me feel such love, both for Her and Lily, and not give me the means to express it? What if it really was sinful, and there was something wrong with me? Lily and I even separated for a brief period of time in an effort to date men (at least we were able to laugh about it years later), but there was no denying who we really were.

In the summer of 1980, Lily got into a car accident and I went to the hospital to be with her. That's when her parents discovered we were more than best friends, and they were outraged. They forbade me from seeing her, and forbade Lily from contacting me. They intercepted my calls and letters to her. When she recovered, she made her way back to me, but the writing was on the wall—we were never going to be able to have the life we wanted without losing the ones we loved. And Lily was terrified of being shunned by her family at the time. My family would have an easier time with my being a nun than my being a lesbian, and I didn't want anyone other than Lily.

You may think I settled for a life I never really wanted, Eva, but I didn't have the choices that your generation has (or I believed I didn't). I had too much to lose, although losing Lily was one of the hardest things I've ever endured. Being a nun has had its ups and downs, especially in the wake of all the scandals of the Church. I have considered leaving the vocation many times. Lily and I recently reconnected thanks to Facebook. She had married a man in an attempt to please her parents, but divorced several years ago. With our parents so aged and the times more tolerant, it may finally be time for us to live the life we've always wanted. I'm not sure. I adore my parish and its people, and I love my Grounds family, too. And I still love my Lord. I don't want to renege on my commitment to Her.

I am praying for answers to this next course of my life. I hope you'll pray for me as well, as I have been praying for you, Kenny, Scott, Minerva, and Norman, and all those looking for the loves of your lives. Just remember that love comes in many forms. Never settle, and know that what one has torn, another can mend.

Most of all, the love you really want is in <u>you</u>, Eva. Don't go chasing rainbows. Just open your eyes and admire their ever-present beauty.

Yours,
Beulah

It took a moment for me to register that "Beulah" was *Sister Beulah*. Never in my life had I received a letter so beautiful, so thoughtfully and carefully written and delivered. I mean, she could've just handed it to me and asked me to read it in private, or mentioned it to me when we were all sitting together while Jan told her story. She could've sent an e-mail. She could've bought a Hallmark card. But no. It was like a secret between a mother and daughter, or sisters. She had wanted it to be special, right down to the LOVE stamp on the envelope.

Minerva and I had once secretly speculated whether Sister Beulah was gay. Stereotypically, she matched neither orientation description. She dressed plainly, her coarse but well-coiffed hair a salt-and-pepper mix, and she wore little if any makeup at all other than an almost fuchsia-colored lipstick that could only look good on her and somehow drew attention not to her lips but rather her long eyelashes. The cross that rested comfortably on her chest was made of olive wood that she bought in the Holy Land, as she called it, and anyone might mistake her for a curio shop owner or a grandmother rather than a nun.

We all loved her dearly, of course. She was a mother hen to us all, listening to all our chatter, comforting any one of us having a bad day, giving us a run for our money when it came to book or movie trivia, and insisting that the Beatles, Elvis Presley, Ella Fitzgerald, and Nat King Cole were "the Chosen Ones." And even though we all called her Sister Beulah, despite her telling us early on not to, I think most of us forgot she was a nun. She was simply one of us.

I reread the letter, carefully smudging away each stray tear before it could drop to the page, blot the ink, and blur the words. *The love you really want is in you, Eva.* Watching Scott sleep for a few seconds, his back to me, I reached out and ran my fingers through his hair gently, hoping not to stir him. He didn't budge. I then turned out the light and offered a prayer for Beulah and Lily, my mother and father, and one for me, hoping I'd dream of rainbows.

19

They're on to You

I WASN'T DUE in to work until later in the afternoon. Normally, this was a good thing. Depending on my mood, mornings off either gave me the momentum to be super productive (as if I had already spent a full, accomplished day by the time I got to work) or to treat myself to pampering and lazy relaxation.

This morning, however, I could neither sit still nor focus long enough to accomplish anything. I felt edgy, agitated, unfocused. I hated days like this, and my frustration only compounded as I wandered from room to room, task to task, without finishing any one thing or setting it all aside.

It was a gray day, too. The kind where the sky is cast in shades of slate, almost purple around the edges of clouds that slide beneath more clouds. Wilmington weather forecasters called for a thirty-percent chance of thunderstorms in the afternoon, and I could practically taste the electricity on the air.

Giving up on the stack of bills I'd barely managed to sort, I grabbed my keys, tucked a pen and a small dog-eared journal into a tote bag along with a bottle of water, and headed out.

I lived within biking distance of the beach, but if I drove straight there and back, I'd have more than enough time to sit by the ocean and let the rhythmic roar of the waves restore my balance. On the way there I kept a watchful eye on the sky, scanning for lightning bolts showing up ahead of schedule or illuminated clouds that might be masking their presence.

By the time I arrived it had started to rain, a fine mist like those manufactured to soak vegetables while thin recordings of Gene Kelley's "Singin' in the Rain" hummed from speakers in grocery stores. I stepped out and sighed, lifting my face to the wetness before pulling my hood over my head and tucking my ponytail in. The beach near NCLA was a mix of white, flat dunes peppered with broken bits of scallop and clam shells and pebbles. Its ocean was a lackluster gray-green today, untamed and creeping far up the shore. The air had a harsh tang of salt, and the mist fell softly. Stillness seemed to settle along the beach, but the ocean roared with each crashing wave, pulling me closer to it as each one receded.

I chose a spot of sand and smoothed out a seat, attempting to pull my NCLA hoodie low enough over my sweatpants to shield me from the dampness, wondering if I should've worn a raincoat instead. I took a few deep breaths and closed my eyes, listening to the ocean beat out its slow rhythm: crash, rush... calm. Crash, rush...calm.

The scent of salt made me crave, of all things, dark chocolate. As I hypnotically watched the waves, images of chocolate almond bark overtook me. I'd make it this afternoon when I got to The Grounds, I thought. Pick up some almonds and roast them over the stove in sea salt and butter; melt some dark, bittersweet chocolate with just a touch of sugar and perhaps a taste of cream; I could also buy some lavender and add that to the mix...*oh, yes...*

Crash, rush...calm. Crash, rush...calm.

I licked my lips. Pulling my knees close to my chest, I turned my head to scan the beach. A runner, still too far away for me to make out his features, beat out his own unheard rhythm on the flat part of the beach close to the surf as each sneaker connected tight legs below baggy shorts to the packed, damp earth. He looked big, broad shouldered, like he might fill up a room with his presence, and could make any color seem saturated. As he drew closer, he looked starkly brighter set against the steely tones of the sky; his inky hair, deep skin tone, heather gray hoodie, and Wolfpack red shorts stood out even through the haze of rain. I hated anyone who could run on a beach—the mere thought made my calves scream. I'd only ever tried it a few times, but I'd learned my lesson: stick to the roads and trails and treadmills and leave the beaches for the truly sporty and exceptionally masochistic. I didn't realize that I'd been staring at his sneakers kicking up small clumps of sand as each foot lifted off, leaving craters for footprints, until he slowed down and waved.

It took me a good five seconds to realize it was Kenny.

I blinked, squinted, and tried again. Still Kenny.

I waved awkwardly as he passed, his stride restored, my hand hanging in the air as I watched him reach the other end of the beach, slow down and stop. He doubled over, hands on his knees, sides heaving, and checked his watch before loping back to the spot where I sat.

"Hey," he said between breaths.

"Hey yourself," I said. "What are you doing here?"

Stupid, stupid question.

"Getting some air," he said, leaning his head back and forcing his breath to return to normal. His hair had darkened and slicked into thick chunks thanks to the rain and sweat. "Mind if I sit?"

I made a gesture of invitation over the sand; he plopped down and began stretching.

"I love running on the beach." He reached for an out-stretched leg, grabbing his toes only after bending the knee a bit.

"Nobody loves running on the beach," I remarked. "Especially in a sweatshirt. Or the rain," I tacked on after a beat.

He eyed his hoodie as if inspecting the way it hung loosely on his shoulders, the front of the neck cut into a V, and shrugged. "Never know when the rain will turn cold."

I pulled the bottle of water from my tote bag and handed it to him. He opened and chugged half of it. "Maybe you shouldn't be running in the rain," I said. "I don't." I never ran in any weather that required more than shorts and a light tank, and I often wished I was daring enough to be one of those women who skipped the tank and ran in a sports bra.

He shook his head, switching to the other leg. "That's the best time to run."

"Suit yourself."

He returned the cap to the bottle. "You run?"

"Not in the rain."

He smiled and stared straight ahead.

The ocean raged. Our silence was neither awkward nor uncomfortable. Still, I wasn't disappointed when he broke it.

"OK. So I don't love running on the beach," he confessed.

"I knew it," I said. He grinned and switched to a butterfly stretch. "So why do it?" I asked.

"Why not," he answered, using his elbows to try to force his knees toward the sand.

Another minute of silence passed.

"I nearly drowned when I was ten," said Kenny.

I turned to him, shocked, but he kept his eyes on the water.

"We were on vacation at the ocean. There were storms coming in from the coast, and the waves were crazy," he said as he glanced over his shoulder, "a little like today, actually. Anyway, I was swimming even though my mother told me not to, and the undertow got me. I wasn't strong enough, and it had never occurred to me to be afraid of the ocean before. I'd never thought about the fact that if I washed out, I could swim forever and never find a shore. That my parents would never find me— not even my body. That my best hope might be being eaten alive."

"Kenny!" I shuddered, trying to imagine a smaller, weaker version of him soaked and scared and lost between waves. "That's awful!"

"Ever get salt water up your nose?" He didn't wait for me to answer. "Well it's ten times worse to breathe it into your lungs. It hurt so bad I stopped fighting—I just, stopped. Couldn't think. Next wave knocked me into a rock, and my last thought was that even if I could scream, no one would hear me through the waves."

He stretched his legs out in front of him, crossed his ankles, and leaned back. "My dad had been running on the beach. He was a master athlete—marathons, triathlons, all that stuff. He said he saw a flash of color right before I went under. I woke up on the beach, just me and him. And you know what he said to me? 'That was a stupid thing to do.'"

"That's a bit harsh."

"No, it wasn't," Kenny countered. "It was an honest, loving response. A way for him to lessen the trauma of it for me. He wasn't mean, wasn't afraid; he just called it like it was. And besides, he was kind of right. I mean, my mom told me not to go in. And maybe I should've been upset at him, but I wasn't. I appreciated it. No one had ever spoken to me so bluntly before. I think it was the first time I ever felt like an adult."

"No one's ever spoken to me like that. Well, not till you, I guess."

He acknowledged this with a crooked grin before resuming his story. "The next day my dad took me running on the beach. I think he knew how scared I was. Day after that we went kayaking. Then swimming. And when I told him I was scared he said, 'You can be, if you want to. And sometimes you should be. But you never *have* to be afraid.' I liked that. It meant I had a choice."

"He sounds like a great guy," I said.

"He is," Kenny answered. "I think you'd like him. He's funny, too. More blunt now than ever before. And if he thinks he's got you, if you even think about blushing, he just goes in for the kill. Drives my mom crazy, but it's all in good fun."

"Any brothers or sisters?"

"Nah," he said, "one was more than enough for my parents. I made sure of that."

It was hard to imagine Kenny giving anyone trouble—even as an angsty teen—and I wondered what his family looked like, what they felt like, what they did on Christmas Eve, how many anniversaries and birthdays they'd spent together. I loved collecting images of other people's families, piecing them together in my mind as if I could parse out what might have become of my own.

The mist blew back into our faces. I looked at him for only a second, and yet, in that second his aura magnetically pulled me into him, sweeping me away like one of the waves. I resisted the urge to brush his wet bangs aside, to wipe the moisture off his face with the back of my sleeve, to wrap my hand around his neck, pull him to me, and kiss him.

"I gotta get going," Kenny said, standing, snapping me out of my split-second trance. "So I'll leave you to your thoughts.

What were you thinking about before I interrupted you, if you don't mind my asking?"

"Dark chocolate bark with sea salt, almonds, and lavender."

He smacked his lips. "Totally not what I expected to hear. But I'm glad I ran into you today."

"Yeah, me too," I said, feeling the cold dampness of the sand beneath me for the first time.

"Stay out of the water though, OK?" he teased. "I haven't seen anyone else around."

"I have to be at work soon anyway," I said as he turned away. "See you soon!" I called out, watching his shoulders sway with each sandy step, and I found myself hoping I was right.

⌒◯

Later I was glad for the morning reprieve; it may have been the only thing that saved my sanity at The Grounds where the line never let up, the cookies burned, the supplies were running low, and I barely got to say more than hello to my customers.

For the past two weeks, Norman had been saving his wit for the clientele, his smiles for Samurai, and his business-related talk for me. Meanwhile, Scott and I continued to keep a low profile. I went out of my way to be as nonchalant as I had always been with him, not lingering at his table too long to talk to him, not looking in his direction, that sort of thing. He did the same, casually placing orders at the counter and sitting at a table near the front window rather than closer to the counter, as he used to do.

Taking a deep breath that morphed into a frustrated sigh, I was wiping the countertop for the hundredth time as Norman brushed past me with a tray of half-empty mugs and plates and muttered something about a mess of crumbs to no one in particular when the phone rang. He grabbed the cordless off the back counter on his way to the kitchen.

"Eva!"

"Why are you yelling?"

He extended the phone to me. "Would you please talk to the paper guy? I've had it with his attitude."

I scowled and took the phone as Norman left the kitchen growling about why I didn't dump their asses since the napkins were thinner than Kleenex.

When my shift-from-hell finally ended, I headed straight home, staring like a zombie at every red light and stop sign along the way. Once there, I dropped my keys, tossed my clothes on the bedroom floor and slipped on a T-shirt, ate a cup of yogurt for dinner, and willed myself to check my e-mails. Scanning through the inbox list consisting mostly of Facebook notifications and vendor advertisements, a message Minerva had sent earlier this afternoon caught my attention.

E-mail to: eva@thegrounds.com
Subject: They're on to you

> Not sure what the world looks like from the other side of the counter, but it's looking pretty grim from this side, Eva. I've been trying to catch a moment alone with you all day, but it's just not working, so I've been forced to resort to undercover reporting, as it were.

They're on to you. Hell, anyone with half a brain is on to you. It's the way you're so meticulously normal. The way you never look up when Scott enters, but wait till he's already halfway to the counter—as if you're not even interested. The polite smile, the professional hello, all the while your eyes are glittering like a maniac and I swear I can see the phero-mones just pouring off you.

Oh yeah, it shows.

I was hoping it was just me, knowing what to look for, you know? But it's not. Yesterday, when you weren't here, Jan asked me if you were OK since the big, bad blowout scene. I said of course you were, but she insisted that something seemed different. Then, Tracy said that she was "sure" there was something "going on" between you and Scott. When they confronted me, I said something about how I wasn't sure. 'Cause, you know, I'm not technically 100% sure what is going on, so it's not a total lie, right? And you know how bad I am at lying. I figured trying for a half-truth was way safer than going for a full lie. And what was I supposed to say—"what makes you so sure?" OK, so that would have worked, but fishing for clues would've been obvious.

So Kenny came in yesterday and we started grilling him about where he's been the past few days and blah, blah, blah. So Jan starts asking him to weigh in his own opinion.

Anyway, Kenny seemed most interested in how you went home with Scott. And no one saw Scott all weekend, and we all know he's a big Saturday-morning-large-iced-coffee-kinda-guy. So then Spencer starts speculating (say that ten times fast!) and Tracy's trying to get them to keep their voices down, and Jan's pissed at Dean (he said Scott was a "lucky bastard," and Jan got all upset). And all the while I'm doing my best to look busy so they don't ask me point blank whether you're sleeping with Scott (can you imagine what would've happened if they had asked me?? *shudders*), and poor Kenny's about to get whiplash trying to follow the verbal volleys going back and forth, and Norman doesn't butt in once.

And just so you know, yesterday the Topic of the Day was how Scott's been coming in later than he used to and no one sees him leave. As in, he's suddenly staying till closing. As in, he's probably leaving with you. As in, he's probably leaving with you to go have sex. And we both know it's only a matter of time before "probably" becomes "obviously." (And I can tell that Dean wants to ask me something—he keeps looking my way, shitshitshit!)

So, in conclusion, it's out there, and it's about to hit the fan.

Min.

I sighed loudly and buried my face in my hands, then brushed my hands through my hair and let them linger, holding my hair in place like a ponytail. Kenny was at The Grounds yesterday and I'd missed him? Why didn't he mention it this morning at the beach? He didn't even offer a hint. Then again, I'd been less than forthcoming about my own situation.

Damn.

Drained, I wrote back.

E-mail To: mbrunswick@ncla_alum.edu
Subject: Re: They're on to you.

Min-

Shitters. I don't even know where to start.

I could just call you, but dammit, the phone is all the way on the other side of the room—not house, mind you, but room. Yes, I am that tired. As in my-body-is-a-hunk-o-jello, tired. And I'm going it alone tonight, if you know what I mean.

Well, there goes my illusion of customers not talking about me behind my back. Holy crap. And here I thought I was doing so well, playing it so cool. Geez, have I really been that oblivious? (Don't answer that.)

And what's up with Jan and Dean lately? Is there ever a time when Jan isn't mad at Dean anymore? And what's with the lucky bastard comment? Please don't tell me he's a member of the Club.

So what should I do? Should I make some announcement, like Joel and Maggie did on

Northern Exposure, when they announced to everyone at the Brick that they just had sex because they figured it was written all over their faces? Or should it be like on Gilmore Girls, when Lorelai gets through saying that she's not ready to let the town know that she and Luke are dating, and then proceeds to walk into the diner to get some coffee, thinking it's still closed, and walks in—wearing nothing but Luke's flannel shirt—to find it full of customers? (Good grief, I have got to stop watching so much TV.)

Sigh. I'm too tired to think about any of this right now. And Scott's not here to massage my neck (he's pretty good at it…). And by the way, you think you're not 100% sure what's going on between me and Scott? Neither am I. I'm maybe 60% sure at best, but those are still pretty sucky odds.

Say hi to Jay for me.

Eva

I sent the e-mail knowing the subject of Kenny had not been addressed. I wished I had an answer for that. I wished I'd been the one to tell him about the blowout and going home with Scott. But mostly I wished he'd said something to me about it earlier at the beach.

I'd barely had a minute at The Grounds to tell Scott not to come over tonight, that I was simply wiped out and needed to be alone. But I was missing him, too; we'd already gotten into a pattern of him coming to my place (I had more room, and it was furnished with more than milk crates, an old couch, and stereo equipment), renting movies from Netflix, and vegging out on the couch until one of us (usually me) fell asleep, or skipping the movie and going straight to bed and having sex.

Despite my eyes growing heavier by the minute, I logged on to WILS and stared at it. I'd not posted anything new for close to a week, telling myself that The Grounds had been busy and I was too tired to write. But the truth was that I'd been at a loss for what to say. Was I even still single? Did I want to be anymore?

Leaving WILS blank, I shut down my laptop and placed it on the end table beside me, turned out the light, closed my eyes, and fell asleep in my reading chair.

20

The Bigger Fools

MY FOUL MOOD began after Norman's call from The Grounds, shortly before closing. I was at home, watching *Julie and Julia*. It's hard to be in anything but a good mood when watching *Julie and Julia*, but Norman managed to kill it quite effectively.

"Eva, it's me. Listen, the coffee people delivered a shipment today."

"The 'coffee people'? You mean International Organics?"

"Yeah, whatever," he said, distracted. "They were running late, so it just got here two hours ago, and we were slammin' busy, and I would bring it in and inventory it, but I'm taking Samara out for dinner tonight, and it's already late enough, don't you think?"

I let the silence hang long enough for him to become uncomfortable.

"I mean, I really don't want to keep her waiting, you know?" he said.

"Yeah, no, um, it is…late."

I tried not to stew about the fact that this was as late as both of us ever left, that Scott waited for me and maybe Samara should learn to do the same, that he'd not found the time in the past few hours to do the shipment, or even about the fact that I just plain didn't like Samara.

"Thanks, Eva. I know you don't like to leave such things unfinished, but she's already here and she's been waiting for hours anyway…"

Those very same hours you couldn't find the time to bring in a few boxes of product?

"…and since you open tomorrow, I thought I'd let you know it'll be here waiting for you."

He sounded excited and oblivious. I, on the other hand, sounded pissed. "Great," I said. And I was sure he knew it, too, although he pretended not to.

"OK, well, thanks again. Have a good night."

"Yeah, sure. You too."

I turned off *Julie and Julia* and went to bed sulking. And no one ever sleeps well feeling bitter and wishing they'd skewered their coworker and friend with a line about responsibility and dedication and relationship expectations and making exceptions and…and…and…

⌒♈

The radio annoyed my eyes open with a terribly perky song when my alarm clock went off. I woke up feeling more than bitter—I downright *hated* everyone and everything. I bashed the clock into silence but couldn't fall back asleep.

It all went downhill from there.

I burned my store-bought bagel. The butter dripped down my hand and onto my carpenter pants, which was when I noticed I'd gotten deodorant on my shirt. I had to change my outfit entirely, and nothing looked good. I was late and crabby, having settled on crappy jeans and a faded NCLA T-shirt, and I smeared mascara beneath my eye while fighting with my hair, effectively giving myself a stunningly bedraggled look in one moment of brilliant clutziness.

Blasting the Clash as loud as my ears could handle them remedied my mood somewhat; I took a little perverse joy in Joe Strummer bleeding out of my open windows before seven a.m. I even came close to smiling—that is, until unexpected roadwork at the intersection before turning onto The Grounds's street delayed me even further. I could've gotten there faster if I'd hoofed it.

By the time I got to the shop, I was seething. Five boxes of fair-trade Columbian coffee beans awaited me in the narrow hallway separating the café kitchen from the back alley exit. I wondered how much time I had to plot Norman's death—could I have him successfully killed and disposed of by two this afternoon? Or did he come in at three on Wednesdays?

I was being irrational and knew it. Still, the extra hour of plotting would be helpful.

One by one, I dropped the boxes next to the island in the center of the kitchen. It had rained most of yesterday and overnight, and they were crusted with dried mud from the delivery guys leaving them in the alley.

Would getting pummeled by a rolling pin be too cliché for Norman? How 'bout if I rigged the microwave to blow up when he went to heat up someone's muffin?

I smeared the mud across the linoleum with my sneaker. Let Norman sweep it up. Or maybe I'd just leave the entire shipment there for the God of Romance to inventory when he got in, since he was supposed to do it last night anyway. Or maybe Samurai would come in and he'd tether himself to the front counter—well within ogling distance—all day, thus distracting him from his duties, which was what likely happened yesterday, I was willing to bet.

Fine.

Jerk.

I slumped against the counter and surveyed the damage.

Who was I kidding?

It wasn't Norman's lack of motivation the night before that had gotten under my skin. It wasn't even Samurai's never-a-strand-out-of-place hair or the way her shellacked nails always matched her shoes. It was watching Norman swoon over someone who spent her days prattling to a friend named Kiki (or Gigi, or whatever the hell her name was) on her cell phone in public, who convinced Norman to stop wearing his Chucks simply because she didn't like them, who just plain didn't deserve a second look from him.

And it was watching him be so overt with his attention to her while she remained unimpressed, while Scott and I continued to sneak around like teenagers who'd been forbidden to see each other.

Suddenly I wondered who the bigger fools were.

The thought was still nagging me when Norman came in just before noon. He met me behind the counter.

"You're early," I said.

"I felt bad about sticking you with the shipment."

Ahh, Norman—one minute I was plotting his death, the next minute I wanted to hug him. My foul mood began to dissipate.

"That's OK. Forget about it. So how was your date?" I asked.

He turned to the sink and washed his hands. "Wouldn't you like to know."

I took a breath. "I'll tell you how my date went if you tell me about yours." It was the first time I'd said anything about Scott and me in public, let alone to Norman. I shrugged my shoulders as if to say, *Might as well.*

"'Bout time you fessed up to that. Not like it was a well-kept secret. About as obvious as a bald guy wearing a toupee."

"I kinda thought maybe Scott already confided in you."

"Yeah, he caved. Scott's a crappy liar. He tried his best to be evasive, though. When are you both gonna totally come out?"

"I don't know. I guess keeping it secret is pretty pointless by now."

"Post it on WILS," he suggested.

"Maybe," I said.

As if on cue, Scott walked in.

"Or you can announce it together right now."

I gave Norman a threatening glare.

Scott walked up to the counter. "What's new?" he said, feigning nonchalance, but giving me a look that said, *I am so dying to kiss you.* I returned the look with a flirtatious grin—I couldn't help myself. And yet, I suddenly became self-conscious, realizing how stupid I was to think that I was fooling anyone when my face revealed all.

"So," I said to Scott, a little louder than necessary, "what'll it be?"

"Surprise me," he said as he tossed a ten on the counter with a wink, "and keep the change."

I turned away from Norman's huff in an effort to hide my goofy grin, not wanting him to see just how much I enjoyed Scott's cheeseball playfulness when it was one of the few things I'd heard Norman tease him about.

Plating a turkey chipotle wrap and apple muffin to accompany an extra-extra iced mocha for Scott, I stole a glance at Norman. He was staring into the parking lot. I followed his gaze but saw only parked cars and a mother trying to wrestle her toddler into a car seat.

"You OK?" I asked. "You look tired."

He shook his head as if to clear it. "Oh, yeah. Didn't get much sleep last night."

I laughed. "I'll bet."

He smiled weakly as I crossed the counter to bring Scott his snack. I allowed myself to linger at his table for a moment to watch Tracy migrate from Dean's table to the empty chair next to Dara, who was nursing her coffee and regaling the other Regulars with stories about a stray kitten she'd adopted two nights before.

When Dara left, Tracy brought a few empty plates to the dish bin. "There's one woman I don't envy."

Norman raised his eyebrows. "Looks like it's really taken a toll on her."

"Apparently she's high maintenance…and talkative."

Norman let out a sharp laugh.

"The kitten," Tracy clarified, "not Dara."

He shoved his hands in his pockets as Tracy turned back to Dean's table. "Just my type," he muttered. "I like her already."

I studied him: his collar was rolled in on one side, dark bruise-like circles tugged at both eyes, and a thin stubble roughed out his chin.

"Are things OK with you and Samara?" I always had to pause for a split second to keep myself from calling her "Samurai" in front of Norman.

"Things are good with *me*," he answered. "And that's all."

The comment took a moment to register. "Oh, Norman, I'm sorry." I gave him a quick hug that he didn't return. "When?"

"Last night. Should've seen it coming. Apparently it's been shit for a while."

"Are you kidding? You guys seemed so…" Surgically attached? Smitten? Disgustingly gooey? "…good."

He shrugged. "Looks can be deceiving, I guess. Anyway, let's not make a big thing out of it." He glanced at my hand. I hadn't even realized that I'd left it resting lightly on his arm.

I pulled away as if burned. "OK, sure. I'm sorry."

"S'OK." It was unnerving seeing Norman so lackluster.

"No really, I am. You're a gem, Norm-o. This just confirms my suspicions," I said. "The girl's as dumb as a post."

Norman guffawed. "Thanks." He then opened his mouth as if to say something else, but reconsidered and closed it again. "We still on for the meeting?"

"Yeah," I said, glancing at the clock behind us. "Susanna will be in soon."

Norman nodded as his stomach gave a feral growl. "Sorry," he said as he rubbed it absently. "I forgot to eat breakfast this morning…and dinner last night, come to think of it."

"So eat something!" I waved a hand at the tray of wraps in the case.

He made a face. "Don't really feel like it."

I left him standing at the counter, bypassed the kitchen, and went straight to the office. I picked up the phone, tapped the number for Minerva's cell, and waited while it rang.

"Hey," she answered. "I'm on my way in, what's up?"

"Can you do me a huge favor and stop off for a can of tuna first?"

"Like, tuna-fish tuna?"

"Yeah. Maybe two cans."

"Please tell me this isn't for a cookie recipe. Whatever it is, Eva, no matter how good it looks, I'm telling you right now—"

"Good God, Min, what do you take me for? I'm not *that* bad…"

"Are you forgetting the 'Breakfast Burrito Cookie' fiasco?"

"There was a problem with that recipe. I had nothing to do with that."

"Yeah, yeah, doomed from the start. So you said. You had *bacon* in there, for crissakes. So why tuna?"

"It's for Norman."

I could almost see her raising an eyebrow. "What, is he having some sort of craving or something? 'Cause if so, he should get his iron levels checked. Or better yet, just get a multivitamin or something."

"It's his almond biscotti," I cut in, knowing she'd understand.

"Oh," she answered. "Everything OK?"

"I'll tell you later," I replied. "So when can you get here?"

"With tuna? About fifteen."

"Perfect. Bring the receipt, and I'll see you then."

I had a double batch of caramel swirl brownies in the oven by the time she got there, and I managed to procure the tuna while Neil was distracting Norman with funny tales from the nine-to-five world.

By the time Susanna came in, I had two tuna melts (minus the mayo) sizzling on the stove.

"OK." Norman froze just inside the kitchen, as if stopped by the wall of salty-scented frying butter. "I'm ready for the meeting now, if you want." His eyes turned to the sandwiches. "Are you making tuna melts?"

"Well I can't very well have you fainting in front of the clientele, can I?"

He nodded in agreement. "Bad for business." Hesitating for a moment, he crossed the kitchen to return the hug I had given him earlier. "Thanks, Eva. Really."

He took a bite, and any signs of stress—be it from hunger or heartbreak—left his face. "I still don't know why you don't do tuna-salad stuffed pitas," he said upon swallowing. "They'd sell just fine."

"Because mayonnaise is disgusting and I won't go near it with a ten-foot pole."

He laughed. "What is it with you and your food phobias?"

"It's not a *phobia*."

"You don't like coffee, you treat mayonnaise like it's fungal…"

"Tell me there's no food you won't eat."

"Not without a little ketchup, no."

I laughed, encouraged by his returning humor, but I don't think I'd ever looked forward to a weekly meeting so much. I was glad for the opportunity to be able to overtly study him and look for signs, for any reason at all, to give the Samurai a piece of my mind.

21

I Spill My Beans

NORMAN SEEMED GLAD to be able to fully dedicate his attention to something unyielding, like our agenda.

Actually, it was more of a glorified to-do list than an agenda. We always met once a week to go over all business pertaining to The Grounds. Usually, the meetings were routine: reviewing inventory, making sure bills were paid on time, considering new suppliers or products if any came our way, et cetera. But lately the meetings were about bringing more money into the business. Most days, with the exception of holidays and the occasional torrential downpour or tornado warning, we were slammin' busy. Since opening, The Grounds was finally breaking even rather than operating at a loss. Our intake went right back into salaries and benefits for Norman, Susanna, the revolving door of seasonal part-timers, and me; making sure the place was up to health code and green standards; and, within the past year, updating the coffee machines and kitchen equipment.

To increase revenue, Norman came up with the idea to make T-shirts that said *I spill my beans at The Grounds*. Minerva had a friend who was a design student from her undergraduate NCLA days, and we commissioned her to design the T-shirt in exchange for three months of free coffee. She created a cup spilling coffee beans over a saucer, and The Grounds's name along with the slogan in both men's and women's styles—taupe scoop neck and cap sleeves for women, and basic tee for the guys. We gave freebies to all the Originals and Regulars, twenty percent off for six-month regulars ("new Regulars," we called them), and the rest sold for fifteen bucks a pop. They went like hotcakes. Baseball caps followed at ten bucks a pop. Pretty soon we had requests for different colors and other merchandise: decals, mugs, tote bags, the kinds of things a sizable donation to National Public Radio would get you. We even started selling them through The Grounds's Web site.

But I still wasn't satisfied, so this afternoon I consulted with Norman in our little closet of a back office.

"What are the options?" he asked.

I took in a breath. "Well, one is to extend the business hours at least one night a week."

The thought of staying even later made me shudder with dread; I already spent twelve-hour days here at least once a week, and it was becoming clear that little in my life was non-café-related.

"Or we could expand the café and reduce the size of the reading room," I said. "Most days we're bursting at the seams as it is."

"That could work," said Norman. "But that's going to take a lot more capital, not to mention we'd probably have to close for the expansion—knock out the wall that divides the café and the reading room, for starters."

"True. Besides, I've always wanted to keep the setting small and intimate, to be open fewer hours than the chains and develop the very atmosphere and rapport we have with our clientele. Even though expanding the café would likely fit more people, more isn't necessarily better."

He nodded in agreement.

I groaned. "What do you think, Norman? What should we do?"

He was quiet, mulling over the puzzle. Then he sat up straight—I could almost see the light bulb appear over his head. "We could start hosting open mic nights and readings for local authors in the reading room. In fact, I don't know why you've never considered it before, especially being so close to campus."

"I didn't think the space was big enough."

"We could make it work. Just redo the reading room. No one's ever in there, and it's not really user-friendly. It could use a makeover."

I raised my eyebrows at the word *makeover*.

He continued, "We can replace the chairs, add a couple more bookcases, more extension outlets for laptop hookups, fresh coat of paint…"

As Norman spoke, my mind's eye sketched a floor plan of the reading room, mentally moving the old furniture out, sampling color swatches, taking before-and-after photos.

"…and it won't cost much, especially if we get some of the Originals involved."

The more he spoke, the wider my eyes opened, so much that I thought they might pop out. "You mean, like have a painting party or something?" I asked.

"Sure, why not? We can invest our time and energy without losing money or the intimacy."

I sat there and looked at him, dumbstruck for a moment. His face turned into one of worry.

"No good?" he asked.

"Norman, you're fabulous."

Giving in to impulse, I jumped up, threw my arms around him, and hugged him, nearly knocking him over. He laughed and hugged me back.

"Wow," he said, "got any more dilemmas that you need to bounce off me?"

"This is perfect! We'll have another book drive—this time for *us*—and paint the bookcases, perhaps buy at least one more. Then we'll get rid of the couches and anything else not nailed to the floor—come to think of it, we should pull up the industrial carpet, too—and then buy some secondhand comfy couches and chairs from Craigslist, paint, new rugs, and have a Grand Reopening, or something like that. We'll put out punch and cookies and have a little party!"

I was talking a mile a minute.

"Breathe, Eva! Breathe!"

"A month, Norman—do you think we can get this up and running in a month?"

"I think we can do it in less time than that. Thirty-six hours tops if we close and get volunteers to help—I'm sure the gang would be willing to pitch in."

I squealed with delight and hugged him again.

"Shall we keep this under wraps or make a formal announcement?" I asked.

"I don't think you'll be able to conceal this one, Eva. You're positively glowing. If you walk into the café right now and say nothing, they'll think we just had sex."

"Good point," I said, laughing. Then I added, "I gotta go tell Minerva!" *And Kenny,* to my surprise, popped into my thoughts next.

"And Scott," Norman said more solemnly. "He'll be in soon, no doubt."

"Of course," I said, deflated. "Let's go out to dinner tonight after work and get the ball rolling on making plans for what we need to do and when."

"Sounds great. Where shall we go?"

"Mike's is always good," I suggested.

"Cool. It's a date—you know what I mean," he quickly added.

I walked back into the café beaming. Sure enough, Dean asked, "Did you two just have sex back there, or what?"

ᴄ⁓ᴐ

Later that evening, as Norman and I split an entrée of mussels, we made plans for the upcoming makeover, each of us jotting notes in little memo books. When finished, we closed our notebooks, pushed our plates away, and took swigs from our beers. Our eyes locked for what was probably no more than a second; but it was the kind of second that felt much longer, and I kept my focus on him.

A former army brat (although you could never tell by looking at him) and only child, Norman had spent most of his childhood moving from place to place until his father transferred to Fort Bragg and stayed there until he retired. He attended NCLA on a scholarship, fell in love with the Carolina coast, and having had enough of suitcases and cardboard cartons, made Wilmington his permanent home.

I had liked Norman Bailey the moment he entered the construction trap that would eventually become my second home as well as his. He was laid back and amiable—well groomed to the point that I thought he might be gay—and shared my vision for The Grounds. It was like great jazz, Norman and me. We could finish each other's sentences, anticipate what the other was going to say before a word was even uttered, work in rhythm, and not miss a beat. Being at The Grounds every day wouldn't be half as fun without Norman there. If I was its heart, then he was the lungs.

Prior to his coming to work for me, he had managed the trendy independent bookstore in downtown Wilmington; thus, his freakish knowledge of all things literary matched my own. When I'd asked why he wanted to leave the bookstore, he'd replied, "They've gotten too snobby for their own good, and they can't laugh at themselves anymore." I later found out that he had lied; the owners fired Norman after he publically blasted a customer for calling a guest author "a hack" during the Q&A part of her reading because she was self-published.

"Hey, asshole," Norman called out, diverting the attention away from the author, who had started to cry. "I'll bet you can't even write your name without having to spell-check it." The audience of about thirty people applauded Norman. When the customer threatened him to "step outside," it took two store employees to stop Norman as he unpinned his name tag and said, "Let's go," heading for the door without even batting an eye.

Oh yeah. I liked Norman.

And so did our customers. You could see it on their faces as he quickly memorized their names and orders, already knowing half of them from the bookstore (including the Originals). The girls from NCLA flirted with him just as much as he flirted with them, although he was only eight months younger than I. And despite his feigned womanizer persona, I could tell he was as monogamous as they came, and romantic to the hilt. He fell in love hard, and nursed his heart when it was broken.

It's not that I never felt attracted to him, or that I never considered what it might be like to go out with him. But I just couldn't picture us working as smoothly together otherwise, and I needed him as a manager more than a lover. And yes, occasionally we flirted with one another. How could anyone not flirt with Norman? One look at those puppy-dog eyes and you had the urge to give him a hug.

Without warning, a nervous laugh escaped me as I caught myself actually checking him out.

Norman smiled. "What's so funny?" he asked.

"Nothing," I said, taking another sip of beer and averting my eyes. "I just felt like laughing, that's all."

"I have that way with women."

"Do you know this is the first time we've ever hung out together, just the two of us, outside The Grounds? How did that happen?"

"We tend to have opposite schedules," he said matter-of-factly.

"But you know, I like hanging out with you, Norman."

"I like hanging out with you, too."

We both got really quiet, and a look came over his face, as if he already knew what I was about to say next.

"Can I ask you something?"

"Uh-oh," he said.

I laughed again, this time more anxious and less boisterous. "Nah, it's not an 'uh-oh'—at least I don't think it is."

"You're not going to fire me or anything like that?"

"Of course not! How could you ever think that?"

"So what do you want to ask, Eva?"

I stalled, folding my napkin, fidgeting with my flatware, my nerves getting the best of me.

"Scott said something to me the first night we hooked up that has kinda bothered me. Well, maybe not 'bothered,' but it's definitely been on my mind."

"Uh-oh," he said again. I didn't laugh this time.

"He said you had a crush on me."

Norman took in the words for a second, then lightly hit his fist on the table and leaned back in his chair.

Uh-oh.

"He said that?" His face darkened, creases forming between his brows and at the corners of his mouth. I'd never seen Norman angry. Irked, maybe. Stressed from work, sure. But not angry.

"He may have said that he *thought* you had a crush on me," I said, as if that might keep him from exploding. "I can't be sure. My head wasn't exactly clear that day."

"Asshole," he muttered. "I apologize for my language and I know he's one of my best friends and your boyfriend, but sometimes he's just an immature asshole."

"He's not my boyfriend," I corrected.

Norman looked at me, confused.

"I mean, we're obviously seeing each other and stuff, but I don't think we're really all that formal or official," I rambled.

"Then what are you doing, besides the obvious?"

I stared at him blankly.

"Was he right about what he said?" I asked.

Norman leaned back again, beer in hand, took a long swig, and let out a deep sigh, which set my insides doing cartwheels.

"Look, Eva. I don't want things to get awkward between us, especially since we work so closely together and you're my boss. I respect you as a boss and a colleague. You've never once treated me like an employee or a subordinate—you've always treated me like an equal, a partner. You have no idea what that means to me."

"I've never even thought of you as a subordinate."

"So you can understand that I would never dare cross a line."

I wasn't sure how to respond. "Well, I appreciate that. But…" I started.

"*Crush* is a strong word, Eva. I don't believe I have a crush on you."

"But you have feelings?"

He looked away searching for words, not quite returning his eyes to my own when he did.

"I think...I think I'm *taken* with you. Or intrigued. I don't know, I can't put my finger on it. I do find you attractive, and I thoroughly enjoy your company and wish we could hang out like this more often, but..." He trailed off again in search of words, but this time he looked me squarely in the eye. "But I don't think it's meant to be."

I looked at Norman at that moment—really looked into his eyes—and both fell in and out of love with him in an instant. It was as if our entire relationship—or the possibility of it—passed before me. We were seemingly perfect for each other. He was warm and sensitive and funny, and natural in all the ways I wasn't. We liked the same books and films and TV shows and music. And yet, despite all this, we weren't going to be a couple, ever. We were never going to act on those deep feelings of affection for each other that, up until that moment, I had never let myself even acknowledge, much less feel.

"You're right," I said. "I know you're right. Why, though?"

"I'm not sure. Maybe we're too much alike."

"Maybe." I sipped my beer again. "What do you think might've happened if *you* had taken me home that night?"

"Exactly what happened between you and Scott, and I'm glad now that it wasn't me. I'm not gonna lie to you—I was disappointed at first. But I think it would've been a disaster. It would've changed *everything* in an instant. You went home with the right guy."

"I guess," I said, bothered by my uncertainty.

"Anyway, if it makes you feel any better, you have my blessing. I knew it was bothering you these last few weeks."

"Was it bothering *you*?"

"You wanna know what's been bothering me? That you didn't tell me. Of course you were gonna tell Minerva, but why not *me*?"

Hearing the hurt in his voice, *his* hurt, my eyes brimmed with tears. I didn't realize how much we'd been holding back.

"I'm so sorry. I didn't mean to hurt you. I was afraid of how you felt, afraid you'd be angry at me."

He nodded slowly. "I can understand that," he said, "given what Scott told you."

"I love you, Norman," I blurted. I hadn't even said those words to Scott.

He smiled softly in understanding, his eyes glassy as well. "I love you, too."

Norman leaned in. I thought he was going to take my hand, and it seemed to want to be taken, moving forward to meet his before I consciously pulled it away and moved both of my hands into my lap.

"Are you happy, Eva?"

I looked down at my lap and took in a breath before facing Norman and his question. "I think so," I said. "I really don't know."

"That's not very reassuring."

"No," I replied. "I guess it's not."

We split the check (he insisted after I'd offered to pay and charge it as a business expense—work meeting) and then walked out into the parking lot together, his arm affectionately, platonically around me. It was comforting. We then hugged—something we'd never done before, at least not like this. But it felt right, and we both knew we needed to.

"See you tomorrow," I said.

"Back atcha."

I drove home in silence. The moment our eyes had locked, Norman and I witnessed our relationship change for the better, evolve into something deeper. I knew there would be no signs of awkwardness between us in the coming days, no trying to avoid the subject or getting around each other feigning politeness. The very realization of this unloosened the knot in my stomach that had been so tight for the past few weeks.

At home, I checked messages, read e-mails, and looked at WILS. Stared at it. Put my fingers on the keyboard, hoping they'd move on their own.

Nothing.

I went to bed and cried.

22

The Horror

OH, THE HORROR

I have seen Minerva study for four different kinds of anatomy exams at once. I've heard her stories about holding human brains in her hand. Real, dead brains. I've known Minerva to be able to cook a Thanksgiving dinner for ten people, clean up, and then go write a paper on the origins of DNA discovery. The woman doesn't carry a golden lasso, nor can she deflect bullets with accessories, but dammit, she's up there on the list of efficiency in the face of pressure, save a meltdown every now and then.

I have also seen Minerva look all sorts of haggard—final exams haggard, daylong labs haggard, two-straight-weeks-working-on-nothing-but-cadavers haggard; but *this*—this was above and beyond. She had dark circles under her eyes. She had never-before-seen frown lines running like rivers across her forehead. She had hair breakage.

She trudged in and up to the counter, shoulders hunched as if carrying a backpack full of rocks; yet she only held her wallet, keys, and cell phone. Her first words came out in pants of breath, as if she'd just run a marathon.

"I just found a pair of socks in my silver-ware drawer." She paused for a breath. "Clean."

"Well," I said, exhaling a mock sigh of relief, "as long as they were clean…"

Norman leaned against the back counter as if to steady himself. "I'm afraid to ask how they got there," he said.

"Blame it on multitasking gone all wrong. I was trying to fold laundry, empty the dish-washer, and polish the silver at the same time; in retrospect, probably not the smartest idea. Anyway, the drawers were all open. They must've fallen in there while I was relocat-ing the pile to the bedroom. Didn't even see them until today, just as she was pulling into the driveway. Had to make sure the silver was polished enough."

"Who?" Norman asked.

"My mother-in-law."

And instantly, everything fell into place; for, when up against the in-laws, Minerva waves the white flag. This much I knew.

"I didn't know your in-laws were coming to visit," I said.

Minerva looked like a cornered animal. "Neither did I. Not until yesterday, that is. Can you believe that? Only twenty-four hours' notice."

I searched for something intelligent or com-forting to say, but "Why?" was all I could muster.

"Labor Day weekend," she answered.

"So you put socks in the silverware drawer," Norman said.

"I didn't *put* them there; I *found* them there."

He looked confused. "Won't she find them?"

Minerva looked at Norman with impatience. "Well obviously I removed them, idiot. I switched the silverware out with the silver when I heard she was coming."

"For what occasion would you be using silver?" I asked.

"Cici only uses silver when she eats."

"You're kidding me," I said, incredulous.

Norman blurted, "Cici? I'm sorry, did you just say *Cici?*"

Minerva's face darkened. "She makes me call her Cici," she said through clenched teeth. "She's a Cynthia, but she told me calling her Mom would make her feel old."

"What does Jay call her?" asked Norman.

"Mom."

"So…"

"So what she meant was having *me* call her Mom makes her feel old."

"Ahh."

"But Cynthia was too formal," she said.

"So the only logical choice was *Cici?*" pressed Norman.

"Hey, don't look at me—I didn't choose it."

Norman leaned in, resting his chin on his hands, eyes all lit up, like this was the hottest gossip of the year or the plot of some new serial on TV. "Who is this woman?" he asked while I looked on sympathetically.

"Old money Boston. Real high society. I think one of her great, great something-or-others was one of the original tea-dumpers."

I was a little surprised. Jay never struck me as a polished-silver-old-money kind of guy—he wears hemp, for chrissakes, and spent an entire week begging Minerva to let him have a "worm farm" in his compost heap—and Minerva rarely talked about her in-laws, except in metaphors referring to nightmares.

"So where'd you get the silver from?" I asked from behind the counter, making her an extra thick mocha latte with extra whipped cream in an extra large mug.

"Cici's old set," replied Minerva. "Engagement present," she continued, shooting Norman death rays as he erupted into a laugh, which then broke into a cough.

I attempted a hint of validation. "That's sweet," I said while sending Norman a *shut up!* look; he ignored me and continued coughing between laughs.

"No. It's not," Minerva snapped. "She did it so she can sigh every single time she eats; I never have them polished the way she likes."

Norman managed to take a breath. "Oh come on, she can't be that bad."

"She's the poster child of evil. The sum-total of the stereotypical mother-in-law. I won't eat any apple she hands me. She—"

I set the mocha in front of her. "Here," I said. "You need this. Trust me."

She nodded and opened her wallet, exhaling a "thanks."

"So," Norman resumed, "back up. Why didn't you pick up the socks when you dropped them in the first place?"

"Because of the toilet," she said.

"Excuse me?"

"The toilet. I'd forgotten to scrub it."

She hovered over her mocha, as if fortifying herself with the scent of it, while Norman looked at me, his eyes pleading for me to explain the connection; but I shrugged my shoulders, just as stymied.

"I spent twenty-five minutes scraping mold off my toilet," she said to the whipped cream.

"Now that's something you don't often hear over mochas," I said to Norman.

"It's powder blue—the toilet. Don't ask what the landlord was thinking; I don't want to know, especially since the rest of the bathroom is yellow. It was like that when we moved in. And it molds every week—the fan in there sucks...or doesn't, actually. So I cleaned it nonstop at first, but lately I've been letting it go...and grow. I know, I know," she said as she held up a hand, "totally gross, and if I had any pride left after dealing with that woman, I'd never admit to it. But, see, Jay's got this weird thing where he thinks the toilet is so ugly that mini polka dots are some sort of improvement."

"Jay?" I asked. "Environmental engineer Jay? Has six color-coded recycling bins Jay?"

"Again, don't ask. I don't pretend to know. But there was no way in hell I was going to let Cici lay eyes on it."

She took a sip.

"I also had to code my to-do list on the off chance I forgot to take it off the fridge before they arrived."

"Smart move," I said.

"What does a coded to-do list look like?" asked Norman.

She huffed. "For example, 'organize book-shelf' actually means 'dig up that picture of the whole family at the Christmas charity and put it in plain sight.'"

His laughing fit returned. "They go to *a Christmas charity*? Who dresses up as Santa?"

"Norman, you are so not helping," I said and turned my attention back to Minerva. "'Straighten up' is code for 'hide the mess somewhere else,' right?"

She grinned and nodded in gratitude of my validation. "'Organize kitchen' translates to 'scrub till your knuckles bleed.'"

At that point, it became clear that the mocha wasn't going to cut it. Minerva needed serious reinforcements.

I entered the kitchen as Norman asked, "So, are you taking them to any good charities while they're in town, or are you slummin' it and just going to the country club?"

I couldn't hear Minerva's response—if there was one—but I grinned when I heard Norman yelp. Smacked him with a stack of paper menus, I guessed.

Looking around the kitchen, I considered my options. A batch of butter cookies was baking in the oven, nearly done. I had intended to do the traditional raspberry jam sandwich thing, but that was altogether too teatime for the poor girl. She needed reassurance. She needed strength, but not too much. Sending her home too wired would be a recipe for all things hideous. She needed sanity.

And so I quickly whipped up a glaze consisting of mocha-malt and confectioner's sugar in a saucepan, adding butter at the last minute in homage to Paula Deen. Snapping off the heat of the oven, I drizzled the glaze straight from the saucepan to a few cookies in swirls so tight that they almost looked like petals. In a last minute addition, I placed chocolate-covered espresso beans at the cookies' centers, and stepped back to view my work. They reminded me of black-eyed Susans or some sort of rare, edible daisies. Comfort, kick, creamy...the perfect pick-me-up.

I presented them to Minerva as Cici's Pick-Me-Ups (although I wrote "Daisy Pick-Me-Ups" on the menu board—because when it comes to mother-in-laws, you can never be too safe). They did the trick.

"By the way, Minerva, how'd you manage to escape the wrath of Cici and come here?" I asked.

She popped an espresso bean into her mouth and said, "I told her I needed to go study."

"But you don't have your books."

She grinned slyly. "They don't know that. It's the one time I would *rather* be studying."

Just seeing Minerva so frazzled had made me want to check my own blood pressure; but the next night, when I read her e-mail—her ranting, venting, I'm-not-gonna-make-it-send-the-straightjacket-and-bring-drugs e-mail—it really hit home for me. She'd sent it from her bathroom, sitting on her mold-free blue toilet. It was the only place she could get away. And while I won't disclose the contents of that e-mail, let me just say that most of it was in block caps, consisting of profane epithets and threats of biochemical warfare made almost entirely of Tilex, Listerine, and other under-the-sink cleaners.

But here's where my confession comes in: while I was totally commiserating with and feeling her pain, I was, in truth, thinking one very selfish thought the entire time: *Thank God it's not me.*

I've never had to deal with in-laws. Shaun's mom and dad lived on Long Island, and I only met them for lunch or dinner a couple of times. We actually spent holidays apart—I'd go stay with my sister and Shaun would stay with his family and we'd just coordinate the big meal and that was it. I've never had to host anyone. I've never had to subject my home to the scrutiny of a white-gloved finger or a watchful eye. I've never had to polish silverware or check the china for nicks.

Nor do I want to.

Mind you, Minerva has the stereotypical mother-in-law from hell. (And I can't help but wonder how that stereotype came to be a stereotype in the first place. I mean, what makes mothers-in-law such dragons? Most of the time they seem perfectly acceptable as just plain mothers. So what happens after the I-dos? Does a switch flip in their brains? Is some kind of scary hormone released? How did *in-laws* come to be synonymous with *evil*?)

Shaun's parents and family were always friendly and generous. They welcomed me in their home, complimented me regularly, complimented Shaun on his good taste in women, etc. But I wonder: had Shaun and I tied the knot, would that have changed? If so, in what ways? Would Shaun's parents have suddenly begun to make more trips down South, possibly purchase a summer home in Wrightsville Beach or Emerald Isle? I bet they would've. The prospect of grandkids—no matter how remote—does strange things to a person. Or would his mom have started to insist upon taking me shopping because my wardrobe was in need of spiffing up? Would they have approved of my career change?

And I can't help but obsess over the Jeanette—oh, they must *love* her. They liked me, but I'll bet *she*'s getting the heirloom silver, and *she*'s going to be included in the latest family portrait, and *she*'s the one his mom is bragging about right now: *My son's bride-to-be has a* doctorate *in philosophy and wrote a* serious *book—not like his last girlfriend. She only had a master's degree and wrote a novel and now serves coffee for a living...*

Sadder still, Shaun never would've had mother-in-law issues on my side. No husband of mine ever would. And I would subject myself to a firing squad of mothers-in-law-from-hell if only to have my parents by my side if I ever walk down the aisle; if only to have my father give me away; if only to have my mother dance with my groom at the reception.

What really disturbed me as I witnessed Minerva's meltdown was how it was suddenly so clear to me that my relationship with Shaun was so *noncommittal*, and we both seemed to prefer it that way. I liked not having to worry about splitting myself in two for every holiday or getting the guest room ready just short of using those ultraviolet light sensors to detect the presence of microbacteria. And Shaun liked only having to attend the occasional wedding or graduation. It was just plain easy this way for both of us, him especially.

And yet, I realize now that all along I wanted so much more. I just didn't want to put in the work to get it.

So I'm left with a real dilemma now. I seem to want to have my cake and eat it, too. I want all the perks of marriage—the shared companion-ship and expenses, the vacations, the dining out—without the sacrifices and compromise and headaches. I want one guy promising me that it's only ever gonna be me, and I want the ring to prove it (not that that guarantees anything); but I don't want to file jointly, and I don't want to share bank accounts, and I don't want to be Mrs. Someone Else's Last Name. Or worse still, Mrs. Perino-*hyphen*-Someone Else's Last Name. Worst of all, Mrs. *His*-First-*and*-Last Name. Ugh. Heck, *Mrs.* just sounds old to me. My mother was a Mrs. It worked for her. But I didn't even like being called *Professor* Perino most days.

Perhaps being single is relative; because as far as I'm concerned, I'm married to The Grounds. Totally 100% committed. And I'm per-fectly willing to take the bad with the good because it's all worth it. To spend each day with familiar faces, with friends and former students and colleagues and the things I love most—books and cookies and conversation—is sheer joy. It's

```
a place to be and to belong. It's my place. My
playgrounds. My stomping grounds. My grounds.
    So what stops me from going the whole nine
yards with a man, then? Why was I so willing to
settle for so little, when I clearly wanted so
much more? And what do I want now?
```

I reread the post, deleting the paragraphs about Shaun and the Jeanette and a line I'd added at the end: *Were we ever a real couple, or were we two single people who shared a bed and had great sex?* Because as I read that line, what had immediately followed was, *My God, isn't that what I'm doing right now?*

I called Min but got her voice mail. Without leaving a message, I hung up and vowed to make cookie dough truffles just for her the next time she came in. Standing there with the phone still in my hands, I felt my heart sink deep into my chest. The illusion about how good life with Shaun had been, the one I'd lived with all these years, had shattered. And not only could I not pick up the pieces, but there was nothing to reconstruct because there hadn't been much there to begin with. And I don't know which hurt more: losing the illusion or never having had the real thing.

With a sigh, I put the phone down, returned to my laptop, and clicked "Cancel Post." When a warning popped up, *"Are you sure?"* I physically nodded and clicked the onscreen button.

It was way too long, for one thing. Besides, nothing good could have come from it.

Rather than look for new recipes as planned, I picked up a book from my end table, curled into my reading chair, and stared into nothingness.

23

Three Sides

BASED ON MINERVA'S last secret-e-mail-from-the-bathroom, I knew that Cici was flying home this morning. And yet, I was still surprised to see both her and Jay enter the shop just after lunch. Jay propped his sunglasses on top of his head to better read the new menu board from halfway across the room. He seemed single-minded as he scanned the pita wrap options. Minerva stood tightlipped beside him, hair still ponytailed and heavy bags under her dark eyes.

Watching Minerva approach, I couldn't help but wonder if Jay was really as hungry as he looked or simply playing the part of the cheery lunch companion in the presence of his moody wife. I guessed it was the latter but was still unsure if I should commend the guy on his bravado or condemn him for his levity when Norman stepped up to take their orders.

"Hey, Norm," Jay said, still eyeing the board. (Norman liked to be called "Norm" about as much as Minerva liked to be called "Minnie.")

"Hi, Jay." He turned to Minerva. "Glad to see you survived the invasion."

I froze and gave Norman a death stare from the other end of the counter.

Jay's face clouded. "What makes you say that?"

Oh, crap.

As Jay turned to Minerva, I tried with all my might to think of some clever diversion. Short of burning myself on the steamer, I had nothing.

"I can't believe you," said Jay quietly. "You told them."

Minerva's face pinched while Jay's voice stayed hushed. "Is nothing in our life—in *my* life—private? What else do you tell them?" He turned back to Norman, who was doing an excellent job studying the wall farthest from Jay and Minerva.

"Contrary to popular belief, I had a lovely weekend," said Jay to Norman. "And my mother is not a monster or a psychotic drill sergeant or anything else you might have heard."

"Jay!" Minerva said, blushing.

"Don't even," he warned. "I'm sure you said plenty."

"I didn't say any of that!" she insisted, pain evident on her face and in her voice.

"No, let me guess. You bitched about what? The cleaning? The silver? I bet it was the silver." Minerva studied her fingernails, GUILTY AS CHARGED stamped across her face.

"Well, guess what: the house needed to be cleaned, and *you* were the one who decided how clean, and *you* were the one who insisted on silver. You're the one with the competition thing and the perfection thing and all that expectation bullshit, Minerva. That's all *you*. Not her."

Jay fixed his gaze back on the menu board only to draw a few steadying breaths before rounding on her again. "You know what, we're done here. We're not having this conversation center stage. I think these people have been given enough of a show already."

She reached a hand toward him, but he shrugged it off.

"How could you?" he asked, shaking his head sadly. "How could you let them think that I'd let anyone—anyone at all— treat you like that? How can *you* think that?"

I saw the look in Minerva's eyes at that moment, like she didn't know how she could've gotten it so wrong. Minerva, who got As in every class she took, who memorized the periodic table, who used five different color pens when she took notes, was stymied in that moment.

He pulled his sunglasses back down over his eyes. "Get whatever you want; I'll be in the car. I'm not hungry anymore."

Minerva watched him go, blinking hard before silently following him out.

Neither Norman nor I so much as moved until the door closed behind her.

Norman cleared his throat. "Um, Eva? Didn't you want me to check the coffee stock? The coffee people called about the new Jamaican line yesterday and wanted to know if we needed more."

It took a full second for me to shake out of my trance. "Oh. Yeah, that'd be great. Thanks."

"Yeah, thought I'd just go check," he said, ducking into the kitchen. Although I wanted to hate Norman for fleeing while the tension was still palpable, at least he'd been brave enough to move. I pushed myself off the counter and began stacking cups and saucers, hoping the soft clinking would fill the void—left by the Brunswicks' abrupt departure—that was still clinging to the corners of the café. Soft jazz whispered from the speakers above normal conversations of customers oblivious to the fight that had just occurred within feet of them.

My heart instinctively went out to Min. I didn't envy her the ride home, or the inevitable argument that would resume once they got there.

My hands paused between cups as one of my mother's favorite mantras flitted into my mind over the gentle sounds of the café. *There are three sides to every story,* she'd say while

Olivia and I scowled at each other. *Yours, hers, and what really happened.* Cici probably wasn't the monster Minerva had made her out to be. It was only logical—how could anyone so seemingly horrid raise such a genuinely good guy? Sure, Minerva occasionally complained about Jay's quirks and conspiracy theories. But never had I seen Jay mad at her, ever. Never heard him say a cross word to her or even shoot an annoyed glance in her direction. It occurred to me that Minerva wasn't perfect, either. She had quirks and bad habits. She had insecurities. She and Jay had fights.

They had a typical marriage. I just never thought about it like that.

I stacked the last few cups. Why did Minerva think Jay would let Cici keep her like a bug under her thumb? And how did I not set her straight when Minerva had come to me? Regardless of whether Cici was a three-headed monster or an angel, Minerva had turned her into a force to be reckoned with—one she could undoubtedly never win against. To Minerva, that monster was real. I'm sure Cici said or did something once, or gave Minerva a look that made her feel like she was a stain on the carpet. And Minerva—wonderful and strong and spirited as she was—was vulnerable. She had a hard time letting go of disappointments and shortcomings, especially her own. She loved Jay so much that she wanted to be perfect for him, or perfect enough to be with him. And she wanted to be accepted by a woman who wasn't affectionate or open. Besides, she was Minerva—she made everything into a challenge.

My mind continued spinning as NCLA English professor Paul, a new Regular, politely requested a refill of French roast.

Was *I* like that? Was I a perfectionist, or worse, a revisionist? With every year that had passed since my parents' deaths, I was only able to remember every good time, every quality moment of laughter, every hug—and I was able to forget every fight, every neglected tear, every shouted expletive. It took Olivia's kicking me out to make me see that she needed so much more. And it had taken me far longer to come to the same conclusion about myself, about my relationships.

How could I get it so all wrong?

I didn't hear from Minerva that night, nor did I see her the next morning. By lunchtime I was nervous. I didn't want to intrude or make anything worse, but I couldn't help but worry about what happened and how she was. By one thirty I couldn't take it any longer.

You ok? I texted her.

She responded within five minutes. *Yeah.*

Want to talk?

Shop busy?

Before I could answer, she followed with, *Stupid question. I'll stop by later. Need chai.*

I felt a wave of relief.

I'll have one waiting for you.

24

An Offer

HE CAME IN out of the blue. Ed Rush, a former colleague from NCLA and the current writing department chairperson, hadn't been to The Grounds since he'd brought several prospective faculty candidates to show off the "community ties" to the campus. Although he had introduced me by name, he referred to me as an alumna rather than former faculty. I didn't take offense to this—he was probably afraid someone would think I'd left because I hated the department or the college. One candidate, however, recognized me.

"I read your book," he said.

"Really?"

"Yes. Liked it, too. You tell a good story."

"Well, thanks," I replied, a bit dazed. I couldn't remember the last time anyone—including myself—had talked about my novel. "You must have a thing for obscure novels that go straight to the bargain shelf before going out of print."

"You should write another," the man said.

When I left teaching, I left behind all that publish-or-perish stuff. Funny, it had never occurred to me that I could write or publish because I *wanted* to. At the time I was pretty sure I didn't want to.

"Good to see you, Eva," said Ed, bringing me back to the present moment. "How's business?"

"Couldn't be better. How'd it work out with that last batch of candidates?"

"Major flakes," said Ed.

I laughed. "So what can I get you?" I asked.

"How about a large mocha hazelnut coffee and coming back to teach a course?"

"Comin' right up," I said and went to process his order in automaton fashion, until my brain caught up and I stopped in my tracks before turning around to face him.

"What was that second thing?"

"Jenna Jaffe is taking maternity leave for the first half of next semester."

I straightened my posture and dropped my jaw. "I didn't even know she was pregnant."

"We've covered her course load except the short story class, and since that used to be yours, she wanted you to do it. What do you say?"

I was flattered, but dumbfounded. *Teaching? After all this time?*

"Wow. I need some time to think about it, Ed."

"Don't think too long."

"Can't you get a TA to do it?"

"Not at upper level. Besides, you *know* the course. And she specifically asked for you."

"But Ed, it's been *years…*"

"It's like riding a bike."

"Yeah. I suck at biking, by the way. Even the stationary ones."

He laughed. "Call me at my office. I hope you'll do it, Eva. We've missed you."

"You'll know by the end of the week," I said.

"Thanks," he said.

He stood there, not moving.

"You gonna camp out here and wait?" I asked.

"My mocha hazelnut?" he said.

My brain snapped back into café mode. "Ohh! Sorry about that," I said as I finished filling his order. "On the house."

"Thanks. I'll talk to you soon." With that he took his drink, stopped at the self-service bar for a couple of extra napkins, and headed out. I saluted him with two fingers as he turned and exited the café.

Jenna Jaffe had been my advisor and mentor throughout my graduate work at NCLA. When I had begun my thesis project, she encouraged me to submit it to agents and sent the manuscript to her own, who signed me no sooner than I had submitted it to the thesis committee. I owed Jenna a lot. The only reason I was good at teaching was because I tried to replicate the experience I'd had in her classes.

We had also been good friends. I loved her sense of humor; she loved my freakish knowledge of pop culture. Back during my grad school days, I probably hung out with Jenna and her circle of friends and faculty as much as I did with Minerva and Jay, although the two circles never overlapped. When I hung out with Jenna, I felt important, scholarly. When I hung out with Minerva, I felt free, like I was getting a second chance at adolescence without all the angst or acne.

I had always sensed that Jenna disapproved of my leaving my teaching and writing career behind. She had given me her blessing, but only after an unsuccessful attempt to talk me out of opening The Grounds. "It's not that I think you'd fail, Eva," she'd said. "It's that I think you'd be wasting a talent."

"What good is that talent if it's not something I want to do?" I had replied.

When The Grounds first opened, Jenna had attended the grand opening with our colleagues and friends, and she'd stopped by on a weekly basis, enough that I'd had her pegged as a Regular. But weekly had slowed to bimonthly, then once a month, then once every two months, and then I rarely saw her anymore. I wondered when I'd stopped missing her, why we'd drifted apart, if it really was because of my career shift. And I wondered if she had missed me, or when she'd stopped.

~~ↄ~~

Not more than a minute after Ed's departure, Scott, Norman, Beulah, Spencer and Tracy, and Minerva all perched around the counter, surrounding me. I fell back a step and hit the counter with my rear end.

"Yikes! What is this, *The Birds*?"

"Tell us you're going to do it," said Beulah.

"I said I'll think about it."

"What's there to think about?" asked Minerva.

"It's not easy to step into a classroom and fill someone else's shoes, especially when she's got her own style and rapport with her students. I haven't even seen her reading list."

"But you have time to prepare and go over all of that with her," said Tracy.

"Look, if you're worried about coverage, I can handle it," said Norman.

"It's not just the three hours of class time. There's out-of-class conferencing, office hours, reading, grading…It may only be a dozen students, but that's at least twenty hours of work right there, even if it is just for a few weeks. I'm pullin' forty-five to fifty hours here on average."

"So? Hold office hours here," said Scott.

"Yeah," said Norman. "They'll love it. And I'm fine with you reducing your hours. It's only for what, six weeks?"

"Seven," I said.

"It'll be over before you even know it," he said. "Do it, Eva." I took in a breath.

"Scott, go to the NCLA Writing Department Web site and see if Jenna Jaffe has her course syllabus there."

This instruction mobilized the troops: Scott checked out the Web site, Norman took out the calendar, and Minerva wrote a list of things for Jenna to do for the remainder of the pregnancy in terms of self-care.

I spent the rest of the afternoon in the office, preoccupied with mentally composing reading lists and workshop formats and syllabi. Regardless of whether returning to the classroom really was like riding a bike, I was more concerned about whether I'd hate it—or worse, *like* it. I pushed this thought from my mind as Norman reminded me for the third time to draft an ad for a new full-time employee. When I returned to the café, Minerva practically knocked me over.

"Here. I made a list of pregnancy musts for each month, including how to stay fit and comfortable during the last trimester and how to deal with postpartum depression."

"Geez, Minerva!" I yelped. After a calming breath, I took the list and folded it. "Sure, thanks. I'll pass it on."

"So you're doing it, then," she said.

"I think so," I replied.

"OK." She retreated to her table, her textbooks sprawled open in their usual organized chaos.

Moments later, I glanced around in search of Norman and found him emerging from the kitchen, his shirttails smoothed,

holding a paper bag in one hand and a napkin tied to the end
of a stirrer in the other. He approached Minerva's table, slowly
waving his napkin.

Minerva opened and closed her mouth several times, each
clearly more perplexed than the last. Finally she raised her
hands. "I give. What are you doing?"

Norman nodded at his napkin, "Waving the white flag. And
I come bearing gifts. A peace offering," he corrected.

She burst out laughing. "For what?"

Slumping with relief, Norman set the bag on top of her
enormous loose-leaf binder and remained standing, still clasp-
ing his makeshift flag.

"Oh for crying out loud, Norman, sit down." He did as
she unfolded the top of the bag, eyes growing wide. "Is this…
cheesecake from Delmonico's?"

She glanced at me, and I held up my hands and shook my
head as if to say, *I had nothing to do with it.*

"I was a dumbass to open my mouth the other day," he said.

It took me a moment to register that he was talking about
the Cici incident and the scene with Jay, but Minerva nodded
in understanding, her mouth already full. As she closed her
eyes, letting the creamy cheesecake melt on her tongue, I was
reminded yet again about how much first bites are like first loves.

"I didn't…it wasn't…" He tried again. "I'm sorry."

She swallowed. "It's OK. And not just because you brought
me cheesecake from Delmonico's—the grand-poobah of cheesecake—although that is grounds to nominate you for sainthood."

"Thanks. I'd like to take you and Jay out to dinner. I know
I offended him, too."

"I think he'd like that. Let me check our schedules and get
back to you."

She took another bite before flipping open her cell phone. Norman stood up to resume his work, looking considerably more relaxed.

"Cheesecake?" I asked him when he joined me behind the counter.

"Well I couldn't very well give another man's wife roses, could I?"

I hadn't thought of it that way.

"And that meant a mix tape was out of the question, too. And without my two stand-by apologies, I had to improvise."

"Believe me, Delmonico's hits the spot. You done good, Norm-o," I said, giving him a soft punch on the arm.

⌒⊃

That night, I called Jenna. She sounded pleased to hear from me and filled me in on everything. The longer we talked, the more comfortable I felt.

"Oh, I'm so glad you're doing this," she said. "You're one of the few people I trust to do it right."

"Wow," I said. "I had no idea you had such faith in me."

I didn't ask her why we'd drifted apart or suggest that we pick up where we left off or do a better job of keeping in touch. Perhaps it was because our lives were different. She had a husband and a kid on the way, after all. Or perhaps I was afraid she'd say she'd rather not keep in touch with a coffee shop owner whose latest literary achievement was a sporadic blog about being single.

After I got off the phone with Jenna, I called Ed and left a message on his voice mail.

"You got yourself a sub," I said, "and I'm charging you double for your mocha hazelnut coffees from now on."

25

Failure to Thrive

BAD THINGS HAPPEN in threes; everyone knows that. You just never know when and where they're gonna happen.

The first happened to Jan and Dean. Like Kenny, they had disappeared from The Grounds, and their Facebook statuses hadn't been updated for days. The other Originals and Regulars speculated on their whereabouts.

"I say they eloped," I said.

"Maybe they ran off to Fiji," said Norman.

"Nah, Eva's right. They eloped," said Minerva.

"Without telling anyone?" asked Tracy, who was worried.

"That's the whole point of eloping," said Spencer.

"But what if it's something serious? Her dad's not been well lately."

"If you're that worried, hon, then call her."

Tracy pulled her cell phone from her miniscule purse (I always envied women who could fit everything in a purse that size), opened it and scrolled down to Jan's number, then waited as she mouthed to us, "Voice mail."

"Jan, it's Tracy. We're all here at The Grounds and are worried since we haven't seen or heard from you in a week. Please call and let us know you're not lyin' in a ditch somewhere."

Spencer made a face at her. "Did you really have to mention the ditch thing?"

Two days later, Tracy came in looking pale and shell-shocked.

"What is it, sweetie?" I asked.

"They broke up."

"Who?"

"Jan and Dean."

Norman nearly dropped the plate he was carrying. "Jan and Dean broke up?" he said loudly enough for the entire café to go quiet.

"Holy shit," said Scott.

"What happened?" I asked.

"She didn't get into specifics with me—she was too upset, crying on the phone the whole time. We both were, actually. She just said it was over between them and she couldn't trust Dean and he was never as in love with her as she was with him."

I knew that crappy truth all too well.

"Did he cheat on her?" someone asked.

"She didn't say."

The café was hushed, and everyone slowed down, their movements sluggish and automatic. It remained that way for the rest of the day. Like Spencer and Tracy, who had been here since day one, literally, Jan and Dean were more like one entity than two separate people. Losing them was losing something familial, the kind of loss that made you question the people and things you thought you knew.

That night, after my shower and before dinner, I opened my laptop. It was time.

Eva Breaks Silence

Readers, I apologize for my disappearance from cyberland. A lot has happened during the past couple of months, and the writing well had temporarily gone dry. I know this is news to few of you, but surprise: I am seeing someone.

What I like about seeing someone:

The company. I like having someone to come home to, looking forward to the possibility that someone will be there, waiting for me, happy to see me. I like having someone to curl up on the couch with after a long day, someone to share a plate of french fries with at a diner at 10 p.m.

Not dating. The verdict is in: I do not like dating. Rather, I don't like going out on dates. Especially first dates. Especially bad first dates. Seeing someone is different—it's comfortable, it's routine, it's safe. But dating—the stress of the unknown, the effort to impress, the inevitable tension—I don't miss any of that.

But here's the thing: what I love about singlehood is that you never have to worry about losing what's good. You never have to look at your significant other and wonder if he'll be gone tomorrow, be it physically, emotionally, mentally, whatever. You'll never be blindsided by a crushing blow to the head or the heart. You never have to wonder if it was all a lie and you've been a fool all along. Some will tell you that singlehood is a false kind of security, the kind that comes with bars on the windows, a self-made prison, shutting you in from a fabricated fear. But singlehood is safe. Because you can't keep the ones you love. There's no such thing.

If only knowing so was enough.

Thirty minutes later, the phone rang. I looked at the caller ID and answered.

"Hey, Scott."

"I just read your WILS post."

"Already? Geez, the ink's still wet—metaphorically speaking, that is."

"Jan and Dean really shook you up, huh."

I sighed sadly. "Yeah."

"I know. Me too. I'm really bummed out about it."

I didn't respond.

"You want me to come over?" he asked. I was surprised that he was asking since he'd told me earlier that he needed the next few nights to prepare for an upcoming conference in Denver.

"Sure," I said. "Why? Don't you want to?"

"Of course I do. I just...I don't know. I thought you might want to be by yourself."

"I probably should, but no. Come over. Bring ice cream."

"OK."

When he pulled into the driveway, I opened the door, having been standing and waiting there nearly the entire time, and watched him galumph up the walkway and the porch carrying two pints of Ben & Jerry's (Cherry Garcia for him, Chocolate Chip Cookie Dough for me). I practically strangled him as I threw my arms around his neck and squeezed him, the door still open for my neighbors to see. He squeezed back, and I could feel the cold containers on the small of my back.

Hours later, in the darkness of my bedroom waiting for sleep to come following sex, Scott said very softly, almost in a slur, "I'm glad you think this is a relationship, Eva. I want it to be."

"Me too," I murmured, nuzzling him like a cat does its owner.

I really, really wanted it to be.

⌒⊙

Surprisingly, since outing Scott and myself on WILS, no one commented much, but the vibe had definitely softened up at The Grounds. I hadn't realized how tense I'd been trying to cover it up for so long, and how tense they'd all been pretending not to know. It was as if the air were breathable again.

We all missed Jan and Dean, though. Jan kept in touch with Tracy, but my guess was that neither came back to The Grounds for fear of running into the other. Or maybe it was just too hard. After Shaun and I had broken up, I had all but stopped going to the places we frequented.

Since deciding to give the reading room a facelift, Norman perused Craigslist every day looking for used couches and chairs, and he and Scott would take Scott's pickup truck to check them out when one looked promising. An awkward moment came when it turned out that one of the sofa-loveseat sets had belonged to Jan and Dean. Despite it being in near-mint condition, perfect for our space, Norman had turned it down, and I knew why: it was too painful a reminder.

The reading room makeover was keeping us all busy—both employees and clientele were pitching in, whether it was cleaning the floors, giving the space a new coat of paint, looking for rugs and accessories at garage sales and flea markets, or just plain staying out of the way when necessary. It was a family affair. The sense of community warmed me; I'd had that at NCLA as both a grad student and a faculty member, and it was nice to feel the same thing so fully in this capacity.

Still, I found myself missing Kenny with each day he didn't show up. I missed our silly exchanges and his amiable smile. I missed seeing him perched in his corner with a book or his laptop, simultaneously removed from the crowd yet as much a part of the gang as Spencer or Tracy or Scott or Minerva. The space somehow seemed quieter, emptier without him there even though he hardly made a sound when he was.

⌒↺

The second bad thing happened to Minerva.

It was one of those gorgeous fall days—the kind that makes you want to bask in the sun, shop, and eat a pumpkin muffin all at the same time. In short, a busy day at The Grounds. By midafternoon the stream of customers was still flowing, and I'd barely had time to glance at the photos of Jan's new apartment on Tracy's BlackBerry before rushing back to the counter, where Norman was fighting with the blender.

A man in a well-tailored brown suit ordered a tall, extra-extra iced mochaccino. I forgot the *iced* and was busy apologizing to him when I saw Minerva slip in. I waved to her, forgetting the extra-extra, and corrected the drink a final time before giving it to Brown Suit on the house out of guilt. Meanwhile, Tracy hailed Minerva to gush over Jan's sun deck.

"Later," she said. As I assisted the next customer, I watched her fold herself into what had always been Kenny's chair in the far corner, tucking her feet in like a cold cat.

After bidding the customer a good day, I grabbed a Cookie of the Week (the one that Min dubbed the "Chocolate Orgasm" cookie), popped it in the microwave for seven seconds, and headed her way.

"Hungry?" I asked when she didn't look up.

She shook her head.

"Rough exam or something?" I tried again, scanning my memory for exams she'd mentioned recently.

"Not now, OK?" she said, still not looking up.

She looked like death warmed over. Something was *wrong*.

"OK," I said, trying to be amiable. I held out the plate. "Cookie? It's Chocolate Orgasm."

"No thanks," she replied, almost in a child's voice.

No to a Chocolate Orgasm cookie?

I left the cookie on the table next to her and went back to work. We were so busy that afternoon that I didn't see Minerva leave, the cookie untouched, and by the time I got home I was so exhausted that she'd totally slipped my mind until I checked my e-mail.

E-mail to: eva@thegrounds.com
Subject: FTT

Eva,

    I'm sorry to dump this on you, but it's just too much for me.

    I had my first FTT today. Failure to thrive. Convenient how the medical world sterilizes everything isn't it? "Ceased to breathe." "Failure to thrive." As if it somehow makes it cleaner, less soul splitting.

    It wasn't unexpected, but it wasn't easy, either. Almost worse, I think, is knowing it was all in vain. As I was standing there, the assistant in this birth (if you can call it that), I couldn't help thinking about the first birth I'd ever seen. I was four, and my sitter (who was also our herd manager) came in while I was eating a peanut butter sandwich. She told me to go on out to the barn because one of the cows was having a baby. And I remember thinking how odd it sounded. Did she think I didn't know the difference between babies and calves? Taking one last bite, I abandoned my sandwich and made my way to the barn.

    The first thing that hit me was the smell. As in, the smell of birth. If you've never witnessed a birth, I'll do my best to explain. It smells like pungent wet earth, with a tang of blood, which almost turns your stomach. But at the same time there's an almost tangible excitement laced in the overpowering scent—it's almost dizzying, so that even at four years old I knew that there was great power being unleashed in that scent. The power of life.

The cow was bellowing. And heaving and moaning and groaning. She was shaking. I looked at my mother in fright, but she hadn't even noticed that I'd come in. She was too busy talking to the cow, coaxing her, trying to soothe her, I think. The calf was breech, and I remember tasting my peanut butter sandwich again as I watched my mother sink her arm in nearly to her shoulder to try to push the calf back and spin it around. I think that's when my mother saw me. I can only imagine the look on my face. I remember her saying something about getting back inside and maybe next time. She gave me one last tired look before turning to the cow again. Coaxing again. Pleading with the cow, calling her "honey," asking her to try just a little more.

I retreated to the doorway but couldn't make myself leave. Instead I hovered just outside the threshold and leaned back into the barn, unable to take myself away.

The cow fought less and less. Her bellows turned to huffs, and eventually her head just hung in the mud before her. I was terrified for her, afraid we would lose her; I'd never seen anything die before. Been to the butcher's more than once (and hid in the car each time—now there's another smell I'll never forget), but I'd never watched anything actually die. I was sure this was it.

In the end my mother had to sit in the mud and manure behind the cow, brace one leg up on each of her hips and pull the calf out by its hooves.

The calf was dead.

I think we all knew it from the beginning. It looked so small, puckered even. And it didn't smell like birth. It didn't smell like anything. It just looked wet and empty. Lost.

I watched through blurry eyes as the cow slowly got her shaking legs underneath herself and turned not to her discarded calf, but to my mother. She nudged my mom's hand, bellowed softly, and sank to the ground again. It was the most human thing I'd ever see a cow do.

I remember hearing our herdsman laugh, "I think that right there is one grateful cow," as I broke from the doorjamb and ran back inside.

I refused to eat dinner that night, and though I never asked Mom where the calf went, I made a grave at the edge of our field, marked with a stick, and visited it every day for a month even though there was nothing buried there.

Today I hovered by the doorway, unable to do anything but watch as my nurse coaxed the mother, who huffed and moaned and fought with all her strength, even though she knew it was for naught. She had lost her baby the day before, and had to be induced in the seventh month.

I barely remember what really happened, and I'm not sure I even saw it. I was too busy smelling birth and barns and hearing my mother coax that poor, young cow. She was the one bellowing. She was the one fighting. And in the end it was not a human child but a calf that the midwife held, puckered and empty and lost.

I knew an FTT was bound to happen. I know it will happen again. But I can't help thinking that for all the babies I birth, for all the first breaths I hear and all the lives I see unfold, there will never be another like this one. And no matter how many stars there are in the heavens, and people on the earth, none can replace this life, nothing can take its place. Because this life, no matter how fleeting or fragile, was like no other.

But I guess that's the beautiful thing about life: sometimes it isn't—beautiful, or there.

Minerva

By the time I'd scrolled through and got to the end, I was so riveted that I didn't even notice the tears rolling down my cheeks until one of them dropped onto my hand.

I sat on my bed, dumbfounded, not knowing what to think first. When we were classmates at NCLA (which had long felt like another lifetime, a dream, even), Minerva once told me that she didn't care for memoir—she accused the genre of being kitschy, and said she'd do us all a favor by knowing better than to pretend that anything in her life was worth reading.

Clearly, she was wrong. Layers of emotions rolled over me like waves as I read the e-mail a second time. First was the empathy and simplicity of the four-year-old's perspective, the helplessness and pain of being washed away in a flashback. Next were loss, horror, grief, fear, and finally, want. I wanted to drive over to her apartment, walk in without knocking, and hug her like a mom holds a child after the world has let her down for the first time. But it was almost eleven o'clock, and even that wouldn't soothe the hollow ache either of us harbored.

I reread the e-mail, tried to draft a reply, but only managed a few sentences before erasing the entire message. The words sounded too banal, too artificial, too planned. With each attempt, I deleted and tried again.

> Min,
>
> I don't know where to begin. I'm so, so sorry. Why didn't you tell me in person

I stopped short. No need to attack the poor girl. I knew exactly why she didn't tell me earlier, and it was probably the best decision. I tried again:

> I'm so, so sorry. I can't begin to imagine ~~where you're at~~ how you must feel right now

No. Sorry didn't begin to cut it, and I *did* know how she felt. Like total crap. Like she'd just watched death win a battle that was never fair.

Dear Minerva,

You're right. Sometimes life isn't beautiful and usually it's not fair. If you think about it, some of the most beautiful and treasured things in nature are those that are so delicate that they rarely survive the smallest of changes: certain wild orchids, patterns on snowflakes, corals that can't survive even the gentlest touches.

I wish there was something I could do or say to make this even a little better for you, for that family, for the nurse even, but you know I can't. No one can. All I can do is be here for you, and I am. (And for the record, this isn't venting. This is grieving. And I'm glad you came to me.)

This too shall pass.

Love, Eva

No eloquent response could follow something like a failure to thrive, I decided. Hopeless, I closed the laptop and went to bed, feeling empty. Staring at the ceiling, I missed Scott (he had to get up super-early to fly to Denver, thus thought it'd be better if he stayed at his place), missed Jan and Dean, missed Olivia, missed my parents. I even missed Kenny.

The next morning before work, I called and left a message on Minerva's voice mail. She returned it a few hours later, insisting that she was fine and thanking me for my concern, but I knew better than to believe her.

⌒⊙

Two days passed before she resurfaced on Saturday afternoon with Jay in tow. I looked up to find her at the back of the line, pale and wearing sunglasses, staring at the menu board behind me.

I smiled tentatively at Jay.

The line moved up, and as if coming out of a trance, Minerva began to hunt through her purse. "I'll have a chai smoothie, and..."

"Min, you OK?"

First she looked at me as if I'd just insulted her. Then she looked at Jay, as if to say, *You take care of it,* left, and grabbed her usual table, sitting with her back to the counter.

Jay sighed. "The smoothie and Cookie of the Week for her. And can I get a strawberry milkshake?"

I filled their orders and then attended to the customers behind them. When I had a free moment, I joined them at their table.

"How are you?" I asked, my voice full of compassion. I felt very motherly.

"I'm quitting," she replied.

I looked at her, shocked.

"Quitting as in quitting school? As in, *dropping out*?"

She neither nodded nor shook her head, but I knew the answer.

"Min, I know it's—"

"No. I'm done."

"Wow," I said. "Seems pretty final."

"That's because it is," she snipped.

"Don't you think you should give it a little thought? Hold out for another week? Finish the semester?"

She stared at me as if I were speaking Klingon.

"You said it yourself: it's terrible and heartbreaking, but it's going to happen." She shook her head as I spoke. "It doesn't mean you should give up."

"What, this too shall pass?" she snapped. Her words, despite their air of flippancy, kicked me in the stomach with a gale force.

I bit back my anger, knowing she was projecting her own pain and grief, and tried to rationalize for her. "That's not what I meant and you know it."

"Eva! It's done. I can't do it, all right? I've made my decision."

"Well, maybe you should reconsider."

"Not happening."

"What will you do instead?" I asked.

"I don't know. Be a hairdresser, maybe."

My mouth dropped open. "You're kidding, right?"

"Why not? They're creative and they're healers in their own way. And I don't have to give away my firstborn to pay for schooling. I can make back my investment in less than a year if I can get a clientele going. Not to mention all that great product. It's not that far-fetched, you know. I wanted to be a hairdresser when I was a teenager. But all the guidance counselors and my mom kept telling me I was too smart, too gifted, yada, yada, frickin' ya…"

"Maybe because they were right?" I asked.

"Don't insult hairdressers like that."

Later, as they got ready to leave, Jay brought his empty milk-shake glass to the dish bin.

I approached him. "Jay, help me out here."

He smiled in a way that emanated understanding rather than aloofness, watching his wife wipe down the table. "Of course you're right, Eva. She'd be a great midwife, and we all know it. And we've been through a lot to get her this far. But, well, I just can't. She's done, and that's it."

I wondered how many rounds they'd gone for him to be so resigned.

"What if two years down the road she decides it's what she really wanted after all?"

"Then I pity the fool that tries to argue over matriculated credits with her."

"Jay, she's got a gift."

"I know," he said. His eyes were earnest. "But there's no way I'm going to watch her punish herself for every FTT that happens. And she's not the kind of person this will ever get easy for. She's not her mother, and these babies aren't farm animals."

"Maybe she'll change her mind," I offered, trying to instill some hope in myself as much as him.

"She won't," he said sadly.

"I know."

Damn.

⌒ᴑ

For the next two weeks, I waited for the third bad thing to happen. I moved around skittishly, vigilant for books mysteriously falling off shelves, a rain of toads, coffee vendors going on strike, anything potentially cataclysmic.

But nothing happened.

At her insistence, Minerva helped out in the shop just so she could have something to do. She knew it was midterm week at the college, which meant we were short on help since Susanna had reduced her hours. Minerva told me to consider it "volunteerism." It felt more like condoning slave labor to me; worse still, slave labor of my best friend. Yet, I knew she needed something to keep her mind off dropping out and the failure to thrive incident, and she needed a soft place to fall. The Grounds was that place. She did all the shit-work—cleaning bathrooms, the floors, the coffee machines—voluntarily and without complaint, and she was ecstatic when she got to help make the cookies. Her batches even rivaled mine. Almost.

She was a great worker, as always, and I compensated her by letting her make her own hours. Thus, she could work for ten minutes or an hour or four hours, or she could hang out and be a customer, although I refused to let her pay for even so much as a paper cup anymore. Basically, she had free reign of the place. She and Norman had developed an older brother–younger sister relationship, and they loved bossing each other around. I was both delighted and entertained to see Minerva reemerging from her grief until one afternoon when Jay came in unexpectedly.

Norman had just swatted Minerva with a towel for calling him "Normie" and, still laughing, she threw Jay a casual "Hey" over her shoulder before ducking into the kitchen for a tray of pita wraps.

Jay looked stricken. When he pulled her aside a few minutes later, I could tell from their gestures that the conversation was tense. I casually made my way toward them as Minerva put up a hand, cutting him off. "That's great, but I have work to do here." He opened his mouth to try again. "Jay, I said I'm busy. I'll see you tonight." She walked back to the kitchen without saying good-bye.

I fidgeted while he stared at her wake.

"Jay?"

He jumped, seeing me for the first time. I looked at his face—still pinched in frustration—and my shoulders sagged. For all the fun and games, for all her joviality and determination, I knew Minerva was hurting, and we had no choice but to let her hurt. But I hadn't taken into account until that moment what it was doing to her husband.

Wishing I could come up with something appropriate to say to take the edge off his pain, all I could manage was, "Totally sucks, huh?"

"Yeah," he said quietly, "it does." Giving Norman one last venomous look, Jay left, hands shoved into his pockets, nearly bumping into Dean on the way out.

Dean had come in a couple of times but didn't stick around long enough to talk to anyone. Perhaps he thought we were taking sides against him (although we really didn't know anything other than what Tracy had told us that day), or maybe he was avoiding the possibility of running into Jan. On his last visit, I had at least persuaded him to check out the progress on the reading room makeover (I painted a sign that said Play Grounds over the entranceway, with a matching Back Grounds sign for the back office, and High Grounds for the café), and further tried to goad him into staying and participating in one of our surveys.

"We're figuring out who made the best Robin Hood: Errol Flynn, Kevin Costner, the guy who was also in *The Princess Bride*, the fox from the Disney version, or Daffy Duck," I told him. "So far Daffy Duck is ahead by three votes." But he shook his head and darted out. Maybe he missed us just as much as we missed him.

The new-and-improved reading room was ready to be officially christened by the end of the month. It looked better than I could've imagined: a loveseat/sofa set with coffee table, three upright reading chairs, and a set of end tables, giving it an eclectic living-room-meets-library feel. We painted the walls a warm nutmeg color (daring for nautical Wilmington), and the light streamed through the windows onto the tables, warming it even further. We also threw down an area rug from Target over the painted cement floors, and flanked the couch with two restored bookcases. Finally, we checked all the electrical sockets and bought several surge protectors and extension cords. Using Norman's laptop, we made sure the WiFi worked in every part of the room. All that was left was hanging artwork; we'd bought several pieces by local artists.

It was beautiful. We decided to coincide the unveiling with a Halloween costume party.

Perhaps the third bad thing had passed without anyone's noticing. Perhaps someone spilled coffee down the front of their shirt in the middle of a meeting. Perhaps someone made off with a couple of books from the new reading room. But after a while I stopped looking over my shoulder and let the bustle of routine at The Grounds chug along like an old locomotive.

26

Bender

WE WERE EXPECTING quite a turnout for the Halloween Costume/Reading Room Reopening party: Susanna distributed flyers all over campus, Scott did a podcast, and we plugged it on Facebook. I even mentioned it on WILS, reporting that it would be a singles' safety zone—no dates required. We promised free vanilla chai and cookie samples, coupons for one free coffee, raffles for free *I spill my beans at The Grounds* merchandise, and an open mic set in the evening.

Norman and I obsessively checked to make sure we had more than enough of everything, and we asked Minerva to work the full day with pay (Susanna could only do her usual four-hour shift because of her class schedule). Even Scott offered to pitch in.

The place was packed to capacity. We not only ran out of the chai reserved solely for the opening, but also our regular reserve. To compensate, Norman made punch. The cookies were devoured right down to the crumbs. People begged for a free T-shirt or cap. Two local authors booked readings for January. Three people asked if they could book private parties. Even a reviewer for the *Wilmington Weekly* came and checked out the place (and you can be damn sure I gave *him* a T-shirt).

I smiled so much my jaws hurt.

The place was decked out in fake webs and swaths of black cloth. Little black cauldrons full of candy corn sat on every table, and a talking skeleton guarded the door. Norman and I dressed up as the Wonder Twins, Susanna was Raggedy Ann, and Minerva and Jay were Dr. Honeydew and Beaker, respectively. Minerva had dug out silver wire-framed glasses and two lab coats, and translated Jay's *Mee-mee-mee-mee*s all day long. It was the first time I'd seen them playful since the Cici incident. The Originals and Regulars joined the fun. Ed Rush and half of NCLA showed up, faculty and student body combined, some even in costume. I hadn't seen some of my former colleagues in a while, and it was nice to see them, even though I was dressed in a leotard, skirt, bodysuit with a "J" ironed on, knee-high boots—all purple—and Spock ears. Even Jan and Dean stopped by separately, and I couldn't help but wonder if they had specifically coordinated times.

When I came back from the kitchen around four o'clock with refills of chai and pumpkin-shaped shortbread cookies, I spotted Shaun circling the reading room. I froze and nearly dropped both pitcher and platter when we saw each other for the first time since my meltdown in front of the Jeanette, who was nowhere in sight this time. Fortunately, Minerva was close by and took the platter from me, eyeing Shaun coolly as she passed him approaching me.

"What are you doing here?" I asked.

"Followed the crowd," he said.

"So, you actually *would* jump off the Brooklyn Bridge if everyone else was doing it."

"Headfirst."

I couldn't help but chuckle as he smiled.

Shaun looked around. "This is really impressive."

"Thanks."

"I never imagined it could be like this. And you did it all by yourself."

"Don't let everyone who helped hear you say that."

"I don't mean this," he said, gesturing around the room, "I mean *this*." He extended his hands as if he were holding twenty-pound weights in them. "All of it. From day one. I could never do all this. It's so remote from academia."

"Not really," I said. "I see most of the same people. There's just no homework or grading."

"Don't you miss it? Ever?"

"Not really, but funny you should mention that. I'm filling in for a prof on maternity leave next semester. My old short story class."

"That's fantastic!"

His tone came off as patronizing. Then again, it had been a long day for me in pointy boots.

"Well, I've gotta get back to the customers."

He blinked rapidly for a second, as if someone spritzed him with water. "Of course you do. I'm sorry to keep you."

"Thanks for coming," I said, and started to walk away. Just then Scott came over to me, grabbed my face with both hands, and kissed me hard.

"Hey, baby," he said when he released me. From the corner of my eye, I saw Shaun take in Scott's costume with a mix of puzzlement and repulsion. He was dressed as Bender, the robot from the animated show *Futurama*, complete with gray long johns and a hoodie under a plastic gray trash bin, a ping-pong ball attached to a spring on his head as the antenna, and scuba goggles. In short, a disaster.

Scott looked at Shaun defiantly, as if to say, *She's mine*, and extended his hand. "What's up, dude." Shaun shook it, and Scott proceeded to put his arm around me while I fumed. I hated being called "baby," and this display of machismo was too much.

Shaun turned to me and said in blatant sarcasm, "Yeah, so you're obviously busy. I'll let you get back to work."

As soon as he walked away, I gripped Scott's arm and removed myself from its gray clutch, then turned and looked at him, disgusted.

"What the hell was that?" I asked.

"Me? What the hell was *that*?" he retorted, pointing in Shaun's direction, glaring from behind his scuba goggles. "What're you still talking to that loser for?"

"First of all, he is not a loser. Second of all, if you ever call me 'baby' again, you're gonna have to eat your food through a straw for a week, got it?"

"You're still not over him, are you."

"Jealousy doesn't become you, Scott."

"Whatever, dude."

"Call me 'dude' again and it'll be *two* weeks."

He looked like he wanted to hit something.

"I'll bet if Norman came to your rescue, your eyelashes would be fluttering in admiration."

"Rescue? What rescue? Don't think for a second that I needed any help. And leave Norman out of it."

"Fine. You're on your own today," he said. The ping-pong ball antenna thrashed from side to side with every step as he stormed out. I rolled my eyes and resumed my hosting duties.

Within minutes, Minerva sidled up to me. "You OK?"

"Just two more reminders of why I love singlehood, Min," I said after filling her in on what just happened.

She held the mini paper cup of vanilla chai in a toast. "I'll drink to that. For you, anyway." After she gulped the drink, she said, "Is this a bad time to tell you that I'll never be able to look at Bender the same again?"

"Me neither."

Norman appeared after Minerva walked away, two mini-cups of punch in hand, and I hoped this wasn't going to turn into a receiving line of all the Originals asking me if I was OK, if Scott and I just broke up, if I had anything to do with the design and construction of his costume, et cetera.

"How you holdin' up, kiddo?" Norman asked, handing me a cup. Funny he would call me that considering I was older than he was. I wondered if he knew Olivia used to call me that.

"We lost our free help," I said.

"No problem. He wasn't very helpful anyway. Was giving away multiple samples to the same customers. And he was frightening them with those goggles. Poor Bender."

"No wonder why we're running low. Knucklehead..." I muttered. Norman threw his head back and laughed out loud. Quite a sight, considering he was wearing Spock ears and a light purple T-shirt with a Z on it over a dark purple long-sleeved tee and blue jeans. ("No way you're getting me to wear a purple leotard," he said.) All day the clientele had mistaken him for Sheldon from *The Big Bang Theory* instead of Zan, which was fine by Norman.

"Can you imagine if we'd charged for all this shit today?" he asked in a hushed voice.

"We'd be looking at an empty space," I said.

"Maybe. Or maybe we could've closed the joint and ran off to Fiji together."

"What is it with you and Fiji?" I asked.

"Pipe dream," he answered.

"Make it a real one and I just may take you up on it."

We eyed each other, knowing what was coming, and fist-bumped. *"WONDER TWIN POWERS: ACTIVATE!"* We then clinked cups and downed our punch like shots.

The crowd finally started to thin out after the open mic, about an hour before closing. I leaned over the café counter and rested my head on my arms momentarily. Every muscle in my body was about to give out. Minerva came up from behind and put her hands just where my shoulders met the nape of my neck, kneading them hard. I picked up my head.

"Ow! Geez, Min! What're you giving me, the Vulcan Neck Pinch or something?"

"It'll feel good in a minute. I learned it in class."

"They teach you this in Midwifing 101?"

"Soft tissue manipulation."

"Which is Vulcan for…"

"Massage."

"Seriously, they teach you that?"

"It was an elective. It's good for the mothers when they're in labor." She continued with the treatment while I leaned back and closed my eyes.

"I'm glad you were here today, Min. And I can't thank you enough for helping out. You should sue me for what I'm paying you today."

"I would've done it for free. I don't know when it happened, but The Grounds became my baby, too."

I opened my eyes and turned to face her. "Consider yourself the honorary godmother," I said. She smiled that smile of quiet satisfaction. That Minerva smile. Then she looked past me, and her eyes filled with childlike excitement behind her Dr. Honeydew glasses. I turned around to see what she had fixed her gaze upon.

Kenny.

She ran around me and practically jumped into his arms. Dressed in a black thermal henley, baseball cap, and faded blue jeans, he laughed and hugged her tight as he turned his eyes to me. I approached him slowly, my joints creaking with each step.

"You OK there, Jayna?" he said to me.

"Do I know you?" I asked in mock seriousness.

"You look like you went twenty rounds with a cappuccino machine."

"And lost," Minerva added. "So?" she said to Kenny, playfully punching his upper arm, "what gives? Where've you been, stranger?"

"Yeah," I said, trying to act nonchalant. "What brings you here?"

"I was hoping you'd be dressed as a Robert Palmer girl."

I could only imagine the shade of pink my face was turning. Kenny kept his gaze on me.

"You missed a helluva blowout," I said.

"Nah, I was here earlier—you were busy being the hostess with the mostess."

"And you didn't come over to say hi? I'm insulted."

"Seriously, you were preoccupied."

Had he seen the conversation with Shaun, or the confrontation with Scott? Or both?

"The place looks awesome, Eva. You have a lot to be proud of."

My tired eyes brightened. "Thanks."

He pointed to the side of my head. "Your ear fell off."

I flinched, feeling for the remaining Spock ear before pulling it off. "Thanks."

He turned to Minerva. "Hey, can I talk to you for a sec?"

She raised an eyebrow. "Sure."

He took her by the arm and pulled her to his old corner. Itching to read their lips, I watched them in hushed chatter. He handed her a scrap of paper and a pen; she scrawled something and passed it back to him. I pretended to be busy pushing in chairs when they returned to me.

"Well hey, I gotta go," said Kenny. "Sorry to keep it so short."

"That's OK," I lied. "You two take care of business?"

Did I sound as jealous as I was? I wondered.

"Yeah. Thanks, Min," he said to Minerva.

Min? He called her Min?

"No problem," she said. "See you, Kenny." He looked at me while he hugged her again, a flood of words behind his hazel eyes, but I couldn't decipher them any more than I could read his lips moments ago.

"Seeya," he said. I couldn't tell if the words were directed to me, or her, or both of us.

"Thanks for coming," I said, the phrase on autopilot now.

"Wouldn't have missed it for the world." I watched him do a low-five handshake with Norman before leaving. Then I turned to Minerva, hands on my hips.

"*Min?*" I said.

"What," she replied.

"I don't think I've even heard Jay ever call you Min."

She mirrored me, putting her hands on her hips. "Seriously, Eva, you think you own the rights to it?"

"What did he want?"

"He needed a referral for a graphic designer and wanted the name of my friend who did the design for all The Grounds stuff."

At the last second, her forced focus fell off my eyes, and I pounced.

"Then why did he have to ask you out of earshot?"

"He didn't wanna have to get into why he wanted it."

"Did he tell *you*?"

"Not in so many words. 'New project,' was all he said."

"And you gave him her number?"

"Um, actually, I gave him my number and told him to call me later so I could give it to him."

Minerva was a crappy liar. Why did he *really* want her number? Minerva and Kenny had always been friendly with each other whenever he came to the café, nothing more. Perhaps he just wanted to catch up with her. But why the secrecy?

For a fleeting moment, I considered the possibility that they were planning an affair. Despite their playfulness today, it was obvious that things were far from blissful in the Brunswick marriage. I suppose every marriage goes through peaks and valleys, and it seemed that as of late, Min and Jay's had been passing through valley after valley.

No. She would never betray Jay. Not with Kenny or anyone else. I admonished myself for letting the thought even enter my mind.

Five minutes before closing, Norman and I sat together on one of the new couches, exhausted, my head on his shoulder as the last of the customers straggled out. Minerva flopped down on the other side of him. Instantly, Jay appeared.

"Mee mee mee *mee*."

Min drew in a breath, and with momentous effort, stood up.

"Jay wants to go."

Finally, after closing and locking the doors behind them, I turned and leaned against them and faced Norman.

"I can't deal with cleaning or closing out tonight," I said. "Let's just blow the place up."

27

Admit It

THANKFULLY, SUSANNA OFFERED to open The Grounds the following morning since we had all pulled iron-shifts the day before. Norman dragged himself in at twelve, while I staggered in around two. Minerva didn't come in at all. You'd think we'd been out drinking all night, the way we were dragging our bodies around, popping aspirin, asking customers to speak slowly.

"I'm getting too old for this shit," Norman and I whispered to each other repeatedly all day.

Scott came in late that afternoon. He looked marginally better without the dopey costume. Truth be told, he looked like hell—hair matted, eyes bloodshot, face unshaven and dark, shirt wrinkled. We'd not spoken to each other since our fight at the party. Granted, I'd been asleep during much of the elapsed time, but he'd left a voice mail and texted me twice.

"Hey, Eva," he said.

"What's up," I replied, avoiding eye contact with him.

"You never called me back."

"I never knew you called," I lied.

"I left messages."

"I went into a coma the minute I got home."

He started to come behind the counter until he saw the look of death I gave him—aside from Minerva, *no one* came behind my counter uninvited. Not even God herself.

"Look, can I just talk to you alone without the whole damn world listening in on us?"

I huffed and looked at Norman, raising my eyebrows, and excused myself. Then I led Scott into the office.

"You seem to forget that this is my place of business," I said in a hushed voice. "That I *work* here. I can't just drop everything on a whim for you."

"You do for everyone else."

"Let's not get into this right now."

"I just wanna say I'm sorry, OK? It was a stupid thing to do yesterday. But dammit, it makes me crazy to see you talk to him."

It took me a moment to register who "him" was.

"You mean Shaun?"

"Who else?"

"You have nothing to be jealous of, Scott. It's long over with Shaun. You know that."

"You just deserve so much better than him."

"I have better than him."

The sad thing for Scott, unbeknownst to him, was that I was referring not to him but to Minerva and Jay, Norman, The Grounds, Olivia. What's more, I hadn't been able to stop thinking about Kenny. *That look* he'd given me right before he left.

"Are we cool now?" asked Scott.

"Yeah," I said, refraining from a display of affection. "Now let me get back to work before I crawl under my desk and take a nap."

To my surprise, Scott left while I was in the kitchen. When I came out to find him gone, I looked at Norman.

"Said he had work to do." Norman then looked at me as if to say, *Everything OK?*

I nodded and rolled my eyes.

"He could've at least given you flowers," said Norman.

I burst out laughing.

Dating Rules Addendum: Rule #7

Male or female, it is not cliché to give your sweetheart flowers after a fight. Daisies'll do. Or a single rose. Or one of those bouquets that the grocery stores sell. It's not so much the action as much as the thought behind the action. It's hard *not* to smile upon the sight of flowers. Unless you've done something monumentally stupid, like cheating or committing a felony, flowers are always appreciated.

But afterthoughts don't count. If the moment's over, it's over. Save it for next time. Better yet, shoot for no next times.

～ↄ

Our grand reopening of the new and improved reading room attracted new business while the Originals and Regulars remained fixtures. Minerva was still helping out twice a week, although she was also making plans to go to hairdressing school despite my attempts to talk her out of it. She already owned a pair of good sheers and had been cutting Jay's hair since they met. In typical Minerva form, she thoroughly researched the schools in central and southeastern Carolina, visiting each one and comparing costs and services and job placement records following graduation. The Aveda Institute in Chapel Hill was her favorite, but she knew it would involve moving, and even though Jay offered to relocate, she didn't want to. She interviewed local salon owners to find out which schools they preferred and why (and even started working at one salon two days a week as a receptionist) before selecting Carolina Cosmetology School three towns over. She registered for the next rotating session, to begin in two months, giving her plenty of time to change her mind without losing her deposit, I told her. But she *seemed* certain. She was determined, if nothing else.

In preparation for her eventual departure and my teaching job in a couple of months, Norman took on the responsibility of hiring another full-timer—we were long overdue for one. He was meticulous about finding the "right" person, which I appreciated. What's more, Norman had started dating a woman he'd met at the Halloween party: Jeannie with the Jimmy Choos, we called her. Actually, she was Drop Dead Gorgeous Jeannie with the Jimmy Choos. The men couldn't stop looking at her long legs; the women couldn't stop looking at her shoes. She came to the open mic and blew the doors off with a short Southern fiction piece that had everyone in stitches. Minerva and I much preferred Jeannie to Samurai—she was smart, sassy, and stylish, thus we gave Norman our blessing.

Scott and I made up following the confrontation with Shaun and the opening and went back to our usual pattern of hanging out after work, mostly watching DVDs from Netflix before going to bed. Lately I'd been falling asleep on the couch midway through the movie, exhausted. But Scott never seemed to mind. He'd keep his arm around me while I rested my head on his shoulder, and oftentimes he'd carry me to bed (unless it was just easier to leave me on the couch), kissing my forehead good night.

My business was thriving. My friends were content. My relationship was back on track. In short, everything was just right.

Everything except me.

"I'm exhausted," I said to Minerva one day while we sat at a table during a break and picked at the same blueberry muffin. "Do you think I'm just burned out?" I asked.

"Maybe you have an iron deficiency or something," she replied. "When was the last time you got a checkup?"

"About six months ago."

"Then you should go again. Go to the lab where I interned. They're the only place from where I could have blood drawn without going green and feeling woozy."

I pushed the muffin plate toward her, signaling that I'd had enough.

"You could be pregnant," she suggested.

"Oh, please don't say that. Not even as a joke."

"When was the last time you, you know, got your monthly bill?"

I laughed. "Is that an official medical term?"

"Well?"

I didn't dignify her question with a response. "What if it's not a physical condition?"

Minerva tilted her head so as to peer at me from above her horn-rimmed glasses instead of through them.

"Eva, can I ask you something without you getting mad at me?"

Of course, at this request, my insides tightened as I sat up straight. "Would it stop you if I said no?"

"Are you happy with Scott?"

"What do you mean?"

"You know what I mean. It seems like you've been going through the motions with him since day one."

Despite her soft tones and worried eyes, I was offended. "What, I'm supposed to have some gooey, I'm-in-love look plastered on my face twenty-four-seven?"

Minerva looked at me matter-of-factly. "Well, yeah."

I crumpled the napkin I'd been toying with and tossed it next to the plate. "You know, I've decided that the whole 'romance' thing is overrated. It goes away. No romance ever truly lasts. Show me a couple who's just as romantic as the way they were the day they met."

She extended her hand, as if for me to shake it. "Minerva Brunswick, pleased to meet you."

I refused her hand and gave her a skeptical look, wondering if she was ignoring the obvious tension between her and Jay, in denial, or merely trying to prove a point.

"I mean a long-term couple," I said. "Twenty years in. Did you know that my parents almost didn't make it that long? And that's the reason my mother had given me. She said when the romance died, so did the marriage. And I thought, 'How freakin' stupid.' She didn't even know my father well enough when she married him to determine whether he'd be a good friend. It took her getting sick for them to fall in love with each other all over again and to figure out who they really were. That's why I look for my best friend above all else. Like you and Jay."

Minerva studied me intently.

"Wow," she said, her tone serious. "That explains a lot."

"Explains what?"

"I just never thought of it that way."

"How did you think of it?" I asked.

"I thought he had a kick-ass poem. And I thought he was attractive."

"Well geez, Min, that that clears it all up."

Minerva looked at her watch. "Break's over."

Frustrated, I went back behind the counter, unable to dispel the deadweight that seemed to have taken root in my stomach sometime during our conversation. About an hour later, before she left, Minerva came out of the reading room and behind the counter.

"By the way, Kenny says hi."

My heart lurched into my throat. He'd gone back into hiding since the party, and it took all my resolve not to ask Min for his number and call him myself.

"When did you talk to him?" I asked. It came out more like an interrogation than a question.

"He called me," she replied.

"You two have gotten very cozy lately."

"He's a friend."

"He'd be mine, too, if he started coming back to the shop. What, did he find a Starbucks that he likes better?"

She shuddered. "Eiw. No. He's just really busy. He's starting a new business."

"Well, when he wants to tell me about it, he can come in and tell me about it," I said, not even trying to hide my disappointment this time.

Minerva shot me a sly look. "Admit it. You like him. Just own up and go do something about it."

My mouth dropped open. Before I could even draw a breath, Scott came in and approached us, and I found myself glad that he didn't want to kiss me hello.

"How's it goin'?" he asked after Minerva left. I shrugged in response.

"Tired," I said, disappointed by my own predictability. "As usual."

I filled his order and brought it to his table.

"Hey, why don't we go out to dinner tonight after I get done here and take my shower," I suggested. "We haven't done that in a long time."

"It's Thursday, Eva. Must-See-TV night? New episodes of *The Office* and *30 Rock*."

"So? We'll TiVo them. Come on, I'll get dressed up and everything. I'll even wear those red stilettos you love so much," I wheedled and coaxed. He picked up his head from his laptop and looked at me to consider this.

"Wear them during *30 Rock* and things could get really interesting."

I became annoyed. "Scott, I'm asking you to go out with me tonight. I don't ask for much. When was the last time we did anything that didn't have commercial interruptions or a rewind button? When was the last time we went out on an actual date?"

Come to think of it, had we *ever* been on an actual date?

He got visibly annoyed as well. "You know, you're not the only one who works hard. Just because I work from home and get to sit most of the day doesn't mean I don't get tired. Honestly, Eva, you have no idea what kind of work I do, or how it makes my head hurt sometimes. Sometimes I don't wanna do anything that requires more thinking than 'pass the salt.' Sometimes I'm shot, too."

I faltered for a moment; he'd always been so laid back it never occurred to me that his work was stressful.

Ashamed of my oversight, I tried again. "I'm not asking you to rewrite the Constitution; I'm asking you to *dinner*."

"Tomorrow, OK? I'll take you anywhere you want to go."

"Yeah," I got up from the table and started to walk away, deflated. "Sure."

That night, as Scott and I sat on the couch watching *The Office*, I tried not to think about all that Minerva had said. What did she really mean by *that explains a lot*? I leaned against Scott, my hair still damp, and closed my eyes. Then I opened them and looked at him for a second and it hit me: *This isn't going to work. Ever.*

28

Coming Apart

FOR THE SECOND day in a row, I kept my eyes peeled on the front doors, hoping Kenny would amble in and up to the counter like he used to. My heart nearly leapt out of my chest when, while filling a customer's order, I caught a glimpse of a black henley shirt out of the corner of my eye and thought it was him (and sank even deeper in my chest upon realizing it was someone else).

Also for the second day in a row, my body dragged in lethargy, and I chalked it up to the post-party crash, my adrenaline reserves spent, not to mention the revelation I'd had the night before that my days with Scott were numbered. Sitting in the back office during my lunch break, I poked at my salad and checked my phone for messages. Hardly anyone other than Scott or Olivia ever called me, mainly because just about everyone I knew was a Grounds customer, but the ritual was a way to kill time in the dingy little office when I was too tired to read or too busy to hang out with the Originals. To my surprise, my phone signaled that a voice mail awaited me, and I studied it with curiosity as I proceeded to play the message. Ed Rush, sounding stoic and serious, asked me to call him. At first I thought that perhaps he'd found someone else to cover for Jenna's short story class next semester, someone within the department, and didn't need me after all, but his voice sounded too urgent for that.

I dialed the English department number—I still had it memorized—and Ed's secretary picked up on the second ring before connecting me to him.

"Hello, Eva," he said, the tone of his voice matching the one in the phone message.

"Hi, Ed," I replied. "What's up?"

"We've got a little emergency here. As of yesterday, Jenna Jaffe was ordered to go on immediate bed rest. Apparently there's something wrong."

I took in a breath. "Is she OK? Is the baby?"

"Both she and the baby will be just fine if she follows the doctor's orders to a tee."

I breathed a sigh of relief.

"So what can I do to help?" I asked.

"I need you to fill in for Jenna for the remainder of the semester, if you can."

Before I could raise an objection or even get a word in, Ed steamrolled on. "We're in a real crunch with budget cuts and salary reductions here. Most of the faculty are already over-loaded with course schedules and classroom enrollment caps. I know you've already spoken to Jenna regarding next semester's agenda, which isn't too different from this one. Please, Eva, it would really help us out. She's already cancelled this week's class, and there's only four weeks left of the semester, two after Thanksgiving break. And of course we'll compensate you for it."

Money was the last thing I was thinking of. Since deciding to host Thanksgiving for the first time here in Wilmington and proposing it to Olivia, all I could think about was trying to pre-pare the house for company, cook food, and entertain my guests. And that was without considering how busy The Grounds got during the holidays, when students would camp out and cram for finals or finish writing term papers as a change of venue from the library or their dorm rooms. Besides, ever since the makeover and the party, the reading room was filled to capacity. Still, I was torn—I didn't want to leave Jenna or Ed in a lurch.

"Ed, it's not that I don't want to help you out. I just…I need to work it out with my manager. It's a busy time of year for us, and I don't want to throw him to the wolves."

He sighed in frustration, and I understood all too well that it had little to do with what I'd just said and everything to do with the sum-total weight of responsibilities that he juggled on a daily basis as the department chairperson. This was only the latest fire he had to put out, one in a line of fires.

"I understand," he said, "and I wouldn't pressure you if we weren't in such a jam. But I really need an answer ASAP," he said, pronouncing it "ay-sap."

"Can you give me an hour or two?" I asked.

"Sure. That would be great."

"OK, then I'll speak to you in an hour. Do you know if Jenna is taking any calls?"

"As far as I know, yes."

Despite his answer, I had the nagging feeling that she shouldn't be disturbed. As I ended the phone call with Ed, I returned the Tupperware lid to my salad and pushed it away, my appetite replaced by a to-do list twirling in my gut like a tornado.

I exited the office and returned to the café to find it nearly empty, the lunch rush subsided, save Neil (who lately had been staying well past his twenty minutes) and Jan on her lunch break in festive Snoopy and Woodstock scrubs. Minerva had also arrived and was wiping down tables, while Norman was leaning against the back counter, taking a breather.

"Hey, Norman, can I talk to you for a sec?"

"Sure."

I went to one of the tables and sat down, where Norman joined me, a look of concern on his face.

"So I just spoke to Ed Rush on the phone, and it turns out that Jenna Jaffe has a problem with the pregnancy and needs immediate bed rest."

Just as the words "bed rest" left my mouth, I heard a quiet gasp behind me, and I didn't have to turn my head to know it came from Minerva.

"What's wrong?" he asked. "Do they know?"

"He didn't say."

"*Placenta previa*," I heard Minerva utter under her breath, barely loud enough for me or anyone else to hear.

I turned around in my seat. "What did you say?"

"Sorry, I didn't mean to eavesdrop." I waved a hand, dismissing her concern. "It's most likely placenta previa," said Minerva. "It's when part of the placenta detaches from the uterine wall."

Norman's face went pale as she continued.

"It's usually minor, but he means it when he says she needs *immediate* bed rest. If she puts any stress on her body, the tear can get bigger, she can lose blood, basically succumb to internal bleeding, and the baby could suffocate."

"Oh *God*, Min," I said in horror.

"Really, she'll be fine as long as she stays in bed and is as immobile as possible, getting up just to use the bathroom and shower. She'll even carry to term and the baby will come out just fine, but they'll likely have to do a C-section."

"I think I need a glass of water," said Norman.

I went behind the counter and soaked a clean dishtowel under the sink, wrung it out, and folded it in a long rectangular shape, applying it to Norman's forehead.

"Wow, Norman," said Minerva. "I had no idea you were so squeamish. What are you going to do when your wife gets pregnant?"

"Geez, Minerva, I gotta crawl before I can walk, ya know? Let's just see if Jeannie and I make it past the three-date mark."

"Anyway," I said, glad at least that Norman's color was returning, "I need to fill in for her for the remainder of this semester, and I wanted to make sure it was OK with you."

"Why wouldn't it be OK?"

"It's a lot of work, Norman, and it's the holiday season. You know how it gets around here."

"Look," Minerva said, taking a seat, "I'll fill in the missing hours, if that's your biggest concern. Eva, you can't not do this."

"She's right," said Norman. "It's only for a few weeks. We can pick up the slack. You've put in fifty- and sixty-hour weeks here long enough. It's time for me to take one for the team. Really, I want to help out."

I kissed him on the cheek, and felt the cold, damp towel stick to my hair as I did so.

"You're too much, Norman, you know that?" I said.

"Maybe you can get Jenna to name the baby after me."

"It's a girl," I said.

He paused to consider this. "Bailey is a nice girl's name."

I smiled in agreement. "So, Drop Dead Gorgeous Jeannie with the Jimmy Choos..."

"Lordy, that's a mouthful."

"Three dates?"

"Third one's tonight."

"Looking good?"

He held up his hands to reveal crossed fingers.

"I hope it works out, Norman. You deserve happiness."

"Yeah, singlehood really isn't my thing. Not that there's anything wrong with it…"

"Yeah yeah yeah…" I patted him on the shoulder and went back to the office to call Ed back. He thanked me profusely, apologizing for the last-minute ambush and offering me Jenna's office on campus for course preparation and any other administrative tasks I'd need to handle.

"Jenna will be very relieved," said Ed. "It'll be one less thing for her to worry about. I'm confident I'm speaking for her as well when I say the course is in good hands."

I smiled, and my eyes stung. It was if my parents had just told me that they were proud of me, and I couldn't help but wonder in that instant if they would be proud of the life I'd made. Would they approve of my being a coffee shop owner, an entrepreneur, or would my father be disappointed that I didn't stay in teaching? Would my mother have preferred I'd settled down with a family of my own, like Olivia? Would it have even taken me so long to figure out what I wanted to do had they not passed away? Would I have followed the same path?

In that instant I felt lost at sea, alone and adrift, the boat bobbing up and down, and I clasped the edge of the desk to steady myself. I could hear Norman's voice echoing, *Singlehood really isn't my thing*, followed by, *Not that there's anything wrong with it*…trying to figure out which one applied to me.

⤳

Scott arrived carrying two bags of Chinese food takeout, and as I ritually retrieved two plates from the cabinets and two beers from the fridge, he sorted and opened the boxes, trying to make small talk with me. When he'd had enough of my one-word answers, he asked why I was so quiet.

"Just thinking of everything that's been goin' on, I guess," I replied, filling him in on Ed Rush's call and Jenna's condition.

"You've been burning the candle at both ends, huh," he said. I nodded. Looking down at the food, I immediately lost my appetite.

"I'm sorry, I can't eat any of this."

I took him by the hands and led him out of the kitchen and outside to the deck. I sat on the patio chair and stared out into the horizon, trying to avoid saying the words. Scott sat in the adjacent chair, waiting.

"Just say it, Eva," he said after the silence had passed long enough. His tone was neither demanding nor impatient. I was pretty sure he knew what I wanted to say, and he was giving me permission to say it. Or perhaps he just wanted it to be over with, like ripping a bandage off in one fell swoop.

"I can't do this anymore," I said, my voice soft, yet matter-of-fact.

"I know," he replied in the same tone. "I've known it for a while. I was just hoping you'd change your mind."

"I should've talked to you about it sooner, told you it wasn't working out."

"Yeah, you probably should've. But I don't know that I would've listened. I would've tried to convince you to give it more time."

"We both know I didn't get into this with you for the right reasons. And even if it hadn't been on a rebound, even if you'd asked me out conventionally, or if I didn't know you and replied to your Lovematch-dot-com ad, it still wouldn't have been for the right reasons."

"Was it about him?" he said, not mentioning Shaun by name.

I shook my head. "It goes back further than Shaun. It was about *me*. I thought I was in such a good place when I wrote that first WILS essay."

"Was it a lie?"

"Not exactly. I'd rationalized that I was doing just fine, when all I was doing was distracting myself from wanting all the people I'd lost to come back to me."

"A lot of people care about you, you know," said Scott. "Including me."

"Oh, I know that, and I care about you, too. I just...I don't... I don't feel the way you're supposed to feel when you're in love with someone." I could hear Shaun saying those same words to me, almost verbatim. "I'm so sorry. I wish I didn't have to hurt you like that. I've been on your end of that statement before, and I know how crappy it feels."

He looked down. "It's OK," he said, and I could tell that he was forcing the words. "I know you're not trying to be mean or intentionally malicious or anything like that. It's just the cold, hard truth, that's all." He studied his hands for a moment. "It does suck, though."

"Yeah, it does," I agreed.

"I'm sorry I couldn't give you what you needed," he said.

"Same here."

Scott stared past the backyard, beyond the trees.

"Do you know we never went to the beach together?" He pointed outward in the direction of the beach. "I mean, it's right there, right at our fingertips, and we never took advantage of it."

"I know," I said. "I used to be that way with New York City. I grew up about an hour away by train and could go in any time

I wanted. And because of that accessibility, I took it for granted, thinking that it would always be there, whole and unchanged."

"We should have gone to the beach," he said.

We sat on the deck for a while, saying nothing and avoiding eye contact. I felt my hand slip into his, almost without my willing it to, and we stayed like that even longer, still silent. His hand felt warm in mine, a lifeline of some kind. Perhaps it was to keep me from falling into my own reverie with a picture of an incomplete skyline, a portrait with two missing faces, a future with no way to come back.

Finally, Scott stood up.

"I should go."

I stood up as well. "Yeah. Wanna take the food with you?"

"You can have it. I've lost my appetite, too," he said sadly.

"Have it for breakfast tomorrow," I offered. "At least take the Kung Pao—it's your favorite."

He looked at me and a smile escaped him, followed by one of my own, and we embraced. It was a moment of genuine caring and knowing we'd both be OK.

"Thanks, Eva," he practically whispered.

I whispered back, "You gave me exactly what I needed. You really did. I just didn't need it for that long."

We continued to hold each other.

"Does this mean I have to stop coming to The Grounds?" he asked. He almost sounded like a little boy. "Please say it doesn't. I don't want to end up like Jan and Dean."

I squeezed tighter. "Of course not—your friends are there."

He let go and looked me directly in the eye. "Are you one of them?"

I couldn't help but look away, regretting it instantly. He looked down, utterly defeated, as pangs of guilt washed over me.

I thought about the charade with Shaun—how many months I'd clung to a fake friendship under my self-induced false pretense that it would return to something more. Shaun must have known on some level that I still loved him, must have seen the desperation and longing for him that I failed to hide—after all, everyone else could—and pretended not to. No. I wasn't going to put Scott through that. Hell, I wouldn't wish it on my worst enemy.

I resumed eye contact. "I really want to be," I started, "but I have no idea what that means."

My answer took me by surprise.

"It means we don't hate each other," he said before tacking on, "and we don't go out of our way to avoid each other, either."

"It should also mean that we don't pretend things aren't awkward for a while," I said, "or that things could ever go back to the way they were before, as if we never had a sexual relationship."

"A damn good sexual relationship," he pointed out.

I agreed with a chuckle. "Yes indeed."

He took in a quick, deep breath. "OK, then. I'll just get whatever stuff I have here and let myself out."

He turned to reenter the house, but abruptly stopped and whisked around.

"This may sound totally stupid, but this is probably the best breakup I've ever had. Thanks."

I let out a contorted laugh, not knowing what else to do. "You're welcome," I said.

He extracted his keys from the front pocket of his jeans, removed one from the ring, and extended it to me. I took it from him and stayed out on the deck, the key tucked tightly in my fist, until I heard the front door close and his car pull away from the driveway.

Which side of the door are you on?

I've heard the expression, "When God closes a door, She opens a window." But what if there was no God or no windows? If there was just a door, which side would you be on?

One side puts you in the open world, the place full of possibilities—new faces, new places, new ideas and experiences at your fingertips. In the wake of a breakup, that world is a scary place—so vast, so unexplored, so far from your little patch of land where you know every corner and crevice and could navigate your way around with your eyes closed. And it's so easy to linger there, to stay close to it, hanging out by the fence with the hopes that you'll get back inside again. I know; I've been there.

Or you can be on the other side of the door—the side that keeps you trapped inside the box, a prison of your own making. One without locks, but you don't dare step outside. I've been there, too.

I ended a relationship today, and although I'm the one who closed the door, I can't help but feel like I'm on the other side. Only this time, I want to go out into that vastness, go exploring, step outside the box. The word *single* conjures up feelings of solitude, aloneness. No wonder some people think singlehood is a sucky place to be. Few people want to be alone, especially if they've been with someone else for a long time. They don't want to venture out into that big world all by themselves.

But young birds would never learn to fly if their mothers (or in my case, sister) didn't push them out of their nest. They need to use their wings.

I didn't close the door on him; I opened the door for me. And this time, I pushed myself out of the nest, and my shaky, fragile wings are spread. Who knows where they'll take me. Or you.

29

Thanksgiving

I'D SPENT THE morning and early afternoon in a hectic whirl—every movement toward the greater goal of a family-style Thanksgiving. I typed up a schedule of events that was invaluable—both a to-do list and timetable that I checked and double-checked throughout the morning while the Macy's Parade marched on in the background.

Once upon a time I'd looked forward to the days when I would have a family and host dinner parties and family get-togethers at my own house. Too young to see beyond my idealistic world, I'd imagined myself in a red checkered apron, smiling at my doting husband (presumably either Michael J. Fox or any one of the cast of *The Outsiders*) and setting outstretched dining tables with a spread deserving of magazine feature photos. And yet, year after year it just seemed to make more sense for me to go to Olivia's rather than host my own Thanksgiving, even when I'd been with Shaun.

So last month, when I'd decided to do just that (the thought of hosting a *family* dinner thrilled me to the core), I'd enthusiastically made a list of ten guests (myself included) and called them one by one, starting with Olivia. She hedged at first, complaining about flight and hotel arrangements, but seemed to warm up to the idea.

"I'd love to not have to deal with all that crap this year," she said.

I winced at the word *crap*—since when did having family over amount to crap?—and Olivia seemed to have picked up on it. "I mean," she backpedaled, "I'd love to help you out."

"Yeah, that'd be great," I answered, already excited at the thought of a full house.

Minerva and Jay had declined on account of her suggesting that they spend the holiday with Jay's parents. I think it was her idea of penance for the Cici incident. I understood and silently hoped that she wasn't setting herself up for another failure.

Beulah also politely declined on account of other plans. I'd never actually talked to Beulah about the letter she'd sent me, or responded to it. But since then we'd had an unspoken bond, a communication without words that invoked a mutual understanding. It was as if we "got" each other, and giving voice to it would've been redundant. So when the look in her eyes told me that she'd be spending the holiday with Lily (their first in years), I couldn't be happier for her.

Scott had also been on the guest list, but for obvious reasons, that invitation never went out. Norman, however, was looking forward to it just as much as I was (it was too early in his relationship with Jeannie for them to be spending major holidays together, he explained) and even offered to bring dessert.

OK, so it wasn't going to be the extended dining table. But six would suffice.

I'd been in my kitchen two nights before with Mom's battered copy of *The Joy of Cooking*, the bible of all cookbooks, complete with singed corners marking the failed flambé and a rather ominous brown stain on page 483. Flipping it open with a dull thud on the counter, I'd fanned through the pages, but instead of seeing the parade of recipes march before my eyes, I saw the parade of Thanksgivings past, smelled the sour pan drippings for the gravy, heard Dad's and Olivia's laughter above the hum of beaters. Motivated by memory, I listed of all the classics and necessities: turkey, stuffing, and potatoes (of course), cranberry sauce in a can, green bean casserole, and, to add a Southern flair, biscuits, cornbread, sweet potato pie, and fried corn.

As I'd preheated and prepped, mixed and stirred, braised and baked and boiled, I tried to pin down exactly what made our family dinners so *us.* I wanted to re-create all the silly traditions that made our family unique, to feel some semblance of having a family unit again. When setting the table (a yard sale find when I was with Shaun, polished into something of a well-loved antique), I tried to recall every golden turkey, every crowded place setting, every pie-induced bellyache of my family's history, but I came up short. The more I thought about it, the more I remembered how mad Mom got whenever Dad snagged a bite of whatever she was prepping. How Dad was never pleased with that year's turkey, perpetually convinced that he'd bought the previous year's someplace better. How by the end of dinner we were so tired it hurt to speak to one another, much less peel ourselves off whatever couch or chair we'd collapsed into to face dishwashing. How I always tried to negotiate with Mom regarding leftovers: fewer hot turkey sandwiches awash with undeserving bread, more potato pancakes.

The lack of more pleasant memories disturbed me.

I had finished preparations with twenty minutes to spare—a miracle! The table set, turkey happily roasting away (as happy as a dead bird could be, I suppose), I changed out of my sweats and T-shirt, running a mental checklist.

As Olivia and crew arrived, followed by Norman, I doled out hugs and hellos, remembering the ritual when we were kids: our parents, Olivia, and I standing at the door like a receiving line at a wedding as aunts and uncles and cousins processed in with covered dishes and bottles of wine. Just like Thanksgivings past, we all congregated in the cozy kitchen. Olivia sliced the French bread she had brought and set it in a basket, and I tucked Norman's infamous seven layer bars (the only thing he knew how to bake, which he described as "so good, why bother learning to make anything else?") out of eyesight from Tyler and Tara.

At dinnertime, as the hungry pack grazed from kitchen to dining room, Olivia laughed at the Mayflower place cards made from cracked walnut shells (it wasn't as fun to make them by myself as when we were kids, the Elmer's glue running down our arms and on the tablecloth, to Mom's dismay). But, like a tickle in the back of my throat, the inability to conjure a truly happy family memory nagged at me as we passed platters and dishes and bowls around, each of us holding one as the next scooped heaping portions onto already brimming plates. Only the green bean casserole dish remained heavy by the time it circled back to me. I looked at it in dismay—we'd always had green bean casserole. Taking a generous scoop in an attempt to mollify the green bean gods, I scanned the plates: Olivia and David hadn't taken any; Tara had pushed a few forkfuls to the far outskirts of her plate just to please her mother; and Tyler outright refused, suspiciously eyeing the dish as if it might attack, like something straight out of Calvin & Hobbs. Norman had taken a tentative scoop and politely ingested a miniscule forkful. He managed to swallow without so much as a wince, but followed the bite with an immediate chug of cider.

The serving spoon was still poised in my hand, hovering above my plate, when I suddenly saw the monstrosity as it was: stringy, French-cut frozen green beans swimming in cream of mushroom soup. Awful.

"Blegh," I said. "Green bean casserole? What was I thinking? Liv, was it always this bad?"

"Worse," Olivia laughed. "I think the panko upgrade is a nice touch. As much class as it could hope for."

"I like it," Norman said.

All heads turned to him.

"The crust, I mean."

"What was the crust before?" David asked, giving the casserole a dubious look.

"Funions," Olivia answered.

We all looked at each other in horror before bursting into laughter. I surveyed the faces around the table, faces I'd seen primarily at work or on bank holidays. They were faces of people I loved, sure, but I couldn't help but feel as if Olivia and I had forfeited sisterhood when I filed taxes as an independent North Carolina resident. Following our parents' deaths, she and I went to aunts and uncles' or cousins' houses before she started hosting her own gatherings with her nuclear family and sometimes David's. One year, when David's parents hosted, they invited me knowing I had nowhere else to go. I'd felt so guilty accepting their pity. The memory still left a bitter taste in my mouth, masked by the perfectly mashed potatoes and the twice baked stuffing, although I felt somewhat bolstered as Norman took a polite second helping of the fated casserole, despite not touching it.

Norman. He was the one with whom I shared the most meals, regardless of whether we were eating BLTs (no mayo) behind The Grounds's counter, out of sight from the customers; sitting on stools in the kitchen with nachos and salsa delivered by the NCLA campus food court; or grabbing slices of Greek pizza while crammed in our cluttered office. He probably could read me best out of anyone here, maybe even out of anyone at all, save Minerva. After turning down my invitation, Minerva had secretly confessed to me that she'd rather have dinner with my family than Jay's, or even her own. And I knew she included Norman with Olivia, et al., in "family." Drowning my turkey in a lumpy river of gravy, I imagined how Minerva must feel sitting at a table full of people with whom the only thing she shared was her husband and name. And yet, I could almost relate. Just like the speed dating night, Norman was the one at the table who made me feel most at ease. Olivia had even pulled me into the pantry prior to dinner to ask about Norman's and my relationship status.

"He's cute," she remarked. "Very John Cusack."

"Not happenin', Liv."

Throughout the meal, as Olivia tended to Tyler and Tara while David and Norman talked college football and steered clear of politics and religion, I couldn't help but wonder if this was as good as it gets.

After dinner David turned on the TV to watch football and Norman offered to help us with the dishes. I shook my head, sticking a bottle of beer in his hand and pushing him into the other room. He looked at it, then me, as if I'd handed him a strange torture device.

"After all that food I ate, you're giving me a *beer*?"

My dad always had a beer following the big meal. It just seemed natural, involuntary, to hand one to Norman.

"I don't have any room left," he said. "One sip of this and I may explode."

"So don't drink it. I just thought you might like it."

He grinned and gave my shoulders a quick squeeze. "Dinner was fantastic, Eva. Show-stopping."

He twisted the cap off the beer bottle—I always loved that crisp *pfft* sound it made—and toasted me with it. "Thanks."

Olivia and I had always been on Dish Patrol when we were younger, and it seemed only fitting to carry on that tradition, too. We stood side by side and settled into a rhythm in front of the double-sink—one filled with Palmolive-sudsy water, the other with pots and pans and dishes and flatware, the dishwasher waiting for us to cram as much as we could into it.

"It wasn't perfect, was it."

"Dinner?" Olivia asked, dunking a large pot. "I thought it was great." She hesitated. "Except for the casserole..."

I shook my head, rinsing off a stray serving spoon. "No. I mean you and Mom and Dad and me. Our family. *We* weren't perfect."

"Oh," she said. "No, we weren't."

"What did we fight about?"

She shrugged. "All sorts of stupid things. The stuff everyone fights about." Olivia scrubbed at a bit of already-dried mashed potato. "Remember the time you stole my bra and I caught you wearing it stuffed with a pair of my socks?"

I cringed and laughed at the same time. "The one with the pink hearts? Yeah, sorry about that, Liv."

She laughed as well. "It was my favorite. I could've killed you."

"Was that before or after you read the notes Beth and I passed in class out loud—at the top of your lungs, mind you—while walking home from the bus?"

"After," she said. "Might've been what prompted it."

"I was so mad I cried."

She nodded. "I remember."

"And remember the time you hung Lacy Stevenson's underwear from the tree outside and Dad was mortified?"

She laughed even harder. "She always left something at our house after a sleepover. Seriously gross."

I giggled, remembering her feeble explanation. "You just wanted to air it out—"

"Yeah, and leave it somewhere where she could find it." Olivia paused to hand me the now de-potatoed pot. "I don't know if Dad was more upset that it was hanging in his front yard, or that it was black and silky."

"Poor Dad."

Unable to fit the pot in the dishwasher, I set it aside as Olivia continued. "How about the time when Mom got offered that big promotion and Dad didn't want her to take it?"

I stiffened. "I'd forgotten all about that."

Our mother had been an executive administrative assistant. Not just a secretary, but one of those I-can't-live-without-you assistants. An organizer extraordinaire. Sometimes she worked nights and weekends, much to Dad's objection, although Olivia and I handled cooking responsibilities far better than he did, even when we were twelve and sixteen years old.

The promotion was for vice president of something or other, and would've meant a company car, an extra month's vacation time, a huge bump in salary, and a lot of travel. But our dad had put his foot down. I couldn't remember why, although I seem to remember the word *neglect* in the midst of angry exchanges.

"They didn't speak for a week and a half, I think," said Olivia.

"God, dinner that week must've sucked."

"Mom stopped eating at the table after the third night."

How had my memory so completely failed me?

"What happened?" I asked.

Olivia shrugged. "Dunno. But she told me that being a mother was always her most important job. I don't think I believed her at first. Not until she got sick and I saw how she worried about what was going to happen to us. She feared that more than dying, I think. I can fully understand it now, of course."

"Wow," I said, trying to take it all in.

Olivia continued. "At the time I was so angry—with both of them. She'd worked so hard and deserved the promotion as well as the extra money and perks. I thought Dad was being selfish, as did she. But I think I would've made the same choice if I were in her shoes. Being a good mom is more important than anything, really."

The words churned in my stomach and left me feeling more like a foreigner, a citizen without a country, than I had since Dad's diagnosis and death shredded the last piece of family we had left. When I was younger I'd likened myself to Little Orphan Annie, but even that felt like a faulty comparison now. After all, she was never portrayed as lonely or wanting, and she made out great with Daddy Warbucks. Besides, she had the sweet voice and the cute curls and the scruffy dog going for her. Being an orphan was about as romantic and glamorous as a hermit crab. Not only was I an orphan, but even after all this time, I still had no real family of my own. Not like Olivia.

"You're a good mom," I said, desperately wishing the same could be said of me.

Olivia's voice was bitter. "I had plenty of practice for the whole mom thing."

"Hey," I said, "I never asked you to be my mother."

"No, but you needed me to be."

I shook my head. "No. I needed *my* mother to be my mother."

The running faucet sounded like a waterfall between us. I don't think either of us had ever acknowledged this, that we had each made demands on the other without asking. Nor had we ever realized how deep our mutual resentment ran. The soapy water thinned, bubbles bursting one by one and breaking off in little islands.

"Thank you, though," I offered. "You did a good job under the circumstances."

I thought I saw her brush away a tear. Or maybe a stray bubble, or wisp of bangs.

"Sorry I made you my guinea pig," she said quietly.

"Sorry I let you."

I studied Olivia's reflection in the window as she swirled a finger in the suds, and I saw the thought register on her face a split second before she scooped a handful of remaining suds and flicked them at me, sloshing my arm.

I gasped, then plotted. "Hey, Liv? You've got something on your cheek."

"Wha—"

"This!" I smeared a handful of bubbles on her.

When Tyler came skidding into the kitchen a few moments later to find both of us shrieking with laughter, drenched in lukewarm water and remnants of suds-bombs, he took stock of the situation and backed away, retreating to the safety of the living room.

"Mom and Aunt Eva are having a suds fight!" he announced.

"You'll have a whole new appreciation of it when you get older, kiddo," I heard Norman reply. By this time Olivia and I were slipping on the floor, soaked, and squealing with laughter.

⤳

Norman was the last to leave, and no sooner had I waved good-bye and he'd gotten to his car than I called his cell phone. I stood in the doorway, watching him.

"I'm not taking that casserole," he said after the second ring. "I don't care how bad your fridge smells."

I laughed. "I wasn't calling about the casserole."

"Good," he said, "'cause I'm not taking any."

"OK, OK already."

The dome light in his car dimmed, obscuring his form.

"So can I go now?" he asked in mock impatience.

"Yes," I said. As he shifted into gear and backed out, I peered at his headlights. "But I just wanted to say…" I finished putting my thought together. "Norman, you're more my family than they are."

He took a moment to answer. "Wow," he said softly.

"Yeah," I paused. "And it's both special and sad, you know?"

"Yeah, I know."

I could imagine him nodding as his car waited at the end of the street, turn signal pulsing like a heartbeat. He turned onto the main road and was gone in seconds.

"Happy Thanksgiving, Zan."

"Same to you, Jayna. Enjoy the day off tomorrow. See you Saturday."

"Yep. You too."

"And thanks," he said. "It's good to have a home that isn't going anywhere any time soon."

"See ya," we each said and disconnected.

The quiet of the night seemed oppressive and pounding, made tangible by the sudden absence of anyone in my home or on the street. It settled into the house, and I took in a breath, feeling exhaustion mixed with relief that the day was over. Cleaning the kitchen had been twice the work following Olivia's and my suds fight, but it had been worth it to find my sister for a moment.

30

The Potato Shack

ON THE TUESDAY following Thanksgiving, at three minutes before seven o'clock, I locked the doors and then went to work on register closeout while Susanna cleaned. From behind the counter, I heard a rapping on the glass door, and when I looked up from the register till, Susanna called, "It's Car Talk Kenny."

I stopped counting. "Kenny?"

"Want me to let him in?"

"Tell him to hold on a sec," I said, counting the change again. When I finished, I grabbed my keys from the counter and let him in.

"Hey," he said. "You free tonight?"

I looked at him, dazed. "What?"

"You goin' out with anyone tonight?"

I laughed at the notion that I would go out anywhere. "No."

"Good. Wanna have dinner with me?"

It was then that I got a good look at him. For starters, his hair was short and styled. Gone were the uneven wisps, and it even looked darker—less sandpaper and more walnut-colored. The cut flattered his features, bringing out his eyes and defining the bone structure of his clean-shaven face.

My eyes moved away from his face only to take in the rest of him—he wore a light blue oxford shirt tucked into dark blue jeans, with a brown leather belt and Nubucks to match. Instead of lanky or gangly, he stood tall and towering, professional. His presence was full, powerful, dominant, not unlike the man I'd seen running on the beach months ago.

In short, *Wow.*

"Is this—are you asking me out on a date?" I asked. "On a Tuesday?"

He nodded. "Guess so."

"I reek of coffee."

"I'm not taking you to Tavern on the Green."

"I really, really need a shower," I said.

"So I'll follow you to your place."

During the seven-minute drive to my house, I checked my rearview mirror every few seconds to make sure he was behind me, driving his sun-kissed orange 1970 Volkswagen Karmann Ghia convertible. The famous Karmann Ghia. The one that had Click and Clack on *Car Talk* so excited. He pulled into the driveway behind me and followed me to my front door. All I could think about was how messy my house was. But I couldn't very well let him wait in his car.

"It's a mess," I warned him as I unlocked the door.

"I'll only look at the clean parts," he promised. We entered and he took in the rooms one by one. "Nice."

"I've got some decent DVDs over there," I said, pointing to the entertainment center. "Not that I'm gonna take that long, but, well, help yourself."

He perused the DVDs on the shelf in front of him, bending slightly. I then headed to the bathroom, where I hastily showered and mentally ripped apart my closet in search of something to wear. I figured jeans, a V-neck sweater, and boots would suffice.

After hastily blow-drying my hair and applying some makeup, I returned to the living room to find him channel-surfing. When he saw me, he stood up, his hazel eyes sparkling.

"I like," was all he said.

A bout of shyness overcame me as I smiled. "I'm clean, at least."

He turned off the TV while I got my leather jacket and scarf.

"Where are we going?" I asked.

"Dinner," he replied.

I rolled my eyes, feigning exasperation. "Obviously. Where?"

"You'll see."

We walked out to his car. He opened the door for me, and as I sank into the seat and pulled the vintage seatbelt across my shoulder and lap, I put my nose to the backrest and inhaled the scent of leather before catching myself.

"What are you doing?" he asked.

I blushed. "My uncle used to drive a Triumph—the smell of these seats reminds me of him taking my sister Olivia and me out for Carvel ice cream when we were kids."

He seemed pleased with my candor (and yet, I realized that I would've been repulsed had one of my Lovematch.com dates engaged in such behavior) and peeled out of the driveway. We talked mostly about the Karmann Ghia—he was sorry it was too cold to put the top down—and his *Car Talk* show appearance en route to wherever it was he was taking me. Fifteen minutes later, we pulled up to what looked like a small house with a flat roof.

"What's this?" I asked.

"The Potato Shack," he said.

He opened both the car and restaurant doors for me. The walls inside the Potato Shack were decorated with aged black-and-white photos of potato farms. We talked as a server escorted us to our table.

"I thought you'd appreciate this," said Kenny. "The original owner of this place was a Long Islander and his dad was a potato farmer. He moved down here—"

"The son?" I interjected.

"Yes, the son of the potato farmer moved down here because he could get the beauty of the Atlantic coast for half the cost."

"Good slogan."

"And he opened this place in honor of his dad, using imported Long Island potatoes."

"I didn't think there were any left—potato farms on Long Island, I mean."

"I think his family still owns a small plot."

I opened the menu, scanned it quickly, and looked up at Kenny in confusion.

"This is the appetizer menu?"

"No, this is the whole menu."

"OK, I don't wanna be like a complete idiot, but—"

"Yeah?"

"It's all potatoes."

He grinned playfully. "Isn't it great?"

"No salads? No steaks or burgers?"

"Smashed, roasted, fried, baked, scalloped, skinned, take your pick."

"How'd they stay open during the no-carb fad?"

"I highly recommend the smashed with cheddar and bacon. You'll have died and gone to heaven."

"With all that cholesterol, yeah."

He laughed.

"What are you getting?" I asked.

"The fries with meat sauce," he said.

I looked at him, half-stunned, half-repulsed. "Meat sauce as in spaghetti-and-meat-sauce, meat sauce?"

"Yep," he grinned.

"You're kidding."

"Trust me, they're awesome."

The server took our orders, and we sat in momentary awkward silence while the Beatles' *Rubber Soul* album played in the background.

"Where've you been, Kenny?" I finally asked, surprised by the pain in my voice.

He turned his gaze down before looking me squarely in the eye. "For one thing, I started a business," he answered.

"So I heard. Doing what?"

"A small press. I'm the guy that does everything everyone else can't do. Designing and maintaining the Web site, formatting files, budgeting projections, business proposals, you name it. I'm even drawing a salary."

"Wow," was all I could say. "You could have told us. I would've given you a complimentary cookie or something." (God, did that sound stupid.)

"That's not the main reason I stayed away." He paused. "I didn't want to see you and Scott together."

This confession gave me a crappy feeling. I suddenly felt guilty, responsible for his absence. And yet, I also felt a twinge of disappointment and anger.

"Why didn't you say anything?" I asked.

"It was too late."

I couldn't help but concede the point.

"Did you know we broke up?"

He nodded. "The grapevine managed to wend its way to my ears. Why'd you think I asked you out tonight?"

"And you thought a month was enough time for me to get over it?"

"It's not like Scott ever swept you off your feet."

"How do you know?"

"Did he ever take you to the Potato Shack?"

I quickly scanned the place. "You consider *this* a romantic place?"

"Hell, yeah!" He grinned and took a swig of beer.

I changed the subject.

"Did you know that you're the first Kenny I actually like? No guy named Kenny has ever been a nice guy. Actually, it's the Ken's who seem to be the assholes."

"You don't say," he said, amused.

"You've never noticed? In real life and on TV. Watch *Law & Order*. The criminals are always named Kenny or Ken—"

"Always?"

"—and they're all weasels. Then, of course, there's Ken of 'Barbie and Ken' fame."

"Hey, you can't judge a guy by his plastic hair."

"Still, I'm glad you're not a Ken. But you should really consider changing your name," I teased.

"To what?" he asked, eyebrows raised.

I took a sip of my cocktail to buy time. He leaned back in his chair, crossing his arms, grinning in anticipation.

"What's your middle name?" I asked.

"Richard. Kenneth Richard Rhodes," he said, the tone of his voice formal and deep.

"Richard Rhodes…" I tried, accentuating the Rs. "Well, the alliteration works well."

"But…?" He could tell I wasn't sold.

"I don't know; 'Richard' sounds too distinguished for you. Like you should be running a hedge fund."

"Gee, thanks," he said, and quickly added, "I agree with you, though. What about Rich?"

"Nah."

"Rick? Or how 'bout Ricky?" he asked.

I made a face. "That might be worse than Kenny."

"How about Chad? Or Chase? I've always liked that name."

"Not unless you're planning to be a yuppie financier. Are you planning to be a yuppie financier?"

"Not in the near future."

"Then I'm sorry to say, I think you're a Kenny."

"You're just going to have to live with it. I do." He paused for a beat before continuing. "Do you like *your* name?"

I tried to recall if anyone had ever asked me that before, and none came to me.

"I love my name; I just wish I had an easier time with the spelling-pronunciation deal."

"I like your name, too. Your name definitely suits you—it's pretty, and different from what you'd expect."

Of all the compliments I'd been paid from dates of the past year, none rang so simple, so authentic. Perhaps because he'd said it not in an effort to impress me, but as an observation. That alone made my insides turn into Jell-O.

Our orders arrived, and I dug in. Kenny was right; the cheddar-and-bacon-smothered smashed potatoes were out of this world. I let out one orgasmic moan after another, and he smiled at me in satisfaction, his eyes saying, *I told you so*. I even tasted his fries with meat sauce and was surprised by how good they were, too.

I resumed the conversation, switching to a more serious track.

"We've missed you at The Grounds. I swear there's been a drop in sales since you went MIA."

He looked sad for a moment. "I've missed you guys, too."

"Minerva quit school."

"I know," he said.

Of course you know. You've been having clandestine conversations with her.

I changed the subject without warning. "So what are you going to publish on your small press?"

"For starters, my novel."

My eyes widened as I forced myself to swallow. "You wrote a novel?"

He nodded.

"Why didn't you ever say anything?"

"You never asked."

"You could've just casually mentioned it—it's far more important than whether you like peas or the letter H."

"I wanted to save the good stuff for the date. Aren't you glad I did?"

"Idiot," I said, shaking my head. He raised his eyebrows up and down just like Groucho Marx and smiled slyly before taking another bite of his fries.

"What genre?" I asked.

"Literary science fiction mixed with a little bit of pop culture."

"So what's it about?"

"A journalist finds out that there was a portal into the past and future in the Port Authority station that was destroyed when the towers came down on September eleventh, which means that countless people wound up trapped in either time dimension. So he sets out to find another portal so he can rescue them."

I marveled at the concept. "Wow," I said. "That is fantastic. I never would've come up with an idea like that. My novel was about an Italian family who emigrated to New York City after World War II. Nothing nearly as imaginative as yours, but it got good reviews. Limited audience, though."

"I know, I read it. Very Adriana Trigiani."

This time I nearly choked. "When did you read my novel?"

"When I first started coming to The Grounds. I took it from the shelf."

"You stole my book?"

"Pretty much, yeah."

I looked at him, dumbfounded. "You wrote a novel without telling anyone, and you robbed The Grounds."

"I brought it back."

"Anything else I need to know?"

"I named my protagonist Chase," he said after a pause.

"And was he a yuppie financier before he became a reporter?"

He finished the last of his fries. "You know," he said when he finished chewing, "you should join us."

"Join who where?"

"You should work for our press. I'll bet you're a good editor. We could use another one. Or you can write another novel and we'll publish it."

I shook my head dismissively, not even giving myself a moment to consider the idea.

$$\backsim\!\circ$$

After dinner, Kenny drove us to the boardwalk in downtown Wilmington, where we walked slowly along the water's edge. The night air gave me a chill, and I zipped my jacket and hugged my arms.

"You cold?" he asked.

"A little."

He put his arm around me and I got another chill, this time on the inside.

We stopped walking and looked out at the water, the sun long gone. Kenny stood right behind me, pressing his body slightly against me, one hand gently resting on my waist.

I turned and looked up at him. His eyes wore an expression of contentment. I craned my neck to reach his lips, and he lowered his head to meet mine. The moment our lips touched and I tasted the salt from the fries, he cupped my cheek with one hand and pulled me to him in an embrace with the other, while I ran my fingers through his hair at the nape of his neck. We stood for what felt like hours in an embrace.

"I should have done this a long time ago," he said more to himself than to me, it seemed.

Eventually we made our way back to the Karmann Ghia, and Kenny drove me back to my house, holding my hand the entire time. When he pulled into the driveway and put the car in park, we kissed again and then sat and looked at each other for a moment.

"I hope you don't take this the wrong way, but I don't think I should invite you in," I said.

"And I hope you don't take this the wrong way, but I would've said no if you did."

He opened his door, got out of the car, and circled to my side. "I had a wonderful time tonight," he said, holding my door open.

"Me too. In fact, it's the best date I've been on in a really long time."

Maybe ever.

"Am I gonna read about it on WILS tomorrow?"

I shook my head. "That blog…" I trailed off. "It was over before it started."

"No law that says you have to keep it going."

I hadn't considered WILS's future any more than I had considered my own.

Kenny kissed me quickly one last time, and I practically floated to my front door as he peeled out once again and disappeared down the road.

As I lay in bed replaying every moment of our date, I suddenly knew that the thing I wanted most was also the thing that frightened me most. And that truth was no longer willing to be ignored.

31

Poutine

THE FOLLOWING AFTERNOON, Minerva met me for lunch at the Blue Moon, a full-service diner in NCLA's Student Center that was packed at all hours with a mix of students and faculty working from laptops or reading newspapers at the counter, studying or just hanging out in the booths. The retro-fifties décor consisted of chrome fixtures and black-and-white tiled floors, and the menu matched the theme by focusing mostly on burgers and fries and milkshakes. Even the jukebox in the corner contained Chuck Berry and Buddy Holly records.

We stared at our menus.

"You know, I can really go for some poutine," Minerva said to herself, not looking up from the menu.

"Some *what*?" I asked.

"Heaven on a plate," she said, still looking at the menu, "smothered in cheese and gravy."

I sat up straight. "You've got my attention."

She proceeded. "French fries with cheese curds sprinkled on them, covered in thick gravy."

I cringed. "I never liked the word *curds*," I said, folding my menu.

Minerva wasn't listening. Her eyes were closed, and she was practically purring. "Warm, salty, ooey gooey, cheesy, coronary fantasticness." She brought herself back to reality. "Poutine. Very *Québecois.*"

"We're in the *South*, Minerva. You do remember that, don't you? The closest thing you're going to get to French is the fries."

"But it's comfort food. Cheese? Gravy? Potatoes? How much more Southern can you get?"

She stared at the menu for another ten seconds, frowned, and closed it.

"So I had a date with Kenny last night," I said.

She looked up, dropped the menu, and opened her mouth.

"You move from comfort food to 'I had a date with Kenny' with no notice? No transition? How does your brain work, Eva?"

Before I had a chance to answer, the server came to the table holding his order pad. He turned to me first. "What can I get for you?"

"Burger. Medium-well. No lettuce or onions. Tomato on the side. Bun lightly toasted. And an ice water," I recited.

He scribbled on his pad and then turned to Minerva. "And you?"

Her eyes narrowed, and I could tell our waiter was in for it. "You have fries?" she started.

"Of course."

"And gravy and cheese?"

"I think so."

"OK. So I want you to put it all on a plate and bring it to me. Please."

The server looked at her with hesitation. "Are you sure?"

"I asked you for it, didn't I?"

"All of it...just, on a plate?"

"You got it."

He stared at the menus before looking at me, as if asking me to translate, before looking back at her. I raised my eyebrows at him, then her, amused.

"I'm not sure we can do that," he said, tilting his head to the side.

Minerva laughed out loud again. "Listen…" she said as she squinted at his nametag, "Chris, I'm having a craving. Fulfill it and you can charge me the world."

I tried to come to Chris's rescue. "Just bring her an order of fries with some gravy and shredded cheese on the side, please."

"Okey-doke," said Chris, who was probably thinking our tip money was so not worth it.

"And a Coke," she called out as he was leaving. Once he was out of ear- and eye-shot, I burst out laughing. She sighed. "Really, how hard is it to put some cheese and gravy on some fries?"

"I'll bet you can get it at the Potato Shack."

Minerva made a face. "The *what?*"

"The Potato Shack." I said it as if I'd known the place my entire life. "That's where Kenny took me for our date."

"He took you to a *shack?* After all that?"

"It's a restaurant. He brought me there because they use Long Island potatoes. Or at least that's why I think he brought me there. They serve nothing but potatoes of all kinds and styles. I'll bet you could find your little delicacy there, although I'm guessing they wouldn't call it by your frou-frou French name. He had his fries with meat sauce." I smiled at the memory. "It was cute."

"Well, OK." Minerva grinned like the Cheshire cat, and immediately I became suspicious.

"Wait a minute…did you say 'after all that'? After all *what?*"

"So how was it? The date, I mean."

"Don't think you can distract me. What did you mean?"

"We'll get to it. Promise. Now tell me how it went."

I grinned like a happy idiot. "It was…" I searched for the right words.

"That good? Please don't say 'dreamy.'"

"I wasn't going to say 'dreamy.'"

Chris the Server brought us our orders. My bun was untoasted, and the tomato was on the burger. Min's sides of gravy and cheese were in tiny cups more suitable for salad. She frowned and let out an ostentatious sigh.

"Steady," I said.

"Isn't that what you wanted?" he asked.

"Can you bring me two more of these cute little cups?" she asked.

"Um, I'll have to ask."

"Thank you, that would be great," Minerva cooed.

Moments later, Chris returned with two more cups of gravy and shredded cheese; he set them at the edge of the table and hurried away before either of us could ask for anything else.

I couldn't help but laugh. "You and your putin cravings."

"It's pronounced *poo-teen*, not 'putin.' We're talking pota-toes, not Russian prime ministers. You should serve this at The Grounds."

"Keep wishing on that one."

I shrugged and watched with mild interest as Minerva dumped all of the cheese onto her fries before drizzling the gravy on top. It looked terrible, but she was obviously pleased.

She savored her concoction for a moment before continuing. "He really cares about you, you know. He has for a long time."

I took a sip of my water in an effort to hide the giddy grin that pinched the corners of my mouth upward.

She continued, "In fact, I've been rooting for Kenny since day one."

"*Since day one?*" My eyes narrowed. "When, exactly, was day one?"

Minerva folded her napkin, tucking it under the rim of her plate.

"I told you not to rule him out."

"And what did you mean by '*after all that*'?"

She looked like she was trying to decide whether to break her silence.

I folded my arms. "Say something."

She sighed. "Do you remember how Kenny and Sister Beulah and I used to always sit together and hang out before he started his venture with the small press—he told you about that, yes?"

"Yes, *finally*," I emphasized, waiting for more.

"Well, I caught him looking at you one day, watching you. So I asked him about it, and he told me that he kinda had a thing for you but begged me not to tell you."

"And you *didn't*?" I said.

"He's my friend, Eva. How would you like it if I broke your confidence? Anyway, he was about to go for it and then you messed it all up and went home with Scott after the incident with Shaun and the Jeanette."

I opened my mouth. "No."

"Yes."

"NO!"

"*Yes.* So he stopped coming around, and figured he'd just get over it. But he missed you and everyone at The Grounds. So when he came in for the Halloween party, he saw the fight you got into with Scott when Shaun was there and asked for my advice. The rest, yada yada yada, is history."

I couldn't believe my ears.

"So what'd you tell him?" I asked.

"I told him that you needed a kick."

"A kick?"

"A swift kick."

"Thanks, Min. What'd he say to that?"

"He said, 'Then call me Adam Vinateiri.' Do you know who Adam Vinateiri is?"

"He's the friggin' president of the United States."

"He's the best kicker in the NFL."

"He's the best kicker in the NFL," I repeated. "So last night was Kenny's swift kick?"

"Did it work?" she asked.

I crumpled my napkin and tossed it on the plate while Minerva waited. "Something feels off, like I'm not ready."

"Because of Scott?" she asked.

"No."

"Because of Shaun?"

"Hell, no." I paused before adding, "It's *me*."

Minerva nodded. "Oh."

"OK," I said. "Now, what about yours?"

"My what?"

"Your swift kick. It's overdue."

She shrugged and checked her watch. "You have to get ready for class soon," she said.

We flagged Chris for our check. I slapped a five-dollar tip on the table.

"Didn't Adam Vinateiri retire from the NFL?" I asked as we exited the diner.

Minerva shrugged. "How the hell would I know?"

As we walked across campus back to her car, I looked around; the view was postcard-perfect. Trees lined the sidewalks and dormant flowerbeds lined the perimeters of the brick buildings. The Southern sunshine cast shadows as it began to sink.

"I forgot how gorgeous this campus is at this time of year," Minerva said.

I nodded in agreement. "You don't miss med school at all?" I asked.

She said nothing and stared straight ahead, her lips clamped shut.

We reached the car in silence. She paused, her door half open.

"Look, it happened the way it happened and that's that. I think Kenny's got enough regret for the both of you. But now that you know, maybe you'll think about how much more time you want to go by."

It took me a moment to register that she had changed the subject. If she hadn't been so clearly projecting her own situation, the words might have stung.

"If only it was that simple, Min," I replied.

"It is."

⁓◯

Despite my anxiety about returning to the classroom, especially with so little time to prepare, Ed's prediction of its ease came true. Stepping into the familiar smells of wood and musty air felt like a step back in time, perhaps through Kenny's fictional portal. The students' short stories ranged from historical Carolina settings to Midwest white, upper-middle-class protagonists to plots of Mexican migrant workers hiding from the INS. I felt somewhat like a fraud, my only creative writing in years consisting of suddenly stupid and insignificant ramblings about singlehood. After my first day, I'd gone home intending to draft a short story of my own, but came up blank.

Just as class finished five minutes after six o'clock, I exited the building with four of Jenna's students—two on each side of me—and crossed the quad heading towards the parking lot. The discussion from the workshop had spilled over into the hallway and during our walk. I had always liked when this happened, when the story was too intense to put down, to let go, to stop discussing.

Clouds and a chill had set in, and a group of students ran from the student center in the direction of the residence halls, some looking panicked.

"What's going on?" I asked as a student nearly collided with us on his skateboard.

"Dorm's on fire!" he yelled and swerved, pumping with his foot to gain speed.

32

Fire

THE STUDENTS AND I exchanged glances, in shock for a moment. At first, I thought of Shaun as well as my colleagues from the English department, then Minerva, as if my brain was performing a database search of people I might know who could be affected—or worse, involved. When thoughts turned to the horrid image of students, I gasped. *Susanna!*

I dropped my briefcase and took off toward the residence halls as one of Jenna's students called out, "Professor, wait!" But I didn't. I must have run three-quarters of a mile before I came to one of NCLA's oldest dorms, a hulking brick monstrosity designed to stand up to hurricanes but faltering in beauty. Light orange flames and putrid, sooty smoke spat out two of its windows on the second floor. Shattered glass littered the sidewalks and grass like a mosaic. Students were running around, crying, covering their mouths, searching for roommates and friends, and talking frantically on cell phones. The sirens practically deafened me as firefighters and campus police rounded people up, led them to safety, and maintained order using bullhorns and two-way radios. I called out Susanna's name and stopped students. "Susanna Swanson? Do you know Susanna Swanson? Is this her dorm?" I shouted at anyone who would listen. As I pushed through like a New Yorker on a subway platform, a campus police officer blocked me and took my arm.

"That's as far as you go, ma'am. This area ain't secure." His accent was thick, his voice baritone.

"You don't understand."

"I'm sorry, ma'am, I just cain't let you through."

About a hundred feet to my left, I spotted Shaun gathering students and elbowed my way to him.

"Shaun!"

He whisked around. "Eva?"

"I can't find Susanna! She's my employee at The Grounds."

I lost my breath and leaned over to catch it.

"Easy, Eva," I heard him say. He held my arm and placed a hand on my back to steady me.

"They won't let me through," I said between gasps.

"They won't let anyone through. There are at least three people trapped, and they're pulling them out."

"Oh my God, Shaun. They're just *kids*."

"It's gonna be all right," he said in a resolute, yet wavering voice.

"What are you doing here?" I asked, knowing the question wasn't rational, but rationality had been trampled by sneakered feet and screaming sirens.

"Same as you—making sure the kids are OK."

I picked my head up, still breathing heavily, and saw him: the Shaun I was once in love with. Ages ago. Eons. Lifetimes.

And then I saw Susanna.

They were taking her out on a stretcher, an oxygen mask strapped to her face. I shrieked when I saw her and ran like gangbusters toward the back of the ambulance, its doors open, ready to speed off. I reached the stretcher and called her name. Her face was smudged with dirty gray ash mixed with sweat and tears, her right arm burned.

I blocked the EMT. "Please, you have to let me ride with her. She's not from around here. Her mother is in Virginia. I'm the next best thing."

"Out of the way, ma'am," the EMT said, his voice monotone and commanding.

Susanna pulled down her mask. "Let her come, please," she sputtered. The lead EMT nodded and barked instructions at the others. First they carefully boarded her, and then I climbed into the back before the doors were pushed shut. Once inside, the ambulance sped away.

As the scene shrank from our sight, I did my best to assure Susanna that she was going to be all right. When the ambulance arrived at Cape Fear Hospital, I jumped out while the EMTs wheeled her in, leaving me behind. I pulled out my cell phone and called Minerva, forcing myself to speak slowly when she picked up on the first ring.

"Min? Everyone is fine, but I need you to come to the hospital. Susanna's been hurt in a fire on campus, and I want someone here who can speak to the doctors."

"I'm on my way," she said in the same manner as the EMTs. The phone beeped to signal that she'd clicked off.

I stared at my iPhone, still clutched in my white-knuckled grip, until the screen dimmed into power save mode and went blank. My finger hovered over the power button as I mentally Rolodexed through a list of friends, family, anyone to call. The names spun before me, but I called none.

Sinking into a chair in the far corner, I felt invisible as the world swirled around me. The sounds of the ER doors churning open and closed seemed filtered, dulled and distorted, otherworldly. Meanwhile, the waiting room filled with a small collection of college students in jeans and trendy sloganed T-shirts, some already armed with flowers and little teddy bears.

I closed my eyes for a moment. The scent of disinfectant—sharper than the smoke that clung to my clothes—transported me to hospitals from another lifetime, an adolescence long gone, waiting rooms I'd frequented until they'd felt like home, beds I'd sat vigil at. It was not unlike the sour smell of sterile cleaners that invaded our house-turned-hospice even after my parents were gone. Those rooms had been still, frozen in the limbo of people who had nothing left to do but wait.

Here, however, the air jangled with activity, vibrated with noise, pulled taut by people weaving past each other as they set about busy tasks that swam around me. Nurses squeaked by in crocs of every color, leaving behind blurs of medical lingo and codes and snappy matching scrubs. Phones rang, receptionists tapped pens, a troupe of policemen escorted a stretcher, the sheet turned down beneath a face mostly hidden by tubes. Was it always like this? I wondered. Above me, the news and weather cycled on a lone TV hanging from the corner: a rash of Christmas-shopping-related thefts, increases in rush-hour traffic, and an unusual cold snap approaching.

I closed my eyes again and sat among it all, invisible. Or so I thought, until I jumped at the sound of Minerva's voice.

"You wouldn't believe how jammed it is out there. Otherwise we'd've been here sooner."

I stood up and hugged her. She held me tight, seemingly impervious to the chaos around her. Or was it only chaotic to me?

"Eva, you're shaking."

"One minute I had this great class; the next minute someone yelled that the dorm was on fire."

"Do you know anything?"

"The EMTs were talking all medical-speak, and none of it to me. I think she just has smoke inhalation, but she may have burned her arm."

"Did you call her mother?"

"I don't have her number."

"One of my professors is a resident here," she said. "Let me see what I can find out."

"In maternity?" I asked.

"I'll be right back."

Moments later, Jay entered the ER.

"You wouldn't believe the commotion out there..." he started. "Where's my wife?"

"Trying to find someone who knows something, I think."

He clapped his hands together and rubbed them like the villains do in the movies. "Excellent," he said in a cool, Montgomery Burns voice. "Now we're getting somewhere." Then he turned to me. "Are you OK? Your face is a shade of green I've never quite seen before."

He took off his coat and draped it around my shoulders before we sat down.

"She's really in her element," said Jay of Minerva. "I've missed her."

I didn't answer him, but I knew what he meant.

Fifteen minutes later, we spotted Minerva as she made her way to us. We stood up, and she curled against Jay; surprise flickered across his face as he folded her in his arms.

"What'd you find out?" he asked.

"Not much, actually. You were right," she said to me. "She has smoke inhalation and a second-degree burn on her arm and part of her hand. Nothing too serious, but she did pass out, so they're keeping her overnight. We'll be able to see her soon, though—I got around the family-only thing, at least."

"You rock, Min."

She shrugged modestly and said softly, "Thanks."

The waiting room filled with friends of Susanna's, some of whom I recognized as customers of The Grounds, and the two other girls pulled from the fire. They were trying to piece together the events based on hearsay. The stories ranged from a tipped-over candle to a bong gone bad to the building's faulty wiring to a conspiracy theory of the school committing arson in order to get the insurance money to build an on-campus apartment complex in its place.

About an hour later, a woman who knew Minerva escorted the three of us to Susanna's room. Her face had been cleaned off, and the oxygen mask hung around her neck so that she could use it if needed. Minerva and I stationed ourselves on opposite sides of the bed like security guards after taking turns hugging her.

"Sweetie, is there anyone we can call?" I asked.

"They called my mom. She's on her way. Boy, is she going to be pissed."

"Hardly," I said.

Her expression turned to one of worry. "What if my insurance doesn't cover this?"

"Don't you worry about that," I said. "We'll take up a collection at The Grounds if we have to. Hell, we'll throw a bake sale that will make the Halloween party look like a church social. And don't you worry about your shifts, either. Min will take over for you, right Min?" I glanced at Minerva, who nodded in response. "And Norman's probably training a super full-timer as we speak."

Susanna smiled and nodded in acknowledgment before closing her eyes.

"We should go," said Minerva to Jay and me. We each kissed her good-bye and left one by one; I smoothed her hair and squeezed her hand.

In the hallway, I took slow, deep breaths and touched the wall to recover my balance after a light-headedness passed as quickly as it came.

"Hey, can you guys give me a ride?" I asked Jay, returning his jacket.

"No problem," he said, then left us in the lobby while he got the car. While we waited, I suddenly gasped, startling Minerva.

"What is it?" she asked.

"My briefcase. I dropped it before I took off."

"I'm sure someone'll find it," she said.

"I was with a couple of my students when it happened."

"So they probably have it. Really, Eva. Don't worry about it. In the scheme of things, what does it matter?"

"You're right," I said. "I'm being ridiculous."

We stood in silence as Jay rolled up and pulled over to the curb.

"It's good to have you back," I said to Minerva.

33

The Key

IT WAS CLOSE to ten p.m. when I got home from the hospital. Shaun's car was in my driveway, and he hopped out as we pulled in.

"What's he doing here?" asked Minerva.

"He was there," I answered, tired.

Thanking Jay and Minerva, I trudged zombie-like to the front door and unlocked it. Shaun followed me.

"Where were you?" he asked, worried. "I left messages for you. I called The Grounds, I even called the hospital…"

"Turned my phone off," I replied.

"Your friend—is she OK?"

"She'll be fine. The other two girls are OK as well."

"I'm glad," he said.

"I'm going to bed now."

Shaun looked at me, slightly dazed himself. "OK. Do you need anything?"

"Bed."

"Oh, um, I have your briefcase. I found it on the way back to the faculty parking lot."

Of all the people to find my briefcase, it had to be Shaun. He went out to his car and carried it back. It felt heavier than usual when he handed it to me.

"Thanks," I said, setting it down.

"Are you sure you're OK?" he asked. I lifted my head to look at him, concern seeming to crinkle the edges of his eyes. Hesitating only for a beat, we drew to each other like magnets and kissed.

How quickly it all came back—the way our kiss felt, the angle we tilted our heads, the positions of our hands and lips, how good it all was. How good it felt to breathe him in, to let my shoulder support his head as he broke the kiss and lingered in my arms. As Shaun's hand remembered its way down my back, I found myself wondering if he touched Jeanette this same way. Did his hands take the same route? Did his lips pucker the same way? Had mine when I was with Scott? With Kenny?

I opened my eyes and pulled away.

"You'd better go," I said, smoothing my blouse and crossing my arms. "Jeanette is probably worried."

"Eva..." he started.

"No. She's feeling the same way you and I are. It could've been any of us."

He remained frozen.

"Go," I said, pushing him toward the door. "Really, you need to go."

He turned and slowly marched back to his car while I closed the door without watching him drive away. I left the briefcase leaning by the door and peeled off my clothes piece by piece as I made my way from the foyer through the hallway and into my bedroom. Rather than the all-too-familiar smells of coffee and vanilla extract, tonight they smelled like charcoal and disinfectant. I crawled under the covers. The room had never been so eerily silent. Or dark.

I lay perfectly still, listening to the rhythm and volume of my breathing and trying to piece together the inky shapes and grizzly shadows of my suddenly unfamiliar room. I would've given anything just to have Olivia to rub my back like when we were kids.

The darkness felt like it could choke me. Once again I scrolled through my mental Rolodex.

Perhaps I should call Shaun and tell him to come back. We could spend the night, just this once. He wanted to—I knew he wanted to.

No. I couldn't do that to Jeanette. To me.

Or maybe I should call Scott. He'd want to be there for me. He'd been there for me the last time I was down and needed someone.

No. I couldn't use him like that again. Besides, he never really saved me from my loneliness so as much as diverted my attention from it.

What about Kenny?

No. Kenny deserved more from me. Much, much more. And I couldn't just jump into bed with someone at the first sign of discomfort any more than I could work until I was too exhausted to notice that I was lonely.

Norman? Minerva? Olivia? Beulah?

No.

Breathe.

I wasn't fourteen years old anymore. Bad things happened. Things beyond my control. I didn't need to run into the first pair of open arms. Didn't need to climb under the security blanket of someone's protective hug, even if just in a phone call.

Slowly my muscles began to unclench, and bit by bit my body relaxed into the mattress beneath me. People got hurt or left for no good reason sometimes, and no amount of work or food or sex could distract you forever. There weren't enough lemon tortes in the world to make it all nice, not enough cookies to give away so that you'd be loved. There weren't enough customers to nurture to make up for the mother who left when you needed her guidance and advice, and not enough men in the world to make up for the dad who was simply incapable of being the anchor you needed. There weren't enough blogs or books or countertops or kitchens to hide behind. Life was unpredictable and untamed.

And then I got it: The thing I both feared and craved was *unpredictability*. It was the key to life. The key to romance.

And suddenly it didn't seem so bad.

Why had it been so scary? I cast my memory backwards and almost immediately thought of my mom. No one saw her cancer diagnosis coming, least of all her. She possessed none of the typical symptoms; she wasn't a smoker or drinker, had no genetic markers, maintained a fairly healthy diet and exercise regimen. If anything, life had become predictable for her. She had almost left my father because of it. Breast cancer seemed a cosmically cruel way to turn things upside down, however. She once told me that it saved her marriage. I thought the meds were making her talk crazy. I wondered if my father agreed, and his own cancer was the result of his guilt and stagnation.

Hadn't The Grounds become predictable? Hadn't my routine with Scott—and Shaun—been predictable? As long as he was *there*, as long as he didn't abandon me, all was well, regardless of whether we were happy or not.

And wasn't Kenny's unpredictability the very thing that attracted me to him?

The epiphany seemed to be brightening the room. Sure, I'd had a few tough breaks in life. But I'd survived them. More than that, even. I created something meaningful, made a difference in people's lives, be it in the classroom or behind the counter. When it came right down to it, hadn't I been OK all along?

Tonight I had to spend the night with no one but myself, I decided. And I thought about the advice Kenny's dad had given to his frightened little boy long ago. I had a choice. I could be alone. But I didn't have to be lonely. And I certainly didn't have to be afraid of it.

～っ

It was well after eleven o'clock the next morning when I opened my eyes, squinting in the sunlight forcing its beams past the window shade.

I'd made it through the night alone, without shedding a tear, without someone to hold, without running away.

I'd made it through. And I was hungry.

34

Good Things

I THINK SPENCER had been planning it for a while, and I was thrilled that he chose to do it at The Grounds with all of us to witness it. It was cute, actually; he had conspired with me to make a mini red velvet cake, and we carefully wedged the ring on top, like a candle. I served it to him and Tracy nonchalantly and crept away. We all held our breath as Spencer popped the question, Tracy squealing before saying yes, and then we erupted into applause. I could feel my eyes stinging until I saw Tracy lick the cream cheese frosting from the ring, which just cracked me up.

I had no doubt that the dorm fire spurred Spencer's timing. So many of us were connected to NCLA in one form or another (not to mention how much we all loved Susanna). And even though it could have been so much worse, we all walked around in a haze for the first couple of days afterward, saying little, feeling that vulnerability that one feels after a confrontation with mortality. Even for those who hadn't been anywhere near the building, the fire had reminded them of what *could* happen, of how old (or young) they really were, and how much they cared about who they knew and where they lived.

Susanna had been released the day after the fire and stayed with her mother at a nearby Comfort Inn. Her dorm room, along with the entire floor, had been completely destroyed, while the upper and lower floors sandwiching it had been badly damaged. The entire building's residents were relocated to the same Comfort Inn. And yet, many students—residents and commuters alike—gathered outside the burned building to survey its damage, collect eyewitness accounts, and offer support to its displaced residents. At Norman's suggestion, The Grounds made and sold special five-dollar cookies: giant shortbread stars smothered in white or dark chocolate ganache. All proceeds went to the displaced students, and Minerva transformed the tip jar into a collection for donations. Additionally, we set up a box under the Christmas tree in the reading room for linens, backpacks, school supplies, and other college essentials.

When I wasn't at The Grounds, I was on campus grading and conferencing with my students so that they could finish the term—they'd had only a week left in the semester anyway, and many professors exempted students who were somehow connected to the fire from final exams. Minerva and Norman filled in for me, as did the new full-timer, Simeon: a chunky, twenty-five-year-old Starbucks defector who won a latte-serving contest. By the end of the week, he knew all the Originals and Regulars (and their orders) and had confessed to being a follower of WILS since breaking up with his college sweetheart. He had close-cropped dreads and mocha skin that perfectly offset his red-framed glasses. Sporting tattoos on his arms and neck, he only wore T-shirts—even in winter—each one bearing some sort of quote, expression, or decal, and still managed to look well-dressed. Oh yeah. He fit right in.

Since the fire, I'd spent days rehearsing exactly what I was going to say to Minerva when the moment presented itself; I could recite it in my sleep. So on an unsuspecting Monday, when she parked herself at her usual table and was about to unload the contents of her messenger bag, I marched over armed with the Cookie of the Week. Setting the plate down, I remained standing, hands on my hips.

"Now listen here, Minerva Brunswick," I lectured. "You are never going to be able to have absolute control over what happens to a mother as she's giving birth, and FTTs are going to happen whether you like it or not. But your *not* being a midwife won't stop it, either. Dammit, Min, you're a healer. You're not a hairdresser, and you're certainly not a coffee-server."

She opened her mouth and had barely uttered, "Eva, I..." when I held up my hand to block any more words she might dare attempt.

"You heard me. Not to say that you're bad at it or anything. But it's not what you're supposed to be doing. You're going to be the best damn midwife Wilmington has ever seen. I am hereby firing you, and if you don't get your ass back in med school, then I'm going to pick you up, carry you into your lab, and tether you to the table. So there. That's it. Even though you were never technically hired, you're fired. It's for your own good."

As the last words lingered in the air, I looked down to see that Minerva had pulled the neon green binder she reserved for boards notes out of her messenger bag, accompanied by her highlighter.

I sheepishly pointed to the binder. "Is that..."

She nodded in slow motion, silent.

"So, you're..."

She nodded again, pausing several beats before resuming speaking.

"I go back in January, when the next tri starts. Just thought I'd catch up."

I stood still, hapless and stupid.

She studied her highlighter before looking back up at me.

"Sometimes I'm just consumed by this overwhelming desire to be part of something beautiful in the world," she said. "Something so good that it touches people, really changes them." She put her highlighter down and nailed me with one of her classic, piercing Minerva looks. "And it's not because I want to be known as That Person who did That Thing. It's because I want to know that somewhere someone is smiling, and even if I never see them or never know it, I was a part of that."

I stood quietly for a minute, honoring and absorbing her words.

"You could be a florist for that, you know."

"Yeah," she said, "or a hairdresser. But I'm going to be a midwife."

I fidgeted with the plate on her table, swerving it in different directions.

"So, my little speech just now was totally useless," I said.

"I wouldn't say totally."

"Well, in that case, I'll let you get to your studying."

"Oh, and Eva?" she called as I was about to walk away. "I quit."

My smile widened. "Fine," I replied, feigning annoyance. "Oh, and Min?" I said after a beat. "You're forbidden behind the counter now that you're a customer again."

"Right. Like that ever stopped me."

"I love you, Min. You know that, don't you?"

"I've gotta study."

My heart lightened at the sight of her head hidden behind that bulky green binder again. And it was from my peripheral vision that I saw her eyes peeking from behind her horn-rimmed glasses as she called out, "Love you too."

⌒෨

When Susanna returned to The Grounds, she found a Welcome Back sign in the front window, visible from the farthest corner of the parking lot. So as not to exert her arm (which was still healing), she worked the register and wiped down tables. I would've pressed her to stay home and take it easy, but she seemed to *need* to work. I learned quickly to stay out of her way.

Susanna's return coincided with the first launch party of Kenny's new small press, Andiamo Books: a curious choice for a company name without a single Italian in it (not that it mattered; I think I'd been exiled from my own Italian heritage when, as a kid, I confessed to liking Ragu spaghetti sauce). Kenny seemed to read my thoughts and explained the origin. "I love how that word became a theme in your book," he confessed. "Amedo's voice gave the story this rhythm that kept everything going. I liked that. One word with all that momentum."

I looked at him, touched. "Really?"

"I guess I wanted some of that momentum in my life. Well, that and I just really like saying it. *Andiamo!*" He gestured like an Italian would. "It feels good to say. The guys thought it sounded worldly and lacked total geekness. Heck, it beat out Yoda Press and Bagel Books, so you should be flattered."

"I'm honored," I replied. "But I so would've voted for Yoda Press."

James Banks, the author and one of the co-founders of the small press, was a friend of Kenny's, and his novel was a Carolina-based commercial thriller. The reading and launch party was open to the public. I couldn't help but watch Kenny standing tall and proud while James read the first chapter and took questions from the attendees, as if his child rather than his buddy was the center of attention.

After James finished the Q&A and signed books, I sidled up to Kenny as he was wrapping up an interview with one of the local papers.

"So, Mr. Kenneth Richard Rhodes."

"Kenny, please. Only my mother calls me by my full name."

I held up my plastic champagne goblet. "To new ventures," I said.

He held up his own and clicked it against mine. "Here's looking up your old address."

Just as we drank, Scott exited the reading room, his autographed James Banks novel tucked under his arm. He bobbed his head in lieu of a greeting as he made and then broke eye contact with us, and I returned the gesture. "Hey, Scott," I said in the amiable way I had always addressed him when he was nothing more than Norman's best friend, one of the Originals.

Kenny raised his eyebrows after Scott was out of range. "Awkward. How are things between you two?"

"Every day gets a little easier for both of us, I think."

"Norman told me that he reactivated his Lovematch-dot-com profile."

I nearly spit out my drink. "Well OK, then. I guess everyone's moving on."

"So where does that leave us?"

Ahh, Kenny and all his cards on the table.

"Lord knows I've been thinking about you nonstop since our date," I said. "And not just because I'm dying for an excuse to get back to the Potato Shack..." He chuckled. "It would be so easy to just get into this with you, and I want to—I mean, I really, *really* want to."

"I do too."

"But I really don't want to get into another rebound situation."

"What makes you think this is a rebound?"

"I don't. I just…I don't know. It just feels so soon after everything that's happened; I think I just need a little time."

"Fair enough," he said. "I can respect that. You gotta do what you gotta do. Take all the time you need."

Neither of us said anything, and after about ten seconds, Kenny looked at his watch.

"Done yet?"

I sighed, wishing I could laugh it off, throw my cares to the wind, and give in to Kenny, when Norman tapped me on the shoulder.

"Hey, can I talk to you for a second, Eva?"

"Sure, Norm-o. What's up?"

"In the kitchen," he said.

A look of concern spread across my face, and I left Kenny to resume mingling and networking with the other attendees as Norman and I headed for the deserted kitchen.

"Is everything OK?" I asked.

"This is probably the worst time to talk to you about this, but I just can't wait anymore."

"Oh my God, you're leaving, aren't you," I said.

"No! Hell no, I would never quit on you like *this*."

"Are you engaged?"

"No!"

"Are you wanted in a foreign country?"

"Geez, will you shut up with the twenty questions and let me tell you?"

I straightened my posture. "OK. I promise I'm listening. What's up?"

"I want to buy half of your business, Eva."

35

The Proposal

I DROPPED THE plastic champagne goblet.

"Say that again?"

"I want to buy half of your business."

I reached out for something to lean on and made contact with the kitchen island, listening to Norman's voice as if he was speaking from a distance.

"I've been here since this baby opened. And even though it isn't technically mine, I've always felt a part of it. More than just an employee. This is a special place. Mostly because you made it special, Eva. But I want a piece of it—" He quickly admonished himself. "That didn't come out right. You've always treated me like a partner, and I want to make it official."

After standing in a stupor for several pounding heartbeats, I finally opened my mouth. "Wow," I said. "Talk about coming out of left field."

"I'm sorry to spring it on you like this—I guess I'm just caught up in the energy of Kenny's new business and all the other change that's been going on. Suddenly it felt like a brass ring that was about to pass me by if I didn't seize hold of it."

"Yeah, I know the feeling," I said, dazed. A curl of something heavy—fear, maybe?—started to unfurl in my stomach.

"I've got enough for a down payment and have already secured a loan. And not for nothing, but I can tell this hasn't been your favorite place to be lately. I'm not saying you don't love it anymore—I know how you feel about this place—but I think you need a break from it. Think about it, will you, Eva? You can take some time off, write another novel, go back to teaching, the sky's the limit. I'm not trying to push you out or anything. I just want you to see that you have options, possibilities that you may never have considered before."

The more he spoke, the more I felt like I was being immersed in a tank of water while bound in chains, my head woozy. I could hear Norman's voice echoing as he spoke, banging against my eardrums, and my heart rate sped up double-time.

"Eva?" I heard Norman asking from a distance. His firm hand grabbed my shoulder as he asked, "You OK?" My eyes moved from his hand to his arm and past the shoulder to the concern in his eyes.

"I can't do this right now," I said. "In fact, I need some air."

I brushed past Norman and out the back door into the alley. *The nerve of him*, said my inner voice as I paced; I stopped and instructed myself to take a couple of deep breaths. *The Grounds is* my *place. Mine.* I resumed pacing, flickering in and out of a pool of a light from a lone streetlamp as my brain alternated between protecting my most treasured possession and trying to rationalize both Norman's and my actions. Minutes later, Kenny appeared in the dank space between building and streetlamp.

"Geez, Eva, you look like you saw a ghost. What the hell happened?"

Before I had a chance to ask how he knew where I was, he said, "Norman told me you needed some air."

My words came out a mile a minute. "Norman wants to buy in. He wants half The Grounds. Ready to sign today, just like that."

Kenny sat on the curb, the same spot we'd sat when he'd brought me lunch months ago. "Well, I guess it was only a matter of time. Why are you so upset about it?"

I paused, trying to make sense of my reaction and find words to match. "I don't know. It was as if someone told me he wanted to take away my child or something. I just freaked out."

Kenny nodded without judgment. "I can understand that. But it wasn't just anyone, it was *Norman*. And I'm willing to bet that most people think you're already co-owners," he continued. "Why not make it official?"

I studied the way that the light threw his features into sharp relief, exaggerating the planes of jaw, nose, and cheek, but didn't answer him.

"Norman offered you a partnership, right? Not to buy you out completely. He still wants you around, and not that I blame him…" he said with a half grin. "He's asking you to marry him, metaphorically speaking, and to be The Grounds's adoptive father. That's huge. It requires a lot of trust. And it's been really easy for you to treat him like a partner all the while knowing he isn't one, that he has no rights at all."

I folded my arms as a breeze blew through the alleyway. And then it hit me: I knew what was bothering me.

"The Grounds is the only thing that was ever *mine*—no one told me to open a café, no one cosigned the loan or told me how to run a business. I navigated that path all my own, mistakes and all."

"You mean it's the only thing in your life that you've been able to control."

"Exactly."

"You've been on your own for a long time, and you built some pretty tall walls. And I understand why you did. But you don't need them anymore, and you know it."

He'd hit the nail on the head, and suddenly I didn't want to be talking about it anymore. I stood up and stretched. "I do know it."

He stood as well.

"Thanks for listening," I said.

He hugged me. "You're welcome."

I wanted him to hold me and not let go, to kiss me and whisk me away in his Karmann Ghia. When he let go, he looked into my eyes for a moment, and I swore he was thinking the same thing. But then he broke into a half-crooked smile and told me he had to go, and I reluctantly let him.

I lingered in the alley for a minute or two, taking a couple of deep breaths and listening to the sound of traffic. I knew I'd overreacted and hurt one of my best friends and most-trusted coworkers. I also knew that his asking me to be a partner had changed everything, made me acutely aware of how much a part of The Grounds he already was, of what I'd known all along: Norman deserved to be my partner from day one.

Steeling myself, I took one last deep breath and opened the back door; there was no preventing the inevitable.

He was in the office, his navy blue pea coat over one arm, keys in hand.

"Hey," I said. "You leaving?"

"I was going to leave you a note," he said, his voice perfectly even, firm, businesslike. He kept his eyes focused just past my head. "The espresso maker's acting up again, and a guy asked about hosting a poetry slam. Told him I'd have to talk to you."

"Look," I started. "I know I shouldn't have run out on you like that, and I'm sorry. You didn't deserve it."

"Apology accepted," he said. I could tell he was still wounded.

"I don't think you're plotting some hostile takeover. You just took me by surprise, that's all. It's a big deal."

"Yes, it is. And my timing was bad, I know. So I'm sorry for that."

"I just need time to think about it, OK? This is my life, ya know."

"Mine too."

Those two words pierced me—not once had I ever considered The Grounds as something so personal to anyone but myself.

"I'll think about it, Norman. I really will."

"That's all I ask, Eva."

And yet, I already knew what my answer was going to be.

36

Nothing to Lose

WITH THE SEMESTER officially over, I met Jenna Jaffe at her house to consult about each student and show her the final drafts of their short stories. I also delivered a care package of homemade peanut butter cups, her favorite. Sitting cross-legged opposite Jenna, propped up against a stack of pillows, I felt more like girlfriends having a sleepover than colleagues having a meeting. Still, it was nice to talk so collegially about something other than coffee vendors and payroll projections. I hadn't missed much when I'd left teaching, but the conversations about the writing (more specifically, the *language*) had always stimulated me, and I hadn't realized how much I'd missed Jenna as a friend, much less a mentor.

When we finished and I got ready to leave, she looked at me inquisitively.

"Eva, are you sure you don't want to teach part-time on a regular basis?"

I shrugged. "The Grounds keeps me pretty busy."

"I know how much you love it there, but it's just…you're good at this, too. And writing. I'd thought for sure you'd be on your third novel by now."

"It never felt right to me. But with all that's been happening lately, who knows." I paused for a moment. "Are you afraid?"

"That something's going to go wrong with the baby? The doctor says the odds are way in my favor, and I'm doing everything right. But I think the minute you find out you're pregnant, the fear never really goes away. It's part of parenthood."

"How do you live with it day in and day out?"

She smiled. "I'll let you know when the baby is born. But my guess is that you have two choices: either let it control you, or channel it into the everyday things you do. The dorm fire was unsettling, to say the least. You do the best you can to prevent another fire, but you don't give up lighting candles forever, right?"

With that, I leaned over and hugged her, then smoothed my hand over her belly. She expressed her gratitude one more time for my helping her out, said it was one less thing she needed to worry about, and bit into another peanut butter cup as I exited her room and let myself out.

The next day I went to Jenna's NCLA office to enter the final grades into the college's computer network. Just as I pumped my fists in the air and congratulated myself on a job well done, a forceful knock on the open door nearly startled me out of my seat.

"Final grades done?"

"Geez, Shaun! You scared the hell out of me! I didn't even see you there."

"Sorry," he said, and smiled. "You look good behind that desk. Just like old times."

"Anyone would look good behind this desk," I said, caressing the smooth finish of Jenna's mahogany desk, handcrafted especially for her by her father.

I hadn't seen Shaun since the night of the fire, and the memory of the kiss sent shivers from my toes straight up to my crown all over again. He plopped into the chair to the side of the desk facing me, holding his faded leather jacket, and slouched just like a student. And yet, seeing him there, dressed in a snug T-shirt and faded Levi's blue jeans (my preferred outfit of choice for Shaun—it perfectly displayed his pectorals), I felt no tingling in my chest, no pangs of longing, no sighs of regret.

"So," I said, "are you done, too?"

"Yep. Last final was two days ago. Finished the marathon of term papers, too." He twirled his ring of keys around his index finger.

"And?"

"And I'm impressed with how much these kids' writing skills have improved."

I nodded and let the silence hang in the air for a second, wondering who was going to speak first. Just as he took in a breath and started to speak, I tried to jump in first.

"Listen, Shaun..."

He put his hand up to block my words. "Hey, can we go somewhere and talk?"

His request took me off guard for a moment.

"You don't wanna talk here? I can close the door."

"Nah, it's too academic in here. Let's go for a walk or something. It's a beautiful day today."

"OK," I said. I closed and locked Jenna's door behind me, put on my coat and sunglasses, and we left the building to step out and into the spectacular December day. Not a trace of cold, not a cloud in the sky, and some trees still refused to shed their fall foliage, even with Christmas right around the corner. As if on automatic pilot, I found myself accompanying him across the courtyard and stopping at the bench swing by the pond—one of our favorite places to relax and enjoy the campus. We used to go even on Saturdays and spend hours feeding the ducks and talking until our throats hurt.

As we simultaneously sat on the bench, our body weight pushed the swing back, gravity forcing our feet off the ground. Across the pond, a swan picked at a blade of grass, sending tiny ripples toward us.

"Shaun, I just wanted to say I'm sorry for the meltdown at the shop," I said, breaking the silence. "I was mixed up back then, and I had no right to behave that way."

He shook his head. "I'm the one who's sorry."

"For what?"

"I took you for granted," he said and gave a short sigh. "Being with you was always so easy. I was just expecting something else, I think. I was expecting it to be harder, to be more work. I was expecting to have to do more to win you over. You know, like chase you. Drama. Excitement. A challenge or something."

The chains of the swing squeaked conspicuously as I tried to construct a response. "Sorry to disappoint you," was about all I could muster. "You did ask me out and get my number first, if that's any consolation."

"I don't think it hit me until the Halloween party."

"What hit you?" I asked, confused.

"When I saw you with that guy..."

"What guy?"

"You know, the one dressed as the tin man reject, or whatever he was."

"Bender," I said, shuddering yet again at the image of Scott's disastrous costume.

"He was supposed to be *Bender*?" he said, baffled. "Oh well... anyway, when he kissed you...I mean, I knew you were seeing someone because you had mentioned it on your blog. And I didn't expect it to, but it kind of upset me."

My mind raced: *He still read my blog. Seeing me with Scott upset him. He was envious. Should I tell him that Scott and I broke up?*

"Look, Shaun, I—"

He interrupted me again. "I figured if you ever got involved with anyone I'd be fine with it. But, Eva, I haven't been able to stop thinking about it since then, or you. And then, the night of the fire, when we kissed…"

"I'm really sorry about that," I said. "That never should've happened."

"I'm not sorry. In fact, I'm not even sure I can marry Jeanette."

"Whoa, Shaun…" I pulled away from him and put my hand up as if he'd made a move on me at that moment.

Wow. It had happened.

That thing I'd wanted all along, my very reason for putting myself through all those Lovematch.com dates and the speed dating and posing as Wilmington's own Carrie Bradshaw, had finally manifested. And irony of all ironies, it had happened when I wasn't trying so hard. At some point I'd stopped wanting Shaun, stopped waiting for him deliver himself to my doorstep. And yet, there he was.

And of course, irony of all ironies, I didn't want it anymore. Didn't want *him* anymore. Didn't need him. Didn't need a reason why it didn't work out, why he preferred Jeanette to me, why I wasn't good enough. Because suddenly, the answer was crystal clear. I *was* good enough. And it didn't matter. The problem was exactly what Shaun said—it had been too easy. I mistook safety for contentment. Shaun must have needed that safety, too. I was never going to leave him, and he knew it. He was never going to have to work that hard. I'd just assumed that he was as content as I thought I was, and for the very same reasons. I guess that the thing that brought him so much ease was the also the very thing that made him finally opt out: I was predictable. *We* were predictable. And we were never going to be otherwise.

And at that moment it was crystal clear to me that I was no longer afraid of the unpredictable, of what I couldn't control. I knew exactly what—and who—I wanted, and what I needed.

I was about to tell him all of this when I spotted a gangly figure wearing a heather grey hoodie and maroon baseball cap heading in our direction, slowing down as he recognized me. The blood rushed from my face.

"Oh no," I said in almost a whisper.

"What?" said Shaun, and he saw me watch the figure, now in full focus, stop and take in the view of my ex-boyfriend and me, our bodies angled on the bench swing to face each other. I jumped off the swing, leaving Shaun swaying and jiggling, trying to steady himself.

"Kenny, wait!" I called as he shoved his hands in his pocket and turned to storm off in the opposite direction. I ran and caught up to him, tugging at his arm. "Kenny!"

He turned to face me, and the look on his face was so full of hurt that I thought my heart was going to break.

"Don't tell me," he said, his voice full of sour sarcasm, "it's not what I think."

"It's not," I said, knowing how shallow and empty the words sounded.

"Really, Eva? Really? Because I'm thinking a lot right now, and none of it is good."

"What are you doing here?" I asked, realizing that that further incriminated me, as if I were blaming him for catching me in the act.

"I came to see you, actually," he said. "Stupid me, wanting to do something sweet and spontaneous like see the woman I'm crazy about. So how long has this been going on?"

"Nothing's going on, Kenny. I haven't seen him since the night of the fire. We were just talking."

"Right. Talking. At the pond. About what?"

"That's none of your business."

Oh, you are so not helping yourself, a voice inside me said.

Shaun approached us.

"Who are you?" he asked Kenny, exerting a macho, what-are-you-doing-with-my-girl voice. I hung my head and covered my eyes in embarrassment.

"I'm her *friend,*" Kenny said, matching Shaun's machismo. "Or so I thought."

"Well, you're upsetting her," said Shaun.

That did it.

"Will both of you apes just shut up?" I yelled. "Geezus, you think you own me? First of all," I said as I turned to Shaun, "he is not upsetting me. Second of all, you and I are no longer involved, and we're never going to be involved again. You have no right getting all Superman on me, acting like you're my bodyguard or something. And *you,*" I said to Kenny, "how dare you stand there and judge me as if you just caught me in the sack. You and I are no more committed to each other than Shaun and I are."

"That's not my doing, is it."

"Oh, get off your high horse! Why'd it take you so long to ask me out? If you were really my friend, then why'd you disappear the moment I started seeing Scott rather than talk to me about it? Didn't it occur to you that I'd miss you, that you'd hurt my feelings by disappearing without a trace? And why'd you call my best friend and ask for her advice like we were in junior high school instead of coming straight to me and taking the risk yourself?"

I raged on, barely pausing for breath. "You sit there lecturing to me about commitment and being brave and 'all or nothing,' but I don't see your courage. I see someone who's afraid to fail, to be vulnerable like everyone else."

My accusations hung in the air as the three of us stood silent, painfully aware that we each wanted to be somewhere, anywhere else, far from the others' presence.

"Well, I guess I got my answer," Shaun said quietly, looking at the grass. "Take care of yourself, Eva."

He slipped away, neither acknowledging Kenny nor giving me the chance to say good-bye to him. A gust of wind blew at that moment, and Kenny dug his hands even deeper into his pockets as tufts of his hair were pushed to one side. I brushed my tangled hair out of my face and folded my arms. We stood close, facing each other yet taking turns shifting our focus from the ground to some other campus building.

"You're right," he finally spoke. "I'm scared to death."

"Of what?" I asked.

"That you don't want what I want."

I couldn't help but laugh. It was like hearing a tape recorder of myself.

"Well, if you can't trust my feelings for you, then no amount of attention I give you is going to satisfy you. And I'm crazy about you, Kenny. You have no idea how much."

"Then what's taking you so long?" He sounded like an impatient child.

"Don't you get it? This is something I really want, and I don't wanna screw it up by going in half-baked. Don't you want me to be good and ready?"

The sunlight soaked my skin and warmed me from the inside out. I reached up and cupped his cheek with my hand, looked into his eyes—those gorgeous, hazel eyes—and smiled.

Kenny moved his head away from my hand. "What happens now?" he asked.

"What do you mean?"

He looked defeated, frustrated, scared. I, however, had never felt so sure or fearless in all my life. "I'm tired of waiting, Eva."

"So don't."

He looked at me like I was absurd and shook his head, exasperated, before turning away. "Whatever," I heard him mutter.

"Trust me," I called out, filled with confidence. *You have nothing to lose. And neither do I.*

37

Grounds for Merriment

●●●

"HEY, NORM-O," I called from The Grounds's kitchen, "did you post the sign on the door?"

"What sign?" he called back.

"I made a sign."

"What, 'Closed Early for Drunken Mischief-making'?"

"Yeah, right." I emerged from the kitchen, rummaged through a box, and handed Norman the sign I'd made earlier that day: *Closed early on account of Grounds for Merriment.* "Go put it up! And let me know when Minerva and Jay get here."

Norman did as instructed, and I put out trays of Christmas cookies followed by a platter of cold cuts and sandwich condiments with Kaiser rolls. Next, I returned to the box and fetched a headband topped with felt antlers. Crouching in front of the display case to capture my reflection, I adjusted the antlers atop my head and went back to setting up the food, finishing with an assortment of wine. I balanced the bottles in one hand while trapping the box between my opposite arm and hip and made my way to the café counter just as Minerva entered.

"We brought the eggnog," said Jay, carrying a punch bowl after Norman unlocked the door and locked it behind them, "and I warn you, it's not for those with weak constitutions."

"Hey, Eva, I brought…" Minerva stopped in her tracks, then started again: "…What. The. Hell. Is. On. Your. Head?"

"You can't very well have a Christmas party without the proper attire."

"You didn't wear that *thing* last year," said Minerva as she pointed to the antlers.

"Right, and what kind of party was it?"

"I can't remember."

"Exactly." I rummaged through the box a third time, pulling out several elf hats, a red nose, and sleigh bells. "Norman, if you'd do the honors," I said as I handed him Vince Guaraldi's *A Charlie Brown Christmas*. Before he turned for the CD player, I grabbed his arm. "Wait!" I dangled a red nose. "You have to get dressed."

He glared at me. "I'm already wearing a very humiliating Santa tie. What more do you want?" Before he had the chance to duck, I slid the elastic band around his head, resisting the urge to snap the nose into place.

"I sometimes think about having you killed," he said plainly, quiet enough that only I could hear. "You do know that, don't you."

"Yes, but then you'd never get your Christmas present."

He put his hand to his chin and stroked it in consideration, as if to say, *Good point...* "By the way, I forgot to tell you that Car Talk Kenny is here."

I perked up. "He is?"

"Yeah. Said he wanted to talk to you about something."

"Oh," I said, feeling the flutter in my chest. "Well of course he's here. He's part of the Secret Santa Club." I hadn't told anyone besides Minerva about the incident at the pond, and I'd assumed he wasn't going to show up. We hadn't seen or spoken to each other since, and for all I knew, he wanted to tell me that we were over before we'd even started; that he met someone else in the campus parking lot that same afternoon and they were running off to Fiji together; that he was considering becoming a Buddhist monk, et cetera. I tentatively peeked into the reading room and saw him in conversation with Beulah and Spencer and Tracy. He caught me spying on him and raised his head in acknowledgment before returning his attention to Tracy's story. Somewhat relieved, I looked around at the rest of the Originals and Regulars.

"Where's Scott?" I asked Norman.

"He had to go to some company Christmas thing," he replied.

"It's not…I don't mean to be narcissistic, but it's not because of me, is it?"

"Nah, he's OK with all that. Really, it was business. I think he would rather be here, though. Lord knows I would if I were him," he said.

I laughed and grabbed a small stack of napkins along with a band of sleigh bells, which I rang to call everyone to attention. "Let the Grounds for Merriment party begin!"

The sea of elves, reindeer, and Santa hats cheered and raised their cups.

"We have anisette snowflakes dusted in powdered sugar, spicy sugar cookie Christmas trees, gingerbread people—all single, of course…" They all laughed. I continued, "Date nut truffles, candy canes, and my new favorite: chocolate peppermint sticks for stirring cocoa. And speaking of, we have both hot white and traditional cocoa, along with Jay's 'you'll-fail-a-breathalyzer-test' eggnog, wine, and soda. The Secret Santa gifts are all under the tree in the reading room, and the dreidels are next to the menorah."

In no time the party moved to the reading room. It came as no surprise to me that Beulah knew what the symbols on the dreidels stood for, and taught everyone. She got a rousing game going using the cookies as loot. You'd think we were shooting craps at a casino, the group was so raucous. I stood at the entrance and watched the action, loving every minute of it. Simeon and Susanna won the biggest pot, and Jeannie with the Jimmy Choos promptly bit every head off her gingerbread specimens before adding them to the game.

When the game was forfeited and the loot redistributed, Norman announced that it was time to open Secret Santa gifts, assigning Neil to the all-important task of Chief Elf Distributor. As the Originals and Regulars opened their gifts (although, truth be told, there wasn't much secrecy since almost everyone blabbed to someone or other about who drew whose name), Kenny appeared beside me to ladle another serving of eggnog and filled my cup as well.

"Wow. You were totally right about this eggnog. I may have to spend the night on that couch over there."

"I'm glad you're here, Kenny."

"Me too."

"I didn't think you'd show up after what happened the other day."

"Yeah, I wanted to talk to you about that."

"We will," I promised. Then I looked at my watch. "But would you excuse me for a minute?" I left his side and went back to the reading room to find Norman. "Hey," I said, after taking in a deep breath and tapping him on the shoulder. "You have another present under the tree. Delivered by Santa himself, I heard."

I tried not to become unsettled by the sudden silence in the room.

"I do?" he said more with surprise than excitement.

"Yeah. Go get it."

Norman went to the tree, the Originals and Regulars watching him in anticipation, although they didn't know what awaited him any more than Norman did. He pulled out a shirt box wrapped in classic *Rudolf the Red-Nosed Reindeer* paper. "Is this it?" he asked. I nodded, my antlers bobbing.

He shook the box cautiously. "Are you sure there's anything in it? It feels empty."

"Wait! You have to open the other one first."

"There's another one?"

I raced to the tree, got down on all fours, and reached around with my hands until I found the little box tucked under the skirt. Crawling backwards, I pulled myself to my feet and handed the gift to him. He tore the paper right across Hermie the Elf's face, opened the box, and burst out laughing upon sight of the artifact.

"What is it?" asked Tracy.

"It's a pinup girl floaty pen," said Norman as he took it out and started tipping it in different directions so that her bathing suit floated right off her body, his eyes widening. "Ohhh. Hello, gorgeous. I stand corrected. It's a *Bettie Page* floaty pen."

"What's a floaty pen?" asked Spencer.

"This." He held it up to show everyone, the guys in particular. "This is going to give me hours of pleasure, and I don't just mean writing."

"Well, you can start on the other present," I said.

"Other present? Oh, right. The empty one. I got distracted by the…" He waved the floaty pen before passing it off to Spencer, who tilted it to the side and let out his own *Hel-lo...* "Don't get too attached—I want her back," said Norman as he unwrapped the second gift, this time gouging out the eyes of one of the Misfit Toys and ripping the rest of the paper in one forceful pull. He slid his fingers under the bottom sleeve of the box, sliced the Scotch tape, and lifted the top off. He then lifted the tissue and went silent when its contents registered recognition.

Norman drew in a breath.

No one moved for several heartbeats.

"What is it?" asked Dara, almost in a whisper.

Norman drew in a second breath and opened his mouth in an effort to answer, but came up blank.

He looked directly at me, still silent. I could hardly catch my own breath.

"Whaddya say, Norman? Wanna get hitched?"

"Hitched?" said Beulah.

I could feel Kenny's eyes on me, smiling in approval.

"It's..." Norman's voice broke. "It's the paperwork for me to officially become a full partner of The Grounds."

I think Minerva and Susanna were the first to squeal with delight, followed by Tracy and Dara, while the guys wooted and patted Norman on the back. He made his way through the congratulatory hugs and handshakes to get to me, where he planted a big kiss on my lips and squeezed me tight. "Thank you, Eva," he whispered in my ear; I could feel the wetness of his cheek on my lobe. "You have no idea how happy this makes me."

"Better than the floaty pen?"

He let go of me. "It's a close second to the floaty pen."

"I don't know why I didn't do it sooner. You were already my partner."

"I'm gonna do right by this place. I promise."

"*I know.* Well, what are you waiting for? Go get Bettie and sign the papers!"

After taking one final peek, Jay handed Norman the pen, and with a shaky hand Norman signed his name and initials in all the designated places while everyone erupted into applause. He then hugged me again, and we posed for pictures: a woman in reindeer antlers, a guy in a red nose and silly Santa tie, and a contract. Partners.

The party continued until well after the last of the goodies were gone, and everyone helped clean up a little, though I instated a no-tipsies-carrying-glass policy after Spencer nearly dropped an entire stack of plates. As the last of the Originals left (I made sure everyone was OK to drive), I locked the doors and Norman and I walked to our cars, Jeannie on the other side of him, their arms interlocked, a comfortable smile playing on his face.

I halted. "Norman! Where is your nose?"

He raised an eyebrow. "You dress me up as a reindeer—" he started.

"As Rudolph, the Elvis of all reindeer," I corrected.

"—with a foam nose that smells like paint, and then you actually expect me to wear it in public? Wasn't the Santa tie bad enough?"

"Suit yourself. I'm not your boss anymore."

I watched his face as the thought registered. Without warning he let go of Jeannie and grabbed me in a final bear hug, pinning me against his shoulder before ducking into her car with one last floaty pen salute.

As they pulled away, I spun around and slammed straight into Kenny.

"Oomph!" I said as he grabbed my shoulder, steadying me. "Sorry, I didn't see you there." I pushed my hair away from my face and tucked it behind my ears.

"Didn't mean to scare you."

We stood in silence for a second.

"So, about the other day…" I started.

"Forget it," he said.

"I don't want to just blow it off."

"No hard feelings." He seemed impatient.

"Look, Kenny, I just want to tell you that I—"

He put two fingers to my lips and shushed me. Then, drawing his other hand from his coat pocket, he opened his fist to reveal the sprig of mistletoe that had been hanging in the café.

I shifted my glance from it to him. "Those things only work if you're standing under them, not if—"

He leaned in, pulled me to him, and kissed me.

"Merry Christmas, Eva," he whispered into my ear, and he backed away slowly to his own car, leaving me standing there, dumbfounded.

38

Resolute

FOR THE FIRST time ever, I chose not to spend Christmas or New Year's with Olivia. Perhaps it was because she had already made the trip to North Carolina for Thanksgiving, and that alone was quite a production for a family of four. Perhaps it was because nothing could top the Grounds for Merriment party—seeing Norman's face as he found the partnership papers, Kenny's kiss, my friends playing with dreidels and opening their presents.

The truth was that wanted to be alone. I *chose* it. I wanted to celebrate myself.

On Christmas Day I attended mass with Beulah and Lily, who had kind blue eyes and a warm handshake despite the chilly day, and afterwards they came to my house for lunch. We made deviled eggs and hoagies and set up a carpet picnic in my living room, watching *A Christmas Carol* (the George C. Scott version, although we liked the Alistair Campbell version better) and shared stories of Christmases past well into the evening.

After they left, I sat on the couch, in the dark, admiring my tree—my first since I'd lived with Shaun. It had always been my parents' tradition to decorate the tree in stages: lights one day, ornaments the next, and tinsel or garland on Christmas Eve, topped with a star. Olivia and I had kept up the tradition, finishing the decorating when I arrived, except we'd replaced the star with twin angels. I decorated my tree in stages as well, with baubles that Shaun and I had collected, ornaments hand-made from baker's clay and cookie cutter shapes, and a new set of collectibles from the Claymation shows of our childhood that I'd found on eBay. Beulah and Lily's gift for me was a new angel.

⤲⟋

New Year's Eve was an equally quiet, solitary affair. I made myself haddock topped with equal parts crabmeat and butter, roasted some broccoli, and sliced focaccia bread to dip in olive oil. Lately I'd been cooking full-course meals just for myself and eating at the table rather than the couch, where I so often scarfed down my dinners while watching TV. I set the table for one with my best plates and linens, and dined by candlelight.

It had been so long since I'd eaten mindfully, savoring each bite, closing my eyes as I chewed and reveling in the flavors as they mixed in my mouth. I dined with silence as a companion, actually *listening* to it, without a book or screen to distract me. Even my thoughts spoke softly.

I decided to save the slice of flourless chocolate cake for later, perhaps when the ball dropped, or just after the stroke of midnight.

After dinner, I spent the evening sorting through the ever-growing stash of recipes that I'd found or created throughout the year, making piles of "finally make this," "make this again," "make this every day," and "burn without regret." From there I further classified them into meats, poultry, fish, sides, entrees, breakfast, et cetera, and put them all into the recipe box that had belonged to my mother. Only slightly bigger than a five-by-seven index card file box, it was now yellowish-white, adorned with flaked and faded pink and blue flowers that Olivia and I had painted when we were children, presenting it to her for Mother's Day.

By around ten thirty, my recipes were fully sorted and stored, and I had a new stack to try during the upcoming week, including two more sit-down dinners. I zapped on the TV, and as *The Honeymooners* marathon on TV Land was in full swing, I contemplated making a resolution but flicked my wrist in a tossing motion and said "Nahhh" out loud, chuckling. I'd always opposed New Year's resolutions on the principle that so many people seemed content to only commit to self-improvement and new beginnings once a year. What about the rest of the year? Why not quit smoking in July, or de-clutter the basement in November and keep it that way all the time? By seventeen, I'd decided to boycott New Year's resolutions altogether. But at thirty-four, my boycott seemed more like a thinly veiled excuse for not holding myself accountable for much of anything, and letting status quo form and pass without protest.

Maybe it was time.

This year, I began as the TV blathered on, *I resolve to devote less time to screens and more time to trees.* I was a bit rusty at this whole resolution thing, and continued out loud. "I will eat sitting down." Better. "I will be spontaneous. And I will do my best to be OK with it."

It was a start. A good one at that.

At 11:58, I switched the channel to see the ball in Times Square drop, and was in bed by 12:16. I think I fell asleep smiling, and never did eat my cake.

39

Forget-me-nots

ON THE SATURDAY before his birthday, I kidnapped Kenny under the guise of taking him out for a matinee and met up with Spencer and Tracy, Norman and Jeannie, Scott, Minerva and Jay, and Beulah for laser tag. I can't remember the last time I laughed so much or was so full of adrenaline as we blasted away at each other. Norman and I in particular had a good time saying, "I am your father, Luke," every time we found ourselves at a standoff. All the while, eighties music echoed throughout the caverns, and Kenny, appropriately, was the last man standing, pumping his fists in the air to "Eye of the Tiger."

After laser tag, we took over two tables at Mia's Pizza, and from there we went next door to the bowling alley that sported an embarrassingly large bar and "flashback disco bowling" every third Saturday of the month. Beulah and I, the two designated drivers, steered clear of the alcohol selection while the rest got pretty soused. I don't think any of us—Beulah and myself included—bowled better than a 110.

Several hours later, we all straggled out to the parking lot, giggling profusely and blowing on the kazoos I'd given out as party favors in Spiderman goody bags (other "goodies" included homemade Mallomars, a jar of bubbles, two Matchbox cars, and a handful of Bazooka bubble gum). After a pitifully rendered version of "Safety Dance" on the kazoo by all of us, Beulah piled

Scott, Spencer, Tracy, Minerva, and Jay into the church's youth group minivan while Norman and Jeannie accompanied Kenny and me back to my car, and I dropped them off at Norman's apartment nearby.

"So," said Kenny, grinning like a mischievous little boy and ramming a piece of Bazooka into his mouth when we were alone, "I guess the next stop is my place?"

I smiled slyly. "Not exactly."

His eyes widened. "There's *more*? I don't think I can handle another surprise."

"It's not really a surprise. You'll see."

As we headed off toward the next destination, I asked if he was happy.

"I'm a little drunk," he said, cracking himself up.

"I'm sorry I didn't invite your other friends and business associates. I don't really know any of 'em."

"That's OK. This was perfect."

By the time we arrived at the beach—dark and deserted and perfectly undisturbed—Kenny seemed to have sobered up. We walked along the shoreline in silence for about a quarter mile, huddled together in the cold, when he stopped and turned to me.

"You didn't have to do all this, you know," he said.

"Yes, I did," I answered.

"Just had to prove that winter birthdays aren't all gloom?" he teased.

"Something like that."

"Well, thank you."

"You're welcome."

We sat on the sand in silence for a while, me wrapped tightly in my favorite cardigan and winter coat, him in his hoodie and leather jacket. The salty wind wreaked havoc on my hair so that by the time we got back to the car, I was a frizzed-out, rosy-cheeked mess. And yet, Kenny looked at me like I was a rare treasure.

He touched my chin and kissed me softly. "Best. Birthday. Ever," he whispered.

I drove him back to his house. Before letting him out, I leaned across him and fished in the glove box for the small package I'd wrapped earlier that day.

"This didn't make its way into the goody bag," I said.

With a questioning look, Kenny tore open the kiddie racecar wrapping paper to reveal a packet of forget-me-not seeds.

"They were my favorites back home," I said softly. "Shortly after our mom was diagnosed with cancer, she planted these for Olivia, my dad, and me, with instructions that we were to think of her whenever we looked at or tended to them. As if we could ever forget her..." My voice trailed off.

He clutched the packet and looked at me.

"Anyway," I continued, "they turned out to be a nice reminder. And no matter what happens between us, I just don't want you to forget me, OK?"

For once, Kenny seemed unsure of what to say; his face clouded as he opened his mouth, and then closed it. He studied the seeds and shook them so that they rattled like maracas.

"OK," he said, his mouth forming a thin line. He nodded. "OK," he repeated softly before sliding out of the car and closing the door behind him.

40

A State of Mind

TWO DAYS AFTER Kenny's birthday, I booked a small suite at a nearby beachfront hotel with a balcony and kitchenette. I'd scheduled time off from The Grounds to prepare for Jenna's short story class (I wanted her to return from maternity leave to an organized course on track with the syllabus) and decided to do it in style.

Each day was an exercise in solitude; in the mornings I jogged on the beach, followed by a shower and breakfast (chocolate crepes and strawberries for breakfast one morning, caramelized apple French toast the next, granola bars with peanut-butter slathered bananas after that, to name a few). Then, after compiling reading lists and planning workshops and drafting the syllabus, I napped or treated myself to a massage or a mani-pedi at the hotel's day spa. In the evenings I prepared more delectable meals: mixed green salads with walnuts and dried cranberries and gorgonzola cheese; grilled salmon with orange glaze and crunchy red potatoes; lemon chicken with fresh thyme and rosemary; all the goodies from my New Year's Eve recipe sorting fest. Finally, I ventured out for a stroll on the beach before snuggling in bed with a cup of chamomile tea and a book.

I slept soundly every night. I fasted from screens all week— didn't watch TV, kept off Facebook and away from my iPhone. I refrained from calling Minerva or Olivia or Kenny. I didn't even call Norman to check in on The Grounds.

On the last evening, I stood on the balcony wrapped in a plush terry bathrobe, sipping a perfectly medium-dry cabernet. The sky was the color of orange sherbet, and it glazed the walls of my room and glinted off the vase of peonies on my nightstand. I poured myself a second glass of wine, filled not even a quarter of the way.

I closed my eyes and breathed in the moment.

This.

This was what singlehood was all about.

It had nothing to do with bubble baths and sit-down dinners, or the ability to go anywhere alone at the last minute without feeling an ounce of shame. It had nothing to do with convenience or even independence.

I got it. And suddenly my fingers practically burned to write. I raced to the desk, opened my notebook (I'd copy it all to my laptop tomorrow, I decided), and scribbled away.

Singlehood Is a State of Mind

It's not about having the bed to yourself or about sharing bathrooms. It's not about who you were with yesterday or whether you've got a date tomorrow. It's not about whether you travel the world or stay at home. It's not about having a ring on your finger or a key to his place.

It's about being sure of yourself, and living out loud with peace and acceptance. It's not the road less traveled but the one that appears in front of you, brick by brick, with each step you take.

Singlehood is about finding and committing to the love of your life. I'm talking about the literal love of *your* life. Being in a place of self-sufficiency, strength, independence, comfort, confidence, and happiness is what matters. No relationship, no matter how seemingly perfect and compatible you are, can give you these things. You have to find them within. You have to bring them to your relationship. Because in the end, you don't have to be alone to be single. And being single doesn't mean that you are alone.

In other words, singlehood is a state of mind.

This Valentine's Day, I'm not hoping for a box of chocolates or a secret valentine or a dozen long-stem roses or anything like that. Instead I'm going to court myself. I'm going to make myself a marvelous candlelight dinner because I deserve it. I'm going to read my favorite books and perhaps write a short story. I'm going to go for a walk on the beach. I'm going to do more at home than clean or sleep. I'm going to do all this because that's what I love, and we all deserve to live with love wherever we find it.

May each and every one of you find the love of your life, whatever that means to you.

Taking my glass of wine, I stepped back out onto the balcony to watch night settle over all of Wilmington, and gazed at the palm trees brushing in the breeze, listened to the surf sing to the stars, and smelled the salty sea. It was as if the world was smiling at me. Or maybe it was just my parents. I held out my wine glass and toasted it all.

41

Valentine's Day

I DON'T KNOW if it was because of the 65-degree sunshine, the fact that it was Valentine's Day, or that I'd just come from a new yoga class, but I felt so energized I'd decided to bike to work. When I entered The Grounds, I was met with the sight of tables covered in deep wine-colored linens and real roses in long, thin vases. Norman had gone all out over the weekend, giving the entire place a robed, classically romantic feeling, avoiding all shades of pink and all things paper and doily. The Originals, clustered at their usual table, greeted me as I passed by them and stopped to tidy the self-service bar, as usual. Tracy rambled to Jan about wedding dresses while Spencer chatted with Minerva and Jay about his applications to doctoral programs. Kenny was already nestled at a table by the window with his laptop, and I could tell he was pretending not to notice me; but the twitching at the corners of his lips gave him away, and my heart did a little flip-flop.

"Hey, Normal," I called to the kitchen, grabbing my apron from the hook. Simeon brushed past me, giving my shoulders a squeeze along the way. "The place looks fabulous!"

Norman came out of the kitchen with a stack of napkins in his hands. "Thanks," he said. "It's gonna cost a fortune to clean the linens, but what the hell. Happy Valentine's Day." He kissed me on the cheek. "How was class yesterday?" he asked.

"Great," I answered, opting not to tell him about the new short story I'd started, or that I had a feeling it was going to turn into a novel.

"Glad to hear it," he said. "We're out of chocolate chip muffins, by the way."

"Aye aye, Captain," I said with a salute and retreated to the kitchen. Once the jumbo muffins were in the oven, I took last night's cookies out of the fridge and transferred them to the display case.

As I slid the display door closed, Minerva approached the counter. "Hey, Eva. I—" She stopped mid breath as her eyes fixed on the display case. "Are those…" She didn't even get the words out, just stood there looking like a kid who just found her lost puppy—eyes all bright and sparkly with a bit of a grin tugging at her slack jaw. "Half-moon cookies?"

"What did you call them?" I asked.

"Half-moon cookies. Why, what do you call them?"

"Black and Whites." I selected one and plated it, and she carried her prize with both hands to her table, setting it down as if it were as fragile as a Faberge egg.

"Guess someone has a thing for Half-moons," said Norman as he swept around the empty tables.

"They're called 'Black and Whites,'" I said defiantly.

Norman had stopped sweeping and now leaned against the counter beside me, chiming in. "Oh, that's right. You're from *Lawn Guyland*—they have all kinds of silly names there. Really, Eva. Don't you think 'Half-moon' is easier to say?"

"And more suitable?" Simeon added.

"Anyone with a little bit of class calls it a 'Black and White,'" I argued.

"Take a poll here and you'll beg to differ," said Norman.

We couldn't help but stare as Minerva began to eat the cookie in a meticulous ritual that I had never seen before: First a bite of chocolate frosting, then a bite of vanilla. Next, a bit of both. Repeat. Chocolate, vanilla, a bite of both, heavier on the vanilla. Again. Chocolate, vanilla, bit of both, a few millimeters less vanilla. It was a science. And she ate the whole thing with that silly, found-my-puppy grin on her face until the very last presumably perfectly balanced choco-vanilla bite.

As Minerva became aware of her surroundings, and the pairs of eyes watching her, she blushed.

"What?" she asked, dropping her crumpled napkin on the barren plate. She hadn't even left a crumb.

"You could use a fork and knife next time, if you'd like," Norman said in his classic matter-of-fact tone. "Or buy one to frame and one to eat if it really gets you going that much."

She fiddled with the corner of her discarded napkin, at a loss.

I started to laugh. "Really? Not the Chocolate Orgasms? The oatmeal spice drops? The toffee chips? Your favorite is *Black and White cookies*?"

She giggled. *Giggled.*

"I had you pegged as a Chocolate Orgasm Girl," said Norman. "Woulda bet money on it."

She shrugged. "Guess I'm outed."

Simeon frowned. "They're not even that interesting. They're just—"

"Don't!" she warned. "They're not *just* anything! These are *Half-moons*," she said with reverence. Minerva leaned back. "The first time I ever had one was on my thirteenth birthday. We'd been in the car for *hours*, driving all day to see my mom's cousin's something-or-other, and got in late. Late, late. And I was sure I'd be sent straight to bed on what was officially the worst birthday ever, but then she brought out these cookies on a plate and insisted that I have one before bed as a birthday treat."

"Aw, that's sweet," said Simeon in a syrupy voice.

Minerva ignored his teasing. "I would kill for this recipe. Where'd you get it, Eva?"

Before I could answer her, Tracy piped up. "You should publish a book of recipes! Why didn't we ever think of it before?"

"And Kenny's new press could publish it," said Minerva.

Kenny crossed his arms and raised his eyebrows in consideration. "It's not a bad idea, really," he said, scrutinizing me as one might a potential investment. I flushed under his piercing eyes.

"Of course!" said Norman. "We could add it to the other Grounds merchandise. I bet it'd be just as big a hit."

"Especially if it had *this* recipe in it," said Minerva, lovingly looking at her empty plate. "With *pictures!*"

"But if people could make all the cookies themselves, then why would they still buy them from me?" I asked.

Tracy gave me an *oh-please* look. "Like I have time to bake. And as if I could ever bake like you!"

"Or anyone else," added Spencer. "Bake like Eva, I mean. Not to criticize your baking abilities, Trace."

"What do you think, Norman?" I asked.

"I think we should all get profit-sharing."

As the Originals began suggesting book titles, I caught myself mentally skimming through recipes in my head, weeding out those that were too simple, too complex, or too similar to someone else's work. Each recipe needed a story to accompany it, I'd realized, and suddenly the idea appealed to me even more. A cookbook was one thing. But a book that highlighted the hows and whys of the recipes, the reasons for their existence, would capture the *feelings* each recipe evoked.

That was something worth writing. And in sharing my stories with each recipe, readers would, in return, create their own. Years from now, grown-ups would talk about how their mom made Daisy Pick-Me-Ups for them after school when they were kids. Or perhaps a woman would win her hubby's heart thanks to caramel truffle brownies. Or the lemon torte would be re-christened as a birthday treat.

I was all about writing stories lately, and I found margins of papers and both sides of napkins scribbled with ideas that had been pouring out of me since the start of the new term. Academia agreed with me this time around. More than that, it *inspired* me.

After the timer went off and the muffins had fully cooled, I transferred all but one to a tray and slid it into the top shelf of the display case. I then placed the remaining muffin on a small plate and sprinkled it with red sugar crystals.

Stalling, I felt a wave of insecurity. What if it didn't work? What if I had gotten it all wrong, or still wasn't ready? What if I'd missed my chance and there was no going back?

Then unpredictability would win again, and life would go on. And that was OK.

I took a deep breath and entered the café, plate in hand.

Near the window, Kenny was packing up his laptop and pulling out a book. He closed his eyes as I approached, inhaling deeply. "Mmm," he rumbled, "that smells *so* good." I stood, as if rooted to the spot, watching him bask in the scent.

I held it out to him. "Split it with me?"

His eyes brightened, then narrowed. "I thought you could eat a whole one of those things by yourself."

"Oh I can," I said, glancing first at the outstretched muffin, then at him. "And I want to. But that doesn't mean I *have* to."

I counted my heartbeats and waited for his response.

He broke into laughter—warm and rich—and all the apprehension melted away until it was just Kenny, me, and a chocolate chip muffin. And in that moment, surrounded by the hum of friends and customers cradled in familial scents, I swear he sounded like chocolate.

About the Authors

Photo Credit: Larry H. Leitner, 2010

Elisa Lorello is the Kindle-bestselling author of *Faking It* and *Ordinary World*. Born and raised on Long Island, New York, she spent eleven years in southeastern Massachusetts before moving to central North Carolina, where she teaches and writes today.

Sarah Girrell has a background in art history, writing, and rhetoric. After moving to Ithaca, New York, to earn a medical degree, she and her husband returned to her native Vermont, where she is a physician and writer.

Elisa and Sarah met at UMass-Dartmouth in 2002, where they quickly discovered a shared love of writing and a humor for everyday life. *Why I Love Singlehood* is their second collaboration and Sarah's authorial debut.